A Booke of Days

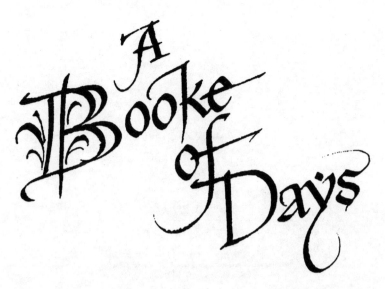

A JOURNAL OF THE CRUSADE

BY ROGER, DUKE OF LUNEL

EDITED AND TRANSLATED BY

STEPHEN J. RIVELLE

MACMILLAN

First published 1996 by Macmillan

an imprint of Macmillan Publishers Ltd
25 Eccleston Place, London, SW1W 9NF
and Basingstoke

Associated companies throughout the world

ISBN 0 333 65747 0

1 3 5 7 9 8 6 4 2

A CIP catalogue record for this book is available from
the British Library.

Phototypeset by Intype London Ltd
Printed by Mackays of Chatham PLC, Chatham, Kent

This book is dedicated to my son,

Eli Stephenson Bocek-Rivele,

who has sent me on my own journey of discovery.

A NOVEL BY S. J. RIVELE

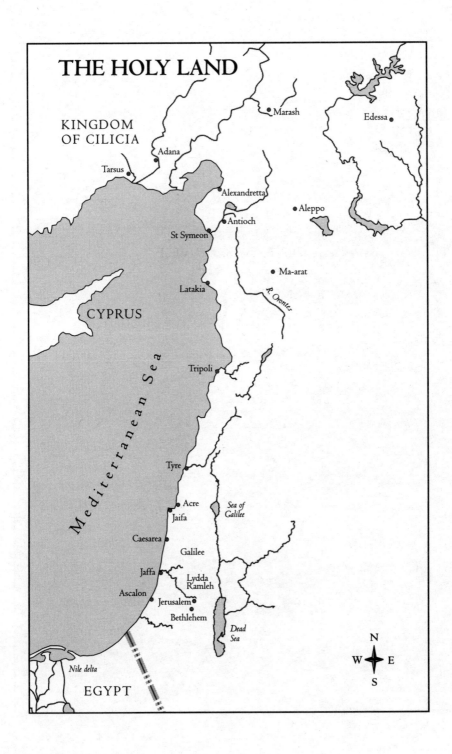

THE HOLY LAND

KINGDOM
OF CILICIA

Marash

Edessa

Adana

Tarsus

Alexandretta

Aleppo

St Symeon

Antioch

Latakia

Ma-arat

CYPRUS

R. Orontes

Tripoli

Mediterranean Sea

Tyre

Acre

Sea of
Galilee

Jaifa

Caesarea

Galilee

Jaffa

Lydda
Ramleh

Ascalon

Jerusalem

Dead
Sea

Bethlehem

Nile delta

N

W   E

S

EGYPT

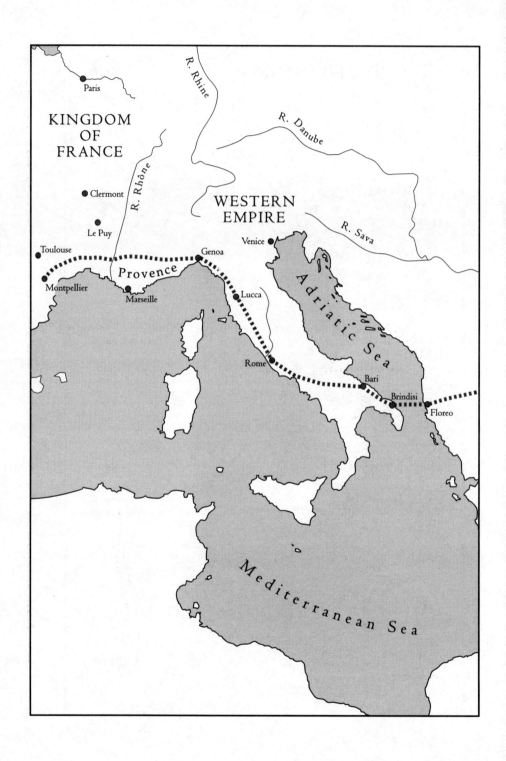

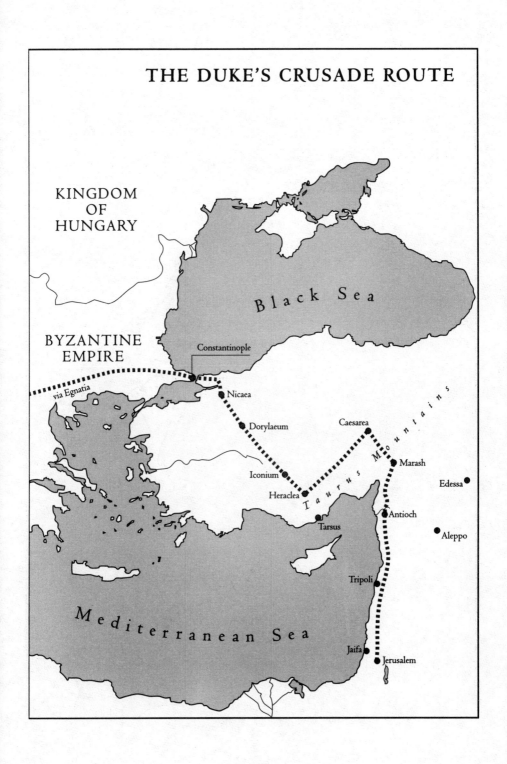

THE DUKE'S CRUSADE ROUTE

KINGDOM
OF
HUNGARY

BYZANTINE
EMPIRE

Black Sea

Constantinople

via Egnatia

Nicaea

Dorylaeum

Caesarea

Taurus Mountains

Marash

Edessa

Iconium

Heraclea

Antioch

Aleppo

Tarsus

Tripoli

Mediterranean Sea

Jaifa

Jerusalem

PREFACE

I am a writer by profession, and a Frenchman by descent. Starting at about the age of six I began, quite spontaneously, to teach myself the French language. I acquired it with so little effort and so naturally that my aunt, who taught languages and was something of a psychic, insisted that I must have lived in France in a previous life. Even then I thought that such talk was nonsense; I do not believe in reincarnation, and I think that all notions of revisiting past lives are the idle indulgence of bored and lonely people.

When I was nineteen, I spent my junior year of college at the famous university at Aix-en-Provence in the south of France. Though I had never been there before I had a powerful feeling of familiarity with the region. I slipped easily into the lifestyle of Provence with its siesta and its slow, lilting speech. Before long I spoke with the local *accent du Midi*, which would be rather like a student from Paris learning English in Mississippi. French students from the north found this hilarious. But to me the southern accent was much more congenial in its songlike rhythms than was the clipped, speedy speech of Paris.

One day after French History class my professor remarked on my last name, asserting that it was a very ancient one, and that he thought it came from nearby, in the region around Lyon. I did not pursue the matter at the time, but put the idea into the back of my head for many years.

Then, in 1990, I was assigned to do a photo essay on the

monasteries of southern France for *National Geographic* magazine.[1] I flew first to Paris, where I visited with friends from my graduate school years at the Sorbonne, before going on to Marseille, Montpellier, Nice, and, finally, Lyon.

While in Lyon I decided that I would pay a visit to the city archives to determine whether my professor had been right about my name. My intention was merely to discover who my people had been, and when and why they had left France for America. I did not expect to find much: a reference in a public record, perhaps a birth certificate, or even, with luck, an etching or a photograph.

No sooner had I mentioned my purpose to the archivist, Mme Germaine Bézert, a small, slender, energetic woman in her fifties, than she was on her feet, checking through yellowed files and pulling books from the shelves with amazing speed. 'Rivelle ... Rivelle ... I know that name,' she kept insisting. 'But not from here, not from Lyon!'

Within half an hour, and over my protests that she not put herself to any trouble, she had found it. 'Roger l'Escrivel!' she exclaimed. 'Of course, Rivelle! Mon dieu! You are not the lineage of Roger of Lunel?' She studied me closely. 'Indeed, it is in your face, monsieur, indeed. But you shall know for sure. Listen, you must go to Lunel. Do you know it? It is in the Cevennes mountains north of Montpellier.'

I explained that I was on a tight schedule and an even tighter budget, but she was adamant. 'If you are of the family of Roger of Lunel,' she said, wagging a finger at me, 'then you must know. And so must I. I assure you, monsieur, I will never forgive you if you fail to learn the truth!'

Mme Bézert took a sheet of paper emblazoned with the crest of the City of Lyon and wrote in a very impressive hand that I might be a descendant of Roger of Lunel, and she asked her

---

1 This article became the genesis of a book, published in France under the title *Les Monastères du Midi: Le Style de la sainteté.* (Favel: 1992).

colleagues in the city administration at Lunel to assist me in any way they could.

Lunel is a small city, or more accurately, a large town, in the foothills of the Cevennes, one of the loveliest and most tranquil mountain ranges of France. The town is surprisingly unspoiled, given its proximity to the Riviera, and one can still enjoy there the leisurely style of the life of Provence. From my year in Aix I had come to expect the easy-going, characteristically Mediterranean manner of the people of this region. But when I presented Mme Bézert's letter at the town hall, it provoked a degree of animation I had not yet encountered in the South. The elderly clerk to whom I showed it peered at me over his glasses and asked if it were true. I told him that that was what I had come to Lunel to determine.

The clerk begged me to be patient a moment and disappeared into an inner office. When he returned, he was accompanied by a stout, middle-aged man with a red-veined face and chubby hands. '*Monsieur le maire*,' the clerk said reverently.

The mayor squinted at me a moment, then poked at the letter with a fat forefinger tipped with the flat, dirty nail of a farmer. 'What do you know of Roger l'Escrivel?' he asked curtly.

'Nothing, monsieur,' I replied. 'Perhaps you would have the kindness to tell me about him, as it seems I may be related to him.' The mayor exchanged a glance with the clerk and asked to see my passport. 'Is it necessary?' I said.

'You will do me the kindness?'

I knelt and opened my duffel bag, which I had dropped in front of the counter. First the clerk and then the mayor leaned over to watch me, to guarantee, I supposed, that I was not forging the passport on the spot for their benefit. When I stood up, I nearly bumped heads with them.

The mayor scrutinized my passport a long moment. 'Your name is Rivelle,' he announced.

'Yes. Mme Bézert thought my ancestors might be from here.'

The mayor squinted suspiciously. 'You speak with an *accent du Midi.*'

'Yes, I do.' They thought this over but said nothing, so I went on: 'I believe this Roger was known both as "de Lunel" and "l'Escrivel". Can you tell me why?'

'Indeed, monsieur,' the mayor replied. 'You will be patient a moment?'

I was now becoming really impatient, but again I waited as, this time, both the mayor and the clerk disappeared into the inner office. When they returned, a police official was with them. He approached me and saluted.

'I am Commissaire Delabert,' he said. He was a tall man with a protrusive belly who wore an impressive amount of braid on the epaulettes of his khaki uniform. He held up my passport and pointed to the name. 'You are Rivelle?'

'Yes,' I said, unable to conceal my growing dislike for the questioning.

'Your family lives in America?'

'What's left of them.'

'You are a small family?'

'Very, although we have always been Catholics.'

The three town officials glanced at one another. 'Monsieur,' the commissioner began in a formal tone, 'it may be that you are descended from Roger de Lunel as . . .' he consulted the letter from Lyon, 'the good Mme Bézert suggests. But to know that will take some time. Several days, perhaps.'

I explained as crisply as I could that I had only one day in Lunel, and that I desired simply to know whether this Roger was my ancestor or not.

'Monsieur,' the mayor said, 'at one time Roger l'Escrivel owned most of the land on which our city now stands. But there has been no member of that family here for many, many generations. If you are a descendant of Roger, then there are . . . implications.'

'What sort of implications?' I asked.

'Important implications,' the mayor replied vaguely. 'Will you be so kind as to wait here, perhaps for an hour, while we make some consultations?'

I gave a frustrated sigh and picked up my bag. 'Listen,' I said, 'I haven't seen the town, so I'll go for a walk, perhaps take lunch, and then return. Will that do?'

They all agreed that it would do well, and they wished me a pleasant afternoon.

Normally I enjoy exploring new places, but I found it difficult to concentrate on the Lunel town centre. I had come here looking for an ancestor, and suddenly I had a mystery on my hands. I was half-hoping that I was not related to Roger as I made my way towards the church.

I had recently photographed the twelfth-century monastery of Le Thornay with the tiny, bell-like chapel that was considered one of the acoustical wonders of Europe, and the Lunel church struck me as being from the same era. The outer doors were closed, which I found odd on such a hot day, but when I tried them I was stunned to find that they were locked. I had never encountered a locked church in France before.

I went in search of a restaurant and after lunch I returned to the town hall. No one was at the counter so I walked back to the door, opened it, and slammed it. From the inner office came the clerk, the mayor, the police commissioner, and a priest. 'This is Père Charles,' the mayor said. I shook his hand.

'May I please see your passport?' he asked. He was a tall, thin man in his sixties, and had it not been for his gentle manner, I would have begrudged him digging the passport out again. Père Charles put on his glasses and glanced at it. 'Has your family name always been spelled in this way?' he asked with a kindly smile.

'No,' I replied, 'I believe my great-grandfather altered the spelling. I was told that, to make it easier for Americans to pronounce, he added the final "l-e".'

The priest nodded deeply and returned my passport. 'Monsieur, we desire to be of service to you if we can. What is it you wish to know?'

I repeated that I merely wanted to know if I was descended from Roger de Lunel, or l'Escrivel, as he seemed to be called.

Père Charles removed his glasses. 'Indeed, monsieur, he was called l'Escrivel, and this may be the origin of your name. May I ask your profession?'

'I am a writer.'

A gasp went up from the other three. The priest nodded again. 'That is extraordinary,' he told me. 'That, one might say, is a miracle.'

'Father,' I began as calmly as I could, 'do you mind telling me what all this means?'

The priest stretched out his arm. 'You will do me the honour to return with me to my office at the church?'

'The church is locked,' I remarked drily.

'Ah,' Père Charles said with a smile, 'but, indeed, I have the key. The key to everything.'

I will not go into detail about the three hours I spent in Père Charles's office, for what follows will speak more eloquently than I ever could. Let me simply say that in the little, ancient church of Lunel I learned much more about my family's past, and perhaps about myself, than I had ever anticipated when I spoke with Mme Bézert in Lyon.

Indeed, there was a record, not in Lyon, but locked for nearly nine hundred years in a box beneath the altar of the church of Lunel. It is a record of one man's search for faith – the ultimate locus of faith – and of his passion to preserve the fruit of that search for his posterity.

That I was the intended recipient of his wisdom I, of course, had no idea. But knowing it has given me a sense of self that I might otherwise never have achieved. It has made me humble, and proud; it has conferred on me a sense of history and the present; it has helped me to understand who I am by showing me where, and from whom, I came. It has thrown a light on my past that, I firmly believe, is helping me to see my future.

I share that light with you now, in the hope that it may serve as a guide to your understanding as well.

NOTES ON THE TEXT

What Père Charles showed me was a manuscript dating from the turn of the twelfth century. It was in the form of a journal written by my ancestor, Roger, Duke of Lunel, a leader of the First Crusade (1096–1099). Tradition, arising from the opening entry of the journal, held that it was to be retained by the pastors of the Church of Saint Gilles de Lunel until a descendant of Roger should present himself.

Because the journal had achieved almost the status of a relic, I was not permitted to remove it from the church, although I was allowed to photograph it. This I did, while Père Charles carefully opened and held back the pages. I must confess that his thumb is prominent in many of the photographs.

The journal is written on vellum and the pages are bound with a very fine leather that has survived the centuries in remarkably good condition. This may be due in part to the fact that it has been stored since its completion in a kind of humidor – a virtually air-tight box of oak, covered in silver and lined with cedar. To my amazement, the cedar was still aromatic when I opened the box.[2]

To say that this is a holy book is, to my mind, not an exaggeration. It has kept its secrets of the great expedition to Jerusalem, and of Roger's deepest thoughts, feelings, doubts and revelations,

2 Besides the journal, the box contained three artefacts: a small enamelled crucifix, a jade statuette in the form of a woman with the head of a cat, and a pearl.

intact through half the history of our civilization. Clearly he was determined that, in the course of chronicling his great adventure of war and faith, he would hold nothing back, either from himself or from his unknown readers.

The journal is unique on several counts. It may be the most complete eyewitness record of the First Crusade now in existence.[3] It is also the only eyewitness account of the Crusade written in Old French, or Provençal, the others having been written in Latin. But most importantly, Roger's book is a diary not only of events, but of the effect they had on his own moral and spiritual development. Indeed, his self-analysis can be painfully probing and, at times, almost unbearably frank.

Before attempting the translation of Roger's journal I had only a sketchy knowledge of Provençal, the ancient dialect of southern France. I am indebted to Professor Ronald Akehurst of the University of Minnesota for his instruction in this lovely language, which resembles modern Portuguese more than modern French. I also acknowledge his invaluable assistance in rendering the manuscript into an English that is at once contemporary and reflective of the spirit of the original.

It took me nearly five years to translate Roger's journal or, at least, until I had satisfied myself that I had done it sufficient justice. I have discovered that translation is at best an inexact science, and so occasionally I note instances where a variant reading might alter the understanding of a passage, or where I am not entirely sure

---

3 To my knowledge it is rivalled only by Fulcher de Chartres's *A History of the Expedition to Jerusalem*. Important as this work is, it was written by a priest who accompanied Baldwin of Boulogne and was absent from the main body of the Crusade from October 1097 until 1100. By contrast, Roger's journal covers the entire Crusade and includes first-hand accounts of all of its major engagements.

I find Roger's chronicle superior also to the famous *Gesta Francorum et Aliorum Hierosolimitanorum* (Anonymous), which many consider the principal source book for the First Crusade. Regarding the experiences of the Provençal Crusaders, there is, too, the chronicle of Raimund of Aguillères, whom, as we shall see, Roger met on the march. It is entitled *Historia Francorum qui ceperunt Jerusalem* and, while unreliable, is nonetheless of great interest.

of the intended meaning. In such cases I am content to let the reader decide for him- or herself.

The journal contains many archaic military terms and references to contemporaneous artefacts such as items of clothing, weapons, and equestrian accoutrements. I was helped greatly with these by Dr Danielle Coppola, Professor of Medieval Studies at the Claremont Graduate School, Pomona, California.

Since Roger lived in a world dominated by the doctrines of Roman Catholicism, his diary contains numerous unelaborated references to its beliefs and practices. I have attempted to explain these theological concepts briefly in footnotes. Readers who wish to inform themselves further are referred to the excellent work, *Faith and the Sword: The Religion of the Crusades*, by C. G. Wilkinson (Temple University Press, 1983).

I must also gratefully acknowledge the assistance of Ms Christine Bocek of the Los Angeles Public Library for her help in locating reference sources, and of Ms Mei-ling Tien who not only typed the final text of the translation, but who pointed out to me areas where correction and clarification were needed.

THE BOOKE OF DAYS

OF ROGER,
DUKE OF LUNEL
AND SERVANT
OF GOD

*Begun in the Year of the
Incarnation of Our Saviour 1096*

A BOOKE OF DAYS

AUGUST THE SECOND[4]

I have no children of my own. This is a source of great discomfiture to me. For a man lives through his children, when he is old, and after he is dead. I am now in my twenty-ninth year and, except for the grace of God, it is unlikely that I shall have issue. For my wife is barren, having suffered the haemorrhage in the birth of her fourth child, the daughter of her previous husband.

I shall, therefore, commence this journal in the event that any member of my line, the children either of my sister Gauburge, or the descendants of my lamented stepbrother Michael, should wish to know of me.

I begin today, for I have lately taken the Cross, and shall soon depart on the great pilgrimage to Jerusalem in service to my Lord Raymond, Count of Toulouse.[5] As it is God's will whether I shall return or not, I shall keep this book as faithfully as I can, concealing nothing from it as if I were speaking to my dearest friend. For as Our Lord and Saviour has said: You shall know the truth, and the truth shall make you free.

I shall tell something of myself.

---

4 A note on time and the dating of the entries: It was the Roman Catholic Church's need to determine the date of the moveable feast of Easter that prompted the adoption of our modern calendar. In Roger's time the old Roman and lunar calendars were still in use, as well as other systems for calculating dates such as counting the number of days to and from important religious festivals. In dating his entries, Roger is by no means consistent, using one or the other calendar and occasionally the old form of kalends, nones and ides as well as other archaic references. These I have translated into the modern system.

Note, too, that in Roger's era, calculating the hour was an imprecise business. Since Christians were required to pray several times each day, hours were expressed in relation to these prayers, which were called matins, prime, terce, sext, none, vespers and compline. Using these references, I have made approximations of the time of day whenever Roger mentions it. For more on this subject, the reader is referred to J. Y. Soto-Quiroz, *Time in the Medieval Mind* (unpublished doctoral dissertation, UCLA, 1994).

5 Raymond of Toulouse was also known as Raymond of Saint Gilles.

I am Roger, Duke of Lunel, son of Richard of Burgundy, vassal of Raymond of Toulouse. I was born in the year of the conquest of William the Norman over the English.[6] My father was carried off in his twenty-first year by the flux.[7] I was then three years of age and so I scarcely knew him, though I have kept his memory sacred. Upon his death his lands were confiscated by Gaspard, the Bishop of Macon, who accomplished this crime through a trickery of the law, declaring that since my parents were second cousins their marriage was null. Such slanders were put about by Gaspard that my mother was forced to flee with my sister and me to her cousins in Provence. There she married my stepfather, Gilles, Duke of Lunel.

Now Gilles had two sons, Reynald and Michael. When the Moors threatened Saint Jacques, the holy city of pilgrimage, Gilles, taking with him Reynald, his elder son, joined arms with Robert Guiscard[8] to drive them out. Reynald was drowned in the River Arga, being weighted down with his equipments, and Gilles, a dark and brooding man, fell into despair and took his own life.

Michael was but twelve years old at that time and his aunt Drucille, unwilling to allow the transfer of the estate to my mother, connived with her cousin Benoît, the Bishop of Montpellier, to annul the marriage and invest the estate solely in Michael. Thus, my mother, my sister and I once again found ourselves disenfranchised, and we were reduced to the level of guests in our own house.

In his sixteenth year Michael married Elisabeth, daughter of Guy Saint-Roc, who, in the fourth month of their marriage, gave birth to a girl whom they named Magdalene. Elisabeth, being red-

6 1066.

7 This was probably dysentery, caused by impurities in drinking water. It was not an uncommon disease in medieval Europe, even among landed families, and it was usually fatal.

8 Robert Guiscard was a famous Norman knight who, in the late eleventh century, led the effort to expel the Muslims of North Africa, known as Moors, from southern Europe. Saint Jacques de Compostelle, as it is called in French, is a Spanish city famous as the object of a medieval pilgrimage route which crossed the south of France.

haired and of a hysterical temperament, was soon put away in the convent of Montelimar. The marriage was annulled and Michael, believing that his wife's madness was God's punishment for his lust, renounced his inheritance and took holy orders at Cluny.

Upon this, at last, Lunel came into the hands of our family. If there had been hot blood before between us and the family of Gilles, it now became black. Drucille stopped at nothing to injure my mother, even going so far as to enlist mercenaries to burn the farmers' homes and plunder the fields and barns. As I was too young to defend the estate, my mother applied for the protection of the Church and of my Lord Raymond.

As the world knows, it is not safe nowadays for a woman to live alone nor even to travel the roads of her own property. And so, although my mother was in her thirty-third year and had had two husbands, my Lord Raymond arranged for her remarriage. Guy Dru, the man to whom she was espoused,[9] was forty-seven years old and, given his advanced age, nearly infirm. He had had some distinctions in the wars in Spain against the Moors and it was from him that I learned the arts of combat as a boy. He taught me the use of sword and lance, and how to fight from horse.

Under the eye of my stepfather I took to organizing the peasants of Lunel into a fighting force, arming and training them to protect the estate. My mother, meanwhile, was able to prevail upon the bishop to apply the Peace of God to our relations with the family of Gilles. And so for certain periods we were left unmolested.[10]

During these intervals I applied myself to restore the lands of Lunel. Many of the peasant farmers have quit the land, and those who remain are hard-pressed to make their living. I am not a farmer

9 The Provençal word is *espozada*, a term taken from cattle breeding, which literally means 'exposed', as a cow is to a bull. I am told by Professor Akehurst that the similarity to 'espoused' is merely a coincidence.
10 The Peace of God was a decree of the Roman Catholic Church forbidding hostilities between designated groups or families during specific times. The penalty for violating the Peace of God could be excommunication, which estranged one from the sacraments and thus, potentially, condemned the offender to eternal damnation.

nor a cattleman by nature; I lack the patience and do not share the love of the soil that comes with peasant blood. Nonetheless, to comfort my mother who had fought so hard and long to secure the estate, I undertook the work, chafing at the backwardness of the peasants and the slow spirit of the earth. It was in these efforts that I began to meet with the nobles hereabouts. From them I took my education in the ways of the landlord, and from one of them I took my greatest joys and my greatest sorrows.

AUGUST THE EIGHTH

It is now one week until the day appointed by Our Holy Father Urban for the commencement of the armed pilgrimage.[11] I have begun to equip those peasants who are to accompany me as infantry, some fourteen in all. As for myself, I prepare both martially and spiritually. My wife weeps at night.

I have read this account – though scant yet it is – and wonder if I shall have the courage to continue it truthfully, for unless it is *true*, I ought not to have begun it at all. And so I will continue my narrative at the point where I had left it.

I said that I had made the acquaintance of the nobles hereabouts. One of them in particular, Eustace of Valdevert, put himself at pains to help me. Whether this was because I was by birth a Burgundian and he wished to show his tolerance for foreigners, or whether it was because he hoped for some advantage of me I could

---

11 The reference is to Pope Urban II, who called for the Crusade at the Council of Clermont, France, on November 27, 1095. A note on the word 'Crusade': Roger never uses it for the simple reason that the word had not yet been coined. To Roger, the First Crusade was known as an expedition or an armed pilgrimage. It was not until the thirteenth century that the great holy wars in the East were called Crusades, and not until the seventeenth century that the word came into common usage. 'Crusade', from the French *croisade* (from *croix*, meaning cross), derived from the fact that the participants wore a cloth cross on the right shoulder of their surcoats.

not tell. Yet he frequently came to me in the company of his wife, and begged that I should visit them as often as I wished.

Eustace was a good man, plump and very elegant in manner, with a clipped beard and a ready smile. He was, it must be said, too forward in his conversation, especially when he was under the influence of wine.[12] I could not help but feel that despite the fact that he had a wife and four children, he was a lonely and unsatisfied man. It was not uncommon for him to ride the ten leagues from his home to mine merely to have my company.

Jehanne, the wife of Eustace, was a dark and handsome woman. Her nose was long, it is true, but her skin was exceedingly pale and her eyes as black as sinfulness. How often did I find her glancing at me from the corners of those black eyes. Meanwhile, Eustace would be nattering away about barley or wagons or some quotidian stuff while he winked at me, pulled at his cup of wine, and tried to make my mother and sister laugh. But Jehanne and I were caught in our own silent conversation, the fire of her coal black eyes filling me with heat and dread.

I was twenty-two years old and swollen with life, as raw as exposed flesh. She knew it. She was older than I, the mother of children. She had lain upon beds in sweat. The scent of her body sang to me.

I rode out to Eustace as often as I could. At first I took Thomas, my stable boy, and I kept him close to me, but later I went alone. It was on the eve of Michaelmas that she touched me for the first time. Eustace had called a fête for the name day of his eldest son. It was a cool night and, while some danced outside, others retired into the house. Eustace had drunk to excess and he did not notice the absence of his wife. I did, and I went in search of her.

She was in the kitchen near the dry store,[13] and when she saw me she stopped and turned and slipped in behind the door. I was

12 The expression in Provençal is *apres lo vin*, literally, 'after the wine'.
13 A pantry for storing dried fruit and vegetables.

puzzled; I did not know what I should do. I walked to the door and waited, feeling stupid and sure to be discovered. Then the door opened and I was taken in a firm grasp and pulled inside.

Jehanne closed the door behind me. It was dark and smelled of apples and garlic. Before I could speak, a wedge of lemon was in my mouth. 'This is from my garden,' her voice said. Then her hands were on my hips. She pulled me to her and in the fragrant dark she licked the base of my neck. That was all. Then she was gone. I stood in the dark after the door had closed, the juice of her lemon running down my chin.

After that the scent of lemons drove me mad. I was in a fever, thinking of her continually. God help me, I devised plots to murder her husband, and in chapel I prayed ardently for his death. I twisted in my bed at night and even moaned, or so Gauburge told me, for she could hear me from her room. The name Jehanne was ever on my lips. I wept and ached for her. The scent of her was in my nostrils. And at night, O Jesu, I gripped myself and made a prayer of her name and my sinning.

When again I saw her, on the morning of Martinmas at the cathedral of Montpellier, she did not raise her eyes to me. And yet I gazed at her across the aisle so that, I was certain, even His Eminence the bishop must have noticed. I had never lain with a woman, and she was all women to me. Forgive me, my Saviour, but her body was the only temple in which I longed to pour out my worship.

To such extremes will passion drive a man. Yet no one could I tell, not even my confessor, the good monk René. In confession I spoke only of longings, for which he gave me the penance of flagellation. And so each night I stripped off my shirt, took up the birch, and whipped myself and wept, and thought of her. The pain was my devotion to her, the welts were proof of my love, the blood was my seed smeared not within her womb but on my back.

It was an unholy time. I did not see her again until the spring, when I rode to Eustace with my overseer to watch his sowing. He had knowledge of the land that he had learned on a pilgrimage to Antioch, and he had promised to share with me the secrets of the East. Eustace was a pious man and a generous neighbour, and I shook his small hand in full knowledge that already in my heart I had violated his unsuspecting trust.

Jehanne stood in her garden, her skirts tucked up into her belt, bent nearly double to tend her seedlings. The moist soil that clung about her ankles was the most lascivious sight that ever I had beheld. Nothing, not the crude drawings of the schoolboys of the town, not the forbidden book that I had once had to myself for a week as it made the rounds of the local youths, was as lubricious as her naked feet adorned with earth. She turned as I passed by with her husband, the scarf atop her hair disclosing the curve of her cheek, and she paused and gazed at me, and then bent again to her labour.

It was enough. I would have killed Eustace on the spot and taken her. But in that instant he turned to me and said, 'Have you seen my mare? She is great again.'

My mare. My mare! It was a summons to my senses. *She* was his mare, that he rode at will, that had borne his pudgy body a hundred times, that had been great by him. I stared at him mute until he stopped and took my hand and asked if I were ill. He made me sit down and stroked my forehead, remarking on the heat. He asked if I would lie down, and offered me his own bed. I thanked him quickly and left.

I went home angry that night, cursing at myself as I rode the hedgerows in the dark, my horse stumbling, turning to peer at me, and then moving on when I kicked viciously at her sides.

It was in the autumn that it happened. The harvest had proved fair and the bishop called a celebration. There had been none in so many years that all the folk around attended, eager to have the chance to thank God and to indulge themselves. I went only because my sister was by then betrothed to a nobleman of Sète and could not be in his company alone.

Eustace arrived on the second day of the fête. I saw Jehanne before I saw him, wearing an emerald gown tied with cord below her bosom, and a veil aslant her face. I was talking with Thomas and I stopped and stared at her and felt my soul dissolve within me. Though on her husband's arm, she gazed back at me, a cold, hard gaze of challenge. I nearly wailed.

All that day I sought to catch her eyes. There were contests and I joined them all, eager for her attention. I vied with the town youths at lifting sacks, fighting with wooden swords, and standing on one leg balancing a pike. And every time she looked at me I felt myself become more brazen.

That night Eustace drank himself into a stupor. I waited till they had carried him to an inn, and then I went to her. Nothing was said. We were in the graveyard behind the church. I scarcely noticed the other couples in the shadows there. I pulled her to the earth of a new-made grave, her hands were in my clothes, my breath was hot, her lips were on fire. She took me in her hands and folded me into the deep and wet of her. And I lavished my guilt upon her.

Five times I had her in that festival, each time more fervid and more daring than the last. There among the horses of the bishop's stable I raised her skirts and took her like an animal, while she gasped and rubbed herself against me and panted out my name.

Oh God where was Your sternness that I had heard of as a child and feared as I should have feared that of my own father? Where was the fear? Vanquished by lust, obliterated by a desire that carried me away like demons gaggling down towards hell.[14]

On the final night of the festival she came to me in my room at the top of the inn. I had made sure that Thomas was drunk and when, even then, he would not leave my door,[15] I beat him with my belt until he sulked away. Poor boy!

---

14 The expression here is *que devalavon cridan e siblan jos en enfern*. The word *siblan* suggests the sound of a flock of geese hissing. I have thus taken a liberty in making a verb of the word 'gaggle'.
15 A squire, such as Thomas, normally slept outside his master's door when he stayed at an inn.

I perfumed myself, for I had not bathed in four days and nights. There was no light save the torches of the revellers, and their songs came up to me in mockery of the beating of my heart. I did not care. I was so deep in sin that sin itself was buttress to my exiled soul. Never had I felt so pleased with myself, and never had I been in greater danger. Thus it always is with passion.

The door opened and then closed as quickly. She was naked in my arms without a word. Her body was everywhere at once, her mouth upon me like a flood of flesh. The life sprang to my loins. She was atop me. I felt no shame — another man's wife. A friend, a neighbour. I revelled in the thought, and in my mastery of her. She bit at my lips, her nails were in my side, the heaving of her upon me was like the sea, a sea in which I eagerly drowned in lust.

Then *he* was in the door: Eustace, his blouse open, barefoot, his eyes staring in horror. I saw him past her shoulder, and it was a long moment before she stopped and looked at me, and then turned.

'Bitch,' he said to her. 'You have taken him from me.'

He turned his back and left. I did not understand. I looked to her eyes for the meaning of his words. But she began to laugh. To laugh!

AUGUST THE TWELFTH

How painful it has been to write these things. I have decided to lock this book in my mantle chest for fear that it may be found. Yet whom I fear I cannot say, since none of the women or serving people of the house can read. It may be that I fear myself. For, God forgive me, I find myself excited still at the unholy events that it relates.

I left the festival with great foreboding in my heart. Guilt I had yes, but also fear: fear that Eustace would confront me and demand satisfaction. I did not fear the combat, for I knew that, should he beard me,[16] I could easily disable, even kill him. Yet the thought that so generous a neighbour should pay with *his* life for *my* sin tormented me. How we bring evil upon ourselves by ill deeds! And how we relish of those deeds even as we commit them.

Every time I heard a knock at the door I felt the dread, not that I might die, but that I might kill. My lust would make a murderer of me. Eustace would die, and with him my soul. Both would go to hell. And for what? For her! A slut. A common adulteress.

It was my sister, Gauburge, who brought the news to me. She is a plain girl, it must be admitted. Her face is long and unintelligent, her eyes are close, her skin is blotched, her hair not at all supple and rich like that of Jehanne. Yet when she came into my chamber, her face bore such an expression of pain and grief that I thought her beautiful, just for a moment.

'What is wrong?' I said to her.

'Eustace of Valdevert,' she whispered. 'He is drowned.'

I started up in spite of myself. This I had not expected. That he would come to me in a rage, or even in the calm of his revenge, I had a hundred times imagined. But that he should take his own life . . .

Later the monk René gave me the details. After the festival, Jehanne returned to Valdevert alone, her husband having refused to accompany her. When at last he returned to his home, he locked himself indoors and would admit no one. On the seventh day his rooms were found unlocked, but there was no sign of Eustace. That evening his squire found his tunic floating in the river. Nearby on the bank were his wallet[17] and boots. There was a note in his hand addressed to Jehanne which said: 'I go on my final pilgrimage.'

---

16 I have chosen to use a Shakespearian idiom to translate the expression *si m'afrontava*, which would today most aptly be rendered 'get in my face'.

17 *almosniera*, literally 'alms purse'. Since money was only just coming into common use again, the clothing of eleventh-century men had no pockets. Instead, they carried small change in a leather purse attached to their belts, and so it was not a 'wallet' in the modern sense.

Though his body was never found, the bishop declared him a suicide. After the shortest decent interval, I married Jehanne.

It is the evening. I was interrupted in my writing by Thomas, who came to inform me that my hauberk[18] is not yet ready. This annoys me greatly, since I must leave in three days' time. I have had to sell ten hectares of land to the bishop to raise the money for my own and my peasants' accoutrements, and I especially directed the smith to have my hauberk ready in good time. Now he demands more payment to finish it, saying that the labour involved has taken him from his shoeing, and that he has had to hire the overseer's son to work the helix.[19] How brazen the craftsmen have become in recent years.

I was writing about Jehanne de Valdevert, whom I married in my twenty-fourth year. I adopted her four children according to the law, though I have not included them in my inheritance. This is because, God forgive me, I despise them. They are arrogant, disobedient, sullen and brutal children who make clear their disdain for me. They seem to know that I was responsible for their father's death, and they never cease to impugn me by their looks and their disrespect. I find them dirty, ill-tempered and unlovable, and I shall keep them from the land that my mother paid so dearly to secure.

I have spoken little of my mother. She is a saintly woman, very austere in her manner and very righteous in her speech. She is full of good counsel and shares it liberally. Jehanne shuns her, saying that she is meddling and judgemental, and refuses even to eat with her. Mine is, alas, not a happy home.

I am weary now, and will go to bed. Jehanne will come to

18 The coat of mail, worn by knights of the period. Knights of the eleventh century did not wear suits of armour, but rather, a knee-length shirt and leggings made of closely woven iron chain. These, of course, were manufactured by hand, and were extremely difficult and time-consuming to make, as this reference indicates.
19 To make mail, individual rings of metal were bent around an iron dowel called a helix, then cut along one side and interwoven, before being welded shut again. It was a tedious process, and one that any smithy was likely to delegate to a hireling.

me, I know, in the middle of the night. And I will sin with her. For sin it is, in the shadow of her husband's watery corpse.

AUGUST THE FIFTEENTH
The Feast of the Assumption of Our Blessed Lady

I leave today to join my Lord Raymond on the great armed pilgrimage to Jerusalem. Jerusalem! How the word sounds like a trumpet! How it calls to my soul for deliverance! Jerusalem, the holy city, the city of God.

I lay last night with Jehanne as I foretold. How well I know her. She came in to me, her hair caught up, her nightgown flowing about her body like smoke. Her full arms and legs were about me even before I woke. Her breath was in my face. She was crying.

She begged me to take her in the forbidden way saying, 'God knows you may never return, and what shall I comfort myself with then?' And so I obliged her like a sodomite, weeping as I did so, for even there, upon the mantle, my surcoat hung with the scarlet Cross upon the shoulder. I gazed at it as I lay upon her and listened to her pitiful groans, thinking of the remission of sin[20] that will be the reward of all who fall in battle.

In the morning the men were turned out, looking dull and

---

20 The question of the indulgence granted to the Crusaders is complex. However, a brief discussion is necessary, since this was one of the main reasons why men joined the Crusade.

It is clear that Pope Urban II intended that some spiritual inducement be offered to the 'milites Christi', the army of Christ, but precisely what it was meant to be is still open to debate. The Pope had the power, conferred by Christ, both to forgive sin, and to grant remission for the punishment due to sin. This punishment could be of two kinds: either temporary suffering in purgatory, or eternal suffering in hell.

Urban appears to have offered the Crusaders *remission* of sin. What was not clear was whether this meant release only from the punishment for sins already committed, or a permanent release from punishment for all of one's sins, past and future. The Crusaders seem to have believed that Urban was offering them the latter, which would have represented an irresistible inducement to join the expedition.

unprepared, their tunics not so bright as I had imagined, their expressions rather more of melancholy than of fervour. O, Jerusalem, shall we be worthy of you? Shall our faith be great enough to save you?

We are now in Montpellier at the castle of my Lord. Many nobles and knights are assembling with their retinues for the great pilgrimage. In the morning Lord Raymond will inform us of the route we are to take, as well as instruct us in the commands of the Holy Father, conveyed to him through Adhémar, Bishop of Le Puy, the Holy Father's legate. I must go now to the hall where I am to dine with Raymond and those other nobles who have so far arrived.

The same, later

It is now night, and having travelled most of the day and drunk overmuch at dinner I am sleepy, but I will write of my departure from Lunel before I go to bed.

My mother bade me goodbye in her rooms, not wishing to do so in the company of my wife. I had not noticed how old she has become until I kissed her. Her face is drawn and dry and the wrinkles of it read like a story of woe. Indeed, she has not had an easy life, but has been plagued by slanders and quarrels. Even I, forgive me, have caused her grief by my incontinent behaviour.

'You must go,' she said. 'You must fight for God in order to save your own soul.'

She was correct, of course. I have many sins to purge by this endeavour, and I go in the hope that God will receive my sacrifice as atonement. I told her that it is unlikely I would be able to write to her, but that I would try. She looked into my face a long time and nodded, and then she said, 'Roger, my son, I shall never see you again.'

I tried to reassure her but she would not hear it. She held me in her arms and then made me kneel while she invoked God's blessing on me. Outside Gauburge and Jehanne waited for me.

Gauburge was very strong. I have spoken too little of her here. She had cakes for me, wrapped in a scarf sewn with the initials of her name. And she gave to me the crucifix that she has worn around her neck since she made her first communion.

Jehanne was near hysterics. She wailed and moaned and ripped the veil from her hair and threw it under the wheels of the provisions cart. She swore she would drown herself in the river and then, realizing that this touched on her first husband, she fell to her knees and beat the ground with her fists.

I pulled her to her feet and tried to silence her, for she was unnerving the horses, and the peasants were laughing at her. Her face was as ugly as I have ever seen it, twisted and tormented and dirty with tears and soil. She would have ripped my tunic if I had not held her arms like the limbs of a kicking ram. I commended her to the care of Gauburge but she spat and said, 'She does not love me, she wishes me dead. You, all of you, wish me dead.'

I was at pains to mount my horse for her pulling at my belt and my legs. At last I leant down and took her by the hair, bent back her face and kissed her on the mouth. This quieted her, and she set to kissing my knees and my ankles, and moaning like a lost child. I was away before she could forget herself again.

All the long dry ride to Montpellier I thought of the home that I was leaving. It is perhaps because I did not have a father that I do not know how a man should make his home. I have too long been under the dictates of women and of my sins. I have not acted from my own true self. But what is that self? Perhaps this pilgrimage will tell me.

AUGUST THE NINETEENTH

It is four days that I have not confided in my book. Much has happened. My wife Jehanne appeared at the castle, having ridden all night of the day I left. It was a humiliation to me, and the other men did not hide their mockery. I was harsh with her, ignoring her tears and commanding her to return home. When she persisted, and tried to sleep in the passage outside my door, I had her bound hand and foot and sent packing in a cart. I could not show my face all the next day. But at last the good Père René, who has accompanied us as chaplain, convinced me that all was well.

And indeed, it is a joy to be in the company of men. We have our jokes and games, and we can delight in one another's fellowship without the corroding influence of sex.[21] I think, as I watch these good, wholesome, manly soldiers, that all of the sufferings in my life have been due to women, and to my relations with them. It is Godly to be free of them at last. And I reflect that when God took flesh, He chose the flesh of a man.

I attended mass in the cathedral this morning. The Bishop Adhémar himself was celebrant, and in his sermon he preached the pilgrimage in words of fire: The Turk has seized the Holy Land from Christians who call to their brethren of the West for relief. His Excellency Adhémar was magnificent in his golden chasuble and jewelled mitre, the crosier grasped in his hand like the lance of God as he spoke. The nobles were all there in their colours. I too, in my blue and gold, the three stars of my family upon my breast. I swelled with pride to know that I was as good as any man, and blessed of God for the Cross that I wear upon my shoulder.

Later we all ranged around the bishop to hear his invocation. He looked each of us in the eye in turn and said: 'The sepulchre in which they laid Our Saviour is in the hands of unbelievers. Give your fortune, give your blood, give your life if you must, but save your soul. Save Christendom!'

---

21 *l'accion ronjan del dezir.* This is a very difficult expression to translate. The word *ronjan* means to nibble away or to prey upon. To my mind, it is a significant choice of words by Roger. He appears to view sex as a predatory animal, but a small, subtle one that destroys by inches, rather than one that consumes whole. I have thus chosen a word, 'corrode', that perhaps violates the animal spirit of his description, but that implies the gradual loss of integrity.

We all cheered at once: 'God wills it!'[22] Lebaud of Balbec, a rough, bearded Norman knight who wears a necklace made of fingernails, tore his cloak and swore that he would die upon the spot if he did not himself pray at that holy shrine.

The Bishop Adhémar is a noble man, near fifty, quite six feet tall with aquiline nose and dark eyes that pierce the soul. This is a saintly prelate, I thought as I listened to his booming voice, a man of God whom one might follow to the very gates of hell. It is not for nothing that the Holy Father has appointed him as leader of our pilgrimage. At one point, while Adhémar spoke, I glanced at my Lord Raymond, and was surprised to see him glaring at the bishop as though he were restraining a rage. I resolved to speak with him about it, for it seemed to me that he was filled, not with fervour, but with envy.

We have been training for combat in the courtyard of the castle. Lord Raymond leads us, accustoming us to work in unison rather than as single fighters. We practise the wheel and the redouble, the charge and the cembel.[23] Some of the knights chafe at these drills, but Raymond, with his white beard and his fame in fighting the infidel, commands respect.

I should speak a moment of him.

Raymond of Saint Gilles is a man of fifty-five, aged it is true, but as youthful and strong in spirit as any apprentice knight. He has spent much time in the East, and he keeps his body fresh with unguents and rubbings, and with all forms of exercise and spiritual devotion. No one can match him for vigour or for quickness of mind. Even his teeth are strong, and yesternight I saw him rip the backbone from a roasted suckling whole by gripping and thrashing at it with his powerful yellow teeth. He held it high in his mouth, the juices smearing his face, and grinned while we all applauded. He could, I am sure, kill a man with those teeth.

22 *Deus le volt!* The motto of the Crusade.
23 The cembel is a feinting manoeuvre in which part of a force of cavalry makes a sudden move towards a flank to draw off the opponent or to split his force.

His piety is famous. He made the pilgrimage to Jerusalem in the time before the Turks, and he has fought the infidel in Spain, Sicily and Malta. I had assumed that the Holy Father would choose him to lead the expedition, and it occurs to me now that this perhaps explains his snarling at the Bishop Adhémar.

AUGUST THE TWENTIETH

This morning, quite unexpectedly, I witnessed a terrible scene. I was passing out of the castle to attend to my horse when I heard voices raised in anger. Though I should not have, I lingered in the foyer, for I felt sure that one of the voices was that of my Lord Raymond.

'Damn your Holy Father,' he shouted, 'I would be better served by the anti-pope!'[24]

'You watch your tongue,' the other man replied. 'You can be excommunicated as easily as any peasant.' It was Adhémar!

I heard Raymond laugh. 'Don't threaten me with hell, you hypocrite,' he said. 'I know how rich you've become from this expedition. Half the men here have sold you land to pay for their weapons.'

'That money is God's,' growled Adhémar.

'Yes, but you'll spend it,' Raymond replied. 'You and your Holy Father. You want the knights out of France so they'll stop raiding your churches. And you've worked out a clever scheme to get them to pay you for the privilege. Plenary indulgence! They'll pay dear for the remission of their sins before they're through.'

I was scandalized by what I heard. Never would I have expected my Lord to exchange such heated words with His Eminence. I stopped my ears and was about to pass on when footsteps

24 This was the period of the Investiture Crisis. A second pope, Guibert, backed by the German emperor Henry IV, had arisen to challenge the legitimacy of Urban II. To those faithful to Urban, Guibert was known as the anti-pope.

approached the door. I knew that in an instant I would be discovered so I concealed myself.

It was Raymond who came into the hall. 'You are no military man,' he grumbled over his shoulder. 'You may lead this expedition in prayer if you like, but not in battle.'

I could see Adhémar through the open door. 'Our battles will be prayers,' he said. 'And so if I lead in prayer, I lead in battle too.'

'That clever tongue of yours would make a meal for a Turk,' Raymond replied. 'And if you get in my way I will see that it does.' With that, my Lord stalked off into the courtyard. I crept from my hiding place and peered into the room. Adhémar was on his knees, his head bare, praying I supposed. But in a moment I could see that he was clutching at his chest and gasping for breath.

Jerusalem, it seems that you are farther than we know.

AUGUST THE THIRTY-FIRST

A long time that I have written nothing. We have crossed from the kingdoms of the Franks into those of the Italians.[25] So far the march has been a pleasant one, for the most part along the coast through villages and towns where we are welcomed as soldiers of Christ. Notwithstanding this cordial reception, some of the knights do not restrain themselves from pillaging, attacking even those who throw their homes open to us and willingly provision us. It has been a great scandal to my Lord Raymond, who is at pains to stop it.

The Norman knights, especially, know no code of honour. They are Vikings, which shows in their faces and their dress. They wear

25 France and Italy did not yet exist as nations. Both were loose alliances of more or less independent provinces or kingdoms. All of the knights on the First Crusade were referred to as Franks, since the great majority came from the kingdoms of France.

the skins of animals though it is very warm and humid. They are elaborately tattooed, and all the tattoos are vulgar. About their persons they sport jewellery of the most hideous kind, bones and teeth and such. The leader of the knights, Fulk Rechin of Anjou, has sewn his surcoat with pairs of enamelled testicles which, he is proud to say, were severed from the loins of priests. They are horrible things, black and withered like the pods of jacaranda. Their lord is Duke Robert of Normandy, the son of King William of Britain, but he is often absent, going in search of estates, it is said, on which he spends liberally.

The Normans' speech is primitive too, an ugly cross between the Langue d'oil[26] and the guttural grunting of their Viking ancestors. They are for the most part large, fair-haired men, very dirty, with twisted beards and sharp teeth, and they take orders from no one. At night they collect around their fires and sing the most obscene songs which, though they hear them a hundred times, still bring choking laughter. It is sobering to think that William, the conqueror of Britain, was one of these half-men, half-animals.

Yesterday we passed through San Remo, the first of the Italian towns, and the Normans were merciless. The children came out to greet us bearing rolls and wild flowers, but the Normans brushed them aside with curses. That night, when we had camped beyond the town and dark had fallen, they made for the houses. They turned the men out with oaths and their swords and threw themselves upon the women. Rape was king in that trusting village.

When a few of us returned in the morning to fetch water from the wells we saw a horrid sight. Some of the townsmen were slain, lying in the streets with their throats cut. But worse was the condition of the women: wandering about white with shock, or

26 In Roger's France there were two principal languages: 'Langue d'oc' and 'Langue d'oil'. 'Oc' and 'oil' were the two Old French words for 'yes'. Langue d'oc, also known as Provençal, was the language of the south; Langue d'oil was the northern dialect, which eventually prevailed and evolved into French. The modern word 'oui' comes from 'oil'.

weeping in the streets. One girl in particular, who could not have been more than thirteen, I took pity on. Her skirts were bloody and she sat in her doorway as if paralysed. When I approached and she saw the Cross upon my surcoat, she screamed and crawled inside the house, unable to get to her feet.

That night I went to my Lord Raymond with the other men and we reported what we had seen. His face darkened as he heard us out. 'We are not heathens!' he bellowed. 'We go to fight the heathens. Where is Adhémar? Where is the Marshal of Our Lord?' The Bishop Adhémar was summoned and we repeated our stories for him. 'This is your army of Christ!' Raymond shouted. 'You think you can discipline them with prayer?'

Adhémar turned from the pavilion[27] in disgust. 'Do what you must,' he said.

'Now he relents,' Lord Raymond scoffed. 'After a town of ruined women.' In the morning he convened the Norman knights. Those who were guilty of the depredations were stripped of their accoutrements and sent home in disgrace. The others were put on notice that any assaults on innocent people would be met with death. To this Adhémar added his own injunction that excommunication would be instant upon the sentence. Hell, and not the holy city, would be their destination.

Nonetheless, tonight as I write this, the Norman knights are drunk and singing of their conquests. They have invented a new song called 'Sweet San Remo', and it speaks in the most malicious terms of the charms of Italian women.

SEPTEMBER THE SECOND

I should say a word about hygiene. I have never lived close to the peasants and so I did not truly appreciate until now what a filthy

27 The pavilion was the tent of a lord.

lot they are. They never bathe, nor do they have a thought for their teeth, their clothes, or even their evacuations. They urinate just where they are, not even taking the time to loosen their stockings. And when they defecate, they do so in the line of march, with no consideration for their fellows and no effort to clean themselves afterwards. The result is an odour that rises with the heat and can be smelled for a half a league distant. I am embarrassed to lead them into a village or town.

This morning I was so disgusted with them that I took them aside like children and, so as not to shame them, began to teach them in whispers about the necessity of cleanliness. I instructed them in the making of field privies, and the use of leaves to clean themselves afterwards. And I ordered, under penalty of dismissal, that each man bathe at least once a month, and that we never camp beside a stream without their cleaning themselves and their clothing thoroughly.

This has inspired much grumbling among them, but I am satisfied that, in the long run, it will make for a happier and healthier corps.

SEPTEMBER THE SEVENTH

We are passing through the kingdom of Liguria, a most beautiful country by the sea. There are low mountains that remind me of my Cevennes, and vineyards and orchards with every kind of fruit. The men pluck them as they pass, and weave the grape leaves into their hats. They look like Bacchus, with their stained faces and leafy crowns.

There is much time for reflection on the march, and more and more I am given over to it. The fresh sea breeze, the warm, scented air, the regular sound and sway of the march have a settling effect upon the mind. I think of my home, which I miss with pangs I would not have expected. Landry Gros, a Norman knight who sometimes rides with me, an educated man unlike his countrymen, has told me that the word nostalgia means, in Viking dialect, 'home pain'. And indeed, that is what I feel — an absence, a longing for the familiar.

And so all day, as I rode at walking pace before my troops, I found myself composing a verse about Jehanne. It occupied my mind, and I devoted much time and thought to it. I had never made verses before, and found it a pleasant and challenging pastime. I determined, when we stopped, that I would write it down, not because I believe it has any merit, but simply so that I shall not forget it.

> It is three weeks since I
> Have seen you, rapt
> Like Jonah in the tomb,
> Heaving in the deep,
> Mouthed by silent tongue.
>
> I know how beggars feel
> Who sleep in wind.
> I curl and shiver,
> Reaching for your hand,
> Your warmth beneath the cover.
>
> I see what death is now:
> Not loss but longing;
> Not absence but the yearn
> Of once more holding.
> Death is not sleep but dream.[28]

28 Translating Roger's verse has been the most daunting part of my work. In Provençal it has a quiet, lyrical quality that anticipates the poetry of the troubadours. Like any translator of verse I faced two choices: I could render the lines as close to the original as possible, retaining the rhythm and rhyme schemes, or I could find a poetic equivalent in modern English that conveys the spirit of the original. Although I am no poet myself, I have chosen to attempt the latter.

It is strange that I should be drawn to verse at so advanced an age. But I am embarked upon an adventure, and I must be open to new things. A man is a fool who undertakes a journey only to view his own face. It is strange, too, that I should miss my wife so, since she was my reason for leaving. This I ought to explain, for it is not too soon to face it.

I never would have joined this pilgrimage had it not been for Eustace. I coveted his wife, in direct violation of the commandment, and it was that which caused his death. And then, in the wake of that sin, I took her as my wife, in a union that could not but live in shadow. She is barren, of course. But that was to be expected.

It was not the haemorrhage as I wrote before, although she had the haemorrhage. It was the sin – my sin with her. And then the sin of Eustace's death. Yet, Jesu forgive me, I lust for her still, even after five years of marriage, when the blood ought to have cooled, when I ought to turn my thoughts to God and death, looking to my soul and not to my desires. But now, even as I write, I smell her flesh, I feel her warmth, I long for her. The ache is in me and, I fear, can never be expunged. It must be that my blood is cursed, for so hot it stays despite the chill of guilt.

But that sex with her which ought to be the crown of marriage is nothing but carnality in us. There is a corpse in our bed – a pale and bloated corpse and, dear Lord! the knowledge only whets me, makes me coarser, hotter when she lies with me. It is forbidden fruit that savours all the more for poisoned juice. My flesh will burn in hell, but not so hot as it burns within her ivory arms.

That is why I have come on this blessed pilgrimage – for the remission of sin pledged to all who fight in Christ's name. It is my only hope, since I am too old to curb myself, and since I have not the courage or the cruelty to put my wife away.

I do not sleep with her. She has her rooms in the far wing of the demesne.[29] Yet every night she makes her way to me. And, I confess, I lie and wait for her, my heart pounding in my ears. It is a strange game we play of love at a distance.[30] I hide from her where she will find me. She feels her way in the dark, a pilgrimage each night to worship the only God she knows. Alas for both of us!

I must not dwell upon such things. I must be about God's business so that my sins may be wiped away and my soul may bend again towards heaven. That is my task — to cleanse my soul with blood, the infidels' or mine.

September the Eighth

I was carried away last night. I read the passage in horror this morning. And the verse! What on earth possessed me? I went to Père René and begged a penance of him to mortify my flesh, and he ordered me to walk behind my horse on the march today, and not to avoid the droppings of its behind, but to step in them with joy and with every step to say, 'This is what I am' and, 'Such is Roger, the haughty Duke of Lunel.'

I did so, with the result that I am calmer now. And that I had to buy a pair of shoes from a merchant of Savona.

---

29 The demesne was the house of a noble who was not a lord. Lords generally lived in castles. Roger's demesne would have been a one or two-storey house of earth and timber built in a U-shape around a courtyard. The family would have occupied one wing, while the servants occupied another, and the peasants indentured to the family, the third. That Roger took the extraordinary step of exiling his wife to one of the wings reserved for the staff indicates how deeply he was torn by the circumstances of his marriage.

30 *Jonguam un joc estranh d'amor de lonh.* Professor Akehurst points out that the expression *amor de lonh* or 'distant love' would become popular among the troubadour poets. The strangeness here is that Roger has deliberately distanced himself from his wife.

SEPTEMBER THE TWENTY-THIRD

We have arrived at the city of Genoa, and what a splendid place it is! The harbour is deep and clear, and festooned with a thousand sails, and everywhere the homes and shops are open to us. Lord Raymond keeps a sharp eye on the Normans, for the women here are very beautiful and the town is rich with goods. So far they have behaved themselves well, merely stripping naked en masse and charging into the sea. At least they shall be clean.

I went this morning with Count Raymond, Bishop Adhémar, and some other men of rank to be received by the council of elders. We met in a splendid palace overlooking the docks. Arrangements were made that during our campaign in the East we shall be provisioned by the merchantmen of Genoa, who promise that our expedition shall lack for nothing.

The council enquired to know the exact size of our army, and I was surprised to hear Lord Raymond number it at forty nobles, eight-hundred knights, and four-thousand infantry. Together with these are some twelve-hundred pilgrims, men, women and children, who accompany us unarmed. The elders of Genoa have graciously offered to provide for them as well.

These pilgrims I have seen on many occasions while we are camped. They are a ragged lot and, I think, more than a few are criminals. Some act as sutlers, selling food and other necessaries to the men. I am told that they obtain these goods through theft. Two I saw hanged in Liguria, where they were said to have murdered a farmer and his family. I do not know this last to be a fact, but I believe it.

We were meant to go directly down the coast to Pisa and thence to Rome, but Bishop Adhémar has had a letter from our Holy Father who currently is at Lucca to the south-east, and who desires that we should come to him. Thus, after a respite in Genoa, we travel inland to Lucca.

I spend much time in the company of Landry Gros, who has taken to calling me l'Escrivel[31] since he has often seen me writing in my book. He is a good man, more refined than his Norman fellows, though oddly he retains some of their tribal ways. His speech is littered with Viking words, most of them coarse. For example, he calls a doublet 'shit buckets' and his sword a 'gut screw', and women are 'bags' or 'roosts' or 'clap merchants'. Nonetheless, I find Landry to be good company and full of jokes that keep me entertained on the march and during the long nights in camp.

His horse, a powerful sorrel mare, is called Gundestrak, a fine sounding name. I said that it seemed to me to mean 'thunder' or 'lightning strike'. But Landry tells me that in the Viking tongue it means 'vomiting fit'. When I expressed my surprise at this, he assured me that all the Normans give such names to their destriers.[32] Some are called 'Bowels' or 'Piss-pot' or 'Go to Blazes'. It is a custom that they have.

The Normans are very proud of their horses, and Landry did me the honour to say that several Norman knights have remarked on mine. She is a maiden, grey as slate and mottled with a lighter hue. She is powerful and swift, with clear eyes and an instinct for combat, in which I have taken pains to train her. She is brave and steadfast, but very gentle with me. I would not trade with any man, and she seems to know it. She raises her head as we pass the other nobles and even lords, as if to say: 'I am my master's slave, but I am better than any of you.' I call her Fatana.[33]

Landry has invited me to visit him at the Norman encampment and to spend the night there. I am hesitant, fearing that I may fall into some mischief with them and soil my reputation with the Bishop Adhémar. But, indeed, since we have pledged our honour

31 This, then, is the answer to the mystery of Roger's two names. L'Escrivel means 'the scribbler', and the last two syllables of it are, evidently, the origin of my own family name. It also explains the surprise of the officials of Lunel when I told them that I am a writer by profession.
32 Destrier: a knight's war horse.
33 Fatana: Destiny.

not to enter the city after dark, it is so dreary in camp at night that I am tempted to go, just to see what Norman life is like.

SEPTEMBER THE THIRTIETH

Tomorrow we cross the hills into Lucca to meet with the Holy Father. It has been a hot and wearying march, and already some of the men are falling out of ranks and, I suppose, returning to Provence. My Lord Raymond is annoyed with them but I told him that it is just as well; I should not like to have such irresolution at my back in battle.

I must write of the night I spent in the Norman camp. It was the last before we left Genoa, and I went as the guest of Landry Gros who, it seems, is held in great esteem by his comrades. The Normans live more simply than we, even on the march. Their tents are small affairs that are easily pitched and struck, and they travel with few accoutrements. Their animals are fine, however, and they care for them well.

I was introduced to Fulk Rechin, whom I had heretofore seen only at a distance. He is a short, sturdy man with powerful bowed legs and blue, flashing eyes. His voice is loud, and he barks when he laughs. He welcomed me to the encampment and before I could thank him, I had a cup of mull wine in my hands. I remarked that his surcoat was much talked of in the other camps and he told me to the side that they were the testicles of peasants, not priests. 'I am not a barbarian after all,' he said.

It is a rousing place, not like our quiet Provençal encampment.[34] I noted that there were women all about, pilgrims from the group that follows us. They cooked and served and did such other work in return for food, as they occasionally do in our camp. But

---

34 Actually, Roger refers to his encampment as Frankish or French. I have chosen to use the word Provençal instead, since it will distinguish Roger's contingent from that of the Normans while not implying that the latter are not themselves French.

unlike in ours, they did not leave come nightfall as the bishop has required.

For dinner we had pig and calf 'borrowed' from the local farms, they told me. 'We shall surely give it back,' Landry said, 'tomorrow in their fields. And their crops will be better for it next spring.' Indeed, they joke a good deal, and it served to remind me how sullen I have been. After dinner they sang a song, with each man inventing a verse. The song, of course, was about women. I did not understand all of it, but the chorus went thus:

> The juice of the grape
> Cannot compare
> With the juice of the apricot.
> And the juice of the 'cot
> Cannot compare
> With the juice of a Norman slut.
> If the front door is open
> You may drink your fill
> In a foyer as sweet as wine.
> But if it is locked,
> Or the passageway blocked,
> You had better slip in behind.

In the evening we played a game called *sersten slaek* or *slaeg*,[35] which means 'six ball' and which they have from their Viking ancestors. It is a curious contest that is played with six hard leather balls about the size of a man's head. The players are divided into two teams. They stand in a circle alternately, so that each man has an opponent on either side. The balls are thrown across the interior of the circle in random fashion. The object is to catch one ball in

35 To my knowledge this is the first time that this rather peculiar game has been described in modern literature. I imagine it as a form of dodge ball, without the dodging.

the hands and another between the legs. The man who does this first wins for his team.

The balls are thrown with great force at the head and groin, and, I quickly learned, can be very hurtful. But it is forbidden to cry out in pain, and to do so is to be dismissed from the circle. In this way the circle is reduced until only three or four men are left standing. Then the contest becomes extremely fast and exciting. Heads are bloodied and ribs broken, and scarcely a groin escapes intact. But it is considered a great honour among the Normans to be skilled at this game.

After supper there was more singing, as well as games of chance. These games are played with various trinkets, among them bones, cards, dice, and praesteren.[36] I refrained from this, as I had little to wager and no desire to lose what I had, for the Normans are very skilled at such games, and play them with great verve and passion. Landry tells me that under the influence of wine their games can become dangerous, and even deadly.

All the Normans vied to have me spend the night in their tents, but as I was the guest of Landry, I retired to his. I was as happy as I have been since I left on the pilgrimage. My stomach was full, I had sung, played, talked, and laughed. Yet still I felt a gnawing, and as I lay down upon the bed of aromatic leaves, I realized what I lacked. I prayed for comfort but none came, and it was a long time before I could sleep. Then, just as I was dozing, the tent flap was drawn back and two women entered.

Landry and his friends had arranged all. I was far too weak to resist. I do not even know her name and scarcely saw her face, nor would I know her if I saw her this morning. But her body was full and young, and her mouth was wide. It was like bathing after a long thirst; like weeping after a long time stunned.

36 Praesteren: According to Dr Marya Bradley of Yale University's Department of European Antiquities, these were small, pyramid-shaped stones or pieces of wood used in a betting game similar to our modern-day children's game of jacks.

I shall go to Père René before mass and take my penance. And I shall ask him what has been in my mind now that I have sinned so grievously: whether the indulgence granted by the Holy Father applies in life or only in death, and if in life, before we reach Jerusalem or only after.

OCTOBER THE THIRD

We approach Lucca and our meeting with the Holy Father. I spoke to René concerning the indulgence, but he is, after all, no more than a country priest with little learning. He urges me to speak to Adhémar, which I shall do as soon as we reach the city.

I had a dream last night that troubled me, and so I shall set it down. They say that dreams are the whispers of God, and that, though the mind cannot comprehend them, the soul will understand.

I dreamt that I was fishing by a brook in Provence. My line was made of hair, long human hair. I sat gazing at the water when, all of a sudden, a face appeared. It was Eustace, come back from his unmarked grave. He rose up to the bank and knelt beside me. Then he reached into my wallet and took from it the handle of a sword carved from ivory. He frowned at it and wept, and then he swallowed it and slipped back into the brook.

I awoke in fear, for the dream had disturbed me so I could no longer sleep. He haunts me still, Eustace, and visits me even here on the road to our Saviour's holy city. I wanted to tell René, but that would mean exposing my heart to him, and this I cannot do. I carry this secret with me like a hump upon my back, and within my soul it renders me as ugly and disfigured, and incapable of standing upright in the sight of God.

OCTOBER THE NINTH
Lucca

So much has happened – so many wondrous things. We arrived in Lucca two days ago. It is not so beautiful a town as Genoa, but the houses are neatly arranged and the streets are swept and cleaned. Whether this is because of the presence of Pope Urban or not I cannot say.

We camped outside the town as is our custom, for though we are the army of Christ, no elders will allow us to enter their precincts except in twos and threes. The Bishop Adhémar came to instruct those of us who were to meet with the Holy Father on how to conduct ourselves. We are to wear our battle gear and to caparison our horses as if for battle. This has meant the unloading of the wagons, for none of us has worn his mail or outfitted his destrier since leaving Provence.

I begged an audience of the bishop and he consented to speak with me after vespers. At about the seventh hour of the evening I went to his pavilion, which is larger than that of my Lord Raymond, and much more heavily guarded. The watch was insolent to me and, as they were no more than boys, I lashed them with my tongue. I am a duke of Provence, not to be mishandled by a bishop's hirelings too young for beards.

Adhémar received me in a woollen shirt and riding breeches, his feet bare, his hands and face still soiled from the march. I had never seen him without mitre or coif[37] and was surprised to see that his hair is cut as short as a child's. 'I have precious little time for theology,' he said to me.

'I wish only to know what may be the nature and extent of the indulgence that is offered as reward for our pilgrimage,' I told him.

37 Coif: the hood of mail worn under the helmet.

He glowered at me a long while before he spoke. 'Have you come for treasure, or for the Lord?' he asked.

'The Lord,' I replied without thinking.

'Then where your heart is, there shall your treasure be,' he said. And he bent to a basin and began to wash his face.

I had nothing by this answer, but as it was clear he wished to speak no more, I turned to go. His voice stopped me. 'Roger of Lunel,' he said, not looking up, 'if you wish to preserve your soul, avoid the company of the Norman knights. Destruction lies in their encampment.'

I lie awake — it is past the midnight hour — turning the matter over in my mind. It is said that Adhémar has spies in every camp, and now I do not doubt it. I must be careful not to incur his displeasure, for he is the Pope's eyes and ears in the expedition. On the question of the indulgence I remain in doubt. There is a priest who rides sometimes with Adhémar; he is called Raimund of Aguillères. It is said he is an educated man, a poet and a scholar. The next time he joins our march, I shall seek him out.

What I said before, about my reason for coming on this expedition, was not entirely the truth. I have come because I am a Christian, a son of Holy Mother Church. I cannot stand by in silence while the infidel occupies the holy places and mistreats and kills the pilgrims of my faith. I would go even if there were no remission of sin. I would go because Jerusalem is the home of every Christian soul. As such, I am fighting for my home, every bit as much as if the Turks were threatening Lunel.

In ten days I shall attain the age of Christ at the outset of his ministry. God grant that I may be worthy to walk in His footsteps, and to fight in His holy name.

OCTOBER THE TENTH

Annoyances this morning. My hauberk, which I wore for the first time to the audience with the Holy Father, has begun to come apart beneath the arms and in the seam of the skirt. I chastised Thomas for this, although it is not his fault. But I had expected that he would oversee the work while it was being made. He did not, and now I must have it mended in Lucca at a price three times that which I would have paid at home. The wrapping of the hilt of my sword, too, has come loose. This is not so surprising, since it was the sword of my lamented stepfather, Guy. This too have I given to a local craftsman to be fixed and, I am sure, I shall pay dearly for it.

On Sunday last we attended mass in the cathedral. I had hoped that the Holy Father would celebrate, but instead it was concelebrated by Adhémar and the Archbishop of Lucca. This latter was a dark, sharp-nosed man who sipped at the chalice as though it were a bird bath, and who grunted his Latin like a pig in rut. For the most part, Adhémar ignored him.

What was remarkable was the singing. I have not said how much I love music. The choir of monks and acolytes was very good. In our honour they sang in the new style of Limoges in which the voices improvise above the plainsong.[38] Our own monks in Provence sing polyphony, but nothing like this had I ever heard before.

Above the chant the voices ascend, spinning silver and gold on syllables sustained for measure after measure. They rise and twine, dart about each other like blue jays, swoop and soar and spiral themselves to heaven. I was moved to ecstasy, almost to tears, by

38 Roger is referring to the latest development in music, called the *organum purum*, created by the monks of Saint Martial of Limoges. In it, the old-fashioned Gregorian chant was relegated to the level of a continuo, and the voices of the upper range were free to improvise, as Roger describes.

the beauty of it. If the sleeping soul can be awakened it is thus, by music, which is the breath and pulse of God.

After mass His Holiness received our delegation in the chapel. Among our number were my Lord Raymond, Count Stephen of Blois, a very noble, fair-haired man, and Robert of Normandy, whom I saw for the first time. He is not at all like his Norman knights but, rather, looks like a courtesan of Paris. His hair is long and soft, his beard is curled, his features are refined, and he was dressed with an elegance that turned every head. Clearly he is the son of a king, albeit of the Britains, and he affects the insouciance and authority of wealth. Yet when he raised his hand to remove his coif on entering the chapel, I could see an oval scar upon his forearm where a tattoo had been removed. I recognized the shape from my dealings with the Norman knights: it is a common tattoo among them, that of a maiden being mounted by a goat.

I had eagerly looked forward to the audience with the Holy Father. He is a Frank of the Auvergne, and I have been told by those who attended at Clermont that his speech so inspired the gathering which launched our pilgrimage that knights and nobles wept and fell to their knees to swear the oath.

And indeed, Pope Urban is an impressive man, not tall but very regal in his bearing, and immaculate in white and gold, his jewelled crosier grasped firmly in a satin glove sewn with pearls, his mitre taller than the bishops' and heavier with gold and jewels. He wore slippers, I noticed, of scarlet laced with golden thread, and as he advanced towards his throne, six novices bearing up his train, his tiny feet appeared below the chasuble like drops of the Saviour's blood. He does indeed, I thought, walk in the footsteps of Christ, whose pathways in Jerusalem it is our lot to free.

Urban took his throne atop the altar steps, the young priests settling down his robes. He inclined the crosier towards us; we knelt. Every noble held his breath. This was the man who had launched us on our fate, both earthly and eternal. This was the soul that held our souls in thrall. I waited, breathless with the rest, to hear his words, to hear that booming voice that had consumed a thousand men at Clermont.

'Soldiers of Christ!' he began, but what he said was, 'Soldiers of Kuh-kuh-kuh– '. He stuck upon the Christ. He stammered. It seemed as though it took an eternity for him to voice the phrase. At last, with a violent twist of his head, he managed it. I held myself in check, but I noticed some who could not contain their glances.

After an hour I grew accustomed to it, and, after two hours, I found it had a rhythm and ruggedness that appealed to me. His Holiness reminded us of our duty to aid the Christians of the East who had been so badly treated by the Turks. He told of horrors: of women raped and boys made eunuchs and old men forced to labour in the mines. And he spoke of pilgrims seized and taken into slavery, their tongues cut out, blinded, hobbled, and even killed for refusing to renounce their faith. It fired us to determination, and again we took the oath never to return to our homes until we had prayed before the Holy Sepulchre.

'And now G-g-g-od k-k-k-eep you and sp-sp-sp-eed you on your w-w-way,' Pope Urban said and, rising, he blessed us all.

I was deeply stirred, but on the way out of the cathedral I heard the Norman knights making fun of Urban's speech, and I realized that Bishop Adhémar was right – no good could come of my fraternizing with the likes of them.

That night my Lord Raymond honoured me with a visit to my pavilion. I was indisposed, for I had developed a fever and begun to experience an irritation in my member which was like the need to urinate. I kept myself in check while Raymond told me that the Pope wished us to make a stage to Rome for a special purpose that he had confided to him and to the other lords. It seems that hirelings of the anti-pope, Guibert, have occupied the Vatican and are defying all efforts to dislodge them. As we have the army in Italy, the Holy Father said, we should redress this wrong.

I was greatly urged by the burning in my loins to end the

interview, but Raymond was in a pensive mood. He spoke at length and solemnly about the expedition, wondering aloud if we were not being made the pawns and dupes of the Church. I could hear in his voice the heaviness of melancholy.

At last he sighed and rose and wished me a good night. No sooner was he gone than I darted from my pavilion into the woods, but the urine did not come, only a discharge, yellowish and thick as curd. I was greatly in distress and feared for my life, and I cursed the Normans all the more.

Thus passed the day of the audience with our Holy Father Urban.

OCTOBER THE SEVENTEENTH

We are on the march for Rome. I never thought to see that sacred city, where Saint Peter reigned and the Apostle Paul was beheaded. Indeed, this is an adventure that any man might long for, a great seeing of the world to be remembered and retold if I survive.

On that score I have thought a great deal, my indisposition having reinforced the fear of death in me. I drink a potion of berry wine and bark that the good Père René prepares and, praise God, the discharge has subsided. He is a holy man indeed, and I realize now that I never appreciated him for his true worth when we were at home.

Do I expect to die? Most certainly. Do I wish to die? If it is the will of God. For I know that I shall die for my sins, and that my sins shall be forgiven. And despite the wicked life that I have led, I shall be reunited with my Father,[39] there, in heaven.

How do I know this? Just yesternight I spoke with the saintly priest of Aguillères. He is a remarkable man, courtly and well-

39 It is unclear from the original whether Roger is referring here to God the Father, or to his own father, Richard of Burgundy. The text gives some reason to think that he sometimes spoke of the two as if they were interchangeable.

spoken, lettered, temperate, and pious. I would fight at his side or pray beneath his consecrated hands without a thought.

This was the nature of our talk.

I asked him, as I had Adhémar, what manner of indulgence we might expect. He smiled kindly at me and said, 'The blessing of God upon your soul.' I asked him what this meant. 'Liberation,' he replied, 'for even as we are to free Jerusalem, so shall our souls be freed from hell.'

His eyes were blue as sapphires and more deep than I could see in them. What piety was there! 'And this blessed release,' I said, emboldened by his manliness, 'is it to be ours in life or only in death?'

'Is there a difference?' said he.

The question struck me dumb. I had never thought to ask it. I searched for a reply, but Père Raimund put his finger on my lips. 'Think, brother,' he said. 'Do you wake or sleep? If you wake now, then death is sleep, and if asleep, then how shall you have your reward? But if you sleep now, in a kind of dream of life, then when you die, you wake to your reward. Your soul must be liberated not only from hell, but from life.

'And think further, friend: If your life be heaven, then what will you enjoy beyond the grave? But if your life be hell, then how happy you will be to wake from it to life eternal! Be thankful, then, for every setback, rejoice in sorrow, bid welcome to despair, for these are the mirrors of heaven, in which all seems backwards. Turn from them, look inward and see your true face. As it was meant to be seen. As God sees it.'

I nearly wept. I had never looked within myself, but had been distracted by the falseness of the world. I came on this expedition to find myself, and Raimund had touched the pulse of my desire. Perhaps there, at the Holy Sepulchre, face-to-face with the tomb of Christ, I too shall leave my body and ascend again to life.

OCTOBER THE TWENTY-THIRD

We talk a great deal in camp about the Turks. None of my companions has seen them, and there is much that is said that I do not credit. I do not believe that they have horns beneath their helmets, nor do I believe that they mate with she-wolves in the forest at night. This, I think, is superstition.

It is said by many that they eat human flesh, and this may be so. They are very fierce and wild and they do not know God. Some say they worship the devil and especially his wife. I had not thought that the devil had a wife, but surely it makes sense. Much of the evil that comes into this world comes through women, and so it is likely that he has a wife and that she is the patron of evil women. If the Turks do worship her, then it must be that they love mischief.

As for the evil eye, which it is said they can cast upon an entire army, I am undecided. I have heard much about the evil eye, but that is from the old women of Lunel. It is also said that the Turks live in caves, and that they do not urinate as we do, but that the urine seeps out through the pores of their skin, which accounts for their swarthy colour. But all agree that they are very brave and ferocious fighters.

They are heathens who know not Christ or his sacraments, and so they are all condemned to hell. Perhaps, knowing this, they make mock of our religion. The priests say that in Jerusalem they have made brothels of the holy places, and that they strew the hosts of the Blessed Sacrament upon the ground and dance on them. And that when they do, the hosts bleed.

The Bishop Adhémar in his sermon at Sunday mass reminded us of what the Blessed Ambrose said: 'I am a soldier of Christ – I am forbidden to fight.' He explained that by this Ambrose meant that Christian soldiers are forbidden to shed the blood of Christ, that is, the blood of other Christians. But the Turks have nothing in them of the blood of Christ. Their blood is the blood of Satan, and shedding it is not a sin, but relieves the world of sin. It was a powerful argument.

But how can it be? The Turks were created by God. God is Christ. Therefore, they must partake in the blood of Christ whether they acknowledge Him or not. If, God forbid, that girl who lay with me in the Norman camp should get with child, that child would be my blood whether he knew me or not. And if the girl were a Jew or even a Turk, the child would have the blood of a Christian within him. Yes, if God made the Turks and Christ is God, then the Turks have the blood of Christ. And soldiers of Christ may not shed it. And so may I then kill a Turk in the name of Christ?

OCTOBER THE TWENTY-FIFTH

For two days and nights I have been preoccupied with the thoughts I last wrote down. I have wrestled with them, turning them this way and that, but I cannot get the advantage of them. I have been irritable and put out, and I cursed at Thomas and blasphemed this morning when my saddle girths were loose and I nearly was dismounted.

I must not forget myself, especially in front of the men. As we draw closer to the Holy Land, our thoughts must become more pious, not less. Still, the problem I have set myself disturbs me. I must speak with Raimund of Aguillères as soon as he rejoins our column.

OCTOBER THE TWENTY-NINTH

We are camped outside of Rome. Tomorrow a hand-picked contingent of knights and soldiers is to enter the city and attend mass in Saint Peter's Basilica. How this may be possible I do not know, since Lord Raymond says that the troops of Guibert still occupy the Vatican. We shall set out at dawn for mass, but we may be served a battle.

This evening after supper I requested Père Raimund of Aguillères to hear my confession. In the course of it, I spoke of my doubts about the propriety of killing Turks. Père Raimund gave me absolution and penance, and bade me visit with him in his tent. I was happy to do so.

We spoke for several hours, arguing the question back and forth, for he told me to be frank and to play the devil's advocate. At last he took me by the hands and, frowning, looked searchingly into my eyes. 'Brother,' he said, 'if Christ were in His tomb and called for someone to roll back the stone, would you not do it?'

I was warmed to my argument by now and I riposted: 'The gospel makes it clear that He had no need of anyone to roll back the stone.'

'Yes, but if He *chose* not to, and called to you from out of the depths, and it was the only way that you could look into His face, what would you do?'

'I would roll it back,' I said.

Père Raimund leaned back against the saddle that served him as a writing desk. 'Indeed, I think you would. Remember, if Our Saviour wished it, every Turk would be expelled from His holy land, by wind or fire or plague. But He does not choose this way. He calls to us, God's humble soldiery, to roll back the stone from His Holy Sepulchre. That is what we are about. We go, not to kill, but to open; not to destroy but to uncover. We go to roll back the stone. And Roger,' he concluded, his face suffused with peace, 'I believe that when we do, a light will shine forth much brighter than the sun. A light that will fill the world.'

There was such a look of contentment in his blue eyes that I could no longer argue. We go not to kill but to open. We are soldiers of Christ, who fight the battle He has chosen for us. The Turks are in His hands as are we ourselves; He will dispose of us all according to His will. It is as the Holy Father said: God wills it.

I have composed a verse in honour of Raimund of Aguillères:

O gentle soul
Whose saintly eyes
Behold my wretchedness,
When that you kneel
Before our God
I pray you pray for me.

For I am half-devour'd
By the time,
And strewn on space
Like bloodspat
On the butcher's breast.
O I have seen my inmost cleaved,
My heart divided
Love from love,
My brain dissected
Then desplayed,
My very thoughts
Embroiled,
Bled to blanche.

O gentle soul,
Will you not watch with me
One night?
Those lidless nights
When I have felt
The hunger of the dawn
Descend on me
Like worms within the tomb,
When I have tasted all
The savour of the sea
And bloated out until
I drown in my own dreams?

That I have wept and fasted,
Wept and prayed,
I own to you.
I will not hide the hole
Within my heart,
Will not conceal
The cauldron of my soul,
Bubble-deep with dread
And scoured round with fire.

Sweet, gentle soul,
Then pray for me,
For I am orphan,
Offal, onus, os.
You see my bones
Here scattered;
Bones that do not chirp,
But chivy on the air;
The air that is not still
But mocking;
Air that is not only dry
But dust.

And so I plead with you
To pray for me,
To pry me from these depths
To which my mind has dragged myself,
To free me
From myself, my thoughts.
I pray you pray
For peace for me,
Dear soul,
That I may be a piece
With peace;
That I may float upon your prayer

Up to the beams of light,
And in that jointure,
Heaven with the earth,
That I may find repose
Within the fragrant ogive
Of His blessed smile.

I have tonight decided to add to the banner that bears my family crest the motto 'Roll Back the Stone'.[40] I shall keep it before me as my guide to the Holy Sepulchre, and the truth that I hope to find therein.

OCTOBER THE THIRTY-FIRST

It is the eve of All Saints when, the common folk believe, the churchyards open and the dead revisit the earth. I do believe it too, for I think I have seen some myself.

It began to rain last night and has not stopped yet. We armed ourselves before the dawn, though indeed the sun never appeared, and rode into Rome. I expected a welcome in the Eternal City. Instead, there was a sullenness to fit the drizzling sky.

Rome is not a splendid place. There are too many people, and too many of them are poor. There are too many carts, too many broken shutters on the house fronts, too much fallen plaster, too many naked statues covered in grime, too many night lamps hanging from their chains like corpses.

We made our way through the side streets, the people peering out at us from windows like convicts from their cells. Where was the glory of Peter, I thought? Where was the courage of Paul? Was it the rain they were afraid of? Or did they fear what our presence might bring? Rome is an ancient, cowering place.

40 *Ostatz la peira*: This motto still appears below the crest of my family, which is an azure field bearing three gold stars.

The square of the Vatican was empty and the filth of it lay soaking under the downpour which grew heavier as we dismounted. We were sodden by now, and the chain mail ran like rooftops. I could not wait to get inside the church, but I stood my place beside Fatana while the Bishop Adhémar pronounced a prayer upon us, and welcomed us to Rome in the name of his master, the Pope.

According to the custom, we made to leave our weapons with our squires but Adhémar enjoined us to bring them in. Weapons into a church! And the Basilica of Saint Peter! It was as I had feared.

The choir was singing as we entered, a dozen monks, the black hoods over their heads. I soon knew why.

From above, among the rafters, a rain of garbage poured down upon us. It was the mercenaries of the anti-pope, Germans by the sound of their speech. They jeered and cursed and even urinated on our heads as we passed beneath them. Others swarmed onto the altar and stripped it of its candlesticks and linens. They held them up and mocked at us, calling us the dogs of Urban.[41]

The bishop bade us lie upon the floor, which was covered with filth, as he led us in prayer. From the corner of my eye I could see Raimund of Aguillères, whose expression betrayed no pique, but who uttered the responses with a voice both steady and deep. On my other side lay Lord Raymond, whose lips were set and whose fists were clenched, rapping on the stone as if he were keeping time to music.

The soldiers upon the altar began to clap their hands and curse at us in unison. Then from the rafters the chant was taken up, and soon the whole Basilica was filled with their blaspheming. It was too much for Lord Raymond. He rose, strode up to the altar rail

---

41 Fulcher de Chartres also describes this scene in his *History*: 'When we entered the Basilica of the Blessed Peter we found the men of Guibert . . . in front of the altar. With swords in hand they wickedly snatched the offerings placed there . . . Others ran along the rafters . . . and threw stones at us as we lay prostrate in prayer. For when they saw anyone faithful to Urban they straight-away wished to kill him.'

and knelt a moment to cross himself. When he stood again, all the men fell silent. From the nave, we watched in expectation.

Raymond reached out for the tunic of the soldier nearest, pulled him gently to his face, and leaned as if to whisper in his ear. In the next instant his formidable teeth had sunk into the man's neck and with a roar, Raymond ripped out his throat.

It was our signal. With a cheer we rose up from the floor and surged onto the altar. I drew my sword and leapt the rail, seized hold of a man in a flat steel helmet who grinned a stupid toothless grin at me, and drove my sword hilt into his face. He fell, bloodied, onto the altar steps. By now our men were in a frenzy. 'Do not kill them! Do not kill them!' Adhémar was yelling. 'Not upon the altar!' But it was no use.

The monks scattered like frighted sparrows. Men dropped from the rafters to join the fight. We were outnumbered, but the insults had made us crazed. I struck out to right and left, and with every blow more mercenaries fled. It seems they had no stomach to die for the money of Guibert. Lord Raymond trapped a man against the baptismal font and skewered him. He fell into the water, which soon was red with blood. I killed no one, contenting myself to open heads and hamstring men who fled from me like geese. They were cowards and deserved no death upon an altar.

In a few minutes the church was cleared. Instinctively I turned to look for Père Raimund. I saw him standing in the middle of the nave in his simple monk's robe, his arms outstretched, his eyes turned up to heaven. I was told later that he had stood there all the while praying, the fight swirling around him. They say it was his prayers that won the day.

Now it is night. I sit in my tent, the rain pouring down, unable to eat or sleep. Among the mercenaries there were four dead and many injured. On our side, no one was hurt. It was a strange victory, not over Turks but Christians, not in the East, but in the sacred heart of Rome. I find that I am furious – I cannot concentrate. What stupidity was this? Have we left our homes to fight the anti-Christ or the anti-pope? Have we been used, merely so that Urban may return in safety to his house? I am resigned to lose my life for the sake of the Saviour, but not for that of the stammerer.

I would confess myself to Père Raimund, but it seems he had a vision in the church today and has fallen into a swoon. I too have had a vision — of myself knocking in the skull of a man with a flat helmet and no teeth, and of another baptized in his own blood. Yes, I have settled in my soul the killing of Turks. But what of this? I wish that I could fall into a swoon. I shall. God help me, I shall get drunk. Or worse.

NOVEMBER THE SEVENTEENTH

I have written nothing for over two weeks. I have been debauched in that time, spending many nights in the Norman camp, with all that that entails. The Bishop Adhémar this morning threatened to dismiss me from the expedition. I shall curb myself hereafter.

I will relate something of what has happened since the battle in the Vatican.

The Norman knights were not allowed to enter Rome, and so they plied me for details of our fight. I related it all, with every ounce of bitterness I felt, and I laughed and rollicked with them as I told it over and over. The truth is I hate the story, and I rode it like a she-goat, trying to break its back.[42] The Normans, however, took great delight in it. Fulk Rechin pointed out to me what I had not realized; namely, that their lord, Robert of Normandy, who had accompanied us into Rome, had not entered the Basilica. It

---

42 I am guessing here, for I do not understand what Roger means to say. There is a definite sexual reference implicit in his imagery, but whether he means that he is telling the story for all that it is worth, or whether he means that the story itself is insatiable and needs to be exhausted, or whether he intends something altogether different I cannot tell.

seems he slipped away and bought for himself a villa on the Tiber. This is proving a most profitable expedition for him.

After leaving Rome we crossed south-east to Bari and thence towards Brindisi. At Bari our army was divided, Robert of Normandy and his knights remaining there to take ship. We are now near the village of Ostuni, a day's march from Brindisi, where we are to take ship for Floreo[43] in the kingdom of the Bulgars. From there we will march through Macedonia and Greece to Constantinople.

In Bari we had our first word of the pilgrims' expedition.[44] The news is not good. It appears that the pilgrims have suffered greatly on their march, being unprovisioned and passing through mountainous terrain thick with bandits. They had been warned to wait for us. Perhaps when they reach Constantinople they will do so.

It is now three months since I left Provence. I am weary and I have thought often of returning home, but I dare not violate my oath to God. There are those among us, however, who have not scrupled about it. Of the fourteen soldiers I brought with me from Provence, only nine are left. Two have died of disease on the march and the others have disappeared. I suppose they have returned home.

I content myself that, at least, they will bring news of me to my family. I think often of them. My mother, I hope, is still in good health. Gauburge must be married by now. It is strange to think of her with a husband. She is a grown woman, no longer the long-faced girl I played with as a child.

Of Jehanne I think mostly at night. As the distance grows between us I feel her lack more keenly. I will say that, while in the Norman camp, I spent not a single night alone. Nor did I wish to, for I sought to purge the anger from my soul through drink and luxury. Yet, much as I clung to the women and grunted over them,

43 Floreo is probably the modern Vlore, in Albania.
44 Roger refers to the so-called People's Crusade. This was an ill-organized expedition of unarmed pilgrims who, inspired by the Pope's call for the liberation of Jerusalem, set out ahead of the First Crusade under the leadership of the monk Peter the Hermit and the former knight Walter the Penniless. As we shall see, this naive and ragged expedition was a great disaster.

I could not release myself in them unless I thought of her. I tried to concentrate on the body below me, but until *her* body appeared to my mind, until I saw her face and said her name, I could not release myself. I ought to be a slave to Christ. Instead, I remain her slave.

I have seen the Adriatica for the first time, and it is not at all like our sea. It is green, so green that you would think an emerald ship had sunk in it. The country is barren and rocky, and yields only grudgingly to the plough. There are olives here and dry bushes with great thorns. It is a rugged land, and the people are hard and dry. They welcome us like innkeepers, interested only in the business we bring. There are many Greeks among them.

If this place, still Europa, is so harsh, I wonder what Syria will be.

NOVEMBER THE TWENTY-SECOND

We are still in Brindisi, awaiting transport. It is not a pleasant town. The Greeks steal from us shamelessly, either in their shops, where they charge exorbitant prices for their goods, or in our camps, where they sneak into our tents at night and rob us. We caught one and flogged him, and all the time he cried, half in French, half in Italian: 'In the name of God, have mercy on me. They say you possess a great treasure. Who could resist?' And for that insolence we flogged him all the harder. We are soldiers of Christ, poor pilgrims with no wealth except our weapons and our faith.

It seems to me that all the women of Brindisi are prostitutes. They come into the camps with their hair undone and their skirts tucked up to their knees. Even those who appear modest will sell themselves, and their husbands beat them if they keep back the coins they earn.

I must say a word about money.

Here in Brindisi, as in Bari, only coins can be used. It matters little what kind of coin – denarii, bezants, perpers – their weight is all that counts. We have had to learn the use of these coins and, in the process, we have been cheated mightily. A single sheep, which scarcely feeds six men, will command seven denarii, though there is in them full two hundred grams of silver. On the other hand, a woman commands but three.

I seldom go into Brindisi, although, to my annoyance, I have lately learned that Thomas, my squire, has been slipping into town near every night when I am asleep. I found this out one morning when he did not return, and I had to prepare my own breakfast. I assumed he had deserted, when suddenly he staggered past my tent, drunk as a fiddler and with his doublet all undone. I beat it out of him that he has been whoring on the docks, dancing and singing for his pleasure like a common fool. I sent him to Père René who, as I instructed, has given him a heavy penance: he is to wear a whetstone tied to his testicles beneath his trousers.

DECEMBER THE EIGHTH
The Feast of the Immaculate Conception

The climate here is mild, and so the winter does not much affect us. The elders of Brindisi tell us that, given the size of our force – some four hundred knights and two-thousand infantry – it may take time to assemble a fleet to transport us. Meanwhile the pilgrims, about six hundred in number, have contracted for two ships to make their crossing. They have hope of meeting with the Norman force of Duke Robert which, as we have heard, has left from Bari. I, for one, will not be sad to see them go. They have complicated the work of moving and provisioning the army, and their women have had a bad influence upon us, as I know too well.

I attended mass this morning in the church of Brindisi. It is a modest structure overlooking the harbour, much adorned within with metalwork and painted screens. I was surprised to see a number of naked statues upon the altar; indeed, the Italians seem preoccupied with the naked human form. Perhaps this accounts for the profligacy of their women.

I can recall as a youth being intensely curious about the female form. I had seen my sister once, briefly, in her bath and had gaped in wonder so that she shouted and threw the boisec[45] at me. It was a confusion in my mind – protuberance and smoothness – and I determined to learn more. When I was thirteen I gave buns to a plump peasant girl of the estate to show her breasts to me, and as I stared at them she smiled, not mockingly but proud. She invited me to touch them. I put out my hand and ran my fingertips across the nipples. I remember thinking I had never felt a fruit so delicate and ripe and full of life. When she pulled down her blouse I must have looked at her with longing eyes. 'A tart will get you more,' she said.

How I begged my mother to bake that night. It was days before she relented and made a tart of apples. The next morning, early, I stole it from the airing closet and took it to the girl. She was milking. In a moment her face was smeared with crumbs and syrup. 'What more?' I said.

She smiled and scooped up her skirts and leaned back against the trough. I was amazed, and as curious as a scholar. There was nothing there but a gentle cleft downed with moss, as where the nitre seeps between the cellar stones. I watched in wonder as she put her fingers down and spread herself. The deep folds, the dark moisture. And for the first time with a woman I felt myself become excited.

Her name was Josianne and she was, I suppose, sixteen and the beginning of my manhood. I asked if I could touch, and she slapped my hand. 'That'll cost you butters,' she said. I knew what she meant – the butter taffy that we sometimes made at holy days. I made to

45 Boisec: a flat wooden implement shaped rather like a spatula, and used, in the days before soap, to scrape dirt from the body.

go and, in my heat, upset her pail. The milk spilled out, soaking the front of my stockings.

'There,' she laughed merrily, 'you've done it for the first time with a girl!'

It was May and there was no holy day until August. I could not wait. How many times had I cursed the dreary holy days that I had had to spend in church. But now I longed for one! Meanwhile, I thought of Josianne, dreamt of Josianne, made a religion of her naked body in which I worshipped with my memory and hands – three, six, ten times a day. The fever was upon me, but I avoided her, for I knew I could not see her without much pain.

On the Feast of the Assumption I begged for butters. We made them, and I secreted a handful down my blouse. The next day I took them to the cottage where Josianne lived with her parents. Her brother was hoeing in the garden; he was a fat and stupid boy to whom I scarcely ever spoke. I feigned indifference as I asked for her.

'Why,' her brother said, not looking up, 'she's dead these three weeks.'

I was stunned to silence. It seems she had struck her head while bathing in the river and had drowned. I asked him to tell me the spot. I knew it well – we often swam there in the summers. I went and stood a long time and, remembering the butters, I took them from my blouse and threw them in.

I cannot say why I write this story except that, this morning, a statue in the church brought her to my mind, for it was plump and smiling. And the reflection from the harbour played upon it as I prayed.

DECEMBER THE NINTH

Everything is in a turmoil here. Lord Raymond gathered the nobles this morning to say that we shall surely not cross the sea before the Nativity. The weather has suddenly turned foul and the sailors are reluctant to take us, and no amount of bribery can sway them. Lord Raymond has given order that our encampment be moved farther inland, where we may build shelters for ourselves. This tells me that our departure may be a longer way off than Christmas.

December the Twenty-second

We have moved into the hills above the harbour. The men have built me a shelter of wattle, and have made accommodations for themselves for, as I feared, it now appears we shall not be away before the New Year. Ours is a melancholy camp. There is nothing for the men to do, and many have deserted. Of the fourteen that came away from Lunel with me I now have seven. Two boys, brothers from the village, slipped away last night. I cannot blame them overmuch. I wish them God speed home.

We had a visitor this morning, a pilgrim from the band of Peter the Hermit. He was a small man who had suffered greatly by the look of him. He brought the news that Walter of Amiens[46] is dead, and that most of the pilgrims, including his own wife and children, were butchered near Nicaea. He spoke growlingly of the Turks, calling them demons and animals. One of our number asked whether it were true that they had horns. 'Horns they have surely,' he replied, 'but no souls. When you kill them, think of me.'

He begged food of us and then passed on. He was from Caen, and I had much trouble to understand his accent.

---

46 Also known as Walter the Penniless.

DECEMBER THE TWENTY-FIFTH
The Nativity of Our Saviour

How I think of home today! Distance is a great softener, and time a potent healer of wounds. To attend mass in Lunel, to worship with my family, to sit before my own fire – such simple pleasures seem great gifts to me today. Even my stepchildren would give me comfort I think, far from these unwelcoming hills and this useless heaving sea.

I made confession to René and took the sacrament this morning. The Bishop Adhémar, who has found a house in Brindisi where he is waited on by servants, preached a sermon about patience in the service of Our Lord. Indeed, patience is an easy virtue to indulge in when you sleep on feathers and take your breakfast at the hands of Italian girls.

I should not be envious. Surely every day we suffer here, wet and cold and driven down by boredom, is a day of indulgence in the next life. Since I have gained remission of sin, I have decided to offer up my suffering for my father who, I fear, may not have done his penance before his death and so, may be in purgatory. This is for you, dear father! This rain that drizzles in upon my head, this shivering, this rotten meat. May my misery release you into eternal happiness!

JANUARY THE SECOND
The Year of the Incarnation of Our Saviour 1097

A tragedy this afternoon, unexpected and terrible. I am shaking as I write this, for the scenes are still so vivid to my mind.

There was a break in the weather, which for weeks has been raw and stormy. The pilgrims took it as a sign from God, and they swarmed into the town demanding the passage they had contracted for, and the elders, to be rid of them, pressed into service two ageing ships. Into the smaller one, two hundred pilgrims crowded, while the larger of the two took the remaining four hundred souls. The second started first, towed by longboats into the harbour.

Just then a breeze blew up and it seemed to us who watched from the hillside that perhaps, indeed, God favoured them. Then, to our horror, the larger vessel broke in two, split open without warning like an over-ripened peach, spilling its human cargo into the sea.[47] Lord Raymond immediately cried out: 'My God! We must go down!'

In the harbour the elders were assembling every kind of craft, big and small, to make the rescue. I leapt into a boat no larger than a tub, rowed by two boys in wadded coats. As we pulled into the harbour we could hear the cries of the drowning.

In a few minutes we were among the wreckage – broken timbers, women with their babies, baggage and bodies. I spied a young woman, her face barely above the water, and made the two lads pull for her. We came alongside and I took her by the arm. Her wadded coat and skirts were heavy, so heavy with water that I could scarcely lift her. Her face was blue and her eyes were open wide and staring. When I tugged at her collar to bring her into the boat she started as if awakening and looked at me in terror.

'Oh, sir, what are you doing?' she cried.

'Here, take my arms,' I told her. She tried to pull away as if in panic.

'Good sir, please, let me drown!' she said.

One of the boys came to help me while the other steadied the boat. 'Come, take her arm!' I yelled to him.

The woman pulled away, twisting in my grip. 'I have been a sinner all my life,' she said. 'If I die now I'll go to heaven. I beg you, sir, do not deny me my salvation!'

47 Other chronicles, including Fulcher's, describe this scene, though Roger is the only one who indicates that anything was done to rescue the pilgrims.

She was fighting me and her clothing was dragging her down. 'Think of your family,' I said.

Her eyes were calm. 'I have no family, I am alone. But this day I shall be with My Lord.'

And with that she shoved against the boat and slipped my grasp. I watched her face above the water for a moment, unnaturally calm and pale like a flower drained of life. And then she disappeared beneath the waves.

We pulled three people, two children and an old man, into our little craft, rowed them to the shore and returned. But by now the sea was filled with dead, blue and bobbing on the swell. More than three hundred souls were lost this day. Some went to their graves with hymns and smiles on their lips; others, the children especially, with pitiful cries and howls.

It was the most horrible sight that ever have I seen, and as the boat nudged in among the corpses they made a sound, a dull, wet, slapping sound against the bow, like the dropping of stones in mud. It is a sound I fear that I shall hear for a long time in my mind.

JANUARY THE EIGHTEENTH

It is one month now that we have been in Brindisi. More soldiers desert every day, and even some of the knights are going home. Our condition is difficult. The men sell everything they have for food, and the Greeks press the advantage. It is impossible to bathe in the camp. The wells have frozen and the springs are icy cold. The men have stopped shaving, and have lost all interest in themselves. We live like beggars, while Christians, for whose sake we have come, prey upon us.

I now have five men left, but they seem steadfast. They are Uc and Dagobert, brothers of Lunel town; Bartholomew, the tailor's son, a very cheerful, bright-eyed boy who entertains us with his songs; Gérard, a man of my age who attended to my wells and cisterns; and Bernard, a very strong but simple-minded youth.

Also there is Thomas, who remains faithful to me despite my harshness towards him, a practice I must modify. Lately I released him from his penance of the whetstone when he came to my tent and showed me his testicles. Indeed, they were in a sorry state, swollen and red like unripe plums. I let him off with a warning to avoid the women of the town. 'I don't think they'll have me now,' he said, and I thought I heard him crying as he went out.

I have decided to take Bartholomew also as my squire, which makes Thomas jealous. He thinks I do not know it, but he abuses Bartholomew terribly, even kicking him when my back is turned. But nothing angers Bartholomew, who takes the punishment stoically as part of his apprenticeship.

There is too the Père René. He is a goodly man, long-suffering and pious, and a great comfort to us all. Oftentimes I look at him, his plain face resolute, his feet in their sandals tied with cord as black and blistered as those of any tramp, and I tell myself that, if he can bear it, surely so can I. They are good men all. This pilgrimage has worn us down to the core, the unbreachable nut, the better to prepare us for our blessed task.

God grant we may embark upon it soon.

JANUARY THE NINETEENTH

I have thought much about the woman who drowned, and I have written a verse about her.

> O I have seen you
> slip into a dream,
> have watched the night
> close over you
> like breath on glass.

For a moment you nested there
within my arms
like eggs in autumn,
like drops within the leaf.

Were you not my lover,
turning in my arms,
declaring to my watchfulness
your calm intent to sleep?

'Good sir, please let me drown,'
You said.
I could not speak.
But what is death
if not a longing to be held
by silence?

And so I let you slip
into eternity,
your face within the waves,
mute with expectation,
shining with an unreflecting love;
upturned to heaven
whereto you disappeared,
as calm as prayer,
as pale as valleys on the moon.

Of course I never learned her name nor anything about her. Yet I
feel the imprint of her hands in mine. And sometimes, at night,
I hear her voice.

JANUARY THE TWENTY-SIXTH

A terrible time. Three nights ago the temperature dropped to freezing, driving us indoors and under every stitch we have. Within an hour the snow had swirled in, blown by fierce winds from the Adriatica. Below we could see the fires of the town behind the caulked shutters, but on our hillside we shivered near to death.

The storm grew worse and raged day after day. None of us could stir from our shelters, and by the second night our fires had gone out. At last, around the eleventh hour of the third night, Thomas came to my door, begging to be allowed to spend the night within. I could not turn him out, he looked so pitiful, his whiskers caked with frost, his entire body shaking. I admitted him and asked about the other men.

'Good God, sir, they are no better,' he said, 'but worse.'

I put him on the floor under my surcoat and some other clothes from my trunk and went to fetch the men. I found a sorry sight. Uc and Dagobert were clutching each other for warmth, wrapped in all their tattered clothes and quaking beneath a mound of boughs and clotted earth. Bartholomew, poor boy, had the frostbite, his toes and fingers ivory white. Gérard and Bernard had done better, having made themselves a lean-to in the lee of a boulder.

But Père René was the sorriest of all. With no food or fire for two days, he had contented himself with prayer. When Gérard and I discovered him he was nearly frozen on his knees, his hands welded together by the cold, tears hanging on his cheeks like crystals.

We got him to his feet and carried him to my shelter. There all of us crowded in, and the collective warmth restored us. In the morning when I awoke, we were huddled together like children sleeping in a bed. I roused them and we set to rubbing one another's feet, and then I parcelled out my clothing from the trunk.

I had not known how little food there was. Indeed, these men are patient and long-suffering souls. I had a few coins and took them to the village where I beat upon the door of an old Jew, a shopkeeper whose acquaintance I had made. He spoke Langue d'oc and had sometimes translated for me with the locals. The shop was shuttered and as I knocked I remembered it was the Sabbath for them. But I was determined, and at last he let me in.

I must have looked a sight, for he took pity on me and called his daughter to bring me soup and wine. And indeed, I sat a long while shaking at his table, the soup spilling from the spoon until the daughter had to take it from my fingers and feed me like a child.

When at last I was warmed I explained our situation to him. I gave him the few coins and asked for food. He glanced at his daughter and, without a word, she withdrew into the shop. When she returned, she bore a basket covered with an oilskin. I took it gratefully.

Back at the shelter the men had a fire going. I shared out the food the Jew had sold me, salted meat and bread and wine, and they prepared the meal. Then I noticed that there, in the bottom of the basket, were the coins.

I was outraged. To show mercy to a man is well, but no Jew will make a beggar of me. I reckoned up the value of the food, took the coins and such of my possessions as made up the sum – a dagger inlaid with mother-of-pearl, boots of calfskin that I had brought to wear to mass in the Holy Sepulchre, a sword belt of finest leather, and a volume of the devotions of Saint Thomas – and returned to town.

It was the daughter who let me in. I demanded to see her father. The old man came out from their quarters pulling a scarf of black and white around his lengthy beard.

'Sir,' I said with all the dignity I could put into my voice, for my clothes were soiled and my face unshaven, 'there has been a misunderstanding. I found these in the basket.' And I laid the coins upon the counter.

He looked at them and nodded. 'Very well,' he said.

'It is not well,' I objected. 'The food you gave me was worth much more than that. You will do me the goodness to take these things in payment.'

He looked at my possessions, then at me. 'That will not be necessary . . .' he began, but I cut him off.

'I am Roger, Duke of Lunel, son of Richard of Burgundy. If you wish to do me a kindness, you will please remember that.'

The daughter was watching from a corner of the shop. I could see her big black eyes darting between myself and him. The old Jew turned to her. 'See to the value of this gentleman's barter,' he said. 'Reckon it up carefully and give him a receipt.'

'I need no receipt,' I told him. I turned to go but this time it was he who stopped me.

'And I have no need of this.' He held out to me the volume of Saint Thomas. I took it. 'But you will need provisions,' he continued. 'For seven men.'

'Indeed,' I said. 'How do you know this of me?'

'My customers are my business,' he replied with a slight smile. His eyes had a glitter that was not unkind. 'Perhaps we should enter into an arrangement.'

'What sort of arrangement?' I knew the crafty reputation of the Jews of Provence, and I expected those of Italy to be no better. I awaited usurious terms.

The old Jew gestured towards my possessions. 'At this rate, good sir, you will be naked before the spring,' he said. I did not find the remark amusing and told him so. 'Then let me say that you will have no weapons left to fight the Turks. But your men must eat, and I must earn my living.' He paused, stroking his beard and regarding me closely. 'I have need of an . . . assistant,' he said at last.

'A worker?' I asked. 'I shall send my squire.'

'Can he read and write?' asked he. I told him no. 'Then he will not do. I need someone who can keep my ledgers and write my correspondence. Some must be in French, and some in Latin.'

I hesitated a long while. His daughter's eyes were on me, as were his. At last I spoke. 'Only I can do that,' I told him.

'Then those are my terms,' the Jew replied.

'You wish me to work for you?'

'It is better than starving, *mon seigneur*,' said he. 'And suffering your soldiers to starve.'

I could not agree to it; my pride would not allow it. I was scandalized. I thanked him and left.

That night we huddled together in my shelter as the storm blew up again with greater fury. The tailor's boy wept, for his hands and feet were bleeding, and I heard the brothers moan, 'God, what shall we do? What shall we do?' It was the longest night of my pilgrimage so far.

In the morning at first light I went into Brindisi. I sought out the Jew and came to terms with him. He seemed pleased. But my heart is broken.

FEBRUARY THE FOURTH

The weather has worsened but we are faring better. We have food now and good fuel. We are not so cramped in my shelter since Gérard and Bernard have returned to their lean-to, which they have reinforced with materials I purchased in the town.

I continue to assist the Jew, whose name is Mordecai. I work not in the shop, but in an alcove partitioned by a curtain. I arrive at first light, and leave as quietly as I can. One afternoon the Bishop Adhémar saw me and enquired why I was so often there. I blushed and said I had hope of converting the Jew and his daughter. He told me to bring them to him when they were ready for proper instruction. I have lied to a bishop. It is a measure of my shame.

I spend my days at his books, reckoning up the inventory, adjusting the accounts, and writing a large correspondence which he maintains with merchants up and down the coast. It seems he carries on a lively trade not just in victuals but in fabrics, jewellery, pepper, enamels, ivory, and even in medicines. He also trades in money, a thing I have never heard of, exchanging one currency for another and profiting by it somehow. He must be rich, yet he lives simply, and is very modest in his habits.

His daughter is handsome, in a Levantine way. Her eyes are hazel and her features are sharp, but she is a dutiful girl who dotes on him. I often see her hold his hand or kiss the top of his head. Her name is Ruth. She cannot be more than fifteen.

I have sometimes seen him praying, a woollen shawl upon his head, a trinket attached to his arm with a thong. He wears long side curls and a patch upon his forehead, and his body rocks to and fro as he chants. It is very mysterious to me and I always look away for fear of witchcraft. Yet he is gentle and open-handed, and by his accounts I see that he is fair and not demanding of those who cannot pay. I knew little of Jews before I came here. Now I understand less.

This evening Lord Raymond called us into his pavilion and told us to our dismay that we may not be away until Easter. He proposed that any one of us who wishes to return to his home might go, with an oath that he will rejoin the army. Hugues of Béziers and Josseran of Carcassonne have gone. The rest remain. Afterwards Lord Raymond took me aside to where a chest was hidden and, swearing me to secrecy, he opened it. Inside was a fortune in gold. I was amazed. So this was the treasure the Greek spoke of when we beat him!

'I have been saving this for our crossing,' he said. 'I had intended to use it for ransoms or bribes, and to provision our soldiers in the pagan kingdoms. But I know that your men are suffering, and you have been faithful.' He handed me six gold bezants and told me to buy what I needed in the town.

I thanked him but declined the coins, though I did not mention the Jew. In his wisdom my Lord has made provision for our sojourn in the East, and I thank God that I can earn the keep of my men without using the gold that one day may buy their freedom or their lives.

FEBRUARY THE TWELFTH

I am writing this in the shop of the Jew. It is evening and I have agreed to wait here until he returns from a meeting with the elders. It seems the town is to organize a guild to protect against the loss of its ships,[48] and they have asked the Jew to advise them, for he is wise in the ways of money.

This morning, as there was no one in the shop, we found ourselves in conversation. He asked many probing questions about my religion, and the purpose of our expedition. At first I was reluctant to answer, but soon he drew me out and we spoke freely. He is an educated man, a rabbi as he says, which, I gather, is somewhat like a priest among his kind. Though he speaks French, he writes none, but he speaks as well Italian, Macedonian, and Greek. It seems that for a time he held a bank on the port of Marseille, until the Jews were driven from that town.[49]

'I have no great love of Christians,' he said. 'They are no more nor less hypocritical than other peoples, but they are much more prone to violence. Why this should be I do not know.' I replied that we defend our faith. 'Defend, yes,' he said, 'but you also attack. I have seen Christians – priests, and bishops too – invade the ghettos and murder innocent people. And as they did so, the name of the King of Peace was on their lips.' I told him I did not believe it. 'Oh, you may believe it,' he said. 'I have seen it with my own eyes.'

'Not women and children, surely,' said I.

He nodded gravely. 'Them too, I assure you,' he responded. He

---

48 These medieval guilds were the origin of the modern insurance industry.
49 Roger probably refers to the pogrom of 1088, in which hundreds of Jews were slaughtered in Marseille and their property confiscated and given to the Church.

reached into a cabinet and took out a woman's mantle and the linen shirt of a child. He laid them on the table and smoothed them with his hands. 'My wife,' he said, 'and my little boy.'

There was no anger in his voice, just sorrow. Yet he had every reason to despise me, a soldier in the service of Christ. I said nothing. After a long interval he looked up at me. 'You will remember when you go to the Holy Land that my people are not your enemies,' he said.

I promised that I would.

FEBRUARY THE TWENTY-FIFTH

I have enquired the date of Easter, and it is April the fifth. We shall be here another month and more. Were it not for Ruth, the daughter of the Jew, my clothes would be in tatters. She patches and mends and will accept nothing but my thanks. 'It is an honour to attend on the Duke of Lunel,' she says. She is a sweet young girl.

Tuesday last she cut my hair. It was very long and often fell across my face while I wrote. She saw this and could not help but laugh, and when I looked up she quickly put her hand to her mouth. I was indignant, but in an instant I saw that she was blushing and I chided her.

'Please, sir,' she said, still giggling, 'your hair, which is very beautiful of course, is almost as long as mine.' From her sewing things she took a scissors and was so gentle, and spoke to me in such sweet whispers, that I did not feel embarrassed, for no one but my mother or my wife has ever cut my hair. It was a joy to be cared for by a woman, and I told her so. She blushed again and stopped in her work.

'You think of me as a woman?' she said.

'Of course,' I replied.

Her dark eyes glistened. 'My father tells me I am still a girl.'

'You are as fine and fair a woman as any noble lady of Provence,' I told her.

She smiled at me a long moment and then returned to her cutting. As she did so she told me that it was through her that her father had learned of me. She had singled me out, she said, for my noble bearing and my serious mien. This time it was I who blushed, for I was overcome by a desire as shameful as it was sudden. The whores of the Norman camp are one matter. But Ruth is a maiden and a Jew.

I thanked her curtly for her attentions and returned to my labour. I fear that by my tone I offended her, though I had no wish to, but it seems that we cannot even do right by women without causing pain.

MARCH THE FOURTH

Time passes more quickly. I speak often with Mordecai on the long, chill mornings when no customers come to the shop. He makes me tea from a silver-plated pot as large as an urn, and spices it with lemon rinds and cloves that he keeps as carefully as any duchess her pearls. The shop is warm and smells of spice, the beams are thick and low, and there are carpets from the East upon the floor. Never in Lunel on a frosty winter's morn have I been more comfortable.

Our talk ranges over every subject, and I must say that I learn more from him than he from me. He has travelled much about the great sea, from Syria to Macedonia, through France and Spain and in the Holy Land. I ask him for details of Jerusalem: Is it true the streets are of gold and the churches are crusted with gems? He merely smiles and says it is a lovely place of palms and orchards and ancient walls.

This morning he said something so curious that I cannot dismiss it from my mind, and will write it down for future pondering.

We were talking, as we often do, about religion. I have learned much of his, and blush now to think that I thought it witchcraft. It is a deep and sound belief, which Our Lord Himself adopted when He was baptized in the river by Saint John. Indeed, I think that every Christian man ought to study this religion of the Jews, else much of our own belief is lost on us.

But to the point.

'You have in your religion,' Mordecai said to me, 'a practice called confession, have you not?' I said we did. 'And when you confess – I do not wish to pry for I know it is a great secret among you – but when you, Roger, Duke of Lunel, do your confession, what do you tell the priest?'

'My sins,' I said.

He squinted at me. 'What manner of sins?'

I lowered my voice. 'Is your daughter gone?' I asked. He nodded. 'Then I will tell you. Sins of the flesh,' I said.

'Sexual sins?' he asked. 'But do you not confess religious sins?'

'Religious sins?' I said.

'Sins of doubt. Do you not have doubts?'

'Of course,' I replied.

'You do not confess them?'

'No,' I said. 'I discuss them with the priest, but I do not confess them as sins.'

'Must not your confession be true?' he asked.

'Absolutely,' I replied.

He leaned back upon his couch, separating his beard with his long fingernails as he considered this. 'I think,' he said at last, 'that unless you understand that your doubt is rooted in the sins of the flesh, you cannot make a true confession.'

It was an idea so foreign to my mind that I stopped at once to think about it. I have not stopped thinking since. I have discussed it with Père René, but he is as puzzled as I. He advised me to ignore it, being the counsel of a Jew, but I shall keep it in my mind.

MARCH THE FIFTEENTH

The worst of the cold has passed, praise God, and the men stir once again about the camp. We have survived, and have become a band of brothers, so closely have we lived and suffered together these past weeks. I am alone again in my shelter, and I must confess I miss the company of the men, for many were the stories and much the laughter that we shared these winter nights.

One evening, while the snow blew outside and we huddled round the fire, our talk turned to our reasons for joining the pilgrimage. It seems odd, but I had never discussed this with the men, and I was most curious to know their thoughts. Typically, Thomas spoke up first. 'I've come because you have, sir,' he told me. 'For what should I have done at home without a master?'

'What about religion?' I asked.

He shrugged and replied: 'Service is my religion.' The others laughed, which caused him to pout. 'Don't the priests teach that religion is everything in life? Well, I was born to service, and so, service is my religion.'

René clucked his tongue. 'Religion is the duty we owe to God,' he said. 'If service is your religion, that makes Duke Roger your God.'

'And so he is,' replied Thomas. I shushed him, but he went on. 'You're my master, you have the power of life and death over me. You can tell me when to marry and who, where to live, what work to do. You can turn me out or make me rich as you please. What more can God do to me?'

'Damn your soul to hell,' Père René answered curtly.

Thomas wagged a finger at him. 'No, He can't,' he declared. 'Since I came on this pilgrimage, I've got the indulgence!'

We all laughed heartily at this. I next asked Gérard why he had come. He answered: 'Sin.' I was struck by his reply and asked him to explain.

'I'm not a bad fellow as that goes,' he began slowly, 'but I know what I'm capable of. I have a wife and children, sure, and that settles a man. But it doesn't change the nature he was born with.' He paused a moment, measuring his words. 'I reckon someday I might fall, I mean really fall, and then I'll need the indulgence. So I come not for what I've done, but against what I might do.'

We all considered this a moment in silence. I was impressed by the depth of his conviction, and the frankness with which he spoke it. 'But may not the indulgence make it more likely that you will fall?' I asked him.

'Aye,' Gérard allowed. 'But then, that would be as God wills.'

Again Père René took a scolding tone. 'You say that God would lead you into sin?'

Gérard fixed his eyes on him coolly. 'God brought us here to kill. Isn't killing a sin?'

'Not if God wills it,' René replied.

'Then what I do won't be sins either,' Gérard said. 'I think that's how the indulgence works: it doesn't make us any better men, it just takes the sin out of what we'd have done in our lives anyway.'

'He's right,' young Bernard agreed. 'We're all sinners here. I reckon this army's about the sinfullest group that ever got together.' Again we all chuckled. 'No, it's true,' he went on. 'God called us because we're all terrible sinners, and there's so much killing and destruction to be done, and saintly men wouldn't do those things. That's why the bishops preached the indulgence to us – good Christians wouldn't need it. But without it, what hope would there be for us?'

'So you came for the indulgence, too,' I said to him.

'Well, that and my friends,' he answered with a boyish grin.

We turned to Bartholomew, who sat dreamy-eyed, his chin upon his knees, his arms wrapped tightly around him. 'I came for the wonder of it,' he said simply. I asked what he meant. 'Well, think of it, sir: a boy like me, what chance does he have of seeing the wide world? I've never been beyond the village of Lunel, no, nor my parents, nor theirs neither. Now look what I've seen: the great sea, and Genoa, and Rome. And the pope, by God.'

'You never saw the pope,' Thomas scoffed.

'But I saw the place where he stood, and I touched it with my hand. How many tailors' sons can say as much? And I see the Bishop Adhémar most every day, and all the knights and nobles.' He lowered his voice suddenly, his eyes growing big and staring into the fire. 'And Jerusalem, too, God willing. I may walk where Christ Jesus walked, and kneel at His tomb and pray, and then I know He'll hear my prayer – the Lord Himself – and all the ignorance and curses and blows I've lived with all my life won't count for nothing any more.'

Again we all fell silent. Then Père René said: 'Did none of you come for God?'

'Oh,' Bartholomew replied earnestly, 'I'm sure His Excellency did.' And with that, Père René asked if I might share with them my reasons for having come. I was almost too moved by their replies to answer for myself.

At last I said: 'I came to lead you. And I am proud that I have done so.' There was a muttering of thanks and satisfaction around the fire, and thus our discussion ended.

But it has not ended for me. I write now by a candle in my shelter. The shadows tremble on the wattle walls, and my hand, too, trembles as I prepare to confide the true reason I undertook this pilgrimage. Perhaps it is because I am alone after such long durance with my friends, or perhaps it is because I saw the first raw shoots of spring today, the crocus and the hyacinth, and was filled by them with such hope and such new life that I want to end this frozen silence. But not even in confession have I whispered what I am about to say. Only to you, my book, my silent friend.

I have spoken of my relations with my wife, before she was my wife, while her husband Eustace still lived. I have said that when he discovered us in the inn, in the full and brazen shame of adultery, he exclaimed: 'You have taken him from me!'

Jehanne laughed, but I was puzzled. It was only after our marriage that I dared to ask her what it meant.

'It means he was a pederast,' she said, as casually as if she spoke of laundry or her horse. I stood in silence before her. She lay naked on the bed awaiting me. She peered at me in the light of the oil lamp, her grey eyes narrowing. 'You don't know,' she said at length. 'You don't understand what it means.'

I shook my head, feeling childishly ashamed. She stretched her full arms out to me. 'Come, boy,' she said, and smiled darkly. 'I shall be your education.'

I fitted myself to her, drinking in the odour of her body, intoxicated by her sweat and the fragrant undulations of her hips. And as she nested me in her and gripped me and swarmed up to her heights, she whispered in my ear, hot words floating on hot breath.

'He wanted men,' she said. 'He took his pleasure with them. He stroked them, fondled them like girls, they made him rise and pant, they made him lust for them.'

I listened in a silence so profound my ears seemed stopped, or tuned like dogs' ears to the whistle.

'He made me watch,' she said. 'He made me stand behind the curtain. A servant, a stable boy, a labourer: he would put his tongue into the boy's mouth and slip the clothes off him. His hands would find the secrets, dark, forbidden secrets, and would caress them, knowing that I watched.'

'And you?' I said. My voice was strained, my throat so dry that I could barely speak. She laughed a quiet laugh into my eager ear.

'I touched myself of course. I touched me even as he touched the boy.'

I was desperate to hear more and I slowed myself in her to draw it out. 'Go on,' I whispered.

'He would lay the boy upon the bed and love him, with his hands, his tongue, his member. He would plunge him like a woman, be plunged by him, sweat with him and groan with him, and I would bite my lips so as not to groan. There in the light, upon the coverlet, two men in passion, lovers joined by flesh, flesh welded into one. And I behind the curtain, fretting like a bitch in heat.'

I could not restrain myself. I rushed in her, consumed her, lost myself deep within her body, so deep I thought never to emerge again into the light.

There it is. The shame of it. Not that I did not know; not that he desired me. But that I doted on it, the hearing of it, and made her tell again and again the stories of his evil lust and her enjoyment of their strange, unnatural debauch. For months we were not together but I demanded it of her, and I delighted in it desperately. Then, drawn by my curiosity and her insisting hands, she introduced me to that same forbidden pleasure which he took with men and which, it seemed, she doted on, following the example of her drowned and hell-damned mate.

Thus from hell and from the river he rose up to claim my soul. It was his revenge, taken from the grave, taken in my bed where I ought to have been most secure, most pure. Thus, though I banished her to the far side of the house, she came to me while I lay sweating. Thus came I here, to winter on this hillside, to commerce with a Jew, and to chafe for my release from sin either by the sword or by the bearing of this holy cross upon my back.

Oh God, preserve me from myself. For I am sin incarnate! For I am lost if I remain within myself. Take me from myself into Your placid bosom that I may rest beyond tormented life with You, whose fervid eyes and unstained hands yet beckon to my tattered soul.

MARCH THE NINETEENTH

It is today the Feast of Saint Joseph, the father of Our Lord. I attended mass this morning — it is the first we have had together in the church since winter — and took the sacrament. But the host did not console me, and my prayers of thanksgiving were distant in my mind. I thought of my book and what I had written.

When I returned I took it out and read it and was overcome with loathing. For myself, for him, for her. I held the book a long time in my hands, staring at the fire, and made to throw it in. But the burning of my words will not restore my soul.

Can it be true that this pilgrimage will yet undo my sins? Can there be remission in the sword? Can a battle buy eternity? I do not know, but I must hope for it and must believe it, else this expedition may itself become a sin — the bitter sin of hope and expectation.

MARCH THE TWENTY-THIRD

Ruth, the daughter of the Jew, came to our camp this morning. She brought flowers from her garden to cheer the men. 'They are called Rose of Sharon,' she said. 'You will find them in the Holy Land.'

The men swarmed out around her. At first I feared for her, thinking it was lust at seeing a maiden so unexpectedly after so long a confinement. But it was the flowers. They gazed at them like children, some even with tears in their eyes. Those flowers of Ruth were a miracle, reviving the spirit of the soldiers, making them country boys again. They bowed and thanked her. Bartholomew, the cheerful lad, gave her the cross from around his neck in token. She blushed and said she could not wear it, being a Jew.

'You are an honorary pilgrim,' he said with a grin. 'You may wear it as a soldier.'

She smiled and thanked him and put it on. The men applauded.

Afterwards she came into my shelter. I was embarrassed, for it has borne a lengthy time and, I fear, showed and smelled the worse for it. She seemed not to mind, but expressed her fascination with my soldier's things. She begged to touch my sword and gasped as she slid it from the sheath.

'Why, it is a beautiful thing,' she said, 'to do such harm.' She held it in her two hands. It was strange to see such fingers, delicate and small, around the hilt. She hefted it and nearly let it drop. 'It is too large for me by half,' she said, and laughed.

I showed her my mail, the coif and hauberk, and she ran her fingertips over the rough surface, her face drawn in frown. 'Will you die?' she said.

'That is as God wills,' I replied. 'But if I do it will be release, and I shall see my father in heaven.'

'God your Father, or your own father?' she asked.

It sobered me to hear her say it. 'Both, I think,' I said.

She brightened suddenly and asked to see my crown. 'It is said that the crowns of the Franks are beautiful, wrought of gold and rich with jewels. And you are such a great man, yours must be magnificent.'

I took it from the chest. I had not thought to unpack it until Jerusalem, but she was so much like a girl, so like a child of my own, that I was deeply moved. I have seldom worn the crown of my estate – only on holy days and to receive visitors of rank – for, I confess, I am uncomfortable with it. I dislike ostentation, but I bear it as a duty to my name. In fact, the crown is very plain, of silver with the three stars of my family worked in gold. I handed it to her.

'Yes, it is beautiful,' she said, gazing at it with solemn eyes. 'To tell the truth, I had hoped it would not be fancy. It is so much more like you, simple and strong.' She looked at me as if to plead. 'Please, put it on,' she said.

I knew that she meant for me to put it on myself, but instead, I placed it on her hair. She froze as if a chill had taken her, and then looked down. 'I am not worthy,' she said, but she dared not touch it. 'Please, remove it.'

I stepped back and examined her at arm's length. 'You would make a duchess,' I told her, feigning a seriousness, for, to my surprise, I was happy. 'You would surely make any noble proud.'

She glanced up at me and smiled. It was a smile of such pure innocence, of such goodness and simplicity, that I frowned in spite of myself. 'Are you angry?' she asked suddenly.

On the instant I heard a voice within my mind say, 'No, I am in love,' and I was shocked. 'Of course not, Ruth,' I told her, and took the crown from her head.

'That is the first time you have used my name,' she said, smoothing down her hair.

'Indeed,' I responded. 'Please, tell your father I must speak with him. We prepare to leave.'

The look in her eyes defeated me. I sighed, and she noticed it. 'You are not happy to be going?' she asked. I heard a hope within her tone.

'It is always sad to leave a place that you have known,' I answered.

'And people you have known,' she added. 'When will you leave?'

'At Easter; the resurrection of our Lord.' Then, with a bravado I did not feel, I said: 'We leave our wretched tomb to go to His blessed one.'

' "Your wretched tomb?" ' she repeated. Her eyes were hurt, and in an instant she had left. I wanted to call after her, to apologize and tell her . . . Tell her what?

Roger de Lunel, you are an ageing fool, worse than which there is no kind of fool.

APRIL THE SECOND
Holy Thursday

We are making preparations to depart. I have stripped my wattle house and bundled such possessions as I have into my chests, which Thomas and Bartholomew have taken to the dock. As Lord Raymond predicted, we are to leave on Easter day.

This morning I went into the town to say goodbye to the Jew, Mordecai, and to his daughter, Ruth. After all our talks, after his kindness to me – although God knows I gave good value for my keep – I was at a loss. I thanked him and he, me. Ruth watched us from a corner. When I turned to her to say goodbye, she struggled not to weep.

Mordecai walked me a little way towards the camp. 'My daughter begged me for permission to wear the cross your squire gave her,' he said. He chuckled. 'I told her she might keep it in the pocket of her belt as a memento. You must learn to compromise with children, if not with religion.'

'She is a gentle girl,' I said.

'She is in love with you,' said he, 'as girls are wont to fall in love with foreigners.'

I started to protest but he raised a hand. 'Like all young girls, she dreams of being a princess, a noblewoman of Provence. Alas, it cannot be for her. She is a Jew. She will marry a merchant from Genoa or a banker from Pisa. She will have her children and grow old. But I think she will remember you. And that is well.'

He shook my hand and said goodbye.

'If God wills it, I shall see you on my return,' I told him.

'I will pray that it be so.' He smiled at me. 'That way you will be doubly safe. The God of our covenant and the God of yours will guard you.'

Tonight shall be one of my last in the encampment. The men seem lighter; they are anxious to be away. Nonetheless, they have taken the trouble to decorate our camp with wild flowers, in honour, they say, of the Jewish maid. Now the whole dreary, winter-worn soldiers' camp is bright with blossoms. And everywhere I look I think of her and my sudden, silent love.

I smile. There is no bitterness about it, as has so often been the case. It is a love of flowers and blushes, such as a man of my age seldom has. I am grateful to her, for she reminded me of what it is to long and love and yet keep silent. I sometimes think that silence is the one true language of love.

APRIL THE THIRD
Good Friday

Of all the holy days of the year, this is my favourite. Its drama, its grim sanctity are unsurpassed. I never hear the prayer, Recriminations, without blanching. As a boy it shook me to my soul and made me cry. It moves me still. 'Oh my people, what have I done to you, in what way have I offended you?' It is a dagger to the heart; Christ on the cross, upbraiding us, demanding explanation. 'I have given you the fruit of every tree, and you have hung Me on a tree.' His bitterness, looking down the ages, His disappointment. I go to walk in His footsteps. May I be worthy!

We attend midnight mass on Saturday. On Sunday, we depart at dawn. A new life for us, and death to many.

APRIL THE SEVENTH
Aboard ship

I shall write as much as I can, though it is difficult. Men hem me in on every side, for we are packed on this ship like hay upon the wagon.

We sailed with the tide on Sunday, singing hymns and cursing the Greeks who tried once more to cheat us as we left. They jeered and whistled as the tide drew us out into the harbour. How glad I was to see the last of Brindisi, and that hillside where we suffered such a winter. At last we were on our way, the breeze at our backs, the Holy Land awaiting. Then, no sooner had we lost the sight of land, than we were becalmed.

Four days and nights have we lain here, baking under the sun and chilled at night. There are five hundred of us aboard, infantry and knights, the horses in the hold, our baggage strewn upon the decks like coffins. We can scarcely move; the stench of animals and bodies in the lifeless air is overpowering. For hours at a time the sailors whistle for the wind, a low, moaning sound that irritates and, finally, entrances.

Word of it reached the town, and Greeks rowed out in boats to sell us food and drink. The men in their fury beat them off, overturning two of the boats. I for one did not care if they drowned or not. How I long for Provence, to tread the floors of my own house again, to eat an apple from my orchard.

APRIL THE EIGHTH

Still no wind. Some say the expedition is accursed, but the Bishop Adhémar, who ships with us, forbids such blasphemy. My lips are so parched they bleed, and I can hardly speak. My skin is brown and wrinkled as a walnut. I worry for my horse.

Last night, stepping over the bodies of sleeping men, I managed to make my way into the hold. The stench was horrible. Rats run fearless about the lower decks. Two horses have died in the stifling confines of the hold. Their flesh decays and the rats and worms are at them.

I found Fatana tethered to the floor, her eyes as dull as lead. I gave her dried figs that I had from the Jew and she brightened and nuzzled me. For a time I sang to her in whispers. Then I returned to my place upon the deck. If this keeps up much longer, I fear it may break her spirit.

In my reverie this afternoon, when the sun was at its height, I thought of Ruth. My mind drifted to her like clouds and wrapped her and held her there within its smoky arms. I fancied her, a crown upon her head, her long dark hair unfastened, her fine fingers mending my surcoat, her father smiling his approval of our love. I reached out my hand for her to touch her cheek. It was Thomas, and he grunted at me like a pig.

My breath is foul. I disgust myself. The men urinate where they lie. Now, so do I. Someone went mad this afternoon and threw himself over the side. A few went to the rail and watched him drown. I could not be bothered.

APRIL THE NINTH

God came to our aid this morning. With dawn the wind rose, and soon it filled our sails. Men stood and bared their chests to it, and laughed and cheered. It was like seeing the dead arise.

APRIL THE FOURTEENTH

A long time that I have written nothing, but much has happened. We disembarked at Floreo, where we were met by John, the brother of the emperor of the Byzantines.[50] Knowing that he was to meet us, the Bishop Adhémar ordered us to present ourselves properly. When we relayed this order to our knights and soldiers, there was

50 John Comnenus was the brother of Alexius Comnenus, Emperor of Byzantium, and by all accounts a shrewd and successful ruler. As we shall see, his attitude towards the Crusaders was extremely complex, even puzzling. Instead of the few hundred knights Alexius had expected the pope to send, he found himself confronted with tens of thousands of armed Latins within his borders. It was not surprising, therefore, that he should have viewed the Crusade as a mixed blessing.

grumbling such as I have never heard, even during the darkest days of winter. Men cursed and spat, and declared that they would neither wash nor dress themselves until they had obtained proper food and rest.

The Bishop Adhémar cajoled, invoked the name of God, and finally threatened them with eternal damnation. 'Can't,' a voice replied. 'We've earned our heaven.' At that a derisive laugh went up from the decks.

The result was that we men of name took pains to prepare ourselves while the others sat sulking. When at last the ships docked, we brought our horses out and paraded into the town, followed by the filthiest rabble of fighting men the world has ever seen.

What an army the Prince John Comnenus welcomed! They looked worse than beggars, dirty, stinking, and muttering oaths. They marched from the docks straight into camp, erected their shelters and fell to cooking the meat that had been laid out for them. Meanwhile, we joined the prince and his suite.

'Excellent,' he said, without enthusiasm. 'Splendid host. It is exactly what the emperor expected.'

I felt chagrinned, but Lord Raymond sat his horse as erect as if he led the papal guard. He accepted the prince's invitation to dine with him, and we rode to a magnificent pavilion pitched on a height behind the town. I followed close behind the prince so as to observe him. He is the first contact with Byzantium that we have had.

I had expected a man of the East, swarthy and dressed in skins; instead, he is a gentleman in every respect. He is youthful, vigorous and slender. He rides a white stallion of excellent proportions, not so large as our destriers, but clearly bred for swiftness and show. He is dressed in white and purple silk and holds his unreined hand akimbo at his waist as he rides.

He speaks in a high, lilting voice, and laughs often. There is much jewellery about his person: rings, necklaces, chains upon his surcoat, and even upon his horse. He wears pantaloons such as I have never seen upon a man, cinched at the waist and tight-fitting in the leg. His boots are very fine, made of soft leather and pointed at the tip, even turned up slightly at the toe in the new style. He gestures gracefully with his hands, which are very white, and not at all sunburnt as I had expected. In short, he is a prince, and does not conceal the fact.

His pavilion was lavish. It smelled of incense and was lined with carpets of the most beautiful workmanship. There were cushions and low tables set with wine and fruit, cooked fish, meats of every kind, and finger bowls afloat with slices of lime. I must admit that, after our encampment in Brindisi, I was taken aback. Is this how an army of the East provides itself? Have we come to liberate these people from the Turk or from luxury?

Our talk was genial. Prince John promised us the filial love of the emperor, and assured us with many florid phrases that we shall enjoy both his protection and his largesse. And indeed, the proof of it was before us. It was a great temptation to throw ourselves upon the banquet, or at least it was for me, but the Bishop Adhémar, whose ring the prince had carefully declined to kiss, forbade us with his scowls. He asked news of other columns.

'Others there are, indeed,' the prince replied, 'from every direction. Duke Robert of Normandy, who preceded you, is with the emperor. Godfrey of Bouillon, Robert of Flanders, and the very noble Hugh of Vermandois, the brother, as I am told, of King Philip of France, approach Constantinople. So you must make haste, my friends, as much haste as you may to join them.'

'What escort may we expect to Constantinople?' the bishop enquired.

'Oh, constant, constant,' Prince John replied. 'The cavalry of His Serenity Alexius will accompany you every step of the way. They will hold themselves at a distance I warrant, for they shall act as scouts. But you may rely upon them to defend you against the bandits.'

'What manner of bandits?' Lord Raymond asked.

Prince John flicked with his fingertips as though at flies. 'Insignificant. Ruffians. Kuman, Uzes, Pechenegs. They fight with the arcusa[51] and the spiked club. Their swords are of a very crude kind, lacking even a proper hilt.'

'You do not kill a man with the hilt,' Lord Raymond said. 'What of Count Bohemund?'

Prince John fanned himself with a red kerchief. 'The king of Sicily?' he said. 'He disembarks, God save us. He disembarks in Greece and marches north.'

Lord Raymond grunted his contentment. I could not help but notice that Prince John seemed ill at ease.

That night Lord Raymond came to my pavilion. He seemed to me agitated and grim. 'What do you make of this swell from Constantinople?' he asked. I said I thought him a gentleman. 'Gentleman, indeed,' he scoffed. 'He is a parakeet. He sings the sweet songs his brother teaches him. But mind me, Roger, we must watch him like a hawk above our coop.'

I looked into his old, wise eyes, and they were full of strength and solicitude. What an honour it is to serve such a lord. He clapped me on the arms, kissed my cheeks, and departed.

The army rested at Floreo for three days and nights and then set out. Beyond the town we entered a countryside of cliffs and deep depressions. This is the land of the Macedonians, the people of Alexander, and a wild, rugged place it is. If there are bandits, surely they are here, for at every turn men might descend from the heights or spring up from the sunken riverbeds to attack our column. We have guides from John Comnenus, but of his escort there has been no sign.

---

51 Arcusa: a short, wiry bow that fired equally small and slender arrows. It was used primarily for knocking mounted soldiers from their horses, when they would be clubbed or hacked to death.

April the Eighteenth

I was interrupted in my writing last night by Thomas who reported that diarrhoea was general among the men. This is no surprise since, as soldiers will, they gorged themselves at the first opportunity. It was necessary to move the camp to other ground, which took half the night. The result was that we were late away this morning, and no doubt will have to march until after sunset.

April the Twenty-second

It is late but I shall finish the story of our arrival and early march.

On the fourth day of our journey through the land of Macedon we climbed a high mountain pass and descended towards a lake. As we entered the valley, which was rocky and steep-sided, we passed into a fog so thick that we could push it along ahead of us with our hands. The air was heavy as a carpet wound round our faces, and our ears were stopped by the fog. That is why we did not hear them until they were upon us – armed men, whistling from ponies and tearing the fog like tissue before them. They came at us from all sides, swinging short swords and firing arrows into our midst.

There was no time to form a battle line or even to mount our horses. We fought them as best we could, at close quarters when possible, but mostly at a distance through the fog. It was a wild, terrifying combat, blinded with mist and muted with the moisture of the air.

None of my men was hurt, but several in the column were injured and killed. For myself, I saw only shapes and heard cries, the whistles of the bandits, the wailing of the wounded, and then silence. The men were badly shaken. They had come to fight the Turks, not to be preyed upon by wolves. They cursed Prince John and the emperor. 'Where are our scouts?' they demanded. And I, too, had cause to wonder.

Ascending from the lake we were again attacked, but this time we captured one of the raiders. The Bishop Adhémar, greatly incensed, sent for the man. When he was brought, the bishop struck him in the face with the heel of his crosier and he fell to his knees. His Excellency then kicked him in the groin and, putting his foot upon his neck, demanded to know what people he was from. The man, bearded, with a black face and silver coins upon his belt, said nothing.

'He cannot speak our language,' someone said.

The bishop addressed him in Latin, but again he made no reply.

'Try Greek,' Lord Raymond said. Adhémar frowned at him, but did so.

'I am a soldier of Prince John,' the man replied.

We were astonished but Lord Raymond merely smiled and said, 'I thought as much.'

'Why have you attacked us?' Adhémar demanded.

'I do the bidding of my lord,' was the reply.

The bishop ordered the man beheaded and his head left upon a pole in the road. My Lord Raymond was right — the Byzantines are hawks above our coop.

APRIL THE TWENTY-FIFTH

We earn our salvation in this land; it is a place as wild as a dream and every bit as frightening. The trees are black and reach out to clutch at our coats with long fingernails. There are creatures like jackals but much more cunning, black bears and wolves that attack our mules, rivers so swift they cannot be forded, and bandits howling from the cliffs.

We have spoken much about the Greek's confession. Why would the emperor send his brother to greet us and promise us protection only to have us raided by his men? Why this duplicity? Why these lies? It was he who asked the pope for succour; it was Alexius who called upon the Franks for help. Now comes a letter from him, which Lord Raymond has read to us in his pavilion. It pledges friendship and offers an alliance, promising to share with us the spoils of our expedition.

'Share,' Lord Raymond scoffed. 'We fight, he shares. That is the Greek for you! No wonder they lost the Holy Land. They probably offered to "share" it with the Turks.'

We have had no trouble from the Greeks since we left the head of their companion in the road. But sometimes we spy them on the cliff tops, prancing on their ponies and watching us. The road we travel is narrow, skirts many buttresses, and is oftentimes exposed. It is called the Via Egnatia, an ancient Roman road, paved with flint where it has not been washed away. Indeed, the men have found some artefacts of the Romans, helmets and bits of armour, which they collect, and which, though rusted, have become prized elements of barter.

It is curious to reflect on this. Eleven hundred years ago the Romans marched northward on this road, pagans into France. Now we, French Christians, march southward towards the pagans.

APRIL THE TWENTY-SIXTH

This morning we came to a river that is called The Demon, and its name is well-deserved. Never have I seen a torrent to compare. It rushed and rattled through the canyon like an animal unleashed, defying us to cross. We scouted for leagues in either direction for a ford, but there was none. At last Lord Raymond ordered a chevauche,[52] for which I and several others volunteered. I urged

---

52 Chevauche: literally, an overlap. The chevauche was a manoeuvre for fording a river that involved establishing a chain of mounted men below the crossing so that any soldiers swept downstream might be rescued.

Fatana down the bank; she shied at the torrent but I clucked to her and nudged her flanks. Almost at once she lost her footing and would have stumbled but that I threw my weight to the opposite side and righted her.

Seven of us stationed ourselves in the stream. We had to shout to one another to be heard above its roar. When we were ready, past our knees in the foaming current, we signalled to my Lord. He took the rope and started across while men from the bank paid it out to him. He was magnificent, urging his mount on, his head bent low above her neck, the rope between his teeth. More than once both he and his horse disappeared below the waves and we made ready to rescue him, but in a moment he was up again, his white hair streaming about his face, his powerful voice cursing the torrent and calling to his horse.

When he reached the farther bank no one could restrain a cheer. He made the rope secure, swept the sodden mane from off his face, and yelled for them to cross. It was a long and dangerous endeavour; a dozen men were swept away, and we were at pains to save them. One, a mere boy, came tumbling and gulping towards me. I reached down my arm as he pounded against Fatana's flank, and drew him gasping and wild-eyed from the water, half-drowned and coughing. We saved all but two of them, who were swept down the river, I suppose to their deaths.

It was six hours or more before the army was across. By then my legs were frozen and battered from the waves, my back ached and my arms felt as if they had been pulled from their joints. When the last were over and I reached the shore, I toppled from my horse, and it was a long while before I was revived.

The Bishop Adhémar stood over me, frowning. 'You have done the work of Christopher today,' he said.[53] I put out my hand, supposing that he would help me to my feet, but instead he turned on his heel and left. I do not know whether this was deliberate,

53 Saint Christopher, a legendary figure, is said to have carried the Christ child across a river and nearly drowned in the process.

but I cursed him under my breath, and then crossed myself and begged God's forgiveness. He is, after all, the legate of the pope. Yet I now can understand Lord Raymond's anger at him. He is a distant, imperious man.

Tonight I am exhausted and oddly depressed. I am a long way from home, in time and space. I wonder what has become of my estate. I had only just restored it to some order when the pilgrimage was called. I fear it may have slipped again into unsoundness. I often spoke of it with Mordecai, the Jew of Brindisi. 'Do you think others will sit idle while you save the Holy Land?' he said. He asked what provision I had made to secure my property, and when I told him that I had left it with my overseer and my wife, he sighed and shook his head. 'Property must be cared for like children,' he said, 'else, like children, it will go astray.'

I wonder what I shall find at Lunel on my return. If I return.

APRIL THE THIRTIETH

How I despise this country! It is dark and barren and its people are stupid and superstitious. Apparently the rumour has preceded us that we capture and roast human beings, and so the people flee their villages before we enter them. Not two days ago I was leading the advance when I spied a woman in the forest bearing a basket of tubers on her head. I called to her and, seeing me, her eyes grew big with terror and she threw down her basket and disappeared into the woods. It made me unaccountably angry.

But there is worse. Because these people think that we eat human flesh, when they flee their villages they kill the old and weak who cannot run. Many times we have entered one of their miserable little haunts to find the bodies of old people lying in their huts, their throats cut ear to ear. This is done as a mercy, the guides tell us, to spare them the torture at our hands. They are for the most part Bulgars, and a more backward, vile race I cannot imagine.

Look how they live. Their huts are made of sticks chocked with mud. Their clothes are of bark and animal skins scarcely cured. Their leather is as hard as wood, and their weapons are little more than stones and clubs. I have heard their language in the few places where they have sought to trade with us. It sounds like the muttering of morons.

When they approach our camp, they come in a sort of crouch as if we would strike them, their pitiful goods held out in hands so black with grime you would think they wore gloves. Their hair is filthy and tangled, their beards have never known a comb. Some even wear belts of vines, from which the leaves still dangle. They have neither dials nor maps, and so they have no idea where they exist, believing their villages to be the centre of the earth, and we, visitors from another world.

We camped near a place called Rasic, and I made a point to go with a guide into the village to meet these people. It was no more than a few mud huts ranged on either side of an allée.[54] The people peered at me from the windows as I passed, their fires untended, their scrawny animals hobbled to the corner posts. All the length of the allée not a soul was to be seen, except, near the last hut, an old man lying before the fire. I approached him with the guide, who spoke their language.

'Tell him good evening,' I said. The guide translated it. The old man did not reply. 'Say I am Roger, Duke of Lunel and soldier of Christ.'

The old man grunted a single syllable. 'He says "congratulations",' the guide explained with a smirk.

I glared at him, for I thought the answer insolent. 'Ask him who he is.'

The answer came in a sing-song: 'My father's son, the father of my son.'

'From whom may my soldiers obtain food?' I asked.

54 Allée: an unpaved street.

'Your God,' he said.

'Do you not know that we go to fight for God?' I responded, feeling myself grow angry.

'It is a weak God cannot fight for himself,' the man replied. I had a sudden urge to kick him. Instead I asked what he was doing there. 'Waiting,' came the reply.

'Waiting for what?'

'To die.'

From the hut behind came a boy, no more than thirteen, as stupid-looking a lad as I ever hope to see. His mouth hung open and his eyes were blank. He was naked from the waist down, and he scratched at sores upon his legs that bled. I supposed he was the old man's son, and I supposed too that he would one day take his father's place before the fire. I turned to go, but the boy called after me. 'Do you really go to Jerusalem?' he asked.

I turned to face him. 'Yes,' I replied.

He scratched at his hip. 'It's a long way to go to kill strangers,' he said. 'Why do you Christians always go away to rob and kill. You've been doing it to us for a hundred years with your pilgrimages. Why don't you stay home and kill the people you know?'

I was about to reply when he turned aside and urinated on the door post, and I thought the better of an argument with him.

Later I reflected on the encounter and I thought that, if what the boy said is true, perhaps we are responsible for the condition of these people. But how can that be? They have but to move away from the pilgrimage route and make a life for themselves elsewhere.

And then I thought: Why should folk be terrorized by holy pilgrims, forced out of their homes, and made to live among strangers? Perhaps, although we do not eat human flesh, we must take some blame for their backwardness and fear.

MAY THE THIRD

There is a great deal to tell. As it is late and I am extremely tired, I doubt that I shall finish this tonight. Yet in these two days much of importance has happened, and much that has shocked my soul. I write with my surcoat over my head, the candle cradled on my lap, for I must sleep out of doors tonight and we are in a country thick with bandits. I shall relate as much as I can and finish tomorrow.

Three days ago we crossed a mountain called Bulgatus and, on the far side, entered a hilly country which, our guides said, was the land of the Pechenegs, a wild and outlaw people. When evening fell we stopped to camp as usual, and the Bishop Adhémar, weary of the squalor of the camp and desiring a more comfortable site for his pavilion, moved atop a rise some quarter-league off. As his escort was preparing the tent, a band of raiders dashed over the hill and seized him.

The raiders quickly overcame his guards, cutting their throats with short swords, but seeing that the bishop was a man of rank, they clubbed him on the head, knocking him senseless, and threw him on a horse. I gathered some knights and rode after them. The camp of the Pechenegs was across a stream, a jumble of tents and shelters. I stopped my men, for we were only half a dozen and they were two or three-score, and watched them. They dragged the bishop from the horse and threw him to the ground. Some kicked him in the head and ribs. But one, evidently the leader, warned them off. Clearly he guessed the value of their captive and did not wish him killed. A violent argument then broke out.

I saw this as my chance. I formed my men into a battle line and gave the word to charge. We plunged into the stream, whistling and howling, and topped the farther bank. The Pechenegs were taken by surprise. Some fled to their tents for weapons, others we cut down where they stood. I ran down a man who seemed frozen with fear, and slashed another on the back with my sword. Adhémar was unconscious so I quickly dismounted, put him on my horse, and called the other men away. In a minute we were across the stream again.

By this time Lord Raymond had come up with a dozen knights, and he charged into the camp, killing all but those who managed to flee on their mounts. They also killed the horses and burned the tents.

We took Adhémar to my pavilion and made a bed of boughs for him. His head was gashed, blood caked on the open wound, and his ribs were badly bruised. We bound his sides with linen soaked in vinegar and applied a glowing iron to close the wound. He lay unconscious all that night and into the morning, while we remained in camp, alert for raids.

May the Fourth

I will continue my account.

As the Bishop Adhémar was too ill to move, we remained in camp, keeping close watch for bandits. None came. The next night I watched with him in my pavilion until he awoke. He called for wine and I sent Bartholomew to fetch it. His head was terribly swollen and blue, and his eyes could not focus. I begged him to lie still, but he insisted that I tell him what had happened. When I finished my account he lay back, breathing deeply.

'Roger of Lunel,' he said, 'I have never liked you.' I was surprised by his words and was about to tell him so, but he went on: 'I thought you self-righteous and proud. I know all your sins, for the monk, René, relates to me your confession.'

I was stunned. It is a grievous sin for a priest to reveal a confession, and I said so. Adhémar smiled. 'We bishops can do many things that would scandalize you,' he said. 'Especially when we are the vicars of the pope.' He began to laugh but the pain cut him off. I was glad of it.

'You should rest,' I told him. I got up to go but he clutched at my sleeve.

'Stay,' said he. 'There is something I must tell you.' I sat down again, glaring at him. 'That day at the river I saw your courage and your fortitude. And I realized that you are the son of your father.'

'You knew him?' I asked.

'Yes.' He closed his eyes. 'I have watched you these past months, watched and wanted to talk to you. But I could not. For fear, and for pride. Now you have saved my life, and I understand that God wishes me to speak.' He licked his lips and asked again for wine. I gave it to him gladly, for I wished to loosen his tongue.

'I was the cause of your father losing his estate,' he said at length.

I stared at him, uncomprehending. 'That was his enemy, the Bishop of Macon,' I said.

'His enemy, yes,' the Bishop Adhémar replied. 'And my brother.' I still did not understand and I told him so. He smiled. 'When I was a boy,' he said, 'I paid court to your mother. I did not win her; Richard of Burgundy did. I took holy orders, but I never forgot. When your father died, I moved my brother to disenfranchise him. To punish her, you see; to force her to come to me for help. But she did not. Instead she fled into Provence. From pride. That same pride I see in you. Now you have saved my life. You see how mysterious are the ways of God.'

I got up to go, but he gripped my arm.

'Roger of Lunel,' he said, 'I, Adhémar, Bishop of Le Puy, legate of His Holiness the Pope, am making my confession to you.'

'I will send you my chaplain,' I told him. 'Perhaps he will guard your secrets better than mine.'

'You do not understand,' the bishop said, a desperation in his voice. 'On my ordination I confessed to my lord the Bishop of Dijon. As my penance he told me to go to your family and beg forgiveness. I could not do it. Since then every mass I have said, every Eucharist I have received, has been a mortal sin. Now God has brought me to you. I cannot die in my sins. I beg your forgiveness. You must give it to me!'

I looked down at him, shaking off his hand. I was trembling. 'You may die,' I said, 'and apply to God Himself for your forgiveness.' I walked out.

Tomorrow I shall go to Lord Raymond and ask to have the bishop removed from my pavilion. I shall not say why.

MAY THE SIXTH

I have been living these past two days as if in a trance. The Bishop Adhémar is carried in a chaise at the centre of the column, and so I ride ahead with Lord Raymond. He peers at me as if to ask why I am so preoccupied but, God save him, he is too wise a man and too kindly a companion to importune me.

All of the woes of my family, the suffering of my mother and my sister, the exile in which we all have lived, were caused by the prelate in whose army I now serve. No, that is not true – I serve in the army of Christ, who will certainly judge this man for his sins against our family. I must content me with that thought. Though true it is that I should like to beat his brains in with the flat of my sword.

A thought struck me this morning so powerfully that I nearly fell from my horse: If my mother had chosen Adhémar, he would have been my father. And such a father! A man who violates the sacred seal of confession, and who punishes a woman whom he loved by depriving her of her own land. How I wish to quit this expedition. Perhaps he will die, and all will yet be well. But if he lives, how can I go on? I shall speak to my Lord at the next encampment, and be guided by his wisdom.

I add this.

Tonight I called Père René to my pavilion. He bustled in, wiping his little fat hands on the fringe of his scapular, for he had just finished eating. He asked me what I wished. I struck him in the face with my glove. He fell back, startled.

'That is for the seal of confession,' I said. 'Now leave my service.'

He asked to know where he should go. I lost my temper entirely. 'Go to Adhémar, whose faithful dog you have been. Serve the man who already owns your soul!'

Père René struggled to his feet. His face was contorted with shame, there were tears in his eyes and, for a moment, I felt pity for him. Then I reminded myself that this was the man whom I had found half-frozen in Brindisi, whose hands and feet I had rubbed, and with whom I shared my tent and food, the product of my humiliating labour. And all the while he was breaking his oath to God and spying for the bishop.

He begged my forgiveness and pleaded to be kept in my service. I told him to get out, and I turned my back on him. I heard him weeping as he left the pavilion. It hurt my heart. But the man had betrayed me as well as his oath to God. I shall not allow myself to regret my decision. I will harden my heart to it.

I have no chaplain now. I shall make my confession to Père Raimund of Aguillères, who has joined my Lord as chaplain. And when I do I shall watch my tongue, for I no longer know what priests to trust in this army of Christ.

MAY THE EIGHTH

We are near a town called Roussa. Last night I spoke to Lord Raymond, and I will relate what he said.

I went to his pavilion after compline. 'I do not think I can serve the Bishop Adhémar,' I began. He raised a silver eyebrow and asked me to go on. 'I cannot explain why I feel this way,' I said, 'but there is a thing between us that prohibits it.'

'Prohibits?' he repeated. 'You have your oath.'

It was true, and I had expected him to say it, but I wished to confide in him. I struggled for the words, but Lord Raymond raised his hand.

'Adhémar of Le Puy is a swine,' he said. 'He is churlish, conniving and underhanded. That is how he has risen so far in the Church. You need not tell me what he did to you, or to your family. I can imagine.' He came to me and put a hand upon my shoulder. 'Remember Who it is we truly serve,' he said. He looked into my eyes. 'Roger, I cannot spare you. The trials we have undergone thus far are but the tempering of the metal. The real fight lies before us. We shall have Turks at our front, and Greeks at our back, and bishops in our midst. I cannot spare you.'

I promised I would be faithful. He thanked me and wished me good night.

How complex this expedition has become. I thought I saw clearly what I was fighting for and fighting against. But at every turning of the road, my vision grows more obscure.

May the Twelfth

We have had a battle at Roussa. The citizens, vassals of the emperor, refused us entrance and supplies, and sent such disrespectful messages that we demanded the surrender of the town. Instead, they hurled rocks and arrows at us. Our men were so incensed at their behaviour that it took little prodding to convince them to attack.

We formed a battle line, the infantry in front with crossbows, backed by the knights and nobles. Behind a rain of arrows and stones we charged the gates, breaking down the palisade and forcing the entrance. The people fled in terror, but we were so wrought up that we did not stop until we had charged clear across the square. We left scores of bodies in our wake.

We then stripped the town, destroyed the gates, and left the citizens to the mercy of the Pechenegs who, I am certain, will make short work of them. We are sure, too, that word of this will reach the emperor, whose treachery we have already seen. Perhaps he will think twice before sending his hirelings after us again.

May the Fifteenth

The men march more cheerily today. They wear the spoils of Roussa, hats and scarves and even ladies' dresses. They have filled their bellies and drunk too much, but I do not begrudge them; this has been an unholy march across a barbaric land. Any little happiness they can secure for themselves is far less than their fortitude has earned.

This morning I rode with Lord Raymond in the van, having no wish to see the Bishop Adhémar, whose condition has improved to the point where he can ride. He was correct – God's ways are mysterious. We had just come into a plain when we spotted riders approaching us from the north. We made ready for bandits, but soon we saw their banners. They bore the Cross.

I glanced at Lord Raymond, who peered hard into the distance. All at once he gave a shout and galloped off. I followed close behind. From the group of riders came another man, large, with a blond beard flowing in the wind. He and Raymond made headlong for each other. Involuntarily I took out my sword, preparing to defend my Lord, but in a moment the two were careering around in circles, reaching out their arms and shouting. I came up in time to hear my Lord exclaim, 'Godfrey, you old goat!'

It was Count Godfrey of Bouillon, lately arrived from Brabant. His scouts had seen our army and sent word to him but, wishing to surprise his old friend, Count Godfrey had ridden on to meet us.

'Roger,' Lord Raymond called to me, 'here is a man for you!'

I rode up and saluted. Count Godfrey put out his hand. 'Which Roger are you?' he enquired.

'Of Lunel,' I replied.

'He is the son of Richard of Burgundy,' Lord Raymond said.

Godfrey squinted at me. 'Indeed, it is in your face,' said he. 'I knew your father – a brave and Godly man. And a prodigious drinker.' He smiled a broad, manly smile. 'I hope as much from you.'

I liked Count Godfrey at once, and all the more for the esteem in which Lord Raymond bore him. He is a large, broad man with flowing hair and a lengthy beard, bright blue eyes and a booming voice. He fell in step with us, his horse a magnificent stallion of grey, almost a purple hue, who held his head sprightly and high.

'Tell us of your travels,' Lord Raymond said.

Godfrey wrinkled up his face. 'Filthy, abominable,' he replied, 'a wretched land with an even more wretched people. We've killed two or three hundred of them on our march.'

Lord Raymond told him of our trials, of the emperor's treachery, and of the recent fight at Roussa.

'You waited too long,' Count Godfrey said. 'First town we came to on Alexius's soil, place called Selymbria, we pillaged. And I mean a really good rampage too. Destroyed the walls, burnt the stores, disembowelled the young men, ruined the women – and, God, was *that* work! Levelled the place we did, and sent the heads of the elders to His Serenity. Tied up in a bundle like a tribute, parchment greeting and all.' He laughed a good, hearty laugh.

Lord Raymond enquired the result.

'Well, when Alexius opened that tribute our fortunes were secure,' Count Godfrey answered. 'He sent an escort – and not that buggering brother of his, the pansy John – but a score of knights, whom we instantly disarmed and tied down to their mounts. From that point on we had provisions, and no bandits to worry about. That's the only way to handle Greeks.'

Lord Raymond heard him out soberly and nodded. He explained

that he surely would have done as much, except for the presence in our army of the papal legate.

'Not Adhémar the Good Thief! No wonder you've had a time of it. I'd have run his crosier up his arse and carried him between two mules. Did your men go hungry? They should have eaten him.'

I made bold to ask Count Godfrey if he knew the Bishop Adhémar.

'Knew him? Why, I nearly killed him once. That was before he hid behind the cloth. Tried to seduce my wife. Hot-balled little bugger, though I expect the nuns keep him satisfied. Why? What do you know of him?'

He was so open and good-natured that I could not conceal the truth. Before him and Lord Raymond, I told the story of Adhémar and my father. Both men frowned.

'So that is the trouble between you,' Lord Raymond observed.

I nodded.

'Take my advice,' Count Godfrey said. 'First battle we get into in the Holy Land, put a lance in his back and blame it on the Turks.'

'Why,' Lord Raymond said, 'Roger has already saved his life.'

Count Godfrey stared big-eyed at me a moment and then burst into laughter. 'As the Gospel tells us, it's never too late to make good for a sin!' he said. 'At least, I think it's the Gospel . . .'

Lord Raymond nudged me and laughed and, in spite of myself, I too was caught up in the hilarity.

MAY THE SIXTEENTH

At camp this night our armies were conjoined. Count Godfrey's men, including two hundred knights and three thousand infantry, are a jovial, open-handed group of the Lorraine. Their accents are Germanic, and their manner gruff, but they are good-hearted men and full of fun. They drink considerably of Alsatian wine, and no sooner had we arrived at Godfrey's pavilion, than we were *apres lo vin*, singing their songs and laughing at every foolishness.

Godfrey enquired of Lord Raymond the whereabouts of their mutual friend, Bohemund. I have heard much of this lord, who is the son of Robert Guiscard and is the prince of Taranto in Sicily. Both Raymond and Godfrey speak highly of him and I look forward anxiously to meeting him. Godfrey explained that Alexius fears him more than all the others, since he and his famous father invaded Byzantium from Sicily fifteen years before.

'Alexius must be shitting his satin pants,' Count Godfrey said, his beard stained with wine. 'For old times' sake Bohemund's taking the same route he and his father took when they invaded. With luck we'll meet up with him this side of Constantinople.'

Lord Raymond then related the story of Godfrey and the bear. It seems that, as a young man in Cilicia, Count Godfrey, on a hunting foray, found himself confronted by a bear. Having no weapons to hand, Godfrey wrestled with the animal, finally breaking its neck and killing it. Godfrey told us that he has done so several times since, 'to keep in practice'. We answered that we did not believe it. Greatly indignant, Godfrey got to his feet.

'Well then, damn-it, I'll show you,' he said. 'There's plenty of bears about. I'll find myself one!'

In a moment he had charged out of the pavilion and into the woods. We followed with our torches, all of us rollicking and drunk. Half the night Godfrey searched while we joked with him and cajoled him to return, but he would not hear of it. At last he roused a sleeping bear from its den within some rocks on the edge of a ravine, threw himself onto its back, and shouted to us while he wrestled it. 'You see, you want to stay astride the spine, that way he can't swipe at you.' And indeed the bear, a good-sized black animal, much enraged for having been awakened, thrashed ineffectually with its paws while Godfrey rode him and we all stood ready with our swords.

'Now, you want to slip your arm below its snout, like this, like this . . .' Count Godfrey shouted. 'Then, you want to pull back just as hard as you can . . .' He gave a great twist backward and we heard a snap. The bear shuddered a moment, its whole body convulsing, and then fell onto its side. Godfrey shook himself loose from the twitching carcass and rejoined us, smoothing down his tunic.

'If it'd been light you'd have seen better,' he said. He gave us a look of rescued pride. 'In any case, that's the way to do it, unless I'm very much mistaken.'

It was a remarkable show that I remember only imperfectly for all the wine I had drunk. This morning I woke with a fearsome headache, and rode all day choking down a vomit. I must be careful of Alsatian wine; it is so sweet, like scented water. But it is as sly as a woman with money on her mind.

May the Twenty-first

We have had three battles on this expedition, and so far we have killed not a single Turk. First was the fight in the Vatican, then at Roussa, and now at the town of Rodosto. I will explain how this latest came about.

We reached the coast beyond Roussa where the Italian fleet was waiting to supply us. They had brought us grain and fruit and salted meats. We camped immediately to receive the supplies and share them out and, indeed, it appeared that the last stage of our journey would be a happy one.

Then messengers sent by Count Godfrey returned from Constantinople, now only a score of leagues distant. Their faces were grim, and we stopped at once in our feasting to hear their news. It, too, was grim.

Prince Hugh of Vermandois, the brother of the king of France, together with some other nobles, have been thrown into prison at the Greek capital. This so enraged Godfrey and my Lord Raymond that they gave order at once to break up the encampment and make for Rodosto. When our van arrived at that town we found it fortified, its walls heavily manned.

Count Godfrey sent a herald to demand the surrender of the town. Instead, the gates opened and three-score knights, mercenaries of the emperor, charged at us. They broke through the first line, but the Alsatians at the rear formed up and repulsed them. Godfrey then attacked from the front and we from the rear, and together we quickly overwhelmed them.

Seeing this, some of the defenders of the town made to shut the gates, but Godfrey's brother, Baldwin of Boulogne, dashed forward with a handful of knights and cut them down. Godfrey yelled to Lord Raymond to take the town while he finished with the hirelings. In a moment we were galloping into the square, riding down and killing everyone who could not flee. Stones and arrows were hurled at us from the walls, but our soldiers were quick up the ladders. The Provençals seized the place in less time than it takes to tell it.

We showed no mercy to the mercenaries of Alexius but herded them together in the communal barn and fired it. Their screams were horrible, but we were incensed. This was the final treachery of a treasonous king. We were determined to see our comrades freed.

The men were given free rein to sack the town while we rode off, for the stench from the burning barn had become unbearable. On a riverbank beyond the town we halted. Count Godfrey immediately slipped from his horse to the ground, and for a moment I thought him wounded. But Lord Raymond put a hand on my arm. 'It is his way,' he said.

Godfrey dropped to all fours and began pounding his forehead on the ground. Words poured from his mouth, fervent Latin prayers begging for forgiveness. 'Mea culpa, mea culpa!' he chanted over and over, beating his breast and weeping. Then he wailed, a long drawn-out, piteous cry, growled like an animal, picked up two handfuls of mud and flung them into the river.

He stood again while I gaped at him, straightened his bloody surcoat, looked to see that the scarlet cross was in place upon his shoulder, and climbed back onto his horse. 'All right, then,' he said, and he led us back into the town.

That night we sent messengers again to the emperor to inform him of what had happened and to demand the release of the captives. The next morning they returned in the company of the nephew of Alexius, a pimple-faced boy of sixteen. He created some stir among the soldiers for he wore a pink tunic trimmed with gold, a plumed bonnet, and purple slippers. He declared that it had all been a misunderstanding, that Prince Hugh was merely a guest at the palace, and that the emperor begged us to refrain from further depredations.

My Lord Raymond huffed and said that the emperor's misunderstanding had cost Rodosto dear. And, indeed, Alexius' nephew seemed shocked at the condition of the town. Scarcely anything was left alive. The carcasses of animals and men lay scattered in the square and houses, some even hanging from the windows. The women and children, those who had not been killed in the attack, had been forced to flee into the hills. Even as we spoke, soldiers were preparing torches to fire the town.

Alexius' nephew entreated Count Godfrey to stop them.

'Of course we'll stop,' Godfrey said, giving the signal to his men to apply the torches. The buildings began to catch fire. 'We wouldn't dream of harming your town. Just as your emperor wouldn't dream of harming the soldiers of Christ.' He grabbed the nephew by his throat. 'What other entreaties do you have, pus-bag?' he said.

Choking, the nephew conveyed his uncle's wish that Lord Raymond accompany him to Constantinople, swearing that no harm would come to him. When my Lord refused, the nephew told him that Prince Hugh of Vermandois and Count Robert of Flanders joined with the emperor in requesting his presence.

'You go,' Count Godfrey said. 'If Robert is there you'll be safe enough. But,' he added, holding the nephew almost off the ground, 'you will remain as my guest. If I don't hear by tomorrow morning from Count Raymond that he's well and that our people are free, I'll slit your hide and wear it for a coat.'

This evening Lord Raymond prepares to go to Constantinople. He will take with him only four squires, his chaplain, and a few retainers. None will be armed but he.

'I go to the wolf's den,' he said to me in my pavilion not an hour ago. He was scowling so that I begged to be allowed to accompany him. 'I need you here,' he said, and then he smiled. 'With Godfrey on one side and Bohemund on the other, I expect no harm to come to me.' His face suddenly turned sombre. 'But if it should, Roger, save the Provençal army, and rescue the Sepulchre if you can.'

He took the key to his treasure chest from around his neck and placed it on mine. 'The Greeks understand money,' he continued. 'If they will not let you pass the Bosporus, bribe them, give them all I have. If they refuse, then you must return to Brindisi and use the money to buy passage to Syria.' He shook his head ruefully. 'I wish we had done that rather than make this awful march. But the Bishop Adhémar insisted.'

'Why?' I made bold to ask.

Lord Raymond looked at me as a father would his simple son. 'You are naive, Roger,' he said. 'I admire that. Life is a curdling classroom. God will that it never corrupts you so much as it has me.' He sighed and went on. 'This expedition has many purposes. One, to be sure, is to retrieve the holy places from the Turks. But think what opportunity it offers the pope. An army of Latin knights and soldiers in the heart of the Greek schism? Urban cannot have missed that mark. He hopes to bring Alexius back into the fold with a show of force. And Alexius knows it. That is why he received us as he did: half-friend, half-bandit. You will understand better when you reach the capital. Then the theatre will be opened, and we all will have to dance. But to whose tune, Roger? To ours or to the emperor's?'

He kissed me on both cheeks. 'These are good men who have

braved with us so far,' he concluded. 'Bring them through, and they will bring you to the Sepulchre. But remember, they are like children: the more we wish for them the stricter we must be.'

My heart reached out to him. 'God speed, my Lord,' I said.

Raymond turned in the entrance, the fires beyond just catching the silver beard and the keen, dark eyes. 'Put on your dancing slippers, my boy,' he said, smiling. 'I will see you between the lion and the bull.'[55]

I fear for him; indeed, I fear greatly. This land of Greek Christians is as hostile as any I expected to find in the hands of Turks. My Lord Raymond, whom I would follow to the gates of hell, is passing into the gates of Constantinople. I wonder which is the more forbidding threshold.

MAY THE TWENTY-SECOND

This morning we arrived within sight of Constantinople. The first thing that struck me was the colour of its walls – a golden hue that glowed red in the morning sun. We halted by the shore at the foot of the slope leading up to the city, and Count Godfrey descended from his horse. He knelt and engaged in a lengthy prayer which, I have learned, is one of his habits. He prays excessively, especially whenever he has committed or is about to commit some outrage.

We waited for him to rise. I was mounted next to Count Baldwin, Godfrey's younger brother. He is a curious man, tall and wiry and very young. He has the look of a predator, with long, stringy black hair, a sharp nose and even sharper eyes. He seems always about to leap on something and bite it. I have heard rumours

55 Raymond refers to the fact that the entrance to the palace of the Byzantine Emperor was flanked by huge statues of a bull and a lion. For this reason, it was nicknamed the Bucoleon Palace.

that he is a terrible libertine, and that his passage across Europa was marked as much by the blood of virgins as of bandits.

He sat half-crouched in his saddle, making a show of his impatience with his pious brother. 'Let's get on with it,' he said at last in a piping, hard-edged voice.

Godfrey crossed himself and got to his feet. 'Bring the hostage,' he commanded. A guard came up with Alexius's nephew. Godfrey gave order that a cart be brought. 'Well, masturbator,' he declared in a loud voice, 'we have had no news from our friends, and I must be a man of my word. I said I'd have your hide for a coat, and so I shall.'

He motioned to his soldiers to seize the lad, who at once began howling and begging for mercy. Godfrey's men wheeled a cart with long shafts onto the beach, upturned it, and began stripping the boy. Clearly they had done this before. When he was naked they bound him hand and foot to the cart so that he stood almost upright. The soldiers chuckled, for his member, though erect with terror, was tiny, and he was in as much shame as fear.

Count Godfrey approached, made the sign of the cross upon his breast, and drew out his sword. I watched in a horror of expectation, and glanced at Baldwin. I saw his eyes shining.

Godfrey raised his sword high over his head, stretched to his tip-toes, and prepared to split the nephew in two. The boy gave a kind of squeal, closed his eyes and jerked his head aside. Just then a trumpet sounded, and Godfrey stopped short.

'Heralds, my lord!' voices shouted.

It was true. Three messengers came galloping up the beach with banners and flags of parlay. They were from Alexius, and bore letters from Lord Raymond.

Godfrey sighed and let down his sword. 'You shall live to try that yet,' he said, chucking the boy's member with his mailed mitt. The nephew unclenched his eyes, vomited, and then fainted dead away.

Count Godfrey asked me to read the letters, saying, to my

astonishment, that neither he nor his brother reads Latin. My Lord Raymond declared that all was well, and that Prince Hugh and the other nobles have been released. He told us that a place has been prepared for us on the waters of the Golden Horn above the city. The armies of Robert of Normandy, Stephen of Blois, Robert of Flanders and other nobles are already encamped there. We were not to enter the city, but were to join him at the monastery of Saint Cosmas and Saint Damian outside the walls.

MAY THE TWENTY-SIXTH
Constantinople

Much has happened. We are camped on the Horn, and the army is a splendid sight. There are over a hundred nobles, five thousand knights, and more than thirty-thousand men. We cover an expanse that stretches in a great crescent from one arm of the sea right up to the walls of the city. The men, for the most part, are in good order and surprising spirits, for we are provisioned by both the emperor and the Italians. We have lamb and fruit and fish and treasures of the East such as cinnamon and tea. And the water here is pure, filtered, it is said, by a hundred layers of silk.

On Monday last we joined Lord Raymond who embraced us and welcomed us with admonitions to beware of judging too quickly what we see and hear. 'The Greeks have made a show for us, and wish to tamper with our minds,' he said. 'Against our force they oppose their guile. What they cannot win with arms they hope to win with wits.' Then he lowered his voice and said: 'Sign nothing.'

I asked him what he meant, but he wrinkled up his face and whispered 'Spies' and pressed a finger to his lips.

We rested that night and, in the morning, made ready to meet the emperor. We opened our trunks for the first time since our audience with the pope, dressed ourselves in our colours and crowns, and caparisoned our horses. Then, in a stately train, headed by Lord Raymond and Count Godfrey, we rode to the city.

The pathway was lined with guards in exotic costumes, bearing curving swords and lances adorned with the skins of animals. Some of the guards, I noted, were black as tar and, though I wished to express no surprise, I could not take my eyes from them. Their skin shone like obsidian, even the whites of their eyes being dark, and their expression never changed from one of stark ferocity. They are, I later learned, eunuchs in the service of the emperor who long only to give their lives for him, and there are above ten thousand of them.

We crossed the bridge into the city. Its walls are thick and topped with three hundred towers, each armed for combat. Indeed, Constantinople is impregnable, built in a triangle, with two walls above the sea and the third fronting a moat and double ditch and facing a broad plain. It would be futile to attack it from any side.

For some reason I expected cheers when we entered the city. Instead, we were met with a mixture of curious glances and indifference. Constantinople has seen many visitors, and most are more foreign than we. It is a polyglot place, with faces of every hue, clothing as varied as in a bazaar, and smells that mingle the sacred with the profane. There are incense and jasmine and the aroma of cooking pots, the scent of perfume and leather and of a hundred metal forges. This is a busy city – far too busy to take notice of Frankish knights, of which it has, no doubt, seen all too many in recent months.

There must be a thousand churches, all with copper domes and minarets and tiled vaults, and scented smoke, and bell tones rising to a dozen different gods. Never have I seen such orderly streets. My first thought was: Where does the refuse go? I have been told that it is collected every other day from bins distributed for the purpose, and taken from the city to be burned. And it is against the law to throw faeces into the street! We could learn much from these Greeks.

We passed fountains that ran with drinking water scented with lime, and shops with windows of glass, and there were men in aprons sweeping the public passages with long brooms. No animals roamed the streets, and where our horses left their droppings, they were instantly picked up and taken away. I remembered Lord Raymond's saying that it was all a show to impress our minds. Yet I was at pains to credit it, for it seemed so natural to the citizens. But, indeed, how could such a way of life be permanently maintained?

We followed a broad boulevard to the tip of the peninsula where all the streets and passages converged. We soon saw why. We entered a vast open square, which they call the Augusteum. To one side was a magnificent Basilica – that of the Hagia Sofia, or Holy Wisdom. Its domes swelled higher into the sky than those of all the other churches we had seen. They were not copper, but gold, and the walls were shimmering with mosaics of silver and aquamarine. There were scenes from the lives of the saints, and an effigy of the Virgin that sparkled with jewels worked into her robes and crown. Beneath her floated clouds of such lightness that I thought they must be made of cotton wool, but as I passed I saw that they were alabaster and mother of pearl.

Opposite stood the palace of the emperor, called the Great Palace. Its walls extended straight up from the square for hundreds of feet. Beyond it rose a hippodrome of massive proportions in which, it is said, a hundred thousand souls can watch the spectacle. The walls of the palace were decorated with mosaics of the most intricate workmanship. They depicted stern bearded men, the founders of Byzantium, their victories over every sort of enemy, and the many forms of commerce that nourish the city. There were ships of turquoise, and sheaves of grain worked in filigree, and carts laden with every kind of goods, all rendered in shimmering tiles that caught the morning sun and seemed to vibrate with a living pulse.

We dismounted before the palace gates where grooms in turbans and flowing pantaloons took our horses. Godfrey led the way in, followed by his brother Baldwin, Lord Raymond, myself, and our companion nobles. I could not forbear a glance overhead as we passed within the gates, for they towered above us like the portals of paradise, gleaming mahogany doors inlaid with bronze and studded with spikes of silver.

We were conducted by an armed escort as far as the inner court. There the guards, all huge black men in emerald green turbans and tunics trimmed with gold, suddenly prostrated themselves. A bass drum began to beat, shaking me to my innards, and before us two great doors swung slowly open, the mechanism unseen, and without making a sound despite their enormous weight. From within came a powerful scent of gardenia, so overwhelming that my head swam with the sweetness of it. And then a hush fell over the place as if on a signal. We stood awhile within that cloying scent, the warm breeze from the sea swathing it about us like a cloak. I glanced at my companions. Lord Raymond affected indifference, and Count Godfrey seemed positively annoyed. I composed myself and put on a frown and waited.

A small man, elderly, wearing a robe like that of a magician, came towards us from the inner chamber. He bore a staff in one hand, and I saw that it was wrapped in strands of spun gold. He paused a moment atop the steps, took the measure of us, and then bowed deeply. He spoke in Latin.

'My Sovereign, Alexius Comnenus, Autocrat of Christ, commands me bid you enter,' he pronounced.

Count Godfrey belched resoundingly, swept his sword to one side, and ascended the steps two at a time. We followed.

We passed through a lobby as broad as a tithing barn and surmounted with vaults that crisscrossed at dizzy angles, each arch inlaid with tiles of onyx and jade. The place was unlighted, and the pillars made a forest so dense and confusing that we would have become lost if not for our guide. At the far end shone a square of light, and as we approached, peering into the darkness, I saw that it spilled from a small doorway. When our guide reached it he stopped, bowed to us as if to ask indulgence, then turned again to the door and whispered.

At once the door was opened by an unseen hand, and our passage was filled with the amber light of a thousand candles. Our guide stepped aside, bowed again, and gestured us to go in.

Count Godfrey stepped inside, nearly knocking the man down as he did so. It was like entering a tabernacle. The room was low-ceilinged and lined with candles, each in a golden lantern. The floor was one vast slab of turquoise. There was about the place a scent of sandalwood that I found oppressive. At the far end of the room was a figure alone.

It was the Emperor Alexius, seated upon a throne of simplest wood. He wore a robe that descended from a high collar to the base of the steps below him. It too was simple, of blue and green silk. But upon his head was a crown the like of which I had never seen. It was drawn up high in front, twice again as high as his head, and surmounted by a cross of gold from which ropes of pearls streamed down about his shoulders. His face was narrow and rather plain. I judged he was a man of forty. He bore an expression almost of sadness, which turned to courtesy as we approached.

Alexius extended his hands to us. They were small and very white. When he spoke, he did so with an accent that rolled and bubbled like an Eastern spring. 'My friends,' he said, not rising. His teeth were very yellow.

Count Godfrey was the first to speak. 'You got my message,' he said.

The emperor smiled faintly. 'Which one?' he asked. 'Selymbria, Rodosto, or that of my beloved nephew, whose flesh you wished to wear?'

Count Godfrey huffed.

'We greet your gracious Majesty,' Lord Raymond said.

Alexius squinted at him. 'You are Raymond of Saint Gilles?' he enquired.

'By the grace of God,' my Lord replied.

For the first time, Alexius appeared pleased. 'I have heard much of you,' he said. 'I am glad that you have come.'

I expected Lord Raymond to upbraid him for our troubles with the bandits, but instead he merely bowed. He then turned to introduce the rest of us, but Alexius stopped him with an upraised finger on which shone a single diamond. 'I know who they are,' he said.

Count Godfrey grudgingly thanked the emperor for provisioning the army, and then came straight to the point. 'When can we cross?' he asked.

Alexius smiled at him obligingly and responded: 'As soon as you sign the papers.'

'What papers?' demanded Godfrey.

'A formality,' Alexius said. 'You will enrol yourselves as my vassals and swear an oath to render to me any lands formerly of my dominion that you recoup. In return I shall provide you transport, equipments, and supplies, and shall recognize such principalities as you may wish to establish in the Holy Land.'

It was as if Count Godfrey had been expecting this. He shoved his sword aside, put a foot on the lowest step and leaned on his knee. 'Look here,' he said, 'I'm as much as any man for niceties, but we've the Saviour's work to be about, so I'll spare you words. I and my brother are the vassals of His Majesty Henry of the Germans, and my friend Raymond here and his men are vassals to the king of France, whose brother you had the kindness to put in prison. And what's more, we've all taken an oath to His Holiness Pope Urban, so that's an end to any talk of papers.'

He straightened again, folded his arms and fell silent.

Alexius took us all in with a slow look. Then, at last, he stood, arranging the ropes of pearls and smoothing his robe before him. He glared at us a long moment, and then shouted: 'You will sign, or you will stay!'

His voice echoed around the room, even ruffling the candle

flames. It was so sudden and so strident that I was taken aback. Count Godfrey stood his ground.

'I'll take no oath to Greeks,' he said. 'And I'll cross into Syria with or without your help.'

'You will not move from this place!' Alexius roared. 'No ship will take you, no man will raise a hand for you. You will return ignominiously to your homes. And you will explain to your bishops and your families why you allowed Our Saviour to languish in a Turkish prison!'

'You dare say that to me . . .' Godfrey began, but Lord Raymond put a hand on his arm.

Alexius turned to him, pointedly ignoring Godfrey. 'What do you say, Raymond of Saint Gilles?'

'Count Godfrey speaks the truth,' Lord Raymond replied. 'We are already bound by fealty and our oaths. I can, however, as a Provençal, offer you this much: We have in our land a subsidiary oath by which we swear to respect the life and possessions of a foreign lord, and vow to do nothing to harm them.'

Alexius considered this a moment, then returned to his throne.

'We shall speak again,' he said, and he folded his hands and lowered his head in prayer as a sign that the audience had ended.

Godfrey was fuming as we left the palace. 'You may take your Provençal oath,' he told Lord Raymond, 'but I'm from the north, and there it is too cold for lovemaking with foreigners.'

Lord Raymond advised him to be patient and await the arrival of Count Bohemund.

'Bohemund!? He's a Norman,' Count Godfrey growled as he grabbed the reins of his horse. 'Why, the man can't even read!' He climbed onto his stallion and shoved the groom away with his heel. 'I'll take this pansy city before I take that Greek swine's oath!' And with that he galloped back to the gates, nearly running down the citizens in his path.

This night the Bishop Adhémar, who refuses to meet with Alexius, has conferred with the leading nobles to discuss the oath.

At last he made a solemn disquisition, with hands raised to God and intoning like a choirboy, that anyone who, for the sake of the expedition, takes the oath will immediately be released therefrom. When Raymond enquired how this could be, Adhémar summoned all of his theology to reply.

'You are already bound by an oath to His Holiness,' he declared. 'That oath enjoins your body, mind, and soul. It follows that any new oath will be empty, since man is nothing more than body, mind, and soul. Alexius's oath will be but words, and words are nothing but the air, and the air cannot bind a man. And so you will not be bound by his oath, for there is nothing with which to bind, and nothing to be bound. It will be null and void.'

At that point Duke Robert of Normandy spoke up. He is, as I have learned, a shrewd businessman, and very careful of his affairs. 'With all respect, your Excellency,' Duke Robert said, 'may I enquire what will be the case if you are mistaken, and this second oath conflicts with the first? Your original view was that it would be a mortal sin and we all would be liable to hell.'

Adhémar frowned at him as if he were a seminarian raising an awkward point. 'You have nothing to fear for your soul,' he said, 'since the expedition itself carries the plenary indulgence. You may confess your sin to me, and your forgiveness will take effect automatically. Your soul will be safe, Duke Robert,' he added, 'just as the estates you have acquired on this journey are doubtless safe.'

The result of the discussion is that all the nobles will sign the oath save Raymond and Godfrey. The former is not taken in by Adhémar's sophistry, and the latter is not impressed with Alexius. For my own part, I shall follow my Lord and my own conscience. I shall not sign.

MAY THE TWENTY-EIGHTH

Bohemund of Taranto is said to be approaching the city. The effect of this news upon the citizens is unmistakable. Many have boarded up their shops, some have sent their children, wives and daughters away, and the army of Alexius has exchanged its ceremonial garb for battle gear. The walls are all manned now, bristling with spears and arrows, and the city gates are shut up except for an hour or two each morning and evening. It is as though they are expecting a tidal wave.

Meanwhile the controversy over the oaths continues. So far Duke Robert of Normandy, Count Robert of Flanders, Hugh of Vermandois, Stephen of Blois, and the German, Emich of Leisingen, together with their vassals, have signed. The rest remain undecided.

I must say a word about the German nobles and knights, with whom I have had a little contact. Though they keep carefully apart and view the rest of us with suspicion, when they are drunk, which is often, they will force themselves upon us as though we were their long-lost kin.

They are an unusual group, perhaps a bit extreme. Not content like the rest of us to wear a cloth cross upon their surcoats, they have had crosses burned into the flesh of their shoulders. These they never hesitate to show, stopping perfect strangers about the camp and pulling down their tunics to expose the brand. Then you must express your astonished admiration, or they instantly take offence and draw their weapons.

Their heads are shaved to the temples, but they wear long beards which they braid with coloured cloth bearing the names of men they claim to have killed; thus, the longer and more decorated the beard, the more fearsome the warrior. They speak a language that reminds me of dragging a stick over cobbles. It is full of spitting and growling, and even their prayers, which they recite with martial regularity, sound like muttered threats.

They boast a great deal, and of the most heinous crimes. It appears that they took the occasion of the pilgrimage to rid their towns and cities of Jews. The slaughter evidently appalled the German bishops, who tried to prevent it by offering the Jews their personal protection. But it was to no avail. Emich and his knights slew not only the Jews but the bishops as well. Now their names, and the stars of many anonymous Jews, are braided into their beards.

Their armour is of the finest kind, the mail is close-woven and double-chained, and their swords are of excellent quality. They wear the new type of helmet that bears the nasal bar, which is becoming more popular in the army. Indeed, if I go again into the city, I shall see about having mine modified as well. Some wear the aventail,[56] which I am also considering having made.

Altogether I do not like these Germans, and, given my relations with the Jew of Brindisi and his daughter, I resent their stories of persecutions. But they drill incessantly and appear to be a very formidable fighting force, and so I may be glad of them in the days to come.

There are, too, in our encampment, soldiers of other lands. Indeed, it is like a small city, a miniature of Constantinople itself, alive with many languages and customs. There are Danes and Swedes, many Spaniards, and a few men of Britain. These last are a peculiar lot. They are very poorly equipped and worse trained. They quarrel among themselves constantly, and there has been at least one murder among them, over, I am told, a pair of Greek leather boots, the first they had ever seen. The murderer was tied between two trees and used for practice by the bowmen. He remains there still, though one of his legs has come off.

Among them are Scotsmen, and they are a barbaric race. They wear skirts made of skins and great woollen leggings tied round with sinew. They eat only meat cooked to a cinder, and will not

56 The aventail was a mail scarf attached to the coif that could be pulled up to protect the lower part of the face. As Roger indicates, it was a very recent development in body armour.

touch the fruit and spices sold by the merchants who come out to us each morning. They are very dirty, refusing absolutely to bathe in the belief that dirt locks in the soul and keeps it from harm.

Though building material is plentiful, including stone, hewn lumber and even silk, the Scots prefer to sleep in holes dug in the earth and covered with vines. This, they believe, makes them invisible to demons who haunt the sky at night, and who would otherwise descend on them and remove their internal organs while they sleep. You cannot reason this nonsense out of them, for they reply with great indignation in their saw-edged dialect that 'if you wish to awake lacking a kidney that's your business'.

The most curious of the lot, however, are the men of Galle.[57] They are small, dark, and hairy, and they speak a language that makes even German sound angelic. They are horribly tattooed about the face with very warlike designs intended, I suppose, to frighten animals, or enemies as primitive as they. They eat nothing but raw flesh, and, it is said, drink the urine of the dogs that are constantly with them. They wear a vegetable in their caps, a leek I believe, and some say that they worship it. They are strange Christians indeed.

Though I am housed with my Lord Raymond at the monastery, I move about the encampment often, for I enjoy hearing the many dialects and learning the foreign customs. I have bartered and traded much, and have acquired in the process a fine German dagger, and a very clever writing desk of Spanish design which folds over the knees and incorporates two candlesticks, and on which I am writing this now.

The monastery is a delight compared to the life of the pavilion. I sleep on a bed, albeit a hard wooden monk's cot, and I have the luxury of a roof over my head at night together with a pitcher and basin, an armoire and, most interesting of all, a commode. This last is in the form of a copper tub upon which rests a wooden

57 Men of Galle: Welsh.

plank. The excreta are channelled through pipes into a tank below ground which the monks empty daily. They rinse the commode with lime water each morning and night.

There are also shower baths, which I had read of but had never seen, where one stands upright under a flow of water regulated by a lever. The immodesty of it was quickly overcome, and now we nobles often bathe together, splashing water on one another like schoolboys. The Greeks have a thing called sapon[58] which is made from the rendered fat of animals, and which is almost magical in its ability to remove dirt from the skin. I shall surely bring this back to Lunel with me, together with the idea of the shower bath, should God suffer me to return.

As I sit here writing I am moved by memories of my home, though they are not so poignant as before. It is now a kind of dull ache, rather than the sharp nostalgia which I had previously felt. My longing for Jehanne is not a barbed insistence now, but a soft patina of remembrance. This is well, for I would not wish to cross into the Holy Land with the lust for her in my flesh. That is, I suppose, what a pilgrimage is for – not to remove us from our sins but to bury them within us.

My desire for her will always be a part of me but, God willing, perhaps I may yet rise above it and float free, either to my death in the East or to a resurrected life at home.

JUNE THE FIRST

We have had an interesting time. All the nobles save Raymond and Godfrey have signed Alexius's oath. Then, after much discussion, the emperor agreed to my Lord's Provençal oath, which he, I, and the others of our men of name have signed.

The ceremony was held in the Basilica and it was impressive,

---

58 Sapon: soap.

as is everything in Byzantium. Alexius received us in state, and we signed a large and most imposing parchment with ostrich plumes tipped in gold. Then Alexius, with tears running down his face, stood to embrace each of us in turn, calling us 'my sons', and pledging his unfailing fealty to our cause. He swore with arms upraised and in a voice that everyone could hear, that we would lack for nothing. We each of us were kissed repeatedly and a solemn proclamation was made that all within the reaches of the empire were to respect our persons and goods as if they were the emperor's. We were then dismissed with gifts of jewels and silk.

When all this was done we moved the army, excepting the troops of Godfrey, to a place called the Arm of Saint John in preparation for our crossing of the straits. Godfrey remained behind at the Golden Horn, unwilling either to take the oath or to move his army. Alexius cut off his supplies, hoping to force him to submit, but instead, Godfrey attacked Constantinople.

We followed his progress with increasing alarm and dismay. It was clear that he sought merely to intimidate Alexius into withdrawing his demand, for no army could have breached those walls. But Alexius was steadfast, neither relenting nor advancing to meet the attack. Instead he remained within the city, resisting all of Godfrey's efforts, while, evidently, taking pains to kill as few of his men as possible.

It was at that moment that Bohemund of Taranto arrived. The long-awaited and much feared onslaught of Sicilian Normans caught everyone by surprise. For instead of coming to Godfrey's aid and undertaking to renew the assault on the city, Bohemund led his force straight to the encampment and made the most obsequious gestures of friendship to the emperor. In view of this, Godfrey, who had hoped for support from him, raised the siege and, together with Bohemund, went again to see the emperor.

Alexius invited us to attend the parlay, for he bears great reverence for my Lord Raymond. Thus it was that in the nave of the Hagia Sofia I met the famous Count Bohemund.

He was not what I expected. He is a short, square, busy man who talks a great deal and never stands still. His mind is always working, as are his hands, his eyes, his torso. He is forever slapping his leather gauntlets into the palm of one hand and pulling them out again with a snap, or turning to some squire and barking a terse order, or telling some ribald story at which he laughs much more heartily than his hearers.

He is scarcely thirty-five years old, with small features, a pinched nose, wide-set eyes, a low brow and very unruly red hair. His dress is an odd combination of his heritage. He wears the skins and silver ornaments of his Viking–Norman ancestors, but augmented with traits of his Sicilian kingdom: cloves of garlic on a leather thong about his neck, a sword belt decorated with seashells, and soft calf sandal-boots laced to his knees. His habit has nothing of royalty about it, but rather it has the look of a clever merchant who has made a fortune for himself among strangers.

It is impossible to dislike Count Bohemund, indeed, he will not allow it. He comes right up to you, stares straight into your face, and will not withdraw until he has made you laugh or found some subject that absorbs your attention. That done, he moves quickly on to the next person or the next question. Within a few minutes he had learned the names of everyone in our party and, I felt, had taken the measure of each of us.

Count Godfrey was much depressed and annoyed by the failure of the siege, but Bohemund assured him that it was all nonsense that could be resolved in an instant. He sympathized, he encouraged, he cajoled, and finally he made Godfrey laugh, and then we all were laughing at Bohemund's good humour, before we realized that the Emperor Alexius was standing upon the high altar scowling at us.

Bohemund made straight for him. 'What's all this about an oath?' he said, his voice echoing through the cathedral. Alexius began to reply with an indignant intonation, but Bohemund went right on. 'Here, where's the paper? Bring it to me. What does it say? Somebody read it to me. Never mind; I'll sign it.'

At a nod from Alexius, a Greek bishop hurried forward with the parchment. Bohemund glanced at Godfrey and, I thought, winked at him. He put aside his gauntlets, took up the quill and made a prominent X. 'Come, come, are there any more? I'll sign whatever you want, here, bring me everything. We'll sort this out here and now.'

The pledge of vassalage was brought and again Count Bohemund made his mark. Then he turned to Godfrey. 'See, there's nothing to it. No harm, no divine retribution. A little X or whatever you can manage, and you have ships, good food for your men, safe passage and, who knows, maybe some women?'

He laughed out loud and turned to Alexius. The emperor was not enjoying the performance, but Bohemund did not seem to notice. He shook the ostrich plume under Count Godfrey's nose. 'Come on, Bouillon, how could you have a better master than Alexius here?' He leaned closer, nudged him with an elbow and added in a whisper, 'What's a paper compared to the estate you'll have in Jerusalem?'

Godfrey glanced irritably at us and at the emperor, who seemed to watch with anticipation. Then he took the plume, stepped forward, and signed. Alexius let out a sigh of relief. He rose, came down from the altar, and embraced Godfrey and then Bohemund.

'Yes, yes, I love you too,' Bohemund said as Alexius kissed him. 'I love all Greeks, Syrians, Jews, Moors, and Turks too, as God is my witness. Now, feed my men, give us fresh horses and a few good ships, and we'll be out of your hair. Eh, Alexius? What do you say?'

'You are my son,' Alexius replied in his rolling accent, the tears streaming down his face.

'I'm my father's son,' Bohemund replied, 'and he would have skewered your guts given half a chance, but that's all water under the bridge, isn't it? We're all friends now, and about God's business.' He lifted his eyes and crossed himself, and then broke into such uproarious laughter that none of us could resist.

Later, when we had dismounted at the encampment, Count Godfrey, who had been very sullen and in ill temper, upbraided Bohemund for not supporting his siege.

'Godfrey,' Bohemund replied, putting a hand on his shoulder, 'my father, the sainted Robert Guiscard who invaded this God-bugger kingdom, once said to me: "The day Constantinople falls is the day the earth itself will fall." Alexius knows that, and he knows we know it. That pen stroke saved a thousand of your soldiers' lives.'

'But what about the oath?' Godfrey said.

'This oath?' Bohemund laughed, holding up the parchment. He called to a soldier standing nearby to fetch a mule. When it was brought, Bohemund kissed the rolled parchment with its golden ribbon. 'My solemn oath to his majesty, the Autocrat of Christ, Alexius Comnenus!' he intoned. Then he lifted the mule's tail and slowly and carefully fitted the paper into its rectum. 'There it is and there it shall stay,' he said, and he laughed again more heartily than before.

Tomorrow we shall cross the Bosporus in Alexius's ships, and shall camp in Asia Minor at a place called Pelecanum, our first steps into the Holy Land. Our pilgrimage is now begun in earnest. Our task is liberation; our goal is the Sepulchre of Christ.

JUNE THE THIRD

I am ill. It is a fever that has kept me on my back for two days. I think it is the water, from which we have to scrape the green slime before we can drink it. How I miss the lime-scented fountains of Constantinople!

I see no one, being unwashed and afflicted with the flux. In panic I examine the stool for blood each day, fearing that I may die as my father did. Oh, father, I know now how you suffered. Surely you went straight to heaven, for this is hell itself. To be

unable to control one's bowels, to live in filth and shame! We proud
nobles of France are no more than ordinary men in many ways. In
some ways, indeed, we are no more than animals.

Since leaving the coast we have crossed a barren land of rubble
and low, flinty hills. Scarcely anything can grow here and the heat
is deadening. We are in a land called the Sultinate of Rum which,
I am told means Rome, though why this should be I cannot tell.[59]
The sultan's name, as near as I can spell it, is Kilich Arselon.[60] We
are accompanied by soldiers of Alexius, mostly engineers who carry
the disassembled siege engines that we shall doubtless employ at
Nicaea. Their general is called Butumites, an elderly man who shaves
his head and eyebrows but sports long moustaches. Lord Raymond
does not trust him, saying he is here to spy for the emperor as
much as to help us.

My men are in tolerable spirits, save for the heat. Gérard and
Bernard have been inseparable since Brindisi, Uc and Dagobert have
become lean and strong from the march and shall make good
soldiers. Thomas and Bartholomew have made a kind of peace. I
think Bartholomew's good humour has finally won him over, though
Thomas has become much more sullen and melancholy than before.

This may be because of the sight that greeted us in the pass
leading towards Nicaea. It was here that the sultan's men massacred
the pilgrims led by Peter and Walter. They left the bodies where
they lay — men, women and children. As we topped the rise they
came into view, thousands of baking skeletons stripped of everything
save the rags that had survived the year's passage.

It was a frightening and pathetic sight. There were the bones

---

59 The Greeks of Byzantium called Anatolia 'Rum' since they considered the
emperor to be the heir of the Roman Empire. Its capital was Nicaea, the closest
city to Constantinople.

60 Kilij Arslan was the son of Suleiman, the great Turkish leader who had conquered
the Holy Land. Kilij, who was not yet seventeen, had defeated the rabble led by
Peter the Hermit and evidently did not take the Crusade seriously. At the time he
was away in the east fighting a Muslim rival, Danishmend, though he had left his
pregnant wife in Nicaea, which he had adopted as his capital.

of babies, some that I saw still clutched in their mothers' arms. Most of the bodies were pierced with the shafts of arrows of the short, lightweight sort that the Turks are said to use. On all were the marks of animals' teeth. There was not an ounce of flesh to be seen.

Clearly these people had no chance, but were set upon in ambush from the hills on either side. The scene is not difficult to imagine: the columns of pilgrims trudging through the valley towards Nicaea set upon by bands of howling Turks. Their horses must have thundered down upon the pilgrims like the waves of the Red Sea. There was no escape. Our men trod in silence through the grisly graveyard. Many muttered prayers; others, oaths. Nicaea will certainly pay for this.

At Pelecanum I met my old companion Landry Gros. I should like his company now to cheer me, but the Normans are the rear guard of the army, and march several leagues behind us. We Provençals are second in the line of march behind the troops of Count Godfrey, with whom my Lord Raymond now shares the leadership of the expedition.

Of the Bishop Adhémar I have nothing to recount. He has avoided my company, from shame I expect. When he heard that I was ill he enquired if I was like to die, saying that he must see me in that case. He was told that it was not so, and he resumed his haughty indifference. I know that he wishes my forgiveness, feeling that he cannot merit heaven without it, and so I am content to withhold it. Though whether I could do so were I dying is a matter that I have much debated with myself. I could wish the man dead, but could I condemn him to eternal torment? That is more than I can say.

I am so weary now, and feel so weak that, even though the sun has only just set, I will go to sleep.

June the Sixth[61]
Nicaea

We arrived at this city, which is the cradle of our creed,[62] yester-evening and have joined the siege. I shall try to make a record of it, though I feel so ill with fever that it is a great effort even to write. It is necessary to take Nicaea since it will protect the rear of our march and secure our line of supply. For the time being we are supplied by the Greeks and Italians from the coast, but as we proceed overland this will become more difficult.

The order of our siege is as follows: Count Godfrey and his brother Baldwin front the northern wall, Prince Bohemund and his nephew Tancred, the eastern, and my Lord Raymond, the southern. As the western wall rests upon the great Ascanian Lake, we have the city surrounded on only three of its sides. Our scouts report that the Turks continue to bring in supplies across the lake, and so we have applied to the emperor for ships to prevent this. Even now they are being dragged by oxen across the hills from the sea, but until they arrive Nicaea will be able to resist.

The first few days were spent in establishing our camps out of range of the Turks' stones and arrows. Gradually we shall move them closer as the siege engines are assembled and the scrofa[63] are erected. Lord Raymond has already made preparations to undermine the tower on the lake shore, believing that the ground there will be softer. Some of our men, together with the Greek engineers, will shortly advance to this purpose.

I am too ill to write more tonight. I shall hope for better health tomorrow, and resume.

---

61 The handwriting in this entry is almost indecipherable. I am guessing at some of the passages.
62 The Nicaean Creed is a statement of the basic beliefs of Catholicism and is recited as a prayer at every mass.
63 Scrofa were portable sheds used to protect the troops as they tightened the siege towards the city walls.

JUNE THE TENTH

I was in delirium for three days at least. The fever continued to weaken me, and though I rallied occasionally and felt almost myself, I was soon stricken again. There is a rash upon me, and the aching in my stomach is more than I can bear.[64]

Lord Raymond's doctor bled me from the stomach, and the blood was thick and black like bile. It relieved me somewhat and I sought to rise, but instantly fell back again, hitting my head. I lay unconscious for some time – I do not know how long. When I awoke, the Bishop Adhémar was leaning over me. My vision was unclear, and I saw him as through a veil. He brought a candle near my face and peered closely at me.

'Roger, you are dead,' said he. I tried to sit up but could not. 'I have seen the doctor and he tells me you cannot live through the night. I have come to give you the unction.'[65]

He kissed his purple stole and placed it around his neck. I licked at my lips so that I might speak, but he began the formula for the sacrament, touching his fingers to my lips, my eyes, my ears, and my forehead. I struggled to avoid his touch, but was too weak. At last he sat again beside me and declared: 'Now you will make your confession to me, and I shall give you absolution.'

He inclined his head over me, but I was unable even to whisper.

'Very well,' Adhémar said, 'I shall anticipate you. I know that you have sinned with women in the Norman camp. I know that you have abused yourself often, and that you have lusted for your wife whilst doing so. I know that you have spoken against me, the legate of his Holiness. I know that you have harboured doubts about this pilgrimage, whether it is ordained of God or is from the pride of

---

64 Dr Coppola suggests that Roger had contracted typhoid fever. It would later sweep the army with devastating consequences.
65 The unction: The sacrament of Extreme Unction, the last rites of the Roman Catholic Church.

men. And I know that you have sinned most grievously with the daughter of the Jew of Brindisi, Ruth; she who cut your hair and came to your pavilion bearing wild flowers. Such other sins as you have committed I also take into account. But this unholy commerce with a Jew, a killer of Christ, would alone condemn you to hell.'

The words infuriated me and I forced myself to speak. 'You lie,' I said.

Adhémar regarded me with a frown. 'Very well,' he went on, leaning closer. 'I shall tell you that I know you murdered Eustace, the husband of your wife. Perhaps not with your own hand, but your adultery drove the poor soul to suicide, which makes you his murderer.' He paused and looked at me, for I was staring at him in horror.

'Yes,' he said, running his hand across my brow which was dripping sweat. 'You see, my child, I have watched with you these past days and nights, and in your delirium you made your confession to me. I understand you now. And you understand me.'

'What do you want?' I managed to say.

'You know. And now you know my terms. Roger of Lunel, you will die this night. This night you will come before the judgement, and you will do so with such a heavy burden of sin that it will surely drag you straight to hell. Unless . . .'

He raised his hand to make a blessing, then he stopped.

'Unless with this hand I absolve you. That, with the indulgence granted to this pilgrimage, will gain you paradise. This night you shall be with your Heavenly Father, or in the arms of Satan. This night you shall see God, or your spirit shall start its endless journey through fire.' He stretched out his hand to me. 'Give me your hand in forgiveness,' he said.

I lay back panting. He could see the hatred in my look. 'No,' I answered.

'You are a stubborn man,' Adhémar said. 'You are the son of your father indeed.' Then a thought seemed to strike him, and he smiled. 'When your father died,' he said slowly, seeming to savour the words, 'my brother, Gaspard, the Bishop of Macon, heard his confession. He received absolution for his sins, which were numerous, but . . .' He paused a moment, raising a brow. 'But he had not the benefit of the indulgence that you have. Roger, your father is in purgatory, suffering all the torments of hell. Given what my brother told me of his sins, I would estimate a penalty of some tens of thousands of years.'

He sat up again and straightened his vestments. 'I have the power to release him from that torment. Give me what I want, and not only will I absolve you, but I shall release your father from purgatory, and this very night the two of you will be together before God.'

He gazed at me steadily, awaiting my reply. I could say nothing. At last he demanded: 'Which will it be, Roger? A few hours more of revenge upon me, or an eternity of bliss for both you and your father? Decide, man, for I will not sit here all night.'

I could no longer look at him. I lowered my eyes. I knew he had won. And he knew it too. 'Bring me water,' I said.

He did so and held my head while I drank. I lay back again. 'Adhémar of Le Puy . . .' I began, but he stopped me.

'Your hand,' he commanded.

I raised it to him and he took it. 'I forgive you for your sins against my father,' I said.

Adhémar breathed deeply, as if clearing his lungs. 'Oh,' he whispered, 'I hear the gates of paradise unfasten.' Then he quickly made the sign of the cross and pronounced the words of absolution. When he was finished, he leaned over me, his purple stole brushing against my face, and kissed my forehead. 'Goodbye, Roger,' he said. 'Commend me to our God.' And he was gone, taking the candle.

I closed my eyes and, alone in the dark, I wept for a long while.

That night the fever broke. I slept, and in the morning I was well enough to take a little food. Thomas declared that it was a miracle, for the Bishop Adhémar had already named me among the dead in the morning mass.

With the help of Thomas and Bartholomew I walked from my pavilion, the first time I had done so in a week. The men came to greet me with smiles and handshakes. Lord Raymond was called, and he too offered me his hand. I asked after the Bishop Adhémar.

'He's preparing your funeral oration,' Lord Raymond said. 'I understand it's very moving.' He smiled. 'Well, it seems he shall have to modify his text.'

A verse occurred to me while I lay abed. I shall write down as much of it as I remember.

> The night has lifted;
> Beneath its skirts I see
> The shadow earth,
> The ground of slumber,
> There where seeds sleep
> And roots conspire,
> Where insects flow like water
> And worms lie naked
> Dreaming of the birds,
> There where I will lie
> Beyond this fever,
> Far beyond the beating heart—
> It is night that I am bound for
> Bounded by—
> The night is my desire.

There was more, something about fire and the soul, but I cannot remember it. But indeed the dreams swarmed over me like worms and insects, and so I am not surprised that the poem should refer to them. I am better now and can make my way about. But the delirium remains in me like the taste of spoiled food, or the memory of a sin that stings years after it has been confessed.

June the Fourteenth

This morning we have had a battle with the Turks, the first of our pilgrimage. The sultan sent a column of relief which attacked our forces on the southern wall. We were ready for them, and we beat them off handily. Our men sent up a cheer as they retreated, leaving scores of dead and wounded behind.

From the prisoners we learned that Kilich Arselon was not alerted to the movement of our army until after we had left Pelecanum. Having no great fear of us, he sent only a small expedition to break our siege. The victory has heartened our men and given us a taste of Turkish tactics, which are unlike our own.

The Turks, who wear light armour and ride ponies, do not mass for the charge as we do, but send squads of mounted archers to the front. These discharge their arrows and retire, being replaced instantly by other squads. In this way they harass rather than affront, hoping to draw the enemy from his lines. When we made it clear that we did not intend to abandon our position, they formed a line of battle and charged. That was their undoing.

We sent our bowmen to the front and they rained down arrows upon the Turks, breaking their lead ranks. Then our mounted men charged. I rode with Lord Raymond and we had hardly reached their line when it dissolved altogether and they fled wholesale. We followed up for about two leagues before satisfying ourselves that they were beaten. Our losses were not heavy, and we gave thanks to God for the victory. But we must guard against overconfidence, since this encounter will serve as a warning to the sultan to attack in greater numbers.

I have had occasion to inspect the Turkish prisoners. They are a dark-skinned lot, small in stature, wiry and well equipped. They do not have horns. Their ponies are excellent, though bred for agility and not power. Their language is gibberish of course, but some few speak Greek and through these we are able to communicate.

They speak of their sultan with awe, almost as if he were a god. Our men treat them badly, but the Greeks, who have lived nearby them for many years, show more compassion.

Since they have been in captivity they have observed their prayers faithfully, rising at dawn to prostrate themselves, washing diligently, and expressing great concern for their animals. We give them the leavings of the camp to eat, and these they sort through, removing all that is offensive to their religion. The rest they clean and cook thoroughly. In this they are like the Jews, who are also scrupulous about their food. It causes me to wonder about us Christians, who eat anything in any condition regardless of its effect on our bodies or souls.

This gives me pause. Is it possible that what we eat may have an effect on our souls? Is this the source of the scruples of the Turks and Jews regarding food? And what does it say about us, the children of God, that we eat every creature, cooked or uncooked, clean or unclean? Perhaps this was the cause of my fever. Perhaps I, too, ought to take heed of what I eat, and learn from these infidels.

I have not seen the Bishop Adhémar, as he has taken command of the right wing of our army. However, I am told that he is greatly changed, being no longer haughty and scheming, but gregarious, straightforward and brave. Where before he remained in his pavilion during fights, he now insists on leading the troops himself, and does so with great vigour. Men who either feared or despised him previously now are forced to admire him.

If this is true, then only I know the cause of the transformation. My forgiveness has made of him an honest man. He no longer lives in the shadow of a terrible secret sin, but in the hope of paradise, which I have purchased for him at the cost of my pride. Indeed, he may even wish his own death, since now he has merited heaven by his scheming. Such is the faith in which we live — buying and selling, barter and reward, bankruptcy or heaven.

June the Sixteenth

Our siege has been pressed nearly to the walls of Nicaea. The Turks within do not cease to pour down stones and arrows on us, wounding many. Uc of Lunel town was struck by a stone upon the foot and cannot walk. I have summoned a doctor for him, but it may be days before he can be seen.

The Greeks have closed their engines to within a few score rods of the walls, and the mangonels hurl massive stones within. It is an awesome sight when one of these machines lets fly. The thick ropes are twisted to a tension that threatens to burst the frame, then the lever is sprung and the boulder goes hurtling with a sound like the ripping of cloth. Some strike the towers and bring down a rain of rubble; others fly straight into the town, and we can hear the crash as they strike buildings or men. At night the city is filled with the moans and cries of the injured. Among them is the wailing of women, though whether from pain or grief I cannot tell.

There are huge bolts too, that are fired from giant crossbows. Some have steel tips and some are tipped with torches. The damage they do must be terrible. The Greeks have set several fires in the city, and from our position we can see the Turks let down buckets to fetch water from the lake. When they do it is sport among our men to fire arrows at them. They tote up the number they have killed and win wagers with them. Sometimes there are fights when a Turk does not fall into the lake but back into the city. To prevent these disputes, which can be violent, the men have agreed that a 'city Turk' is worth one half a 'lake Turk'.

This morning the first of the Greek ships arrived by ox carts. The labour to bring them has been enormous. Long teams of the beasts have dragged each ship more than twelve leagues from Civetot on the coast. We are told that they killed over a hundred of the animals crossing the mountains, and that they had to cut their way through forests of scrub and thorns. And indeed the men who have arrived, mostly Turcopoles, who are Turks impressed into the emperor's army, are exhausted and nearly naked. The backs of some bear the scars of whips.

On Tuesday last the undermining of the wall was completed. The Greek engineers and our Provençals had worked continuously for more than a week at the southernmost tower, digging a deep trench, removing the foundation stones, and replacing them with sturdy timbers. When it was done Lord Raymond gave order for the fires to be lighted. The Turks suspected nothing until the flames had burned through the scrofa and begun leaping up the tower walls.

In a minute the entire structure was sheathed in flame which reached to the very turrets. From within we could hear the alarum cries of the Turks who began throwing water down the walls. But it was hopeless. The flames roared and twisted about the tower, and grey smoke billowed from the heights.

It burned all afternoon and into the evening. Then, as the sun was setting, the tower gave a great shudder, there was a sudden deep groan, and it collapsed. Our men let up a cheer, but Lord Raymond held them back. It was too dark to venture into the rubble. Our forces would have become separated and confused, and the Turks, who waited within with torches, could have cut us to pieces. We shall attack tomorrow morning at first light.

June the Nineteenth

I am within the walls of Nicaea. I shall explain how this came about. I shall try to restrain my anger.

No one expected the city to fall today. No one. Instead of bodies and carnage and burned buildings, instead of smoke and wails and the cringing of the captured, there is order and quiet. Alexius's blue and gold banners fly tranquilly over the walls, and I sit in a cooper's shop with a mound of gold as high as my knees before me. This, evidently, is the way that war is waged in the East.

The morning after the mining of the tower, we all were awake before dawn. We said our prayers in silence, led by Père Raimund of Aguillères. Then we crept silently into position to be ready to swarm the rubble at first light. The sun rose at our shoulders; we were about to give the battle cry 'Deus le volt!' and charge the tower. But no sooner was the sun up than we saw what the Turks had done.

During the night, somehow, they had rebuilt the tower. Where before there had been gaps large enough for men to pass two or three abreast, now there was the masonry, blackened but solid. We stood with our swords in hand gaping at the sight. How they had done it we could not guess, but such was their determination to keep us out that they had laboured all the night long in silence to repair the damage we had wrought.

Lord Raymond stared at the tower in disbelief. 'They are devils,' he said. 'Or the devil labours for them.' Behind us the Turkish prisoners fell prostrate – it is their favourite position – and gave thanks to their God. It was with difficulty that we restrained our men from assaulting them.

We were in ill spirits all day and then, in the afternoon, we received word that a large force of Turks was approaching us from around the lake. We knew at once that this was the Sultan Kilich Arselon come to relieve the city. Lord Raymond sent messengers to Godfrey and Bohemund, who replied that they dared not leave their positions at the northern and eastern walls. Thus it fell to the Provençals to repulse the onslaught.

We left a skeleton force to front the walls and turned about. We could see them massing atop the hills. There appeared to be thousands of them, all mounted, their long pennants flowing above the ranks. We brought our bowmen to the front while we mailed ourselves and stood to our horses.

The sun was low in the sky, making it difficult to see the Turks.

All at once a shout came from the hills and they charged towards us. Our archers fired first and, their bows being longer, they tore many gaps in the enemy line. But still the Turks came on.

When they were within range they fired, their arrows killing a great number of our men and horses. Their assaults continued while we traded blows with them, their short arrows and our longer ones mixed with stones from the machines. The Turks were brave; they were fighting for their sultan who watched from the hilltop. Their shouts and cries were horrifying, but our men stood their ground within the earthworks in which we have lived for weeks.

At last Lord Raymond gave the signal and we mounted. I held Fatana in, for she was eager for the charge. When the Turks were within a hundred rods, the trumpets blew. I lowered my lance and spurred Fatana on, though she needed no inducement; this was what she had come to the East to do, and there was no stopping her. She thundered straight ahead, clear through the line of bowmen, her ears bent back, her thick neck straining with every stride. I could not hold her in.

We hit the Turks square in their centre and it was like the clashing of two great waves. We swirled in among them, swinging and clubbing. It was my first real combat and it was like a dream. There were men all around me, hollering and cursing, the Turks howled and slashed at us with short sabres, arrows were being fired from both directions, and men were falling on every side.

I fought as my stepfather taught me, keeping my eyes open, saving my strength, striking only at the target nearest me, constantly checking my back. I saw a Turk grab at Lord Raymond's reins and I cut the man's arm clean off. I watched it fall, the fingers still gripping the reins, and I heard the man give a shriek. In the next moment I thrust at a stout man on a dun horse, the blade striking just below his upraised arm. Then two more of them were on me and I swung my sword above my head, catching both in the ears.

It was a wild and whirling combat in which faces and horses floated by on a mist of blood. At times I heard nothing, then the silence would be pierced with a cry. I saw men's faces slashed, I saw one man's helmet crushed into his skull with an axe blow. Horses screamed and fell on every side, men were spitted, gashed, and beaten to the ground, only to be trampled before they could rise. I was frenzied and soaked with sweat. I thought of nothing except the next man in my view. My blood was so hot that I heard it swishing in my ears, and I swung and slashed mechanically, feeling no fatigue and, to my amazement, no fear.

At one point a Turk came so close to me that I could see inside his mouth as he yelled. For some reason the sight disgusted me and I swung at him and knocked him from his horse. He rose stupidly, stunned from the blow, and I urged Fatana forward to trample him. She hit him with her shoulder and he went down again, and then a knight drove his lance into the Turk's side. I saw the point go in, severing his tunic and sliding in among his ribs. It would not come out, and I watched in fascination as the knight sought to free it, twisting and yanking at it until the Turk's ribs tore out from his flesh and he gave a yell, put down his hand as if to hold them in, and ground his teeth into the dirt.

When the fight was fully joined the infantry came up. With a cheer they smashed into the swirling mass of mounted men, flailing with their clubs and spears. Every Turk that fell was beaten and stabbed. The infantry soon were drenched in the blood that splashed from horsebacks. They jabbed at the Turkish ponies, splitting their legs and puncturing their necks. It was a mêlée in which every kind of weapon was used, including fists and belts and teeth. At last some Turks in the rear ranks began to turn and run, and when their comrades saw them, they too lost heart.

At this a cheer went up from our men and I yelled at the top of my voice and shook my sword in the air. Blood dripped from it into my eyes and I had to wipe at them to clear them. When the Turks heard our shout, they began to flee and I knew in my bones that we had won.

I spurred Fatana on and every Turk we met I struck with my

sword, some on the face and many in the back. I did not care; they were fleeing and the fury was upon me. My surcoat was so splattered with blood that it stuck to my mail; my face and arms and hands were soaked with it. Everything around me was a blur except the man I was about to kill. The evil of all my years poured out of me into my heaving arm.

We could not catch them on their quick mounts. Into the setting sun they disappeared among the hills above the lake. Some few knights pursued them, and I saw a band of horsemen, the sultan's guard no doubt, charge and strike them down. From the hilltop where the standards had stood a well-aimed volley of arrows cut short our pursuit. But it was enough. We had beaten back the sultan himself. Nicaea was open to our mercy.

Our casualties were fearful. Fully half our force was killed or wounded, and many of the wounds were fatal. Men of Provence lay all over the field, from the battle line clear up to the hills. The worst was at the point where our charge met theirs. A line of corpses of men and animals lay tangled together, in some places two and three deep. Under the bodies stirred living men, too weak from their wounds to free themselves. I saw soldiers hack at corpses of Turks to rescue them, deepening the river of blood that had formed there. In some places our men waded ankle-deep to search for wounded.

I was exhausted beyond anything I had ever felt. Not my body only, but my mind and soul were drained. I rode back towards the city in a daze. Thomas stood by my pavilion, his face blackened, his tunic soaked with blood. 'Oh, sir,' he said, 'Dagobert is killed, his head cut off.' And he broke down and cried.

I gave order for the boy's body to be brought to our encampment, but they were not able to find the severed head. We knew him only from the three stars he wore on his breast as an honour to me.

Gérard has a wound to the buttocks, but Bernard is well and nurses him. It is touching to see the devotion of these two peasants who attend on each other like brothers, almost, one would say, like husband and wife. Uc remains in the camp with a festered foot. Bartholomew has not yet returned. I am told that Père René was killed in the battle. It is said that he walked into the worst of it without arms, as though desiring to be killed. I hope earnestly that this was not because I had estranged him. But indeed, each man makes his own decisions and follows his own path, to life or death.

The Bishop Adhémar is celebrating a mass of thanksgiving in the city square which all of us are required to attend. I shall finish this tomorrow.

JUNE THE TWENTIETH

It is morning and, since there is neither marching nor fighting, I have the luxury to remain in my bed in the cooper's shop. I have found some curious items here of which I avail myself, assuming that the owners will not return. There is a flat bread with seeds that is delicious, and which I eat as I write this. There is also juice of the tangerine, that is as sweet as anything I have ever tasted.

I wrote of the mound of gold before me. I shall explain how this came about.

After our battle we returned to the southern wall, and the Duke of Normandy was sent to make up our losses. The next morning he, Fulk Rechin, and others of the Norman knights made an inspection of our position with Lord Raymond. Duke Robert shook his head in pity as Lord Raymond described the savagery of the fight and counted up our dead. Fulk Rechin responded with growing anger.

It was at this time that the emperor's ships at last made their appearance on the lake. Nicaea was finally surrounded, but still very strong in its defences and, so far as we knew, provisioned for a lengthy siege.

'We may be here all winter,' Lord Raymond observed.

'Either that or risk an assault,' replied Duke Robert.

'The order is already given,' Lord Raymond said. 'It will cost us dearly – more than we can spare, for we will need every man for Jerusalem.'

At that, Fulk Rechin asked whether we had any prisoners. Lord Raymond showed him to the camp where the Turks taken in our two battles were being kept under guard. There were about two hundred of them.

Fulk Rechin begged to speak with Duke Robert to one side. We could not hear what they were saying, but I could see the Duke frown, then nod gravely. At last I heard him say, 'Of course, of course.' Fulk Rechin then returned to us and asked Lord Raymond if he could take charge of the prisoners to effect a plan that might save us both a long siege and a deadly assault. Lord Raymond assented.

Among Duke Robert's escort was my old companion Landry Gros, and I asked him what Fulk Rechin had proposed. 'We have a saying in our language, Escrivel,' he replied. He pattered out some doggerel and then translated: 'Sometimes a warning does more than a war.' And he tapped his head and winked at me.

I soon saw what he meant. When the Normans had relieved our guards, they brought a dozen large wicker baskets, drew out their swords, and waded in among the Turks, who were prostrate in their morning prayers. While the Turks raised their voices to heaven in the rhythmic chant that has become familiar to us, the Normans began systematically cutting off their heads. One by one they took the severed heads by the hair and flung them into the baskets until all two hundred prisoners had been killed. The baskets containing the heads were then carried to the siege line.

That afternoon there was a barrage such as we had never seen before. The Normans loaded the severed heads, still dripping blood, into the catapults, and fired them over the walls. At once we heard the screams of terror from within. When all two hundred had been flung into the city, there was silence for about an hour. Then a flag of parlay was raised above the walls.

'It never fails,' Landry Gros remarked to me.

The nobles, led by Godfrey, Bohemund, Robert, and Lord Raymond, assembled to receive the Turkish emissaries. The gates, which had been barred against us for so long, swung open. To our astonishment, Butumites walked out.

It appears that he had been negotiating secretly with the Turks at the emperor's command. When the Turks learned that their sultan was coming to relieve the city they broke off the talks. Then, after our battle, the talks were resumed, still without our knowledge. The Turks were hoping to prolong them until Kilich Arselon might attack again, but the sultan sent them a message giving them leave to decide their own fate. After the warning of the Normans, they straightaway decided to surrender – not to us, but to the emperor.

To this end, Alexius had come in secret to Pelecanum, where he was being continually informed of the situation by Butumites. Upon hearing of the Turks' decision to surrender, he immediately sent word that no Frankish army was to be permitted to enter the city. Thus it was that Butumites, using the ships sent by Alexius, had secretly garrisoned Nicaea, even as we were preparing our assault.

This treachery infuriated our men, who had hoped to avenge themselves on the Turks and sack the city. It was to prevent this very thing that Alexius forestalled us. It seems he had no wish to conquer a ruined city, nor to allow our leaders to take charge of it. And so our siege of Nicaea ended, not in victory but in betrayal.

To compensate us, Alexius has sent gifts of food and gold to our men and ourselves. Every soldier of the army has been given provisions and a handful of copper coins, every knight has been rewarded with jewels, and each noble has been accorded one-third his weight in gold. Thus it is that I sit here with the mound of gold before me.

I say frankly that I have no use or desire for it. I shall divide it among my men, who may keep it or squander it as they please. They are encamped outside the main gates, and I go out each morning and evening to visit them. Uc can now no longer walk, and the doctor has told me that his foot must be taken off. I have not yet informed him of this, but will do so tonight after he has had the chance to enjoy the emperor's supper. Dagobert was buried before the southern wall of Nicaea in the graveyard established for Franks. Thomas is well, though still melancholy.

Bartholomew has had a singular experience. He became separated from us in the battle and was clubbed over the head. After two days on the field he was discovered by a burial party who flung him into the common grave and were throwing the dirt on him when he revived. His behaviour is much changed. He no longer has the joviality of his former self, but is silent and sits for hours in a kind of wonder.

The wound of Gérard is not serious, but I have learned that he is involved in unnatural relations with Bernard. When I confronted Bernard with this fact he broke down and wept, saying that he had never had a woman and expected never to have one. I ordered him and Gérard to confess to Père Raimund of Aguillères and not to associate with each other again. Still I catch Bernard making moon eyes at Gérard, who mopes around the camp like a scorned housewife. I would send them home, but that would leave me with no soldiers of my own.

Thomas is with me in the shop. He continues to be melancholy and plaintive. He is not much use as a squire, but I have not the heart to turn him out. However, I have lately been approached by a creature who begs to be allowed into my service.

I say 'creature' since it is not possible to determine who or what he is. He is a small, frighteningly thin man above forty whose skin is burned so black that he might be a Moor. He is stooped and weathered from years in the sun, but his legs are strong and he swears to me that he will work hard and be faithful. His name is Mansour. He speaks French tolerably well and says that he is Christian. I believe he is a Circassian from the north, of whom there are many in Nicaea. He has few teeth in his head and lacks two fingers of his left hand which, he says, were cut off by the Turks for stealing. However, he seems quick-witted, and I have need of help. I shall try him for a time, at least for so long as we are here.

JUNE THE TWENTY-SIXTH

Nicaea is a strange town. For the most part the inhabitants are Greek Christians, though there are large numbers of Jews, Armenians, and Syrians. Least of all are the Turks, who now live under the protection of the emperor. This morning the wife of Kilich Arselon was escorted from the city in state. She had recently given birth and, with her new baby and her two older children, she was taken from here to Constantinople, where she will live as a guest of Alexius until arrangements can be made to return her to her husband.

When we learned this there was great indignation within the army, for some of our leaders felt that she should be held hostage against our safe passage to Jerusalem. But Alexius would not hear of it, insisting instead that his honour required her return. Thus the comfort of one Turkish woman is to him more important than the lives of thousands of Christian soldiers. Such is the honour of the Greeks.

I have profited by the time to rest and reflect. Much has happened since my departure from Lunel nearly one year ago. I have now been involved in four battles, two against Christians and two against Turks. Clearly the Turks are the better fighters. They are very brave and fierce, though they cannot withstand a mounted charge by our knights. That must be our tactic – not to fight them on the run, but to wait until they mass and then attack them.

For myself, I have changed a good deal. I can feel it. I see now that while I was at home I was drifting, led on by my desires, with

no fixed end in view. This pilgrimage to Jerusalem, with all its
ferocity and strange encounters, is serving to concentrate my mind.
A man must have a goal, a fixed point before him towards which
he strives and against which he measures his progress. For me it is
Jerusalem, not only as an objective, but also an aspiration. For this
is a soul's journey as much as a soldier's. My soul's aim is the
Sepulchre, and what I shall find when I reach it only the soul can
know. Only she will recognize it when it comes.

My servant Mansour is proving as good as his word. He is hard-
working and diligent, and very solicitous of my welfare. Though a
foreigner, he understands the role of squire better than Thomas
ever did. Bartholomew is now virtually useless. He claims to see
visions and hear voices, and frequently spends the day staring in
wonder at the heavens. Some of the more ignorant of the soldiers
regard him as a mystic. There is a fine line, I think, between
saintliness and a knock on the head.

Yesterday the doctor removed the infected foot of Uc. Four of
us held him down while he laboured with knife and saw to cut it
off. The poor boy screamed and wept and begged us to take him
away or to kill him. I think I shall never forget the noise of the
saw as it cut through the bone, so much like that of the butchers
of Lunel as to make me shudder, realizing how very like the animals
we are.

When it was done, the doctor coated the stump with boiling
tar, which set the lad screaming again. The stump was then wound
in linen, and Uc was lain in the Turk's sanctuary, which they call a
mosque, and which is being used to house our wounded. Word has
come from Lord Raymond that we are to quit Nicaea in two days.
Uc will have to remain here and, if he survives, will be sent back
to Lunel by some means. In that event, I have given him letters to
my wife, mother and sister to let them know that I live.

I should say a word about the Bishop Adhémar. After the battle
there was much talk about his behaviour in command of our troops

on the right. It is said he showed much valour, and that his men are now devoted to him.

I have thought a great deal about our relations. When he thought he was dying he begged my forgiveness; when he thought I was dying, he extorted it. It may be that a man can change overnight, but I doubt it. If it is so, then perhaps it is well that I forgave him, for, though I am no priest, I may have saved his soul. But if this is merely one more of his shams, then I hope he will achieve his end of dying in the service of the Saviour. I am content to leave him to his God.

Tomorrow we start on the long road to Antioch.

JUNE THE TWENTY-EIGHTH

We have marched all day and reached a village called Leuce. It is a sorry place, scarcely more than shacks athwart the road. This is a forlorn country, impoverished and dry, but at least the people do not cower in fear of us. Evidently they have heard about our conduct in Nicaea, and now remain in their homes to trade with us.

This evening our leaders met to discuss the future of our campaign. It was decided to divide the army into two parts, the first setting out tomorrow, the second to remain a day's march behind. The leading group will be commanded by Prince Bohemund, and will include the Normans, the Flemish, the troops of Count Stephen of Blois, and the Greeks sent by Alexius. These last are led by a general named Tatikios, a long-nosed, fiery-eyed man who is said to be of Turkish parentage. He replaces the treacherous Butumites whom we have refused to have in our army. Tatikios apparently has a great reputation as a general of cavalry, but it remains to be seen whether he is any more trustworthy than his predecessor.

Our group will be led by Lord Raymond and Count Godfrey, and, besides their troops, it consists of the French forces under

Hugh of Vermandois, the brother of the king. Despite his great title I have little respect for this man. He is short, pudgy and bald, and spends most of his time fussing over his clothes. He is no soldier, and during our battle with the Turks he kept himself well to one side, waggling his banners and shouting epithets, but doing no damage. His soldiers are the best dressed in the army, but their ability as fighting men has yet to be tested. We keep them in the centre of the column, between our Provençals and Godfrey's Lorrainers, trusting them neither with the van nor the rear guard.

I am back in my pavilion after the weeks of siege and the days in Nicaea. It is musty and filled with the hard-shelled beetles that are everywhere here. Mansour has done a wonderful job of making it comfortable. His blackened little frame is always moving, straightening, cleaning, setting out cushions he has brought from Nicaea, seeing to my food and bedding. I have rewarded him with a measure of the gold given us by the emperor. At first he refused, but when I pressed it on him, he glanced away and tears began to form in his eyes. He took the gold most humbly and retired to his place outside the door of my pavilion, from which he has displaced Thomas who, though he grumbles against Mansour, is afraid of him.

June the Thirtieth

We are encamped in a high pass of the mountains. The first group of the army has already reached the plain. Before us is the town of Dorylaeum, where the roads to the east and south divide. Once there, we must decide which we shall take on our route to the Holy Land.

For the first time I begin to think in earnest of that place, which once seemed so distant, but now lies at the end of the road before us. I thank God that He has spared me to this point, for as I look out from our height I see fires in the distance, and fancy that they may be those of Antioch, the city of Saint Peter, the first capital of our religion. It begins now to become real to me. It begins to take on a life.

Here the air is cooler than in the lowlands, with their endless woods of scrub and thorn. There are wild flowers hereabouts that I have never seen, heart-shaped buds with spots of every hue, and pitcher flowers filled with nectar, and tiny purple blossoms with golden centres. I sit upon a rock, holding one of these in my hands, and gazing at the stars, my sword across my knees, my old surcoat draping to the ground, the Cross upon my shoulder. It is quiet and peaceful, and in the breeze I think I hear the voices of the saints, welcoming me to their holy realm.

A shooting star descends, and on it I wish that I may live to see my home again. But if that will not be, then how sweet to give one's life for a dream of faith, under stars such as these and in the presence of the silent majesty, not of princes of the earth, but of this purple flower, handed me by God.

> Within this bloom I see
> Eternity unfold;
> The will of God is here
> In specks of gold.
>
> What have I done
> To desire so much?
> What debt have I repaid
> To be so full forgiven?
>
> Here in this night
> Alive with fire,
> Thick with angel wings,
> It is not my thoughts
> That gather and conspire,
> It is my soul that sings:

What mind has guessed
The spirit knows:
Though lights may dim,
The door is never closed.

JULY THE SECOND

Yestermorn we set out early on our march. We had not gone far before a messenger galloped up to us, panting and excited. He announced that our lead column had been attacked by a large force of Turks, and was fighting a defensive battle until we should come up.

We wasted no time. The mounted men rushed forward, leaving orders for the infantry to follow as quickly as possible. The heat had not permitted us to travel in mail, and so the baggage carts dashed after us to the ridge line. There, while we armed ourselves, we watched the battle in the plain below.[66]

The Turkish force was huge, many thousands of cavalry that were making their quick feints and assaults on our line in wave after wave. The air was black with arrows, from their riders and our dismounted men who had formed a circle and were fighting on all sides. Clearly the Turks thought they had trapped our entire force.

'We shall have them now!' Lord Raymond shouted. Godfrey argued that we should divide our force and attack from two sides but Raymond overruled him, urging a massed charge. While this was going on our rear guard came up and, to our surprise, disappeared across the hills to the south. We had no time to wonder what they were doing, but mounted as quickly as we could, formed up our lines, and charged down the hill.

The speed of our horses on those slopes gave us a momentum that nothing could have resisted. When we reached the plain we

66 The Battle of Dorylaeum, July 1, 1097.

fanned out into a battle line half a league across, five hundred knights galloping at full charge. A portion of the Turkish force turned about to try to prevent us breaking through to our troops, but we smashed them to pieces. Once we had made the jointure our comrades gave the order to counterattack, and with a blare of trumpets and cries to God we turned on them, driving them on all sides.

At that moment there was a great shout from the hilltops to the west, and a massive wave of cavalry descended upon us. They were outfitted in black and gold silks, with long scarves trailing from their helmets. These were not the soldiers of the sultan but some other race of fighters, and they were glorious and fierce.[67] They came at us like tigers, swinging long curved swords and brandishing golden shields. Our infantry shrank back from their charge, but Bohemund rallied his Normans and turned to meet them.

The sound they made when they crashed together echoed over the plain; it was metal on metal, flesh on flesh, screams, cries and the clashing of arms. Though in the midst of the fight ourselves, we were fascinated by it, and for a moment everything seemed to stop till we should see the outcome. The Normans were in their glory. This was close-quarter combat with a barbarian foe such as their ancestors had fought. Their strength was enormous and their skill breathtaking, but the scarfed soldiers stood their ground.

Now the battle was raging on two fronts, ours against the sultan's men and the Normans' bloody fight. In minutes the two had merged into one, and we were being beaten back towards the foothills. A trumpet sounded and we broke off long enough to let our bowmen loose a volley. This staggered the Turks but they came on still. The battle lines were weaving back and forth across the valley, and with every ebb and flow of the fight more bodies were left behind. Neither side would yield, and it seemed that we should dash ourselves to pieces against each other when, from the hills to the south, came a trumpet call.

67 These scarfed warriors were probably the cavalry of the Emir Danishmend, with whom Kilij Arslan had made a treaty to join forces against the Franks.

Our rear guard, which had separated from us so unexpectedly, now came thundering onto the plain. It was the Bishop Adhémar who, perhaps guided by God, had made this detour to come out on the Turkish flank. The manoeuvre worked perfectly. The Turks, not expecting to be attacked from that side, began to crumple and flee. Nothing their generals did could steady them. Adhémar's men stormed into their lines, cutting them down from behind even as we counterattacked from the front. Now it was the Turks who were trapped, and they panicked almost at once.

What had been a pitched battle became a killing spree. The Turks found their retreat blocked at every turn. It was horrible to see them trying to fight their way out, only to be cut down from behind. At last the scarfed knights made a stand at the centre of the plain, a brave corps sacrificing itself to allow their fellows to flee.

It had been a mighty battle, one that had waged for six hours. By the time we regrouped outside the town it was mid-afternoon. The losses on both sides were heavy, but ours were not nearly so great as theirs. Among our spoils is the pavilion of the Sultan Kilich Arselon with its silks and jewels. These our men have divided among themselves after many arguments and broken skulls.

I have a cut upon my forearm which I do not remember receiving, and Fatana, brave animal that she is, has two puncture wounds to her breast, though she never faltered. The Turks are routed, decisively I think. God grant that this victory may open the road for us to Antioch.

July the Ninth
On the Road to Antioch

We have been five days upon the march. This is the ungodliest country that ever have I seen. I am weak and shall become weaker, and my spirits are so low that I have not been able to rouse myself to write.

After the battle of the plain our leaders met to choose our route. From Dorylaeum three roads led eastward. The northernmost would have carried us into land held by the Turks. The middle road, leading due east and the shortest route to Antioch, crosses a salt desert where, we are told by Tatikios, no water may be found, nor any village or resting place. The final route, that to the south, carries us the long way around towards Antioch, but it offers opportunities for forage, or so he said, as well as skirting the vast salt desert.

Thus, there was hardly a choice. We follow the southern road, and it is hell. This is a land without shade, where nothing grows but thorns and weeds. The soil is chalk that crumbles in your hand, and the sun beats cruelly. Our army is a sight. We look like ghosts, covered in white dust and moving with painful slowness. The horses pant and stagger and the men are bent nearly double by heat and thirst. The Turks have preceded us into this land, and they have destroyed everything in our path. Every farm and village has been burned, every well is stopped with boulders, every field is stripped, every stream is polluted with the corpses of animals.

Though we move southwards, we are still too far from the coast to be provisioned by the Greek ships which, in any case, have been dispatched to seize the coastal towns. Thus, Alexius profits by our march to improve his own position and to recover his lost ports. We are now an army cut off from our base, moving through the enemy's country without hope of supply or rescue.

How the men endure is a mystery to me, but one that inspires admiration. They walk in double file, following each other's backs, concentrating only on the road that lies immediately before them. When we pause to rest they drop down just where they are. A few start fires to cook the meagre meat that is left to them. Others instantly fall asleep to be roused only by the trumpet.

At such rests there is a silence that I have never known in the army before. No one speaks, not even mutters of discontent are heard; only the hot wind from off the hills, and the muted grunts of the animals. I think often of the business we are about: the killing of our fellow men for the sake of faith. And I reflect that there is such bravery about our pilgrimage, such nobility of bearing despite our rags, and such fortitude among our men that if ever soldiers were sent to slaughter for an ideal, these are they, and if ever men are deserving of forgiveness for that slaughter, they are these.

These simple peasants with the Cross upon their shoulders suffer everything for their faith. But faith in what? Who knows? Only each man in his heart can say why he is here. For myself, I know that I came because of my sins. Now I remain because of these good men who trudge before me every fiery day and sleep around me every breathless night, and utter not a word of complaint, though no one ever has been as far from home as they.

The Bishop Adhémar has become the hero of the army. His attack was a feat of brilliance, there is no doubt, and his bravery has become a legend among the men. This terrible sinner, deserving of death and hell, has become a saintly figure by his repentance. He bears himself erect, his haughtiness has transformed itself into nobility. His eyes have the look of heaven in them. Truly he is a changed man. Already his pilgrimage is a success. I wish him well, for only God knows the nature of his accounts.

JULY THE NINETEENTH

Our strength gives out. Many men have fallen by the roadside, too weak or too ill to travel. We leave boys to tend to them, hoping that they will not be set upon by the Turks. A third of our horses are dead, and every horse and mule that falls is butchered. The men are so crazed with thirst that they drink the blood of the fallen animals, and even the urine from their bladders.

I am desperate to keep Fatana alive. It pains me to see how thin she has become. Her eyes are clouded and her flanks are withered in, but she tramps on at my side. I have stripped the saddle from her and left it in the road. It was a gift to me from my stepfather, and I glanced back continually at it as we trudged on, a poor mute heap in the dust. Our baggage train has fallen behind, the mules unable to keep up even with our painful pace. I wear one tunic, and drape another across Fatana's back. My surcoat is wrapped around my head like a turban. But I fear that I shall be stripped almost naked before this stage is through. We cross a land that is surely cursed by God. At first it was salt desert, now salt marshes. These are swamps so deep in powdery slime that we wade through them to our hips. The water is impossible to drink and offers no relief from the heat.

Count Godfrey got drunk the other night and went into the hills in search of a bear. He found one, but had not his customary luck. The bear slashed open his breast and now he too must be carried in a litter. His brother Baldwin commands his force, and the men suffer all the more for his cruelty. He drives them with curses and the flat of his sword as if they were responsible for the bleakness of the land.

Lord Raymond is afflicted with a fever and must be carried in a portaize.[68] He is waited on by his doctor and Père Raimund of Aguillères, and we all fear for him. If prayer is efficacious then surely he will recover, for he has the ceaseless prayers of all the Provençals.

And yet I wonder about prayer. Does God really hear my voice? Does He understand my language? Can He measure my desires, sorting out what is needful and what is not? Does He truly concern Himself with me, Roger of Lunel, thirty years old, son of Richard and Hélène, who wears a soiled tunic and does his business by the roadside?[69] Surely the King of the Universe has more to concern Himself with than me.

68 Portaize: a covered stretcher borne between two horses.
69 The expression that Roger uses is: *caga de latz lo cami*. It is surprisingly vulgar, and I have translated it with a euphemism.

I have seen good men die in the midst of prayer, begging only to be allowed once more to see their families. And I have seen the mean-spirited prayers of evil men rewarded, who asked for nothing but riches or the destruction of their enemies. And do not the Turks pray? Indeed, I have watched them pray four, five and six times a day. Yet were not their heads cut off in the midst of prayer to be flung over the walls? And what if they pray for victory over us, while we, just as eagerly and fervently, pray to annihilate them? Whose prayers then are answered? Which of us may expect a reply from God?

I have been haunted by the arm that I cut off in our battle at Nicaea. In the salt desert, while the sun hammered down, I saw it floating before me. The stump was livid, and the fingers curled towards my face. At night I dream of it. It beckons me to cross the salt marsh, it points the way to Antioch. Shall I follow a severed arm to the gates of Saint Peter, he who rested his head upon the Holy Breast at supper, and then denied Him thrice? Shall I take that disembodied hand in mine and walk with it into the Sepulchre of Our Lord?

Last night in a terrible dream, I devoured it. I ate it like a savage, gnawing at the flesh of the forearm until my lips ran red. I chewed upon the fingers and licked the spaces in between. And when I had swallowed it all I awoke in passion, to find that I had spilled my seed into my palm. What can it mean? What can I mean in such a state as this?

July the Twenty-eighth

We are past the marshes but the salt desert continues. Before us in the distance lies a mountain range, and how we shall get through it I cannot imagine. More than half of our animals are dead; their bones are the markers of our progress across this Godforsaken land. My struggle now is to keep Fatana alive, a task that would be impossible without the help of Mansour.

I do not know how he does it, nor do I enquire, but every evening he disappears, and when he returns before dawn there is water and forage for her, and food for me. He is very clever and cunning at his work. He leaves our camp with nothing but a sack folded into his clothing, and when he returns, before the army is awake, the sack is full. It is not too much to say that I owe my life to this strange creature, whose mystery is matched only by his loyalty. Surely God has sent him to me.

Yesterday I watched a boy die. He was a French lad from Paris, one of Prince Hugh's men. He had been left behind in the road, unable to go on, and when I saw him his face looked so young and so pitiable that I had to stop. We picked him up and put him on my baggage cart, for I could not bear to leave him.

At sunset when we camped I took him into my pavilion. Mansour came in as he always does to shake the white dust from my tunic and clean my hands and feet. When he saw the boy he stopped short, and tears came into his eyes. 'He is too sweet to die, Effendi,' he said. He calls me by the Turkish word for lord.

Indeed, the boy was angelic, all the more so for the extreme pallor of his face and the emaciated lightness of his limbs. He was coated from head to foot with the white salt powder, and Mansour immediately set to cleansing him. With what gentleness he did so. He handled his frail body as lovingly as his mother would have done, and gave to him such peace as made the poor lad smile. He reached his hand up to Mansour's burnt face, swallowed a long painful while, and said, 'God bless you sir, whatever manner of man you may be.' And then he lay back his head and expired.

Mansour closed the boy's blue eyes and crossed his hands upon his slender, naked breast. Then he inclined his head with its twisted turban, and said such prayers as his religion dictates. I was very moved. Never had a youth a more peaceful death. Never had a poor boy far from home a more caring funeral.

The army is much reduced by this dreadful march. Day after day, under the white sun across the flat white plain, we grow weaker and weaker. How we should have the strength to fight the Turks if they appear I do not know. You cannot easily imagine such a place: a sea of white dust, a dust cloud like a mocking ghost rising at our footsteps. The men soak cloths in the brackish water that we find and bind their mouths and noses, for the dust is suffocating. Men breathe it in and choke and cough until they bring up blood. Eyelids are coated with it, it clings to our hair and beards until we resemble an army of old men staggering across a dream.

You can almost hear the sun. It hums in its heat, burning our faces at morning, our backs in the afternoon. Were it not for the white dust we should all be black as Mansour. It breaks my heart to watch men who have come so far drop down in this desert, not to rise again. We can see them for leagues as we pass on, motionless heaps upon the white plain. We have long since ceased to bury them. The crosses on their shoulders will be their markers.

Knights whose horses have died are reduced to walking or, if their dignity can bear it, to riding mules and even oxen. I saw Gaston of Béarn, a young nobleman famous for his dignity, astride an ox, his hands gripping a rope around its neck, an expression of indifference on his face. Normally such a sight would have caused laughter. Here we just ignore it and move on.

We march now nearly naked. I have abandoned everything except my tunic and my sword. My surcoat, my mail and my crown are with the baggage cart. I have given orders that all else is to be removed in order that we may carry as many stricken men as possible. Thus our route is littered with the leavings of the army, and the colours of many a noble Frank lie abandoned in the road.

I write this now by moonlight outside my pavilion, which resembles a snowdrift, so thick is it with dust. Not an inch of its blue and gold stripes is exposed. Mansour lies at my feet, snatching a few hours' rest before he sets off on his foraging. The army is silent. The desert is almost beautiful in the moonglow, white upon white. Yet there is no end to it in sight except the mountains. And they may kill us.

AUGUST THE THIRD

It is a week since I have written, the worst of my life. Beyond the salt desert we came into a land of thorns. As far as the eye could see the stubbly bushes grew, tearing at our clothes and our skin as we passed, drawing so much blood that you would have thought a battle had taken place. Some of the Greeks gnawed at these bushes both for their moisture and their flesh. Soon every man in the army was doing so, though the thorns made our mouths bleed. There was precious little water in the stalks but we were so desperate that we sucked greedily at them.

I found they had the taste of parchment, a bitter, dry taste, but were not inedible. We quickly learned to pluck the thorns off with our teeth and draw out the precious liquid. Then we stripped the brown bark and ate the branches. A little farther on we came to fields of wild cane, and this to us was Godsend. Though the cane was tough and rolled tight as a scroll, we ate it greedily. There was much moisture in the stalks and the crystal sweetness was a great refreshment. Fatana especially savoured it, and I nearly wept for joy to see her devour the handfuls that I brought to her. That, together with the flesh of the dead animals, has kept us going.

Three days ago we reached the mountains and struggled up them to the first ridge line. As I expected, it was more than many of the men could manage. Yet when we reached the height, we found a little spring, and nobles, knights and peasants all gave thanks to God and threw themselves upon it. It was a comical sight, hundreds of half-dead men licking out their tongues at what was scarcely more than a trickle across the rocks. We laughed and wept, splashed ourselves, stripped off our tunics and rolled about in the pitiful little stream. Then we lay panting and exhausted. And the rains came.

They were on us with a crash of thunder and a fierce glowering of the sky. And they were cold, as cold as any winter rain of France, chilling us through to the bone. There was not half an hour's respite between the killing heat and the drenching, freezing rain. It has rained steadily for three days now. We march in it, we pray in it, we sleep in it. Far from reviving us, it has nearly broken our spirit. Men cry openly and curse at the sky, and even curse at God. Some, incredibly, have turned back, falling behind the column in little groups, then retracing their steps towards the desert.

AUGUST THE SIXTH

This evening Père Raimund gave the unction to my Lord. He is not expected to live. He called me to his pavilion to give me his instructions. I was frightened by the sight of him. He was so emaciated that the bones of his shoulders protruded and his face was shrunken like a skull. All of his hair has fallen out, and the flesh of his scalp was specked and pitted. I scarcely recognized him, until he smiled. There were the powerful teeth, as strong as ever.

'Roger!' he said to me. I came close, for the rain poured down, making it difficult to hear. 'The priests have given me the sacrament, but I won't give them the satisfaction.' I told him that I was glad to hear it. 'They think this is their expedition,' he went on in a kind of frenzy. 'But it is not. This is a spiritual quest. They know everything about religion, but nothing of the spirit.'

He suddenly took my arm in a grip that pained me. 'We know,' he said, 'you and I. We have felt it stirring within us like a child in the womb . . .'

He closed his eyes and lay back exhausted. I watched his face, wondering at the strange words he had used. At last he opened his eyes again. There was a grim calmness within them, a kind of determination mixed with dismay. I had never seen such a look in his eyes before. He nodded his head on the sweat-soaked pillow. 'We take the cock of God inside us and we try to hold it there,' he said, 'but He thrashes and pumps and at last He leaves His seed in our souls. And we grow great with it and labour and we are delivered . . . to such as this . . . this pilgrimage. Women . . . women know nothing of this. To be raped by God . . .' His voice trailed off a moment, but then he suddenly shouted: 'Women are the whores of men, but men are the whores of God!'

I thought he was delirious and I made to fetch the doctor, but Lord Raymond grabbed me again. 'They carry it between their legs,' he said, 'and they take our poor, pitiful members in, and they think it some great achievement. Some great love. But we . . .' He gripped my sleeve in both his hands. 'A man's whole body is the womb of God. He seeds us, and we must bear. We bear or die. That is why we have come here . . . to bear the fruit of God. To make ourselves trees, bushes, grain fields.'

I begged him to lie back and be still but he would not. He was possessed by an idea that had to express itself. 'We – you and I, Roger – are the brood mares of God. We must become pregnant. Pregnant with . . . Nothing. These sufferings, these battles, they are meant to empty us. You see, my friend? You must become pregnant with Nothing in order to give birth to God.' His eyes searched the darkened pavilion restlessly, desperate. 'The priests do not under-stand this. They make formulas, bargains, deals – they buy and sell God. But they are barren. As barren as that desert we have crossed, and as slick as the hillsides of mud.'

He grappled my arm until his face was close to mine. His breath was fetid and his voice was panting. 'You must save this pilgrimage from the priests,' he said. 'If one soul, if only one soul reaches the Sepulchre, if one soul grasps the mystery that lies within, then our expedition will be a success. If not . . .' He lay back at last, a horror in his eyes. 'If not, then the souls of all those we have killed, and those whom we have led to their deaths, will haunt us for eternity.'

I told him that I understood, but I knew I did not. He knew it too, and patted my arm. 'I rely on you, Roger. If I die before we reach the Holy City, I rely on you to see to it that this pilgrimage will not have been in vain – to guarantee that it will not become the lie the priests will surely try to make of it. In your heart . . . in *your* heart at least it must be true.'

I promised that I would be faithful. He grasped my hand firmly. 'Now you know my legacy,' he said. 'If I should die, you must carry it on for me.'

I was in tears as I left his pavilion. I walked out into the rain, wiping at my eyes. The Bishop Adhémar, whom I had not seen for weeks, stood before me. 'Is he dead?' he asked. There was no malice in his tone, which surprised me.

'No,' I said. 'Though I doubt that he can live.'

'He hates me,' the bishop said. 'He would not allow me to give him the sacrament.'

'No, he pities you,' I replied. 'As do I.' I walked past him, but he called after me.

'Roger, I am a changed man,' said he.

I turned to him. The rain splashed in our faces but neither of us would allow himself to blink. 'I know,' I said. 'For the man you were was not deserving of our pity.'

The same, later

I have lain awake all night listening to the rain and reflecting on what my Lord has said. It rings so deeply in my soul, it sounds so familiar, yet I am too tired or too stupid to sort it out. The Sepulchre calls to me as it must to him. Yet what is the Sepulchre?

A tomb; a place where, for three short days, the Son of God lay waiting for the world to be reborn.

Mansour has come in to bathe me. He washes my feet, my face, my legs. He does it with all the gentleness of a woman, so that I am ready to fall asleep when he finishes. He never looks at my eyes, but attends strictly to his work. I wonder what he thinks of me, this Frankish nobleman who has come into his world chasing a dream of salvation. He has so often scorned my offers of payment that I know it is not for money that he attends me. 'Why then?' I ask myself. But I cannot bring myself to ask him. Perhaps, like Thomas, I am afraid of him with his quick, efficient movements and his intense concentration. And why should I be afraid of him?

Perhaps it is myself that I fear, and the change that has come over me. It is a change I only imperfectly understand, but surely it is reflected in my limbs, which are comically shrunken and spare, and on which the skin is stretched like that of a boiled chicken. When Mansour removed my leggings tonight and bared my legs to wash them, I nearly laughed. Is this Roger de Lunel, the lord of his estate, the son of Richard of Burgundy?

No, this is an old man with chicken legs as white as chalk and as thin as the stalks of cane. Death does not overtake us from without; it grows within, becoming more and more what we are until we no longer recognize ourselves for the sparseness. I am becoming a stranger to myself, and a reflection of death. I am becoming death, which is not black and menacing, but white, familiar and frail, and covered with dry skin.

Yet Mansour washes me as carefully as if I were some young prince of his native land, running his hands over my withers and intruding his fingertips into my joints as if they were the most precious of machinery. And is that not what we are — the most precious of God's machinery, wound up to do his bidding, and running down towards death?

How I hope my Lord survives. For if he should die, with whom shall I talk? And after whom shall I model myself? Please, God, if

You exist and have a care for our affairs, restore him to health. If not for my sake, then for that of our expedition which, after all, is nothing but Your expedition entrusted to ourselves.

AUGUST THE NINTH

We have passed the mountains and are nearing a town called Iconium which lies at the head of a fertile valley of streams, fields and shade trees. We were so stunned when we topped the final rise and found this view that no one spoke. Then one knight dropped to his knees and began to sing a hymn, and soon others joined him. Many of the men wept openly. Someone said, 'Paradise'.

During the illness of Lords Raymond and Godfrey, Count Baldwin has taken the lead. He rode up to me on the rise overlooking the valley, screwed up his dark little pinched face, and said that the Turks must surely be laying a trap. He therefore ordered that no one descend into the valley until a scouting party could inspect the place and reconnoitre the town. Since there are so few nobles of the van whose horses are fit to ride, I volunteered to go alone.

Baldwin squinted at me. 'Take your squire,' he said. 'Or at least, your little heathen. That way, if they capture you, you can send back for ransom.' Then he smiled a mirthless smile and added: 'And in that case, perhaps you ought to tell me where Count Raymond keeps his gold.'

I thanked him for his concern and repeated that I would go alone in the morning.

AUGUST THE TENTH

Before dawn I dressed myself for battle and rode down from the heights. The valley was long and wide, and deep in cooling shadows.

I made my way through the trees to one side of the road, watching for Turks. In an hour's ride I reached the city, which is surrounded by a low stone wall topped with wooden battlements. The gates stood wide open, and peasants were coming out to work their fields. I showed myself to a group of these, who stopped and stared at me.

At last one of them, an elderly man with a long-handled hoe, approached me. He pattered out something in Greek and, when I did not reply, he repeated it in Latin. 'Are you the Franks who have come from the West?' he said.

I replied that I was one of them. I was about to ask whether there were Turks in the city when he suddenly gave a shout and fell to his knees. Fatana shied, but the man reached out his arms and, to my astonishment, he began kissing my stirrups. In a moment I was surrounded by peasants who took my reins and led me into the town. There the people received me as a hero.

They are Armenians for the most part, who have come here from the north and been badly treated by the Turks. They have thrown their city open to us and are caring for us as though we were their brothers. We have made our camp under the walls and shall enjoy our first good meal and quiet rest since leaving Nicaea.

Lord Raymond is improving, thank God, and Count Godfrey has appeared in the camp for the first time since his wounding by the bear. He came out to us looking unsteady and embarrassed, took off his tunic and blouse, and showed us his scars. There are four diagonal red gashes across his chest and two more upon his neck and back; a most impressive souvenir. His men have adopted them as a coat of arms, painting them on their shields. They have also taken the bear as their emblem.

The Armenian girls come out to our camp every morning and evening. They are not particularly attractive, with oily skin, bent noses, and bad teeth, but they giggle and pose outrageously, and many of the men are smitten. Thomas looks mournfully at them, knowing, I suppose, that I will beat him if he misbehaves. Yet it is a great temptation to lie again with a woman, to feel that pulsing warmth, to lose oneself in the forgetfulness of encircling arms.

For myself, I find that I resist. It has been so long since I have lain with a woman that the feeling of it has gone out of me. It seems to me now strange, almost impossible, that I should ever have been so close to another person. I feel awkward when I look at the girls of the town, and I lower my eyes as if I were a schoolboy again. But the truth is, I think I am afraid of venery, or perhaps afraid of losing the sense of goodness and the inner calm that my long abstinence has earned me.

How strange that is. I have killed in the meantime, I have severed a man's arm and seen another's ribs pulled out, I have soaked myself in the blood of foreigners, but I feel that so long as I refrain from sex I can be good. Yet sex is a warm and human thing, and killing is brutish and cold-blooded. Where has this notion come from? Is it from religion? Indeed, I think it must be, for killing serves the purpose of the Church while pleasure does not.

Now, as I lie upon my back in this fair valley, surrounded by the sounds of the camp and gazing at a blue, unbroken sky, I wonder at the words of Raymond my Lord, that men are the whores of God. Perhaps I am, for I am in His employ and do His bidding even to the violation of myself. But what is the seeding he spoke of? And what did he mean by becoming pregnant with 'nothing' in order to give birth to God? And what did the Jew of Brindisi mean when he said my confession could not be sincere until I see that sex and doubt are one? And what did I mean in my extremity when I wrote that I prayed to God *if* He exists, and *if* He has concern for our affairs?

This is a strange pilgrimage if it takes me away from God and not towards Him.

August the Sixteenth

It is now one year since I left my home. Much has happened, but most of it remains unsettled. We rested three days at Iconium, and even the Norman knights treated the people with respect, raping only a few of the girls but killing no one. We now take the road to Heraclea, the last town before Antioch. If we can capture it and Antioch, the road to Jerusalem will be truly open. Yet surely the Turks will fight to prevent this.

The people of Iconium have replaced our horses and carts, giving us their own and those of the neighbouring villages. They have loaded us down with food for the march, and have taught us to make water skins from the bladders of goats. These they dry in the sun, and then rub with oil to make them supple and strong. They can hold several days' worth of water, and now no man of the army is without one. They are also sending guides with us to show us shepherds' wells that the Turks do not know of, and that will not be poisoned. God bless the Armenians of this land.

I am happy to say that my Lord Raymond has recovered. We rode out of Iconium this morning, he mounting a horse for the first time in weeks. He was much distressed that his own horse had died on the march and been butchered. When he learned that he had, unknowingly, eaten of its meat, he vomited.

Before us lie the mountains that the Armenians call Anti-Taurus. We are told by our guides that they are both steep and craggy, and that some of the trails are little more than footpaths over precipices. I discussed this with my Lord, attempting to distract him from his melancholy as we rode together. He interrupted me with the question 'Did you think I was mad?'

I told him that I knew what delirium could be. He shook his head. 'It was not delirium; it was revelation. The fever burned the clots from my eyes and I saw clearly. You must not share what I said with anyone, lest the priests hear of it and accuse me of blasphemy. But you will remember it, Roger.' I told him that I would, and that I had already given much thought to it. 'And what have you decided?' he asked.

'I await the Sepulchre,' I replied.

He smiled and patted my arm. 'That is all any of us can do,' said he.

AUGUST THE TWENTY-FIRST
Heraclea

Our scouts told us that the town was full of Turks, a strong garrison well supplied, and that the citizens, who are Armenians, were being terribly persecuted. They brought reports of men beheaded and women hanged by their breasts. Even children, they said, had had their hands and feet cut off for stealing from the Turkish armoury and hamstringing their animals.

After the welcome we received at Iconium our men were eager to storm the place. We formed our battle lines in the plain before the city, Lords Raymond, Godfrey, Bohemund and Robert taking the lead. We could see the Turks peering at us from the battlements. Then, as we started forward, the knights in the front, the bowmen and infantry in perfect line behind, they disappeared. We supposed they were preparing their catapults and fires, but instead, when we were a furlong from the town, its gates swung open and the people rushed out to greet us, shouting, 'They have fled! They have fled!'

The Armenians welcomed us as liberators, throwing open their homes and stores to us, and for the first time it began to seem that our expedition might truly be a success. Then the dispute began. The question was our route to Antioch. The argument was over the Cilician Gates.

The leading nobles had gathered in the Bishop Adhémar's pavilion. Tatikios the Greek was also in attendance, together with the elders of the town, an Armenian prince and several merchants. Before us they spread out large maps of the countryside, which showed the routes to Antioch. The most direct leads to the south through the high mountain pass known as the Cilician Gates. A second, leading north-eastward in a great arc, follows the old Byzantine military road through Caesarea Mazacha and the low pass known as the Gates of Amanus to Marash and thence to Antioch.

Count Tancred, the nephew of Bohemund, was the first to speak. 'It's obvious,' he said, poking at the map. 'We take the southern route.'

Baldwin, Godfrey's brother, agreed. 'I've been there. The pass is dangerous, but it's foolish to go so far to the north. Besides, the southern route takes us through Tarsus, the city of Paul. Isn't that a prize for Christians?'

'A prize for you,' Count Godfrey spat. He pointed to the map. 'Once you pass the Cilician Gates there's still the Syrian Gates, and they're in the hands of the Turks. They're steep and narrow. A handful of men rolling boulders down those cliffs could stop the entire army.'

'I'll take Tarsus and drive the Turks out,' Baldwin said.

'You'll take Tarsus and keep it for yourself,' Godfrey retorted.

'So what of it?' Baldwin shot back.

Bishop Adhémar reproached him. 'We are here for God,' he said.

'You're here for God,' Baldwin replied. 'I'm here because my damn brother owns every inch of land in Lorraine.'

At this, Godfrey jumped up. 'You little pig,' he growled.

Baldwin ignored him and turned to Adhémar. 'I want a kingdom,' he said brazenly, 'and you're going to need a kingdom in Syria to protect your pilgrimage routes. Your interests and mine are the same.'

'Our interest is in keeping the army together,' Lord Raymond responded.

Baldwin picked up his gloves. 'I'm going by the Cilician Gates,' he said. 'Who goes with me?'

Tancred declared that he would. On that, Bohemund reached over, grabbed his nephew's collar, and punched him in the mouth. 'Upstart,' he snarled. 'You'd split the army in face of the Turks?'

Tancred wiped the blood from his lips. 'You're already a king,' said he. 'This is my chance.'

'You, a king?' Bohemund laughed. 'Your mother was a filthy whore who bore you in a back alley in Messina.'

'You ought to know,' Tancred said, 'she's your sister.'

Bohemund began punching him again so violently that we had to come between them. The Bishop Adhémar shouted over the commotion: 'The army moves by the north. We cannot risk our entire force in the mountain passes.' Baldwin started to protest but Adhémar raised his hand. 'However,' he went on firmly, 'if these two youths wish to occupy Tarsus, they may do so.'

Now it was the other nobles who protested, but Adhémar silenced them as well. 'They have my leave to go,' he declared. Then he turned to Baldwin and Tancred. 'But remember . . . any towns you occupy must serve the purpose of the Church.'

'And are the property of the emperor,' Tatikios put in.

Baldwin smiled mockingly at him. 'We'll sort that out when the emperor arrives,' he said.

At this the Armenian prince, whose name is Roupen, spoke up. He is a bell-shaped man in black with a long nose, dark-rimmed eyes and plunging moustaches. 'The towns you speak of belong neither to the Church nor to the emperor,' he said in his heavy accent. 'Nor will they belong to these young nobles. They are Armenian, and belong to our people.'

'Your people are Christians,' Baldwin said. 'They should welcome us as their kings.'

Prince Roupen looked at him a long moment. 'How many natures does Christ have?' he said.

Baldwin squinted at him. 'I'm damned if I know.'

Roupen turned to Tancred. 'How many?' he repeated.

Tancred shrugged. 'Three,' he said. 'Father, Son and Holy Ghost.'

Adhémar clucked his tongue at him like a school master. 'Not how many persons, idiot,' he said. 'The question is, how many natures.' He turned to Roupen and nodded slowly. 'You are a Monophysite, are you not?' he said. 'A heretic.'

'Our Lord Jesus Christ has but one nature,' the prince replied. 'Half-human, half-divine.'

'Two,' Adhémar said. 'Fully human and fully divine.'

'Nonsense,' Roupen spat.

'The truth,' said Adhémar.

'Two, three, twenty,' Count Baldwin put in, 'what difference does it make?'

Prince Roupen fixed Baldwin's squinting little eyes. 'The difference is that if you attempt to impose your religion on our people, they will cut your throats,' he said. 'You will find welcome as liberators, not as kings. I advise you to move by the north with your friends.'

'Do it,' Bohemund said.

Tancred and Baldwin scowled at us. 'We have no friends here,' Tancred said, and the two stalked out of the pavilion.

They have moved their forces to the farther side of the town, Tancred taking a hundred knights and three hundred infantry, and Baldwin, five hundred knights and over two thousand of foot. Godfrey is resigned to the defection of his brother, but Bohemund is bitterly angry. He has forbidden anyone of his army to consort with his nephew and his men, and has given strict instructions, backed up with threats, that no one from the city may supply them. We do not, therefore, expect them to remain much longer at Heraclea.

August the Twenty-eighth

Tonight I found my squire, Thomas, weeping by himself. I thought at first to leave him in peace, but his sobbing was so mournful that I approached him where he sat beneath a lemon tree some rods off from our camp. I made to comfort him, but to my surprise he turned on me. 'Who do you think you are?' he said, his face contorted and streaming.

I backed away, astonished. 'You forget yourself,' I told him.

'Indeed I do,' he said. 'I forget that ever I was a man.' He picked up two handfuls of earth and flung them away.

'You have been drinking,' said I.

'I have not!' he growled at me. 'I have been doing nothing that any man might take pleasure from!' And he set to crying again so hotly that I felt I could not leave him.

'You are a pilgrim,' I said, sitting down beside him. 'This anger is unseemly before God and your master.'

He turned to me with such a look of sorrow that I fell silent. 'You have undone me, you and God,' he said. He pulled up his tunic and began to loosen his stockings, saying as he did so: 'Tonight one of the girls from the town came to me. A pretty girl she was, with her hair all in knots. She said she wanted to be with me – be, you know, as girls and men do.' By this time he had unlaced his front and was pulling his stockings down. 'She reached in here . . .' he went on, his voice growing bitter again, 'and she found this.'

He exposed himself to me. I was shocked. His testicles were as withered and black as two rotted figs. He laughed cruelly. ' "Dried fruit!" she called them, "Dried fruit!". And she ran to tell the other girls. Now none of them will have anything to do with me and they all mock at me and ask to see my fruit. They have even offered me coins to show them. Am I a man?' He took the shrunken things in his palm. 'This is what you have done to me, you and your penance. I want to die,' he said, beginning again to sob. 'I want to kill myself, for I can't go on living like this.'

Then he threw himself across my knees and wept uncontrollably, his thin body heaving as if it would burst.

I stroked his head a moment before I got up. Indeed, it is a terrible thing that I have done to him, who never did me harm, and who has borne with me through both my sins and this pilgrimage. What can I do to make it up to him? How can I repay the loss that I, in my righteousness, have caused him?

Afterwards I returned to my pavilion, where Mansour was waiting with my bath. I was brooding and he could see it, and he made bold to ask what troubled me.

'Tell me,' I said, 'can a man take pleasure with a woman without . . . testicles?'

Mansour glanced down into my bath and asked me to repeat. I laughed in spite of myself. 'I speak for another,' I said.

He nodded and went on washing my back. 'Of course, Effendi,' he replied. 'There are eunuchs in the hareem who service their ladies quite handily, though they have been castrated. There are . . . many pleasures that such a man may enjoy.'

'You have knowledge of hareem?' I asked.

'Truly, Effendi. I have worked in them. I have been the trusty of several emiri.'

'The trusty?' I asked.

'A man whom the emir may trust to serve his ladies without servicing them.'

'And tell me . . . what are the hareems like?'

Mansour paused, and I could almost feel him smile. 'They are not like paradise,' he began. 'The women are not all beautiful. For many emiri it is the quantity and not the quality that makes the great man. And yet . . .' He broke off as he raised my arms to wash beneath them.

'Go on,' I said.

He smiled faintly. 'Yet, there are beautiful women in the hareem.

At night their sweat smells like fields after the rain, and their sleeping limbs tussled together are like the roots of young trees on the lake shore.'

'You are a poet, Mansour,' I said. He bowed in acknowledgement. 'And what of their desires?' I asked, feeling myself becoming more relaxed under his washing.

'Ah, they are lustful, breathless women, chosen for that reason. And because they are so infrequently serviced, they pant in their dreams, and they learn to love one another.'

I frowned. 'They behave unnaturally.'

'It is not unnatural for a woman to seek love,' Mansour replied. 'And indeed, there is no harm in it among themselves. From years of neglect by their masters, their fingers and tongues become most skilled. They are very loving and passionate. Many come to prefer the attentions of their own sex to those of men.'

I asked whether he had seen this. 'Many times, Effendi. And many are the times that the master has watched with me through the peephole, and many are the guests he has invited to watch with him. It is a great gift among them to have wives who are skilled in the art. It is a mark of honour. And,' he added, 'it keeps the house in peace.'

'And what of the master of the house?' I asked.

'The peace of the house ensures the peace of the master,' he replied. 'And there can be peace in the house only when all desires are in balance. To achieve peace of the soul it is necessary to have peace in the body, and that can be had only when its desires are fulfilled.'

I laughed. 'You are a hedonist,' I told him.

He inclined his head obsequiously. 'The word, Effendi . . .' he said.

'You argue for the pleasures of the body,' I explained.

'Humbly, Effendi, I argue for the pleasures of the soul, without which the pleasures of the body are meaningless. But the soul is in the body, and to speak to it, the body must be put to rest.'

'How?' I asked.

'Indulge it,' he said, 'for the sake of the soul. If the body is raging like a beast, then the soul cannot be heard. But if it is lulled to sleep by pleasure, then the soul may be free to speak. It is our way here in the East.'

'Very strange,' I said.

'Truly,' he replied, 'there are things stranger than that among the holy places of religion.' I said that it was even stranger that this should be so. 'Perhaps,' he replied, replacing my arm in the water. 'Or perhaps it is fitting. I have seen such things not only in Nicaea and Antioch, but at Jerusalem itself.'

I turned to look at him. He immediately lowered his eyes. 'You have been to Jerusalem?' I said.

'Several times,' he answered.

'What is it like?'

'It is the city of the peace of God — Iheru-shalom. As such, it is the place of greatest desire — the most strange and the most violent. But also the most satisfying.'

'I meant, what does it look like,' I said, for I did not wish to hear it spoken of as a place of carnal desire.

Mansour nodded obligingly. 'It is a beautiful place,' he answered. 'The streets are shaded, the mosques are of gold, the synagogues are as cool and fragrant as pine vales.'

'And the Christian churches?'

'Vulgar,' he replied. 'Heavy, crypt-like things built by the Greeks who house the living in tombs and the dead in palaces, and God Himself in great boxes of stone.'

I laughed and he too laughed, the first time I had heard him do so. There was a kindliness in his laugh that I found familiar.

'You are concerned about Thomas, the squire,' he said. I told him that I was. 'Then, with your permission, Effendi, I shall take him into the city tomorrow night and . . . entertain him?'

I glanced at him again, but as always his eyes were averted. 'Is there something that you can do?' I asked.

He bowed. 'Humbly I tell you, Effendi, there is always something to be done in that way.'

I gave him leave, for I cannot think that God would scruple over one boy's lonely pleasure.

SEPTEMBER THE SIXTH

We will remain here for several more days before taking the road for Antioch. The encampment of Counts Baldwin and Tancred has become a haven for the disaffected. Rainald of Toul and Peter of Stenay have joined them, as well as the vassal of my Lord Raymond, Gaston of Béarn. All hope to become rich by their conquests among the Armenians. Before leaving, Gaston approached me to seduce me to their number. I wished him well and turned my back on him. It offended me that he would even think that I would desert my Lord.

Thomas is looking much brighter these days. He goes into the town nearly every night to carouse, I suppose. At first Mansour went with him, but now he goes alone. I have not the heart to upbraid him, for I never intended that he should return to his uncouth ways. But, indeed, it is better than to see him moping about the camp and making evil eyes at me.

Bartholomew, meanwhile, has become a singular creature. Ever since Nicaea he lives in his own world. He talks to animals and spends hours in prayer. They say that blood appears on his forehead when he prays, though I have never seen it. And he speaks in tongues. To me it is simply gibberish, but to the guileless it is some holy incantation. It is said that he can levitate, and that the soldiers use him to pick fruit from the higher branches. We have a saying in Provence: 'No gift is too precious to waste.' For myself, I do not believe it. I think the boy was so afflicted by being buried alive that he has lost his wits.

I live practically alone and enjoy the fact. I have my spare routine: rising for prayer at prime, practice in combat, breakfast, training the men (Lord Raymond has allotted me ten recruits from Marseille to make up my retinue), prayer at terce, practice in combat with the knights, prayer at sext, breakfast in the town, riding and exploring the countryside in the afternoon, prayer at nones, swordsmanship or physical exercise, prayer at vespers, supper with my Lord and the other nobles, reviewing the men at evening, and then to my pavilion. There is general prayer at compline, after which I write in this book, and then to sleep.

It is a pleasing round that satisfies me well enough, but I find that I am anxious to resume the march. Yet, I will be frank: I am lonely. It is a bitter loneliness that follows on the heels of what was once so passionate, so intense. I have not touched a woman, indeed, I have not touched a human except to kill in full a year. There were the girls of the Norman camp, but that was venery; more like handling meat than passion. And as to love – it had no savour of sweetness in it. Except of course the anonymous sweetness that is always random sex: the sudden discovery of another, the delight in the newness of limbs, the scents, the warmth. The struggle to join with her, so violent, so driven by silence, so certain that in the morning, in the light, it will be memory and nothing more.

But as to love . . . It is so much more than sex. Tell that to a young man! It is oneness, it is being, not just living. It is the stepping outside oneself, which is only shadowplay in sex; but in love there is the true indwelling in another, in her thoughts, her eyes, her affections. To be loved, that is the greatest gift. To love, that is the greatest sacrifice.

I often wonder, indeed most every night, whether Jehanne keeps me in her thoughts. It is a way of living even when we are dead. For, truly, we here in Syria are dead to all the world except our own. But another has the power in loving thoughts to keep the dead alive. Indeed, life is nothing but love in flesh, and so in thought love is its purest; in absence it is its most refined. And so do I wonder whether my wife keeps me alive within her thoughts.

And yet I fear that she does not. I fear even more that she

thinks of another, that another has replaced me in her heart and in her loins. Yes, my book, I tell you that I fear, have feared for months, that Jehanne lies with another. I know her: I know she is incapable of being alone, of sleeping alone. I know her nature is so passionate that she must have a man just to remind herself that she is alive. Absence does not remind with her, it frightens. And to her, thoughts without flesh are nothing. I know she is unfaithful. And yet I hope that she loves me still.

I should go to bed. I should think no more about this. For it only makes me angry and, when my anger is spent, it makes me weep.

September the Fourteenth

Tancred left with his force yesterday. Baldwin leaves today. There was much rancour at Tancred's departure. Prince Bohemund cut the tendons on his nephew's horse and when it fell, he stamped and kicked the young count. He blasphemed and frothed at the mouth, called down curses from God and swore that he would disown him. Then he brought out a sorcerer from Sicily, a wizened man whose face was painted blue, to cast a spell on his nephew's army. The old man bit the head from off a chicken and sprinkled its blood over Tancred's face. Then Bohemund urinated on his nephew, who was unconscious, took out his knife and cut off all his hair.

Count Godfrey, being French, merely ignored his brother.

We leave tomorrow.

September the Nineteenth

We are at the town of Augustopolis from which the Turkish garrison has fled at our approach. It is a market town and filled with provisions. We travel well and our men are so hardened now that we make good time. The entire army can be ready to march on half an hour's notice, and indeed, such notice is rarely required.

There was an odd incident on the road today.

We pass many hamlets, where the people come out to greet us and to offer us food and drink. It has happened so often that we scarcely take notice of it. Most are Armenian Christians, but some are Turks. These latter are shy, and watch us from behind their shutters or veils.

As we were nearing Augustopolis an elderly woman, a Turk by her veil and the bangles about her face, walked towards me. I supposed she meant to hand me a loaf or a gourd, and so I put down my hand. Instead she bit me.

I was astonished and did not know what to do. Landry Gros, riding at my side, struck her with the flat of his sword. She fell, and two Normans instantly ran up and would have disembowelled her except that I called at them to stop.

I dismounted and walked to where the woman lay. There was no fear in her eyes, though her cheek was broken and the two knights stood over her with their swords. She spat out some teeth and muttered something at me in her language. Her mouth was full of blood.

By this time Mansour had come up from the baggage train and was most solicitous of me. I told him to ask the woman what she had said. 'She says to take her teeth,' he told me. 'She says that had she taken off your finger she would have swallowed it. But since you have taken out her teeth, they are yours.'

'Why did she bite me?' I asked.

Again he spoke to her, and translated her reply. 'Because you murder her people and are the enemy of God, and she has no weapons.'

I said that she could keep her teeth, but she merely veiled herself again and walked away. Landry Gros dropped from his horse. 'Escrivel, if you will not have them, I will,' said he, and he put them into his purse, explaining: 'They will make a ring for my daughter.'

The incident has disturbed me, as has so much on this expedition. I am the soldier of my God and the enemy of hers. Yet if they are the same God, which of us does the better service: I who kill for Him, or she who bites me because I kill?

SEPTEMBER THE TWENTY-FIFTH
Caesarea Mazacha

This is a vile town; we could smell it from half a league away. It is a trading centre and market, and so people from all over the world come here, stay awhile, and leave again. The place thus has a transient atmosphere, filled with inns and empty shops and the babble of a hundred languages.

I saw men today as black as tar and every bit as odorous, who wore fantastic headdresses on their long, shaven heads, and whose white teeth protruded like the tusks of an elephant. They sold herbs and animal parts which, they swore, were the most powerful aphrodisiacs in the world. Our men snapped them up and immediately went in search of the whores. They purchase all manner of nonsense from these Eastern peddlers, and so we are welcomed into every market we encounter.

From a merchant of Cathay, a parchment-skinned man with eyes so narrow they seemed perpetually to squint, I did buy something. It is a carving in a stone that he called jada: the figure of a woman with the head of a cat. It sounds silly, but the thing struck me as so graceful, so feminine and delicate, that on an impulse I offered him a gold bezant. He seemed delighted. So, I must admit, was I. She sits before me now on the writing desk, lighted by the candle glow. Her body is slender and curved, and clothed in the most elegant gown. Her hands are clasped at her breast, her feet are bare, and her face has all the mystery and haughtiness of a Persian cat. I cannot say precisely why I bought her, but I am glad that I did.

I have been reflecting that I have remained celibate now for a year. This is the longest time since first I touched a woman that I have had no intercourse. I find, after so long an abstinence, that the idea is distasteful to me. When the women of the town approach I draw away, instinctively I think, for it is almost horrible to me to contemplate that which they propose.

Perhaps I have become a good man in spite of myself. Perhaps I may even be holy, for I value all the more the Cross that I wear on my shoulder and around my neck. My sister is a married woman now. It is strange to think of her, with whom I played as a child, lying with a man, sweating and grunting under him, taking his seed. Indeed, viewed from such a distance as I have acquired, it is a vulgar thing. Yet how I longed for it with my wife, and how I told myself, even in the chapel, what a sacred duty we performed.

I believed what the poets said: that carnal love is a blessed desire fulfilled, that it is the highest and sublimest state of man, the purest expression of love. And the Church! Yes, even the Church in her teachings told me that love between a man and wife is a reflection of God's love for his people. What nonsense! It is not the elevation of carnal love, but the degradation of divine love. The love of the soul, as the love of God, is outside the body. They are two planes distinct. Only a priest who has never groaned atop a woman and listened to her demands for more and more and spilled himself, lain back, and felt that awful sense of loss, of hollowness, could make such a comparison.

If we love God it is because we have no choice; because we are what God is. It is not an act but a being. The love of God is still and silent and centred upon ourselves – the God in ourselves. But to love a woman – that is because we are lonely and disjoint. We are wounded by sin and self, and longing to be healed. The love of woman is an act of desperation, reflecting all the ills we feel, all the violence and separation. The love of God is a state of calm, reflecting that which we truly are, the pure substance of ourselves, the unity with that which is our essence. No – sex and the spirit are disjoint, distinct, indeed, at war with each another. Mansour is wrong: you do not attain to God through indulgence, but through denial.

It seems I have become a philosopher. I am under a spell – the spell of celibacy. Perhaps this is what clerics feel; perhaps this is how saints are made. How far have I come from my bed with Jehanne to this lofty self-reflection. Perhaps this was always my vocation; perhaps this is why God sent me on this pilgrimage. Whatever may be the case, it is amazing how clear one's head becomes, how freely one's mind can float, outside the company of women.

September the Twenty-sixth

Thomas is dead. It is said that last night he fell from the upper floor of a house where he had gone in search of pleasure. I do not believe it. Having seen the house, I am sure he was pushed. I have lodged a complaint with the elders of the town, stating formally that I believe him to have been murdered. In response they have burned the house and imprisoned the occupants. All those they arrested, it seems, were young men.

They carried Thomas to me from the town. His neck was broken. My first thought was a guilty one: he looked comical in the odd angle of his head, and instinctively I meant to chastise him. But then the true guilt stung me, for it was I who sanctioned his pleasure-taking. And I had to turn away from the purple pallor of his face and his swollen, accusing tongue.

Bartholomew, when he saw the body, burst into tears. We shall bury the poor boy tomorrow. Mansour is very grieved, blaming himself, but I assured him that nothing could be laid to his account. What harm could there be in it, I had asked myself. What harm is there ever in self-indulgence! The wages of sin are – indeed, must be – death. How my serene thoughts of yesterday have turned to dust. I fancied myself a saint! No master, insofar as he is master, can be a saint. An accident of birth makes us noble; death reminds us that we are nothing.

Père Raimund believes that, in spite of Thomas's sins, he shall benefit from the indulgence. Church law is a wonderful thing — straight from the brothel to heaven. I have collected his few possessions and shall save them for his family. I am not sure of the fact, but I believe that Thomas was twenty-one years old. In our town the births of peasants are not often recorded.

I look forward to quitting this place.

OCTOBER THE SECOND

A good deal has happened and more is yet to come, so I will make a quick account. Tomorrow at first light I am to set off in command of four hundred knights for Antioch! I thus may be the first of our number to reach the city, and to claim it for our expedition. How this honour came to me I shall relate.

After leaving the regrettable town of Caesarea, we took the old Byzantine road southwards towards Comana. A half day's march therefrom our scouts returned to say that the place was under siege by those same gold-scarfed Turks whom we had routed on the plain. Count Bohemund gave order for his troops to hurry forward while the rest of the army followed, but at Bohemund's approach the Turks gave up their siege and fled. Once again the Armenians welcomed us as heroes.

From them we learned that Counts Tancred and Baldwin have conquered Tarsus as well as other towns along the coast, and that Baldwin was even then advancing on Edessa. This siege by the Turks was therefore a desperate attempt to distract Baldwin from his march. Thus we, unwittingly, have assisted him in his ambition to be king.

We did not linger at Comana but pressed forward towards

Coxon, the last town before the Taurus Mountains. Bohemund, meanwhile, decided to pursue the fleeing Turks, setting off at speed with two hundred knights, hoping to trap them on the plain. We have not heard from him since.

We are now at Coxon, from which the garrison has fled, and the elders of the town insist that Antioch has been abandoned by the Turks! Count Raymond at once ordered me to take four squadrons of knights, nearly all the mounted men of Provence, and make forced marches to occupy the city. I was overwhelmed by this commission.

'Roger,' he said to me, 'if it is true, then Jerusalem is ours. But you must be quick. We have three enemies now – the Turks, who may return, Baldwin, who may try to claim the city for himself, and the Greeks, whose fleet may attempt a landing. We must take Antioch for the expedition. Kill your horses, kill your men if you must. But if Antioch is open, you must seize it.'

The key to Jerusalem is at our fingertips. God grant I have the strength to take it in my hand.

OCTOBER THE SIXTH

We are in the Taurus range, guided by the Greeks, and I pity the men who will have to cross behind us. It is the wildest, most forbidding place that ever have I seen. The cliffs are steep and the paths are narrow and crumbling. We have lost half a score of knights already, and three times as many animals. The poor men and the beasts have either fallen to their deaths or been swept away in the powerful mountain rivers. These are made more dangerous by the rains that have fallen almost continuously. At one moment they are streams in deep clefts, and at the next they are torrents raging over their banks and carrying everything before them.

We have ceased to rope the baggage animals together since a misstep by one drags down the others. On a cliff above a stream so deafening that we had to shout to hear, four mules fell from the heights, pulled one after the other to their deaths. Their cries were pitiable as they struggled to save themselves, and we would have lost four more had I not been able to cut the rope with my sword.

The most terrible of all was the fate of Peter of Castillon, a very noble youth whose parents have been guests in my home. At a turning over a formidable drop where the trail rose steeply, the Greeks had refused to go farther. Peter made his way to the front, declaring that he would show them how easy it was. I still can see the black curls of his hair and the deep blue eyes, smiling with confidence.

He moved sideways along the cliff, feeling his way with feet and hands, until he reached the farther side. Then he called for his horse to be brought, saying that if she could find her way, so could they. The horse was skittish and would not advance. Peter talked to her, laughing and clucking for her to follow. His voice was so soothing and his smile so reassuring that she took heart and came on until the youth could just reach out and take her bridle.

But at that moment, when all seemed safe, the horse lost her footing and began to slip backwards towards the cliff. Rather than save himself, Peter wrapped the reins around his arm, and in the next instant he was dragged downward by the horse. It was a horrible sight, man and beast bound together, falling towards the river so far below that, though it frothed and fumed, it made no sound that we could hear.

We were so shaken by the sight that we retreated and sought another way. At last, farther down, we found a safer path and pushed ahead. Now we are camped beside that same river into which he fell. I am so exhausted that I have not erected my shelter, but crouch beneath a tree, my surcoat over my head. I regret that there will be no grave or service for that youth, but were we to stop for every death, we would waste all our time in funerals.

OCTOBER THE NINTH

We emerged from the mountains yesterday and have ridden hard for two days. We bypassed the town of Marash, pausing only long enough in the outskirts to provision ourselves. We have lost fully thirty men in the mountain crossing, and many more have fallen out since then, their horses broken down or their strength given out.

Command of a large force is an instruction to me. One must lead as much by example as by words. I speak to the men often, encouraging them, chastising them, challenging them. But most of all I keep to the front and am careful never to show indecision or complaint. I find that the strong-hearted will do as I do for the sake of pride, and the weaker ones for shame. The rest are not worth having with us. The result is that, of the four-hundred knights with whom I left Coxon, under three hundred remain.

On the road from Marash to Ravendan, where we spent the night, we found many dead horses and mules. From the colours upon the horses we knew that they were of the force of Baldwin. The people here say that he has taken Edessa and made himself king.[70] And so his ambition is fulfilled. But of Antioch there is no news.

If the city is undefended I shall take it at once, but what of Jerusalem? I have thought a great deal about this question these

70 Tancred was the first to reach Tarsus but he was unable to take it. Baldwin arrived with his larger force and occupied the city. The two men quarrelled and Tancred sent to his uncle for reinforcements. Three hundred Norman knights soon arrived, but Baldwin refused to allow them to enter Tarsus and, forced to camp outside the walls, they were attacked by Turks and massacred to a man. Tancred then withdrew from Tarsus, and set off on his own, capturing the towns of Adana and Mamistra.

Meanwhile, Baldwin garrisoned Tarsus and moved eastward to capture Edessa, an important trading centre. He promised his personal protection to its prince, Thoros, who adopted Baldwin as his son. Baldwin promptly had Thoros murdered and made himself king. With this conquest, Baldwin had penetrated farther into Asia than any westerner since Alexander the Great.

past two days. I have no orders regarding the Holy City from Lord Raymond. But if I take Antioch, what then shall I do? Shall I remain there until the army has come up, or shall I advance on Jerusalem?

It is a difficult decision. I could leave half my force, or even less, to occupy Antioch, and move on Jerusalem with the rest. If that city is ungarrisoned, then I could take it and hold it for the army. But suppose the Turks are there in force. Then I shall withdraw to Antioch. But suppose that in my absence the Turks besiege Antioch. The garrison would not be strong enough to hold it, and my force would be too weak to raise the siege. Then everything would have been lost, and my commission from Lord Raymond would be a failure.

But if Antioch is ours and Jerusalem is undefended or only weakly occupied and I do not move boldly to seize it, then may I not be guilty of the loss of Jerusalem, or of the cost of the eventual siege? What shall I do? In any case my goal is to spare Christian lives and gain victory for our cause. But which is the surest way?

We pride ourselves in achieving great responsibility, without thinking that it entails great risk. And I am responsible for my decision not only to Lord Raymond, but also to God.

OCTOBER THE TENTH

We are stopping near a fortress made of mud and posts. It is the strangest castle that I have ever seen. It appears to be still under construction and is being built with a kind of frenzy, for the walls are thrown up in random fashion, the towers totter on spindly poles, and there are no windows or gates save for a narrow entrance chocked with wattle. I have sent two knights to enquire what manner of men may occupy this fort.

Meanwhile I have made my decision regarding Jerusalem. My reasoning is thus.

If Antioch is undefended I shall occupy it with two hundred knights; with the rest I shall advance towards Jerusalem. If we learn that it, too, is undefended I shall move upon it. If it be open, I shall take it and send at once for reinforcements from the army. If it is occupied by any strength, I shall evaluate their numbers. If they are not great, or if they advance to battle outside the walls, I shall attack. If the city is heavily defended, I shall return at once to Antioch and await the army.

It seems to me a sound plan, and the risks it poses well worth taking. What decided me was the thought that, should I remain in Antioch, and should I later learn that Jerusalem was undefended, I would never forgive myself. Whereas, by advancing with one-third of my force made up of the very best men, I risk only the loss of our lives, without seriously endangering Antioch. Two hundred knights who have crossed the mountains and made this hellish march should be able to hold the city until Lord Raymond and the others come up.

Later

I was interrupted in my writing by the scouts I sent to the castle. They bore rather puzzled expressions, in which I found some amusement, and they begged me to go and see for myself. I shall do so, though I made clear to them my irritation at their report.

OCTOBER THE ELEVENTH

What shall I say of the last two days? They have been the strangest and most frustrating of the expedition. I sit in a shelter made of skins below the Syrian Gates upon the edge of the plain of Antioch. We have made the hardest march that ever has been attempted by knights of Provence. Of that I feel sure. Tomorrow morning we shall move towards the city, yet I have no idea what we may find.

Let me gather my thoughts, for my brain is whirling. I am tired and angry, I have scarcely rested this past week. I would cry from sheer exhaustion if I thought I could do so alone. Yet the men are crowded around me in a narrow defile where we have camped out of the sight of spies.

Yesterday afternoon I accompanied my two scouts into the mud-and-picket fort. What I found there defies all description. It was an outpost of a group of heretics who call themselves the Disciples of Saint Paul. Why this should be I cannot imagine, yet they worship Paul as if he were the Christ himself. Or at any rate, they claim to do so.

What does this mean? I hesitate to tell. In daylight hours they go about blindfolded, in imitation of the blindness of Saint Paul when he was struck from his horse. When I arrived, the greater part of the three-score occupants of the fort had filthy rags wound around their eyes. They would not take them off, with the result that their leaders all attempted to feel my face to assure themselves that I was not a Turk. This accounts for the condition of their fort.

I say more. Their rites are of the most repulsive kind. They despise women, citing the epistles of the saint, who advises holy men to avoid the company of women. They thus suffer nothing female to live within the fort — no she-goat nor bitch, no nesting bird or cow is permitted past the gate. Even the beetles are examined, and the females ones are killed. To relieve themselves, however, they engage — dare I say it — in ritual masturbation, chanting as they do so. Afterwards they flog one another in chastisement. It is a most disgusting spectacle, which I was forced to witness since I arrived at prayer time.

When their group devotion was completed, I enquired about Antioch. The leader, a man named Kalash, a Syrian Christian of mixed parentage whose blindfold was sewn with pearls, assured me that Antioch is well-defended, and indeed, that the emir, whom he called Yagashan,[71] has learned of our approach and has appealed for reinforcements from the emirs all about. Further, he insisted that this Yagashan has imprisoned the leading clerics of the city, is persecuting the Christians, and has desecrated the churches, using them for stables.

It was the very worst news, but coming from a man who had just abused and flogged himself in public and who wore a blindfold on his eyes, I chose to take it lightly. Having provisioned ourselves, we set out again at great speed towards the Syrian Gates, a low pass in the final mountain range.

We travelled all day, crossing the mountains at dusk and, finally, in the darkness. It was an eerie and dangerous undertaking. Each man carried a torch of cloth soaked in oil and tied around a branch. Our column wound for more than a league, and when I topped the highest ridge and looked back, the sight was awesome. As far as I could see, a band of fire sparkled through the dark, bobbing and inching its way towards me, moving gingerly, without a sound, guided by an unseen hand.

I watched for a long time, overcome with the frailty and courage of it all. And the thought struck me: Is this not how God Himself sees our world? Tiny firepoints of souls in the eternal dark making their slow and silent way towards Him, some stumbling, some falling, all feeling their way by faith through a strange and unkind land towards His cherished city.

It was a humbling and frightening idea, and I turned my back upon it and shivered, for I did not dare to put myself in the place of God, even in my imagination.

All night we were spied upon. Bands of two or three mounted men, Turks almost certainly, suddenly appeared upon the farther slopes silhouetted by the moon. I do not think they could have made an accurate count of our force, but to prevent further observation I have camped the men in the last of the canyons above the plain.

71 Yaghi-Siyan, the Turkish governor of Antioch. He was not himself an emir, but was the vassal of his father-in-law, the Emir Ridwan of Aleppo.

They grumble, for there is little even ground and all of it is rocky. Some shepherds, who pasture their animals in the hills, have offered us their shelters, and so I shall sleep tonight within the fragrant skin of sheep.

I asked them news of Antioch, and though they spoke no language that we could understand, they made it clear by signs and drawings that the place is fortified. It was interesting that their symbol for the Turks, as they drew it in the dirt, is a wolf. They drew many wolves with their crooks. I pray it may not be so.

OCTOBER THE TWELFTH

Antioch is fortified. I have seen it for myself. We set out before dawn and crossed the plain as far as we dared. I then took six knights and made a scout towards the city. Scarcely were we in sight of it when we were fired upon; the emir, no doubt warned of our approach, had set up outposts in the villages along the road. We made a rapid skirt of these and dashed towards the walls. They are impregnable, massive, topped by hundreds of towers, and heavily manned. Indeed, we came so close that the machines atop the walls opened fire upon us, hurling stones and iron bolts.

After a wide circuit we returned to our camp where I threw myself from my saddle, dashed my sword to the ground, and stamped upon it. I was furious – indeed, I still am. The other men knew at once what it meant, and they too made demonstration of their anger.

'Let's go kill those masturbators,' said one, and several started for their horses. It was a moment before I realized that they meant the heretics of the mud fort. I called them back and told them that I would return to the army and make report to Lord Raymond.

I left the force in the command of Peter of Roaix, giving him instructions to make sorties to capture as many towns and villages in the vicinity as possible. In this way, there will be no impediment to the army taking up its siege, which now is unavoidable.

It will be as I feared, and not as I hoped. There will be no swift possession of Antioch, but a long and costly siege. I cannot say that I have failed, for it appears that Antioch was never undefended. Yet my schemes of seizing Jerusalem now seem to me the stupidest folly. I am ashamed, not of my attempt, but of my pride. And I regret the loss of so many brave men, especially that of the child of my friends, Peter of Castillon. I had hoped one day to tell his parents that he died for Antioch. Now the most that I can say is that he died for a dream of Antioch.

OCTOBER THE NINETEENTH
Antioch

It is a week since I have written. Today I am thirty-one years old. This morning I attended mass in the chapel we have built in the village nearest the town. It was a melancholy service, for the building of a chapel is always a sign of a long siege. The village had some heathen name; I asked my Lord Raymond if we might name it Castillon, in honour of our comrade.

I shall summarize the events of the past week.

After leaving the camp in the ravine, I began the journey back towards the mountains and encountered our army at Marash. It was in a pitiable condition; the men were exhausted, their spirits crippled. Of the three thousand knights who crossed the Taurus Range, four hundred had perished, and of the infantry, nearly twice that number. Not Nicaea nor the salt desert nor the battle of the plain had cost us so dear. I could hardly bear to break my news to them.

In his pavilion, Lord Raymond shook his head. I had never seen him look so old. 'You have done your best,' he said. 'But, truly, there was nothing to be done.'

That evening Count Bohemund returned from his expedition. He had not found the Turks and had had no battle, but, he declared, that was nothing to his discovery that we had moved on Antioch without consulting him. He slapped his gauntlets into one hand, seized them in a powerful grip and pulled them free again. 'You meant to take the city for yourselves,' he growled.

Lord Raymond straightened himself, his eyes catching fire. 'You insult my honour,' he said.

'You betrayed mine,' Bohemund retorted.

'Honour?' Raymond snapped. 'In a man who sticks his oath up a mule's backside!'

Godfrey stepped between them. 'Raymond was in the van,' he explained. 'He had to make a decision. You'd have done the same in his place.'

'I would not!' Bohemund shouted. 'It's him and that bishop – they mean to use the army for their own profit.'

Lord Raymond would have struck him, but Godfrey grabbed his arm. 'We're all Christians here,' he said.

'While you've been off chasing Turks we've been struggling through the mountains,' Lord Raymond huffed. 'It's a wonder we have an army left.'

Bohemund snorted. 'You could have saved yourself the trouble – I found a way around farther to the north. So your little scheme to cut me out has cost you a thousand men for nothing. That's God speaking – He sees your intentions.'

'What do you know about God?' Lord Raymond scoffed. 'You're as much a pagan as the Turks.'

Bohemund poked at the Cross on his shoulder. 'See this!' he declared. 'I'd give my life for this!'

'If you thought it would get you a kingdom,' Raymond said.

'And I suppose you're in this for the saints and the Virgin and the bloody two natures of Christ,' retorted Bohemund.

At this Count Godfrey lost his temper. 'We're all in it for our own reasons,' he declared, 'but that doesn't mean we have the right to fight one another. God gives men reasons to suit His own purpose. Whatever brought us here serves Him, but only if we stay together.'

We were all stunned by Godfrey's reasoning, for normally he was not an eloquent man. I think Godfrey was surprised too, for he said, 'That sounds logical, doesn't it?' We agreed that it did.

'Good,' Godfrey went on. 'Then we'll have no more quarrelling. In the morning we'll move on to Antioch and besiege the place, and when we've reduced it we'll kill every living thing inside, just as God intended.'

That was four days ago. In that time we have advanced the army to the walls of Antioch, Peter of Roaix having taken all the villages in the vicinity, nearly up to the city of Aleppo. At the crossing of the River Orontes there was a furious battle in which the Bishop Adhémar's troops drove away the Turks and captured many sheep and cattle intended for the city. Thus we shall have provisions for a few months at least.

I should mention that on our march here we destroyed the mud fort and dispersed the Paulicians. Counts Bohemund and Godfrey, having visited the place, decided that the inhabitants were insane and feared that they might represent a threat to our rear. Some of them have been allowed to accompany our army as servants, on the condition that they not wear blindfolds, and that they confine their devotions to their tents.

November the First
All Saints Day

I attended mass this morning, and a meeting of the nobles soon after. The discussion was heated, as all are nowadays.

Upon first arriving here, my Lord Raymond had argued for an

immediate assault to take the city.[72] He was opposed by Godfrey and the Bishop Adhémar, and mocked by Count Bohemund. These urged caution, agreeing only to probing attacks to test the fortifications. Thus, any opportunity for surprise has been lost, together with three- or four-score men in these attacks. They have served only to confirm what we already knew – that the Turks hold Antioch in force, and that its walls are impregnable.

It is a formidable fortress. Backed by a steep mountain, one of its massive walls spans a marsh of the River Orontes, while two others rise straight up the slopes to form a towering citadel. On the other sides the walls are both high and thick, topped by four hundred towers that command every inch of ground below them. These walls were built in ancient times by the emperor Justinian, with all the martial arts of Rome, and have been improved in our time by the Byzantine engineers.

Within the walls are markets, bazaars, palaces, and even pastures for the animals. Antioch might withstand a siege of two years or more, for there are plentiful wells and even a roaring river passing through. Indeed, the walls overarch this river by airy fretworks, enabling free passage into and out of the city. How we are to take the place in our weary and demoralized condition I cannot tell. But take it we must, since it commands the road to Jerusalem.

We have not enough troops to surround the entire city; it would require an army ten times the size of ours to do so. Instead, we have positioned our troops at strategic points – Bohemund opposite the Gate of Saint Paul controlling the main road and bridge, my Lord Raymond on his right at the Gate of the Dog, Count Godfrey on our right at the Gate of the Duke, and the remaining forces –

---

72 It is likely that Raymond was correct. By the time of the army's arrival, Yaghi-Siyan had not yet organized the city's defences, and was himself unsure whether it could be held against the Christian army. It is possible that, had the Crusaders attacked at once, they might have broken his resolution and gained a foothold within the walls.

mostly Germans and Flemish – in reserve. Still two gates, those of the Bridge and Saint George, remain unfronted, and the Turks control the road to the port of Saint Symeon.

This last is of major concern. Were we to take the port, the emperor's ships might provision us from the sea. The Turks know this, and our efforts to control the bridge by which the road crosses the river have been hotly contested. We have appealed to the Christians hereabouts for boats with which we might build a make-shift bridge. This will enable us to move around the Turkish garrisons on the river and take them from behind.

Meanwhile the siege has begun, the Greeks go about their work of assembling their machines, and the shelters spring up again with hardly an order to the men. Winter is coming, and unless we succeed by a sudden assault or some treachery inside Antioch, we shall surely suffer outside the walls, even as the Turks and their prisoners do within.

This was the main topic of the discussion today. Bohemund was adamant that spies and saboteurs must be recruited within Antioch to assist us. He argued that among the Armenians there are many who wish to aid our cause, and that the Syrian Christians in the town would rise against the Turks if given a sign.

It was the Greek general Tatikios who answered him. 'The Syrians have little love for the Turks, it is true, but even less for us,' he said in his heavy accent.

'Then we must make it clear that a Latin prince will take the town,' Bohemund replied.

'They do not accept your pope,' Tatikios said.

'Damn-it, not the pope – a prince,' Bohemund retorted. 'One prince to whom they can look as protector.'

The Bishop Adhémar spoke up. 'You will not rule Antioch,' he said. 'It belongs to the expedition – to Christ.'

'It belongs to the Emperor Alexius,' Tatikios said.

'It belongs to whoever gets in first,' Bohemund growled. He

levelled his gaze at us. 'And if that's me, and anybody tries to take it from me, look out,' he said. And with that he walked out.

I fear this will be a long investment indeed.

NOVEMBER THE TWELFTH

This is proving to be a most vicious and dangerous siege. Every night Turks from the city slip out through the river passage and attack our men foraging upon the slopes. Dozens have been killed in this way. In the morning, when our foragers fail to return to camp, we find them, their heads cut off and carried away, their bodies mutilated. The Turks slice open their bellies and expose the intestines, which are devoured by birds. Often the corpses are emasculated, the genitals stuffed into the open throat. It has a most upsetting effect on the men, and for the first time since our crossing of the salt desert, we experience desertions.

In the meantime, we have taken control of the road to the port. Some fifty knights crossed the bridge of boats and raided the Turkish garrisons on the north bank of the river. Every Turk they found they slaughtered, many while pleading for their lives. I cannot say that I blame them for this. There is a darkness, a raw cruelty about this encounter at Antioch that is unprecedented.

I manage as best I can in our encampment. From long experience I have learned to make myself tolerably comfortable. For the moment food is plentiful and shelter is adequate. Since the death of Thomas and the indisposition of Bartholomew, I have come to rely entirely upon Mansour. His loyalty is touching, and his solicitousness is more than I could have hoped for in a hireling. To reward him I have given him permission to wear the colours of my family upon his clothing. At first he demurred most vehemently, insisting that he was not worthy. But when I told him that he was as much a part of my household as any servant in Lunel, he became suddenly serious and thanked me.

He is such a strange creature. I have never seen him bathe, never seen him wash his clothes, yet he is as fastidious as any housewife and as clever as any overseer of a great estate. He has built himself a lean-to adjacent to my pavilion, which I have reinforced with branches and thatch against the winter. We have even devised a hearth within, topped by a chimney made of mud. I shall fare better than I did at Nicaea, and infinitely better than at Brindisi. I owe much of this to Mansour.

When I mention Brindisi, I wonder what has become of Ruth, for whom I conceived so sudden and unexpected an affection. It is seven months since I last saw her, when she brought wild flowers to our camp. How sweet it would be to see her face. How sweet it would be to see the face of any maiden. I have been so long in the company of men, with their coarse ways and animal crudeness, that I think the mere sight of a young woman's face would cheer me immeasurably.

Last night I had an emission, the first I have had in many months. This is because I have ceased even to abuse myself. I remember that I dreamed many quick and urgent dreams, all jumbled together, including visions of Jehanne, the women of the Norman camp, Ruth and the Armenian girls of Iconium, and even of Mansour. When I woke to find what I had done I laughed quietly at myself. 'Roger,' I thought, 'you have become a boy again. With a boy's purity poured out upon your belly.'

It is a gentle thing to think of. I do not chastise myself at all. I am an ageing man, freed at last from the tumult of women, dreaming the innocent wet dreams of a boy. I have gone back in time, even as we go forward with our expedition. I do not know why, but it strikes me as a gentle, genial thing.

Meanwhile, my confessions become shorter, and I am at pains to think what sins I have committed, except for the killing which is, after all, the purpose of our being here.

NOVEMBER THE EIGHTEENTH

Since we arrived, the Turks have been harassing our rear from their fortress at Harenc near Aleppo. Their sorties against Bohemund's army were very destructive until, at last, the Normans could tolerate them no longer. Two days ago Bohemund sent a hundred bowmen to attack the fort. When the Turks saw this they came out to assault them, expecting an easy victory. That was what Bohemund had hoped for. He immediately charged with two hundred knights whom he had hidden in the hills.

The Turks were taken completely by surprise and, seeing that they could not regain their fort, they laid down their weapons and surrendered. Bohemund then gave order for the bowmen, whom the Turks had expected to annihilate, to fire into them. They did so, killing all but a handful. These Bohemund has taken as hostages.

Harenc now protects the rear of Bohemund's army, and serves as an outpost from which he watches Aleppo. There a large force of Turks has lain immobile ever since our arrival. From what the prisoners tell us, the emir of Aleppo, one Ridwan, has refused to come to Yagashan's aid because of some old dispute between them.[73]

We have thus taken every town and village in the vicinity of Antioch, and have surrounded the port of Saint Symeon. Our men now keep a sharp watch for the fleet of Alexius, or for the ships of the pirate Guynemer, who is said to have provisioned the armies of Baldwin and Tancred.[74]

Of these two we have had some news. Baldwin now makes his

---

73 A year before, Yaghi-Siyan had conspired with Duqaq, the emir of Damascus, to seize Aleppo from Ridwan. They failed, and Ridwan had never forgiven his son-in-law.

74 Guynemer of Boulogne was nominally a vassal of Count Godfrey. Early in the Crusade he had assembled a fleet of pirate ships, hoping to profit by the Crusade. He finally made contact with Baldwin after the incident at Tarsus in which Tancred's knights were left to be slaughtered by the Turks. Guynemer's support enabled Baldwin to retain control of the city.

capital at Edessa, while Tancred has taken Adana and has moved on Mamistra to the north of us. We have sent messengers to both men, requesting reinforcement for our siege. Meanwhile there is some talk that Peter the Hermit, who preceded us to the East, has raised a new army and is making his way to Antioch by sea. If this is true it would be welcome news, for Peter is regarded by many as a saint, and his name has become legend. His appearance among us could not but have a beneficial effect on the morale of our men.

Since taking up our siege, we have been joined by a group of warriors who inhabit the mountains above the city. They are called Tafurs, and no one seems to know who they are nor whom they serve. But they are soldiers such as we have never seen.

To a man they dress in the foulest rags and have not a proper weapon among them. All have unkempt beards and uncropped hair and they wear loose turbans upon their heads. They lead lives of abject poverty, chastity, and obedience to their king, a man called Vlast. His law among his men is absolute, and a more savage-looking creature one could not hope to find. He is very tall and wiry and carries a club inset with razors.

No Tafur is allowed to possess money or valuables of any kind. Those found with them are banished to the hills or to our army. They live only for killing, and the more savage and brutal, the better. They have offered themselves in service to our pilgrimage, and every noble save Bohemund has refused them. Consequently, they are now encamped near the Normans of Sicily, from whom they hold themselves aloof, refusing both payment and provisions. It is impossible to know what religion they practise, though they have boasted to our knights that they, and they alone, are the followers of Christ. To me they seem like murderers, or worse.

I have not mentioned the muezzins. These are the priests of the Turks, who stand in the towers of Antioch six times a day and chant out prayers to the city. It is a complex chant, at times high and impassioned, at others low and mournful. I should like to know more of this chant — what they say and whether it is written down.

It is not improvised, for we have been here long enough that I can recognize patterns that are repeated. At first I did not think it beautiful, as are our Latin hymns. But now that I am familiar with it, I find that I look forward to it, and I sometimes catch myself humming it during the day. It is always thus with religions not our own. We think them barbarous and crude until we listen, and then we realize that they sing the same harmonies as lie deep in our own souls, regardless of the words.

November the Twenty-ninth

It is very cold. I have little of importance to report.

A week ago a fleet of ships from Genoa reached the port of Saint Symeon. As soon as it was anchored, the Germans, who were manning the outposts on the river, charged into the town. They were aided by the guns of the Genoese ships, which caused great havoc. The Turks surrendered almost at once – it appears that they were starving and only waiting for an excuse – but the Germans left not one of them alive.

The port is now in our hands, as are the provisions brought by the ships. This is well, since our stocks are growing scarcer. There is salted meat and flour, but no vegetables or fruit. It seems that these Italians, who had been ordered by Pope Urban to provision us *nearly two years ago*, have used the interval to make themselves rich with voyages all over the Mediterranean.

As a result, the only food left for us is that which was neither sold nor spoiled. When confronted with this fact by Emich, the German overlord, the Genoese commander replied that he assumed we were all dead, and laughed. On this, Emich cut off his left arm at the elbow. The Germans have no sense of humour.

The arrival of the fleet has caused considerable commotion. This is due to several facts. First, Peter the Hermit is here, together with some three-score knights and other soldiers whom he recruited in the north. I watched their march into our encampment, and a more predatory, low-lived band of scoundrels I hope never to see. Their equipment appears to have been looted from graves, their mounts are foul and broken down, and they ride them like rag pickers.

The infantry is nothing more than a rabble. They carry clubs and whips and rusted steel. They wear no colours but the motley of thieves and beggars, and they stink. Their faces are unshaven, their eyes have a dirty look, and they immediately set to scouring the camp for valuables. I have ordered Bartholomew and Mansour to hide my possessions, and to bludgeon any of them that approach our shelter.

As for the blessed Peter, I have had the honour of meeting him. He was drunk when he arrived and smelled strongly of garlic. A thin dribble ran continuously from the corners of his mouth. He speaks the Picard dialect, which gives his French a barbaric quality. I had always heard that he went barefoot and rode a donkey. Actually, he quite resembles a donkey – his face is long and dark and overgrown with stubble – and as for his feet . . . let me say only that they have the stench of holiness about them.

He, together with his *militia Christi*, have been sent by Lord Raymond to front the Gate of the Bridge, it being the easiest to defend, and the farthest from our lines. I do not know how they stand in the way of arms, but they appear well supplied with wine.

Two other events marked the arrival of the fleet.

No one knew it, but Count Baldwin, having established his kingdom in the East, had sent for his wife, Godvere, and their three little children. The lady had at once set out with all her luggage on the lengthy journey, managing to travel as far as Bari before falling ill with fever. Nevertheless, eager to obey her husband's summons and share in his new glory, she continued, taking ship with Egyptians who stole her luggage and abandoned her and her children on Cyprus. There the Genoese found her, destitute and sick, and transported her here with the promise of reward from her brother-in-law, Count Godfrey.

En route her condition worsened. Then the youngest child contracted the fever and died, and the older two, a boy of some nine or ten years and a girl no more than six, also fell ill. Thus did the three pitiable invalids arrive at our camp, hoping to find comfort from their relative. How distressed was Godvere to learn that Godfrey, too, has fallen ill with fever and can no more help himself than he can help them.

I accompanied them from the ship to Godfrey's camp. It was a sorry little progress up from the port, past the bodies of the slaughtered Turks, along the river so fouled by our troops that it cannot be drunk from or even used to bathe.

I rode alongside the cart in which Godvere sat as stately as she could. Her two children lay upon her lap and she stroked their heads absently as she stared at our encampment, with its ramshackle shelters and greasy cooking smoke and endless fields of mud. I could see the horror in her eyes as she took it in, eyes already drained with weeks of fever and anguish for her afflicted children. Here is a woman who came to be a queen, and who finds only misery and sickness, and the stares of sullen soldiers.

She did not cry, and I admired her for that. Indeed, I could not take my eyes from her. She is a small woman, very frail, with skin as white as paper, thin lips, and very large, dark eyes. Her hands, I noticed, as she ran them through her babies' hair, were exquisitely small and fine. Through all her trials she has attended to her nails, and that fact struck me as such an act of courage that my heart went out to her. I would save her if I could, but I saw by the sunken eyes with their purple haloes, that she is doomed. I hope only that the children will survive.

I find, reading back on this entry, that I have achieved a passion. I was cold when I began this; not cold in body only, but cold in spirit. There is a reason for it, which I shall tell.

The third event connected with the fleet that has raised a furore in the camp was the arrival of letters from Provence. Evidently when the pope commissioned the fleet, many of the families of our pilgrims betook themselves to write to their beloveds and entrust their letters to the commander. Despite the unfortunate loss of his forearm, he has delivered them faithfully to us, and as many men as have received them are in delirium. They read the letters over and over – those who can read – and brandish them like trophies, and are even paid to read them to their comrades.

It is a wonderful thing to see the effect of a few pieces of paper with their fragile tracery of writing upon the spirit of the army. Every word is a treasure, every sentence is pored over for hidden meaning. I have seen more than one man weep openly over his letter, and I have seen his fellows, men hardened by every trial imaginable, beg to be allowed to touch the paper. They are relics of a distant world, a living link with home – they have been in the hands that have held our hands in times of peace. There is no man who has one who would trade a thousand jewels for his letter. And not a soldier who has none who would not give a thousand jewels to have one.

There was no letter for me.

DECEMBER THE FIRST

The son of Baldwin, the little boy, has died. I did not see it, but they say he made a sweet and quiet death. Death in a child is so unlikely, like the shadow of a cloud that sometimes falls across a valley when the sun is directly behind it. We wonder with a start where it came from and what it means, and why so fair a place is suddenly so dark. I think that if I had a child and lost him I would kill myself. And then I think, no, it would be unmanly. And I realize I have no idea what it must mean to be a father.

Baldwin has not come, though he has been repeatedly sent for. He is off on conquests still, yet all that he has conquered for is dying here at Antioch. I never liked him, but now that I see those who love him I am tempered in my opinion. Even the nastiest among us may be loved by someone, and that alone may be enough to save our souls. I have reflected elsewhere in this journal that it is not so terrible not to love as to be unloved. Baldwin, I see, is not unloved.

The same, later

I was interrupted in my writing by a squire of my Lord who sent for me. In his pavilion Lord Raymond handed me a paper that had arrived within a packet meant for him. I did not at first understand. 'It is a letter,' he said, smiling. 'A letter from your home.' And so it was.

I raced back to my shelter, clutching the letter in my hands like a beggar his meal. I brushed past Bartholomew, who meant to speak with me, and hurried to light the candle. I was trembling as I unfolded it. 'My husband,' it began, 'your animals are well.'

It was from Jehanne, dated two months after my departure.[75] I will not give its contents here, but shall enclose the letter in this book.[76] It was written in her irregular script with no edge to keep the lines straight, and though it spoke of homely matters, I read it over and over. My breath was short, my eyes could hardly focus. Here were words written by her hand; here was paper she had touched. I nearly cried.

There was news of the estate – the harvest was in progress, the yield was good, the overseer was not drinking, the animals were well. How that phrase delighted me. How it warmed my heart and made me smile: 'Your animals are well.' It was a care she had for me, knowing how solicitous I am of them. There was not a word for herself, but of my animals she had a careful mind. All of a sudden I love her again, the heat I felt for her has returned, the smell and taste of her are in my sense anew. This letter with its

75 The actual date as given by Roger was 'the eve of Saint Bonizet', or 23 October.
76 The letter evidently has been lost.

quaint familiarity has brought her rushing back to me. Jehanne! Jehanne! How sterile I have become. All of the sweet juice of you that oiled my flesh had dried out of me. I had forgotten what it meant to be a man within your arms!

Later still

I have read the enclosure from my mother. It dropped out almost by accident as I turned the letter over. I glanced at it and put it to one side and read Jehanne's letter greedily. Only much later, wiping the tears from my eyes, did I pick it up. I recognized my mother's hand at once, small and tight and looped like lace. 'My son,' it read, 'your sister is no more a maid, but wife. This morning at Saint Gilles she wed the Duke of Sète. Now am I alone, for Jehanne is wholly taken up with the estate, which she has placed within the charge of Abelard, the Duke of Arles's eldest son. I commend you to the care of God. *Maman*.'

That was all, but that was everything. Years ago I had met Abelard d'Arles at the home of Eustace. I had seen him hang on Jehanne and I had hated him at once. She had not talked of him since we were married. But now he was in charge of my estate!

I turned from tears to fury. All those nights that I have lain awake wondering whether she slept alone, knowing she had not. Abelard! That skinny, affectatious little man with his squared-off beard and his mincing ways. That awful laugh and those sympathetic eyes! That coward who managed not to be at home when the emissary of Pope Urban arrived to recruit for our expedition! With his tight hose and his whitewashed teeth and the codpiece that always manages to protrude.

I threw the letter down and left my pavilion, nearly knocking over Bartholomew in the process. 'Master,' he said, 'I have a boil on my foot, may I go—'

I told him to go to hell.

Now I have ridden all night, spurring Fatana until she bled, making a circuit of the city, hoping to meet some Turks. I found none, though I startled every sentry in the army and drew fire from the walls. They must have thought me mad, Christian and Turk alike. Well, mad I was, and even madder now that I have thought more on it.

I cannot sit still. I will ride down to the port and spend the night there. Anything to get away from this damned encampment with its eternal stench of death.

DECEMBER THE EIGHTH
The Feast of the Immaculate Conception

I am drunk. I am drunk. As I have been every night for the past week. As I shall be, by the grace of God, every night that I can manage it.

I am at Saint Symeon, the guest of my friends, the Germans, the English, the Scots and the men of Galle. There are caberna[77] here where we spend our nights. Indeed, I slept in one last night and was awakened when they opened the river gate to wash the floor.

Somehow, I do not remember how, I lost my German dagger. It may have been at cards, for these Germans are religious players of cards. And I have a bad cut above my eye that runs with pus.

Emich of Leisingen and I have become great friends. We have sworn an oath to defend each other in grace and sin. He has terrible cuts upon his face from brawling. An Englishman drew a knife on him and I skewered the man, drove straight through him. I felt badly but his friends assured me he was evil and deserved it. Now Emich and I are inseparable since, according to the Germans, if you save a man's life he is your friend forever.

I have had six women since I have been here. They are not

77 Caberna: underground taverns or cafés. A rough English equivalent would be 'dives', with the specification that they are in cellars.

scarce. The Italian sailors know all the bawdy houses so we get them drunk and they take us there. With Jehanne that makes upwards of twelve women I have had, if you do not count Josianne, the girl who drowned, which I do not since I never got inside her.

She was a sweet thing, perhaps a little plump, but so are these girls who make their living on the port. But what I admire is, there is no pretence about them. They welcome you, they service you, they take their pay and say goodbye. There is no land involved, no vows, no promises to love you. They do their filthy business with you and you part forever. That is the way of it. That is what it ought to mean.

What is a wife? A whore, bought and paid as much as any whore of Saint Symeon. You do not give her money; no, you give her your name, your honour, your happiness. She is well paid. You give her your cock and in the bargain you entrust your very soul to her. She gets you to say you love her, and you say it with all your heart — and then she wrings you like a rag. And your soul pours out upon the floor like dirty water. I would rather have these sailors' whores than any wife. I leave their arms with my purse empty, yes, but with my soul still in my body. I give them money, but I keep myself.

The first one broke my vow to be chaste. She ruptured the holiness I felt growing on me like vines upon the wall. She took me between her plump white hands with their dirty fingernails and swelled me to the bursting and it felt every inch as good as evil. I savoured her like a roast, I was on her like a flash, I was in her like a thought. I pumped and pounded her until she laughed and asked me to go slow. And then I stared at her face, a stranger's face gaping at me with bad teeth, and for an instant I saw Jehanne's face, and I loosed myself into her and wept.

She stroked my head as if I were a child and I lifted myself off her and dropped the copper coins upon the bed and went to be alone. I walked by the sea for an hour, just thinking. I found an oyster on the beach and picked it up and pried it open with my nails, and inside there was no pearl, just the wet white flesh with sticky strings between the shells and a smell of salt. For some reason it horrified me and I flung it out as far as I could into the sea and went back to town to finish getting drunk.

I have made it my ambition to sleep with every whore on the port. And to stay drunk for as long as I am here.

December the Eighteenth

I lost my book for ten days, but I found it again among the sacks in the chandler's shop where I had been sleeping. I was frantic over it, which is odd since I had not known how much it means to me. I had trouble retrieving it, for the chandler had forbidden me to enter his shop after the row I had there with the Scotsman.

It was a stupid thing. I was drunk, as was he; a bearded man from a town whose name sounded like the clearing of a throat. We had gone back to the shop after the caberna closed to finish drinking together with Emich and some Germans. It was nearly dawn and the first birds stirred. The Scotsman said that the birds of his native land were the sweetest singers in all the world. Emich, who speaks their language, translated, and I answered indignantly that the birds of Provence have no equal.

That started it. We began to argue over birds and to imitate their songs, and the Scot said my birdsong reminded him of an old woman breaking wind. I struck him, he struck back, and in the next instant we were rolling on the filthy floor clawing and biting at each other. I bit off the top part of his ear and spat it out and he began to cry. The others cheered and urged me on. I was beside myself. He lay there, moaning and covered with wood chips, clutching a hand to his ear, blood running between his fingers. His skirts were thrown up, revealing fat white thighs and the hairy lumps of testicles.

The sight of him disgusted me and I took up a mallet and

began to beat him. The bloodier his face became the more enraged I was and the more horrified at myself. I would have beaten him to death if the chandler had not called the sailors, who came and pulled me off. I felt myself being dragged away, the mallet still in my hand, my heart racing and my breath coming like an animal's. They hit me many times over the head until I reeled, and then they carried me outside and threw me off the dock.

Someone must have fetched me out — I do not know who — for the next thing I remember, I was in a boat bobbing in the harbour. The sun was in my eyes and it was a long moment before I could see. Above me was a face, the face of a little girl. She regarded me indifferently. She had honey-coloured hair and blue eyes. Her skin was as fair as that of any child of Provence. In her hands she held a clump of seaweed from which, as I watched, she plucked an oyster.

I raised my head and glanced about. The boat was scarcely large enough for the two of us. Why she should be out in the harbour by herself I could not imagine. I raised myself from the bilge in the bottom of the boat, setting it rocking furiously. Suddenly I felt a powerful urge to vomit, and I leaned over the side. The vomit came in long brown strings, my stomach heaved, and I squinted with the retching until my eyes were filled with tears.

Just then a hand grasped the side and a boy of fourteen or fifteen pulled himself up, tossing the wet hair from his eyes. His face was fair and his hair the colour of honey like the girl's. He grinned at me and dropped a handful of seaweed into the bottom of the boat. Then he filled his lungs with air and disappeared again.

I lay back feeling hollow and stupid, watching the little girl at her work. She opened the oyster with the point of a rusty nail, reached in her tiny fingers, drew out a pearl, and threw the shell away. The pearl was large and slimy. She put it into her mouth, rolled it around a moment, took it out again and spat. With an expert's eye she held the pearl against the sun to examine it, and then made to put it in a purse she wore around her neck. But at that moment she glanced at me, frowned, and held it out, saying something in a language I had never heard.

When I did not respond, she shook the pearl at me, urging it upon me. I sat up feeling faint and took it from her. She said nothing more, but looked very seriously at me. I thanked her, and she immediately went back to her work, picking at the seaweed.

I remained with her in the boat until her brother — for so he must have been — had finished his diving. How he bore the chill of that water I shall never know (for he was completely naked), and how he remained for such long periods under water is a mystery to me. I started to make room for him in the boat but he waved me off and, hoisting himself up effortlessly, he stood with perfect equilibrium upon the thwarts behind his sister.

She handed him a cloak with which he dried himself, rubbing vigorously at his skin. He was one of the handsomest lads that I have ever seen, with blue-black eyes and a perfect athlete's form. His body shone in the sun and radiated vitality and youth. It made me cringe to look at him, for I felt so foul and aged and ashamed of my condition. I closed my eyes as he paddled us back to shore, feeling keenly the pain of my own lost youth and the flaccid weight of my sins.

There is no more that I can do to myself. I am alone as I have never been and, as I walk about the town, I feel a stranger even to myself. I, Roger, Duke of Lunel, have become a beggar, a drunk, an old man with worn-out hose and ragged tunic, stumbling from dark to dark, my soul in hiding.

And this because I loved my wife and hated her husband, and killed him, and left her alone to her desires. It is all my fault. I am the cause of my misery. No one is to blame but me.

DECEMBER THE TWENTY-FOURTH

I remained in the town for another week. The Germans kept me supplied with drink and trouble. Barred from all the houses and shops, I slept at the end of the jetty that forms the extremity of the port. It was bitter cold at night, and I covered myself with sacks. Sometimes I wept, sometimes I put myself to sleep with shouts and curses. My skin was chapped, my beard grew in tangles, and I shivered even in the sun.

Then, yesterday, I was awakened by a gentle touch. It was Mansour. 'Effendi,' he said, 'your horse needs care.'

He helped me to my feet and I followed him to where Fatana was tethered in a corral by the harbour master's house. I mounted, and Mansour led me at a slow walk back to the camp.

I am installed again in my pavilion. I have slept a good long time. Mansour has bathed and shaved me. He has cleaned the wound above my eye and stitched it with gut. I have made my confession and attended mass. It was a dark and purging time. I am cleansed. And though I feel scoured and raw, with God's help I shall yet heal myself.

DECEMBER THE TWENTY-EIGHTH
The Feast of the Holy Innocents

At a council on the day after Christmas it was decided that Count Bohemund should take ten thousand men, and Count Robert of Flanders half that many, and move up the River Orontes in search of provisions for the army. The great number of men was insisted on by Bohemund for two reasons, I think.

The first is that his spies inside Antioch have reported that Yagashan has applied for relief to the Emir of Damascus, and Bohemund may therefore meet a force of Turks on his march. The second, which he did not state, but which I think is certain, is that he does not wish Lord Raymond to have sufficient troops to take and occupy Antioch in his absence. His suspicion of Lord Raymond has thoroughly infected his mind, and nothing anyone says can persuade him that the army is needed here. Thus, Bohemund will detach more than half the army for his forage expedition, a thing that is unheard of.

Count Godfrey was absent from the meeting. He remains ill with fever and unable to leave his pavilion. In the meanwhile his sister-in-law, the Lady Godvere, has died. Of Baldwin's family there now remains only the little girl. I have sometimes seen her about the camp, where she has become a favourite of the men. Somehow they manage to find treats for her, and no one is allowed to swear or perform any grossness in her presence. It is sufficient for her to appear with her curls and her immaculate shift for the soldiers to transform themselves. Their voices lower, they smile, they put out their hands to touch her. She is the one note of sweetness in this gruff and melancholy world. I am certain that if, God forbid, she were to be killed or captured by the Turks on one of their nightly raids, the men would instantly storm Antioch.

Now I am told that she too is ill and like to die. The men make little pilgrimages to the tent in which she lies, saying not a word, often leaving flowers or toys that they have fashioned for her. She is an orphan, it is true, but she has fifteen thousand uncles.

Yesterday some fool, one of the Flemish soldiers, declared that a visit to her tent had cured him of flux, and now the word has gone around the camp that she is a saint and capable of miracles. Men with every kind of ailment, from severed limbs to gonorrhea, are flocking to her, and have to be restrained by Godfrey's guards. Still they send in items for her to bless – swords and coifs and bits of clothing – so that now the tent is filled to bursting. But the girl lies unconscious, attended by priests.

The winter rains have started, and the lowland along the river on which our infantry is camped will soon become uninhabitable. Consequently, Lord Raymond has given order for the men to move to higher ground opposite the Gate of the Dog, which they are doing with much grumbling. My pavilion, however, is secure.

I have so far said nothing of myself. I wrote in my last entry that I made confession and took the sacrament. It was to Père Raimund of Aguillères that I confessed, though he is a difficult cleric to find. He spends most of his days wandering the countryside in a kind of fit of exaltation. It is said that, inspired by his nearness to the city of Saint Peter, he eats dirt and drinks only the water of the River Orontes, for Peter must have trod the soil and drunk the water.

When I confessed to him he merely sat in silence on a coil of rope, his face consumed with a smile, saying nothing. I had to clear my throat and cough to waken him from his reverie so that he might give me absolution. For penance he commanded me to bathe in the River Orontes.

I would have demurred, for the river is so foul with the refuse of the camp, but I thought better of it. It was a heavy penance indeed. The next morning I stripped down, waded into the fluid filth that is the river, and anointed my body. The soldiers thereabouts must have thought me mad, but I said nothing and took it as part of the penance. Upon emerging I was so vile I could not even dress, but wrapped myself in a horse blanket and went straight to my pavilion, where Mansour washed the penance from me.

Nothing has been said of my weeks in the port, for which I am grateful to him. We speak with the careful formality of those who share a secret shame. I think this must ever be the case between masters and servants, since they who wait on us inevitably see us as we are. That is the role of loyalty: it takes the place of love in those with whom we share our lives from necessity and not affection. Nonetheless, I decided to make my conduct understood — not to seek his forgiveness, but so that he might understand what had driven me to such excess.

As he was preparing to leave me for the night I invited him to sit awhile and talk. He seemed startled and made excuses, but I insisted. He bowed and folded himself in a corner well out of the light of the oil lamp.

'First,' I said, 'I wish to thank you for your service.' I could see him incline his head, the turban just catching the glow as he did so. 'When you found me on the jetty I was unwell . . .'

'Effendi, please . . .' he said, but I raised a hand to quieten him.

'I had received a shock,' I continued. 'I am a married man. I had learned through a letter that . . . that all was not well in my home.'

He remained in silence a long time. At last he spoke, in a whisper I could hardly hear. 'Your wife is ill?' he said.

'It is not that she is ill,' I replied. 'I think she has been unwise.'

'I see, Effendi,' Mansour said.

'Are you a married man?' I asked him.

'Once,' he said.

'Then you perhaps can understand that news — such news as I have had, especially at such a distance — has an unsettling effect.'

He absorbed this a long time in silence. At last he responded: 'It may be worse face to face.'

Now it was I who had to understand. 'You have experienced this?' I asked.

'You will permit me, Effendi . . . To receive such news at a distance, a man may well wish to be drunk. This I understand perfectly. But I think — forgive me, Effendi — to have it before one's eyes, a man may wish something worse. A man may wish to die. You were fortunate, and I am glad of that.'

I saw the wisdom of what he said and I thanked him for it.

Mansour rose to go. 'The king of Sicily departs tomorrow,' he said. 'You will not accompany him?' I told him that I would remain with Lord Raymond. 'Then I shall prepare your breakfast at the usual hour. I have acquired some excellent rye flour from a merchant of Greece. You shall have fresh bread.'

I could not help myself. 'Mansour,' I said, 'you are surely a Godsend.'

He bowed. 'All of us are sent by God,' he replied. 'To one purpose or another.' And as always he left without a sound.

I felt much better – better than I had after my confession to the priest. It has to do, I think, with the ability of men to talk to one another, to share their experiences and to understand with scarcely a word. That it should be so between myself and Mansour, men of such different cultures and classes and from such different worlds, is all the more reassuring to my mind.

December the Twenty-ninth

We have had a battle. No sooner had Count Bohemund and his force departed than the Turks attacked our lines. The attack began before dawn when the bridges dropped with a great crash and they swarmed out in hundreds to overwhelm our positions. Our men were scarcely awake, most were not dressed, and few were armed. We were taken completely by surprise.

Mansour came running to fetch me but I had already been awakened by the noise. I managed to get into my mail and was buckling on my sword when a Turk appeared at the entrance to my pavilion. He seemed as startled as I was and gave a shout. Mansour too screamed. I pulled the sword from its sheath and struck the Turk in the jaw with the hilt. He staggered and I stepped to him and slashed at his throat. Blood splattered onto Mansour, and he screamed again.

Outside all was in commotion. Men were struggling in total darkness, grunting and flailing at each other. Dozens had been wounded and their cries were on all sides. I looked immediately for my Lord, and saw him mounted upon his destrier rallying the knights. I yelled for Bartholomew but he was nowhere to be seen. Fatana was tethered to a tree some rods distant and I made for her at once. Two men came towards me fighting. One backed into me, struck at me with his elbow, and then received a blow to his head. It was so dark that I could not tell which was Turk and which Christian. The wounded man fell at my feet and I could make out the fur-covered helmet of a Turk. The other man raised his club to strike me but I grabbed his arm and called to him in French. He cursed, split open the Turk's head, and disappeared into the darkness.

I saddled Fatana and mounted as quickly as I could. By now the entire camp was under attack. I rode in among the battling men, trying to reach Lord Raymond. He had gathered around him some thirty knights and was preparing to charge. I hollered to him and he waved me on. When I joined him he gave the signal, and we made straight for the city gates.

The effect of a mounted charge on infantry is remarkable, but this one in the darkness was miraculous. A path was cleared instantly, and in a matter of moments we were at the bridge across the moat where the Turks made a stand. The battle was furious, contained as it was within the narrow space leading to the bridge. The gates were still open and I could clearly see the lights of houses within the city, and even women dashing across the square.

'Antioch!' Lord Raymond shouted. 'Antioch!'

We spurred our horses and forced our way onto the bridge. More Turks appeared from the town, some bearing spears with which they stabbed at the breasts of our mounts. In a moment reinforcements had come up on our side. Above the bodies the standard of the Bishop Adhémar appeared, and in the next instant it fell as the standard-bearer was clubbed from his horse.

We fought at close quarters for several minutes. Men grabbed at my legs and I thrust at them as fast as I could. Gradually we made our way towards the gates, trampling the Turks underfoot or driving them into the moat. 'We're in,' Lord Raymond hollered, 'by God, we're in!' Then all at once a shout went up behind us and I turned to see a sight that stunned me.

It was Père Raimund of Aguillères in his nightshirt, his arms outstretched, coming towards us above the heads of the men. 'A miracle, a miracle!' our soldiers shouted. And indeed it seemed that he was floating free like a disembodied soul, moving with a placid smile towards the gates.

The vision spurred our infantry who crowded onto the bridge until it threatened to give way beneath us. I was hemmed in, unable to advance or withdraw. Then one of the soldiers, straining to touch Père Raimund who remained suspended above us, jabbed Fatana with his sword. She bolted and began turning in circles, then other horses bolted, and in an instant there was chaos on the bridge. Men were struggling to free themselves, leaping into the moat or hammering at one another to retreat.

Meanwhile Lord Raymond and a few knights had reached the gates and were fighting to seize the mechanism. The Turks, realizing the danger, began to rally within the city. I could see a line of archers being formed and I yelled at Lord Raymond to warn him, but too late. The archers knelt and loosed a volley of arrows that tore into the men packed upon the bridge.

At that, sheer mayhem broke out. The men at the gates began struggling madly to withdraw, while the men on the bridge fought just as madly against them. Bodies were flung into the moat, men were being crushed, and for a moment I thought that Fatana too would topple from the bridge. I gave her a powerful spur and drove her back through the mass of bodies towards the camp. That seemed to break the impasse, and our men began streaming back from off the bridge.

The Turks were quick to follow up. One of their leaders, a brave man, rushed onto the bridge alone, waving his curved sword for them to follow. I caught sight of Lord Raymond galloping among the tents, rallying the men, and I made for him, yelling to our soldiers to stop and turn. A few did so, and in a moment we had a defensive line that stood to meet the Turks. They fired another volley of arrows which passed over our heads and then we charged. It was enough. The Turks, confused and disorganized, broke and ran for the bridge.

I thought for a moment that Lord Raymond would try again to gain the city but he called our men up short. We formed again, ready for another attack, but none came. In the next moment, the gates of Antioch swung shut.

'Where is Raimund of Aguillères?' Lord Raymond shouted. He was fuming, beside himself. 'Where is that God-damned fool?' I had not had time to think about him, and I wondered myself at what had happened.

Then he was before us in his nightshirt, his hands pressed to his face, weeping.

'What the hell did you think you were doing?' Lord Raymond said to him.

'We were in Antioch,' he replied with a moan. 'I myself saw the Holy City.'

'You climbed over the backs of my men! You caused a panic!'

'Blessed Peter called to me!' the priest responded.

'Well, you'll meet him soon enough if you try that trick again,' Lord Raymond replied, and he spurred his horse and rode off.

In the dawn light, the bridge was a melancholy sight. Dozens of our men lay dead upon it, and dozens more floated in the moat. The entire camp, from the city walls to the bridge of boats, was littered with bodies. The wounded Turks were killed by our men where they lay, and the bodies were burned that afternoon. The smoke from the bonfires rose for hundreds of feet above the encampment, and was carried by the wind into the city. As it descended behind the walls, we could hear the wails of women mourning their dead. Our men who were killed will be buried in the graveyard we have made on the slopes north of the river.

After the battle I went to search for Bartholomew, with whom I was furious for failing to prepare my horse. I saw a faint glow in his tent and assumed he had hidden there during the fight. I strode up to it and pulled back the flap, ready to upbraid him not only for his cowardice, but also for his uselessness these past months. But when I saw him, I stopped short.

He was kneeling in the middle of his shelter, his eyes upturned to heaven. When he saw me he fixed a gaze of such surpassing happiness on me as I have never seen in human eyes before.

That was when I realized that the grease lamp lay overturned and unlighted in a corner. The glow I had seen — how may I say it — was coming from the peasant boy's face.

DECEMBER THE THIRTY-FIRST

We have had two unsettling occurrences. On the day after the battle of the bridge I was awakened by a rumbling noise and then a violent shaking of the earth. I grasped the edges of my bed frame, for I thought I would be thrown onto the ground. The whole pavilion shuddered back and forth for a minute or two, and then all was silent. I lay terrified, my heart racing. Then Mansour appeared at the entrance to ask whether I was all right. I had difficulty replying.

'You must come out,' he said.

I got up, and at once the shaking started again. The poles of the pavilion swayed like branches in the wind, the cloth whipped as though it would tear itself to pieces. Mansour gave me his hand to steady me. The whole camp was roused. Men stood wide-eyed, their feet spread as if on a ship in a storm. Shelters were falling apart and the horses were yanking madly at their tethers.

'It is the earthquake,' Mansour shouted to me.

No one was killed, though dozens of men were buried in their shelters and many animals were lost. All that day there were more shocks, and with every one men dashed out in fear from their tents. I confess I was among them. I have never felt so helpless in my life.

Then, that night, the sky was illuminated by a curtain of

glimmering lights.[78] It was the most fantastic thing that I have ever seen — broader and denser than a rainbow, and rising straight up into the stars. What it could be I cannot say, but the men believe that the earthquake released the souls of the dead, and it was they ascending into heaven. It may be so. It is strange to think of our poor, simple peasants among the stars. I wonder whether the souls of the Turks are among them also.

JANUARY THE THIRD
The Year of the Incarnation of Our Saviour, 1098

How can it be that another year has come? When our pilgrimage was summoned it was 1095, when I left my home it was 1096, when I reached the East 1097, and now . . .

I must say that Count Baldwin has arrived. He rode in great state into our camp upon an Arab horse caparisoned in gold, attired in all the riches of his kingdom, attended by a retinue of Turcopoles and blacks. His men sounded trumpets to announce his approach, and as he passed through the encampment he scarcely looked at our ragged men, his long nose held high, the silken reins laced between the fingers of his jewel-sewn gloves.

He alighted outside Count Godfrey's pavilion, and when he was told that his brother was too ill to receive him he demanded to see his family. The Bishop Adhémar led him in silence to the graveyard above the river. There he found three crosses, for his little girl had died the day before.

I watched in silence. Baldwin turned upon the bishop and raised his arm to strike him. To his credit, Adhémar did not flinch. 'You are king of nothing,' he said, and he left him to his grief.

For three nights Baldwin slept among the graves; indeed, he did not leave them for a moment, not even to eat. His retainers waited

78 The earthquake, and the aurora borealis that followed, were mentioned by all the contemporary chroniclers.

for him patiently, and then dispersed into the camp where they were promptly beaten and robbed. In passing by the graveyard, I could hear the Count talking to his wife and, at night, singing to his children. I think it is too heavy a price to pay to be a king. This morning he left alone to return to Edessa. He said not a word to any of us.

Meanwhile we have had news of Bohemund. He has met the Turks of Damascus and defeated them with heavy losses on both sides. We have hopes that now they will return with our provisions. It will be none too soon, for in the attack on our camp the Turks set fire to our supplies, which were meagre. I cannot help but feel that spies had told them the exact location of the storehouses, for they made for them directly. Indeed, there are many spies on either side, and some who work for both sides, for they are said to be paid well.

The Bishop Adhémar has taken counsel with himself over the events of the past few days, and has declared his opinion that God is displeased with us. It has not taken much argument to convince us of the idea. The bishop has therefore ordered the entire army to fast for three days and to beg for God's forgiveness. This fasting, too, will not be difficult, since there is scarcely any food left to us.

JANUARY THE THIRTEENTH

A great deal has happened. On Sunday last Count Bohemund returned with his armies. He arrived during the service being conducted out of doors in the pouring rain by the Bishop Adhémar. The bishop in his sermon alternated between pleas to God for mercy and fury at our conduct. Had he not been a cleric I think he would have cursed both God and man. When those at the fringes of the crowd caught sight of Bohemund riding towards us they sent up a shout.

'You see! You see, you wretches!' Bishop Adhémar called out. 'God has answered my prayers!' When Bohemund rode up, Adhémar grabbed the reins of his horse. 'You are sent by God!' he shouted over the downpour.

'Then God can keep me,' Bohemund replied, and he slid from his soaking saddle without a further word.

Adhémar stared at him uncomprehendingly, then he went from one cart to the next searching for the provisions. There were none. Our hearts sank with every canvas he threw back. The carts were filled with wounded, not food.

Bohemund's men regarded us sullenly. They were in a sorry state, beaten down, threadbare, and as emaciated as ourselves. Those of Robert of Flanders were in worse condition. Count Robert himself lay in a cart, half-dead from the battle and the journey back. One of his eyes had been taken out by a Turkish arrow, and he could not walk for a leg so swollen that it had split his hose.

'Where is my forage?' The bishop Adhémar demanded. 'What have you been doing all this time?'

Bohemund turned on him, his narrow eyes smouldering. 'We have been killing Turks,' he said. 'Which is what we came here to do.'

'We came here to liberate God's land!' Adhémar replied. His vestments hung sodden around his shoulders and the rain beat in his face.

'And so you have, I hear,' Bohemund growled. 'Or nearly so. In my absence you tried to take Antioch from me.'

'From you?' Adhémar shouted.

Bohemund strode towards him fearlessly. 'That city is mine!' he declared. 'And no sooner is my back turned than you assault.'

'We were attacked,' said Adhémar.

Bohemund spat at his feet. 'How convenient that the Turks should open their gates the minute I am gone.'

Adhémar was about to reply, but at this moment Lord Raymond

walked up. 'Our men are starving,' he said. 'Your commission was to bring food. You have failed us.'

Bohemund regarded his tall frame scornfully. 'I take no commission from Provençals,' he answered. 'Nor from their bishops. Look to yourself, Raymond of Saint Gilles, and you, Bishop of Le Puy. For I mean to have Antioch, and I will have it.'

With that he strode off into the rain. The Bishop Adhémar watched him go, then turned to us. 'Well,' he called, 'what are you waiting for? God-damn you, go take your communion!'

For the past few days there has been a tension in the camp that no one has seen before. The men scarcely speak to one another, and the leaders, not at all. Our condition is truly desperate – no food, no supplies, dissention in the army, and desertions every day. Men began slipping away under the pelting rain in knots of twos and threes, then in larger groups, now wholesale. Animals drop dead where they stand and are immediately butchered for their scant meat. Some, indeed, are butchered before their deaths. I have had to set a watch over Fatana lest she, too, be stolen and killed. It is said that fewer than a thousand horses remain in the army.

Meanwhile, a few merchants from the Armenian villages reached us bringing gifts of grain and dried fruit, and they were nearly torn to pieces by the soldiers. Now they come armed and keep their distance, setting up stalls in the outlying villages and selling to the highest bidders. A single donkey's load of provisions fetches six, eight, or even ten gold bezants.

This favours us, since Lord Raymond has retained his gold, and pays it out judiciously to obtain food for our men. As a result we are among the few who manage to feed our soldiers at least one meal per day. The Northerners – the English, Scottish and Galles – suffer terribly, for they have neither gold nor barter. The Galles have eaten all their dogs, and the others grub for roots. It is a pitiable sight to see them scratching at the earth, picking slivers out of the mud and thrusting them into their mouths. They began this pilgrimage as primitives, but they are nothing more than animals now. Yet there is a lower depth, as I learned when I happened by the camp of the Tafurs.

They have remained faithfully with the army of Bohemund, and have participated in all of our fights, earning a reputation for savagery and cunning. No one has ever seen them forage, and they ask for nothing from our soldiers, yet they never seem to want. I therefore determined to learn how it is that they survive.

I edged as close as I dared to their camp, leading Fatana who nervously shied away. It is a filthy, ramshackle place; their shelters are no more than skins stretched between poles or heaps of branches bound together. The Tafurs were huddled in close knots of six or eight, little smoky fires burning among them. One group, the nearest to where I passed, crouched like savages over a shank of meat, from which all tore pieces and stuffed them into their mouths. At first I thought the meat was a leg of mutton, for the bone protruded from dark flesh. Then I saw that it terminated, not in a hoof, but a foot, the toenails black and glistening in the firelight.

In the next instant one of their guards grunted an oath at me and waved his scythe to warn me off. I was not slow to depart, for the sight had horrified me. What should we make of such men whom we have accepted into our army as Christian soldiers? Is it conceivable that they, too, are instruments of God?

JANUARY THE NINETEENTH

The Turks continue their raids through the Iron Gate above the river and the Gate of the Bridge, which Peter the Hermit's force guards so ineffectually. The Hermit's men have run out of supplies, and they go begging through the camp for any leavings they can find. Peter himself managed to live quite well for weeks by selling his clothing and locks of his hair as relics to the more gullible soldiers. Now he is no more than a beggar, though still with a haughty mien, demanding food in God's name, and being derided for doing so. I had never thought much of the man but, indeed, it is hard to see him fallen so low, who once was thought to be a saint.

I eat no more than my men: Bernard and Gérard, the pitiable Bartholomew, and the Marseillaises whom Raymond has given me. On rising we have one or two dried fruits, then wheat cakes at noon, and fish from the harbour for supper. These last have become so dear that few can afford them, and more and more men have taken to catching for themselves. And indeed we might eat well were it not for the fact that the filth from the river that spills into the harbour has killed the fish or driven them away.

The Turks, I suppose, must also suffer. Supplies still reach them from inland through the undefended gates. We capture as many of the caravans as we can, but some inevitably slip by. Yet they cannot have much. I would to God they would surrender; then we all might save ourselves. Or perhaps it is we who should abandon the siege and withdraw into Armenia. But then all that we have undergone would be in vain, all the deaths for nothing, and our morale, low as it is, might never recover. We are trapped, though it is we who are outside the walls.

JANUARY THE TWENTY-FIFTH
Cyprus

I am naked in a pool being attended by young monks. They wear coarse black robes and all have long beards despite their youth. They add oil to the water, which is as warm as any bath, and bring me fruit and bowls of sweetened goat's milk thick with cream. I am as far from the camp at Antioch as it is possible to be.

How came this about? I shall tell.

On the day of the Greek feast of Saint Peter the Turks celebrated by lowering the Patriarch of Antioch over the wall in an iron cage.

The poor man hung there, cramped and humiliated, while the garrison yelled taunts at him and us. Our men wished to fire arrows at them, but were restrained for fear of striking the cleric. Thus we watched in silence as the old man, with his tattered robes and white beard, was made to endure the insult.

I noticed that the Bishop Adhémar looked on in deep thought, bordering on reverie. At last he turned his back on the spectacle and, to my surprise, clapped his hands in satisfaction. Now there has been much rancour between the Latin and Greek Churches, but this seemed to me beyond the pale. Indeed, the bishop looked positively gleeful as he returned to his pavilion. That afternoon Adhémar called the nobles to a conference. 'This heretic in the cage may free us from our plight,' he announced, and he then laid out for us his plan.

The Reverend Symeon, the Greek Patriarch of Jerusalem, escaped from that city some months ago and fled to sanctuary on the island of Cyprus. What Adhémar proposed was that we send an embassy to Symeon to offer an alliance. In return for provisions for our army, Symeon would be permitted to resume his throne in Jerusalem, subject to the dictates of the Pope. 'This last detail we shall, of course, keep from him,' the bishop added.

Count Godfrey, who, though weak and very thin, had insisted on attending, raised the objection that was in all our minds: 'Symeon has written an edict denouncing our Church. He is the sworn enemy of Rome.'

'He is a shepherd without a flock, a bishop without a see,' Adhémar rejoined. 'But he does have food and wine and fodder. It shall be more than a fair trade – Jerusalem for victuals. Despite what you may believe,' he concluded with a glance around, 'a fool does not become a bishop. Even in Greece.'

The next morning we took ship for Cyprus. The weather was raw and the sea difficult. I attended Lord Raymond who accompanied Adhémar together with Godfrey, Robert of Normandy, and Hugh of Vermandois. We have brought Count Robert of

Flanders with us on a pallet, in the hope that he may receive medical attention from the Greeks. Bohemund remains holed up in his camp, speaking with no one, surrounded by spies, scheming, it is said, some way to secure Antioch for himself.

On reaching Cyprus we were taken directly to the palace of the patriarch, which adjoins the cathedral. The island is handsome, studded with white cliffs to which rugged olive trees and sage cling like jewels upon armour. The warm breeze and sunshine were welcome to me after the months of wet winter and mud at Antioch. I felt the stiffness of my limbs soften and the roiling clouds that had settled in my mind divide. Cyprus is a curative, and I wish that our men could share in it even for an hour.

The Patriarch Symeon received us with a kindly manner. He was a man past middle age with the customary long beard, much of it white, and with very bright, watery blue eyes. Indeed, his eyes seemed to stream tears continually, so that he kept a linen handkerchief in his sleeve to wipe them. It was, he explained, a disease of the eyes which he acquired in Jerusalem.

We had done our best to appoint ourselves for the visit, but we were dirty and ragged. Symeon insisted that we bathe while he sent our clothing to the Greek nuns to be repaired. These we have not seen; indeed, we have seen no women since our arrival, so strictly are they sequestered. Whether this is for religion or for fear of us I cannot tell.

In any case, I luxuriate here, feeling not so guilty that I cannot enjoy the respite. I have drunk bowls of this sweet milk as I write. Never in my life have I tasted anything as delicious, and I do not scruple to hold out my bowl for the monks to bring me more. They giggle like girls and make signs to one another and gladly fetch it for me. It is more intoxicating than wine, and my skinny body longs for it.

It is so good to be clean again. Never in the camp is one clean. The mud is everywhere, in your clothes, in your food, in every withered fold of your flesh. I encourage the monks to pour the water straight over my head, and they laugh and do so, and I open my mouth and take it in. What a joy ordinary existence is. And how little we appreciate it, until we are removed from it by duty or force. Never again shall I take for granted a soaking bath or the taste of milk, or the company of good-willed strangers.

JANUARY THE THIRTIETH

Our business here is concluded. We ship tomorrow for the mainland where we will await the fall of Antioch. For I now believe that it will fall, and the great jewel of Jerusalem shall soon be in our hands.

Our first night we supped with the Patriarch Symeon, who was dressed in all the finery of his office. He wore a mitre the shape of a chimney pipe and nearly as tall, hung with veils of gossamer and adorned with stars made of pearls. Upon his long fingers were rings of sapphires and rubies, and his robes were sewn with embroidery of silver and gold. The Bishop Adhémar could scarcely compete, although the Greek nuns had not only repaired our garments, but had likewise embroidered them. My own poor surcoat is now more intricate and fine than when it was new in Lunel, and I must confess I felt a bit of the Eastern potentate when I caught sight of myself in the glass.

Symeon studiously avoided conversation about our mission that evening, preferring to talk of his departure from Jerusalem. It appears that the patriarch was secure in his see so long as Ortoq ruled Jerusalem. This was a Turk of some breeding, the viceroy of the bloodthirsty Tutush, whose name is a scourge even among his own people. Tutush it was who murdered his own patron Aziz, the conqueror of Jerusalem. Upon Ortoq's death, however, Tutush became lord of Jerusalem, and from that day no Christian, Latin or Greek, could feel safe.

Symeon mourned the loss of his throne, and his eyes streamed, though whether from illness or grief I could not tell. In a man who weeps continually, sorrow is difficult to discern. Adhémar was quick to assure him that our pilgrimage is his best hope to recover his place. Symeon only daubed at his eyes and nodded sadly.

The next day discussions began in earnest. They took the following line.

Adhémar assured Symeon that Jerusalem would again be his as soon as it fell to our armies. Symeon demurred, wiping his eyes. 'I have presided for twenty years over a city occupied by foreigners,' he said in his heavy accent. 'It is not a happy state.'

'But we are Christians,' Adhémar reminded him. 'We are brothers in spirit.'

'You are prodigals come lately home,' Symeon replied. 'And like the prodigal of the Testament, you expect to take the first place, do you not?'

Adhémar could not help himself. 'That is as Our Saviour wished,' he said.

Symeon smiled faintly. 'Yes, but that decision was made only *after* the prodigal was promised food. You have no such promise.'

It was the very point we had come to settle; Adhémar had walked into the Greek's trap. He gathered himself for the reply. 'It is true,' he said slowly. 'We are in need of food. And you are in need of restoration.'

'Then the path is clear,' the patriarch replied. 'You shall eat and I shall rule.'

Adhémar nodded. 'It must be so. Yet if we do not eat, you cannot rule. And so your throne depends upon our bellies. The trade is equal.'

The patriarch raised a jewelled finger. '*If* you take Jerusalem,' he said. 'You have fourteen-thousand men, of the thirty thousand with which you left Constantinople. Three thousand of horse, eleven of foot, with no food to press your siege of Antioch, and not enough men, horses, weapons, or machines to take Jerusalem.' We all were stunned at his knowledge of our condition, for his figures were almost exactly correct. The Greeks are very cunning in their spies, if not in their battles.

The Bishop Adhémar, who had carefully contained himself, now spoke up forcefully. 'You cannot imagine the miracles our men have performed . . .' he began.

Again Symeon raised his hand. 'Your pride is justified,' he said, 'but it is unprofitable. You will remember that I am the vicar of God's own capital on earth. Not the cesspool of Rome, nor even the fortress of Constantinople can compare to that which I have held in my hands. I am the bishop of Jerusalem: the navel of the world, the footstool of the Almighty, the abode of the souls of all mankind.'

Adhémar tried to interrupt, but Patriarch Symeon drew himself up straight, his voice trembling as he went on. 'The incense you breathe from me is borne from the nostrils of God. The jewels of my fingers are the glinting of His eyes. My words are the echo of His voice, spoke feeble and low it is true, but my whole body is the chord of His throat. Think you that I will suffer your filthy feet to tread upon the destiny of God? He has given Jerusalem to our Church, not yours. Your Church, wherever it may be, is in exile; your pope, whoever he may be, is an interloper in the Holy Land of God.'

Adhémar could no longer restrain himself. 'You go beyond your right,' he said. Again Symeon cut him off.

'No, you go beyond yours,' he replied. 'It is for this that you are starving. For this that your men whore and steal and fight among themselves for trinkets and fish bones. Think you not that the disgrace of your armies has reached to every corner of God's land? Think you not that God's citizens tremble at the coming of your rabble? The Turks we have accommodated in their paganism. But how shall God's servants survive Christians such as you?'

It was not a promising start to our negotiations. We left in anger, following the bishop Adhémar, who swept his robes aside, nearly brushing Symeon's face. That night my Lord Raymond called me to his rooms in the chancellery. 'What do you think?' he asked me.

I told him that there was much truth in Symeon's words. Adhémar had come with no intention of keeping his promise to restore the patriarch to his authority.

'That is why our discussions shall succeed,' Lord Raymond said. 'Symeon knows his worth, and he knows the Latin bishops. Everything was decided before we arrived except that one point. Our host has no intention of returning to a hollow throne.' I asked whether that meant that Symeon would demand a guarantee in writing. 'No,' Lord Raymond replied. 'He knows what Bohemund did with his oath. He knows everything we have done since we arrived in the East. He has the measure of us. He will require something more. Something more subtle. Something undeniable.'

I asked what that might be. Raymond shook his silvered head. 'I do not see it clearly,' he replied. 'But that reference to our numbers was the key. When a bishop talks of troops he means souls. Symeon wants power over our souls. It is the bishop's weapon.'

I knew that it was true, for it was precisely that weapon which Adhémar had wielded over me. I feared we would pay dearly for our food.

This morning we learned of Symeon's terms. He called us to his palace to inform us that a ship was being readied to return us to Antioch. Adhémar seemed surprised, yet determined. He asked brusquely what the patriarch had decided.

'You will be sending an appeal to Rome for reinforcements,' Symeon responded. Adhémar admitted that it was true. Symeon daubed at his eyes. 'The language of that appeal is of concern to me, since it will populate my see with even more foreign troops.'

We held our breath, waiting for him to go on. From the corners of my eyes I could see Lord Raymond smile.

'In whose name will the appeal be sent?' the patriarch enquired.

'The Bishop of Rome,' replied Adhémar.

'That can hardly be,' said Symeon. 'An appeal from foreigners to foreigners would have no spiritual force in this land. Such authority as you have now derives from the appeal of our emperor to your pope. Since the emperor desires that no more of your soldiers come to his dominions, it follows that the appeal can come only from me. Your soldiers will be under my spiritual protection.'

It was as Lord Raymond had predicted: Symeon wished to be recognized as the source of legitimacy for our expedition. From this point, he, and not Adhémar or Urban, would be the spiritual leader of the pilgrimage.

Adhémar was taken aback, completely at a loss for words, and I must say that I enjoyed the spectacle. For once the sophistic bishop had met his match. Food for souls – such was the patriarch's bargain. Adhémar regarded him a long while. 'How would such an appeal be worded?' he said at last.

Symeon put out his hand. A young monk handed him a scroll. He passed it to Adhémar. I could see that it was written in both Latin and Greek. Adhémar glanced through it.

'This is an apostolic appeal,' he said, looking up from the paper. 'In your name alone.'

'For I alone am the apostle of Christ in His city,' Symeon replied.

'Apostle?' repeated Adhémar, incredulous. 'Even His Holy Father the Pope does not dare to call himself so.'

'He does not,' Symeon said. 'And he does well.'

It was not until late tonight that Adhémar acceded to Symeon's demands. The appeal for reinforcements will be proclaimed to all the world in the name of the Patriarch of Jerusalem. He alone shall have the power to excommunicate any members of our pilgrimage who shirk their duties or desert the expedition. He alone shall have authority to dispose of our troops and our conquests in concert with the emperor. And he alone shall have spiritual authority over Jerusalem.

In return we are to have such stores as Cyprus can provide us.

And, I am quite sure, every morsel in his mouth will taste bitter to the Bishop of Le Puy.

FEBRUARY THE SIXTH

The week since our return from Cyprus has been eventful. But first I must relate a conversation that took place before our departure.

It had been decided to leave Count Robert of Flanders with the Greek monks until he should recuperate from his wounds, and my Lord Raymond, Count Godfrey and I visited him in the asile[79] to say goodbye. Count Robert was stoical, though quite gloomy. I had always thought him handsome, a robust, fair-haired man with a broad face. Now he was a shadow, so thin that he was frightening to look at, with a patch on one eye and his shoulder horribly distorted.

We did our best to cheer him, and at one point Godfrey bared his breast to show him the scars which had become infected and had nearly killed him. 'Why, it's a map of the Aude,' he declared, 'as God is my witness.' We all began to chuckle. Godfrey pretended to take umbrage, pointing to the jagged scars one by one: 'Here's the Aube, here's the Seine, and this, bugger me if it's not the Yonne.' Count Robert laughed with us and Count Godfrey, brushing the hair from Robert's brow, bent to kiss him. I saw Godfrey wince with pain as he did so. Lord Raymond and I followed suit.

As we were leaving, however, Robert suddenly raised himself with much effort and took Godfrey's hand. 'Bohemund betrayed us,' he said. We stopped and stared at him. We were at a loss to credit it, but Robert persisted.

'He used us to lure the Turks . . . said he would attack as soon as they engaged us. Instead he waited until we were surrounded and the Turks had committed their reserves. Only then did he attack.

---

79 Asile: a room in which the sick were isolated.

By that time half my men were gone. An hour more and we all would have been killed. He had his victory at our expense.'

He lay back sweating, his eyes rolling up to stare at the ceiling. It was thick with spiders' webs that stretched down to the bedposts. I made to brush them away.

'No,' Count Robert said. 'They will remind me.'

None of us spoke of it until we entered the port of Antioch. Godfrey stared grimly at the massive dun walls stained with the smoke of our fires and the burning of corpses. 'Bohemund's got the fire up his ass,' he grumbled, 'and it's searing his insides.' He turned to us. 'A man like that . . .' he said, but he did not finish. It was not necessary.

The Bishop Adhémar announced to the army our success in securing provisions, which did much to lighten the men's spirits. He was soon enraged, however, to learn that in our absence Peter the Hermit had deserted with most of his men. Adhémar immediately dispatched fifty German knights to seize him and bring him back to the camp. This they did without a struggle, though Peter was roughly used by the Germans. When he was brought before us he was naked from the waist down, and his thighs and buttocks were livid with welts inflicted by the flats of swords.

Adhémar stood sternly over him, his arms folded across his chest. 'They say you are a saint,' he spat.

Peter looked up at him, his long hair tangled in wet strings across his face, his wrists bound before him. For a moment I thought he looked like the suffering Christ. He began to sob, and then to cry hysterically. Adhémar slapped him. All of us were stunned.

'You should be hanged,' he said. 'You thought to usurp the Holy Father's expedition. You thought to make a name for yourself in heaven. Well, we saw the corpses of the pilgrims in the valley at Nicaea, we saw the bones of women and babies that you led. And now, having deserted us, you stand before us and weep and expect forgiveness?'

Peter wiped his eyes upon the threadbare sleeve of his robe. He snuffled the mucus back in his throat and made an effort to stand upright. 'I ask nothing,' he said in a high, thin voice. 'I demand to be allowed to return to my home.'

With that a German knight struck him a blow on the back of the head. Peter staggered but just managed to catch himself.

Adhémar glared at him. 'You do not want forgiveness?' he said.

Peter looked straight at him. 'What need have I of forgiveness?' he replied. 'It is others who have sainted me, not I. I have done only what a man can do. Why should I be forgiven for that?'

Adhémar seemed confused. 'What of God?' he said.

Peter regarded him as if the question were stupid. 'It is God who forgives. Nothing else matters. If I have offended you in some way, I will seek my forgiveness from God, not from you. My soul is in His hands, not yours.'

On that, the Bishop Adhémar turned to glance at me, a kind of dark wonder in his eyes. Words passed between us, but not through our lips. He had coerced forgiveness from me, but it was not I who had the power to release him from his guilt. The realization seemed to shake him, and for a moment he appeared not to know where he was. I could not help but smile.

Adhémar collected himself, turned again to Peter, and made the sign of the Cross upon him, intoning: 'You shall stand for three days and three nights upon the hill above the Iron Gate. If the Turks do not slay you, neither shall I.' The German knights led him away.

I stopped Adhémar as he was leaving. 'Forgiveness is a blessed thing,' I said, 'though not as men forgive, but as God does.'

'You give too much credit to the Hermit's theology,' he said.

I replied: 'You give too little to your own. Can it be that in all those years while you simmered in your guilt over my family, you never sought your peace in God? Did you really wait only for me?'

Adhémar made to move past me but I seized his arm and held it. 'And in all those years, did you savour your sins? Did you enjoy them, in the comforting assurance that you were doomed?' He stared hard at me as I went on. 'Well, you are free of me now – you have no more excuse for your sins. And I am free of you. It is between ourselves and God. And that is as a pilgrimage should be, is it not?'

Adhémar pulled away his arm and straightened his cope. 'Duke Roger,' he replied, 'you should have been a bishop.'

His words puzzled me, but as I write this now, I realize that it was the highest compliment he could have paid me.

It is late and I must see to my men. The first ships from Cyprus arrive tomorrow. Therefore, to celebrate the end of our famine, we shall tonight eat all the provisions that remain to us. It will not be much of a feast, but it will be a happy one. I shall continue the account tomorrow.

FEBRUARY THE SEVENTH

I conclude the entry of last night.

On the night of our return from Cyprus the Greek general Tatikios requested a council of our leaders, at which he announced that he was leaving the army for Constantinople. He said that he had no doubt we would attempt an assault with the coming of spring, and it was therefore necessary to arrange for the transport of siege engines. His news was met with dismay and distrust. Bohemund, who did not attend the meeting, has been putting it around the camp that Tatikios believes we are beaten and that Antioch cannot be taken. When Count Godfrey confronted the Greek with this, he was at pains to deny it.

'You have been victorious so far,' he said. 'I have no doubt of you. I look to your supplies.'

We all responded at once that the emperor has done nothing in this regard all winter. Tatikios apologized in his name; all would be set right once he reached Constantinople. We insisted that he leave his staff behind as hostages. Reluctantly he agreed.

Now that he is gone, rumours sweep the camp. It is said that the emperor has made a pact with the Turks to destroy us, and that Tatikios will return with the Greek army. Others say that Alexius believes we are planning to murder him and that Tatikios has gone to warn him. Still others, that a Turkish army is approaching from the east, and Tatikios has fled in fear. The frenzy became such that a second council was called. This time, to our surprise, Count Bohemund attended.

'You want the truth?' he said. 'The truth is this: Alexius has abandoned us. He thinks we're finished. He's encouraging the Turks to attack; that way he hopes to keep what he has gained by us, even if it means sacrificing Antioch and Jerusalem. And ourselves, of course.'

Count Godfrey squinted at him. 'You believe this?' he said.

'I know it,' Bohemund replied, throwing down his gloves. I thought that his confidence bordered on glee. 'I have people in the city. They tell me that the word has already arrived. When the column from Damascus appears, they will throw open the gates and catch us between them. There will be no escape, for the Greeks intend to blockade the port of Saint Symeon.'

'Tatikios gave us his word,' Godfrey said.

'Tatikios is a Greek,' Bohemund spat. 'And a Turk before that. Take that for what it's worth.'

Godfrey glared at him. 'Is it worth the promise you gave to Robert of Flanders?' he asked.

There was silence. Bohemund stared hard at Godfrey, then at Lord Raymond. 'You weren't there,' he said slowly. 'You don't know what was needed.'

'I know what is needed now,' Lord Raymond replied. 'We must prepare for an assault at the earliest possible moment.'

Bohemund laughed. 'Then I wish you well. For I am going home.'

The words shocked us. Several men spoke at once, but Bohemund silenced them with a wave of his hand. 'I am a king,' he said, 'and a king remains distant from his land at risk. I'm not an educated man, but I know enough history and I've known enough scoundrels to understand that. You men could lose a manor house or an estate; I could lose Sicily which, though it stinks of garlic and unwashed women, is dear to me. I have been away two years. God knows what I shall find when I get back.'

Adhémar reminded him of his oath. 'Remind the Emperor Alexius of his,' was Bohemund's reply. 'As far as I'm concerned, all our oaths are voided.'

Again there was commotion. Lord Raymond spoke up. 'Bohemund of Taranto,' he said, 'we have been comrades for twenty years. I know you. You have abused our friend Robert, you have put rumours through the camp regarding the Greeks, you have threatened to leave . . .'

'And I shall,' Bohemund interrupted.

'You have not done this for mischief,' Lord Raymond went on, 'you have done it for a purpose. Tell us now, as men, what you want.'

Bohemund regarded us a long moment. 'Antioch,' he replied.

'God curse you,' Adhémar said.

'God bugger you, bishop,' retorted Bohemund.

Adhémar reached for his sword. Godfrey put a hand on it. 'Bohemund has been plain with us,' he said. 'Let's be plain with him. If we get into Antioch, it will be on the backs of soldiers from a dozen lands. The city belongs to no one man.'

'Now tell me it belongs to God,' scoffed Bohemund.

'Do you pray?' Godfrey said. The question caught him short. 'When these scars burned in my chest like hellfire,' Godfrey went on, 'I prayed to God. I promised that everything I won would be His if He would spare me to see my wife and home once more. God said yes to me.' He shook his head. 'I cannot now say no to Him.'

Bohemund looked around the ring of faces in the firelight. All of us were silent. He nodded as he picked up his gloves. 'Then I'm off,' he said.

The next day nothing happened. We all watched Bohemund's camp for signs of his army's departure, but there were none. It was as if the Count was waiting for us to change our minds. We did not. And so the following morning his pennants were struck and his soldiers began to load their carts. We looked on in silence, for every man knew that it meant the end of our pilgrimage.

It was in the midst of this that the courier came.

It would be difficult to imagine a man more covered in blood. His features were indistinguishable, his tunic was soaked from his shoulders to his knees. His saddle and the flanks of his horse were bloody, and as he rode into our camp, he clutched a hand to his forehead in desperation.

We tried to help him from his horse but he refused. He panted out that the Turks had moved in force on Harenc, our outpost on the road to Aleppo. The garrison there had been slaughtered; the Turks were preparing to march on Antioch. Then, having delivered his message, he took his hand from his forehead and the flesh of his face rolled down like a sodden cloth. He had been gashed from ear to ear, and suddenly his pink skull was exposed to us. He fell from the saddle into our arms. I never learned his name, but he was as brave a man as any in our armies.

Lord Raymond called a hasty council of war in Adhémar's pavilion. The news was not good. Of the two thousand knights left to us, only five hundred have horses. And of our seven thousand foot, scarcely three thousand are fit for battle. Urgings flew back and forth: some argued for an immediate assault on the city. Others insisted that we withdraw across the river towards Armenia. Lord Raymond favoured an attack on Harenc, while leaving a garrison at Antioch to hold our position.

'Without Bohemund we have not enough men,' the Bishop Adhémar said. 'We dare not attempt it.'

'You have enough,' came a voice from the entrance. We all turned. Bohemund stood behind us in battle attire. 'Raymond is right. We take the knights and as many infantry as can make a quick march and we move on Harenc. The rest we leave here — every man who can stand, and all the dismounted knights. We blockade the bridges and hold them inside the city. Meanwhile, we surprise the Turks on the march.'

Not another word was passed. We all returned at once to our pavilions. We set out tonight to be in position before dawn.

February the Tenth

It is two days since our battle, but I have been too weak to write. I shall attempt it now, but shall be brief.

We left our camp with some seven hundred knights and a thousand of the fittest infantry, and made a forced march across the bridge of boats to the shore of the Lake of Antioch. There between the river and the lake we awaited the Turks, our horses muzzled, their hooves wrapped in sacking, our men in total silence. The knights stood in front in three ranks, with our frail line of infantry behind. All through the chilly night we waited and then, just before sunrise, we heard their hoofbeats.

They were coming, as we expected, around the western shore of the lake towards the Iron Gate, where they hoped to enter the city in secret. To do so they would have to pass directly across our front. We waited for their main body to reach us, and then the Normans and Germans attacked.

They hurled themselves with wild cries upon the Turkish archers, terrifying them in the dim light and throwing them into confusion. But our attackers numbered scarcely a hundred and they soon withdrew, followed closely by the Turkish cavalry. It was our plan. The Normans and Germans drew them into the narrow plain between the river and the lake where our main body waited. Unable to manoeuvre or to flank us, the Turks came straight on. We held ourselves until they were well inside our trap, and then attacked again with our full strength.

They were overwhelmed. Our charge smashed into their front and sent it reeling back. The effect on those behind was devastating. They broke and fled back down the plain, trampling one another and crushing their archers, who had never had time to form. We swept them before us like wildfowl, and indeed, many tried to escape across the river and the lake and were drowned.

Prince Hugh of Vermandois, who had volunteered to command the infantry at the rear, now moved forward to kill the stragglers. These were systematically being put to the sword when Lord Raymond made his way back and forbade any further slaughter. He ordered Prince Hugh to round up the captives and secure the battleground. The Prince replied that he would accede to a request, not an order. Lord Raymond, who was winded and soaked with sweat and grime, repeated his instruction in the bitterest courtesy that I have ever heard. The brother of the king was satisfied.

The front had been so narrow that I had had difficulty closing with the Turks. Since I was still fresh, I offered to lead a flying column towards Harenc to seize the garrison there. Lord Raymond agreed and I quickly rounded up some fifty knights, the closest to hand, and set out in advance of the main column.

Harenc is an ancient fortress upon a hill surrounded by a cluster of crude shacks. I did not wish to allow the Turks time to prepare a defence, and so ordered a charge straight through the village. Our men became separated as they galloped among the hovels, and I was in the process of forming them again when I felt a sudden stinging in my thigh. I glanced down to see the shaft of an arrow protruding from my surcoat. Somehow it had found a chink in my mail and had passed nearly through my leg.

I expected to feel a pain but when none came I called to the others to charge up the hill for the fort. It was in ill repair, with many gaps in the weathered stone, and we were inside before the Turks could flee. They surrendered almost at once.

It was only after I had posted guards upon the prisoners that I took time to attend to my wound. In the charge up the hill or in the brief fight within the fort the shaft had broken off, so that now only a frayed stump protruded. Two of my companions helped me from Fatana and into a room off the courtyard. It was, by the look of it, some sort of storehouse, for sacks were everywhere, covered with vermin and huge, slithering roaches.

A bearded Englishman stood over me, gesturing at my leggings. It was a moment before I realized what he meant. I undid the braces and he carefully removed them. I was feeling giddy and kept on laughing in spite of myself, for I could see the point of the arrow inside my leg, pressing against the flesh just below the groin.

I tried to grasp the broken stump of the shaft with my fingers but it was too short. By now I was growing light-headed and feared that I might faint, for the flush of the battle had worn off and the first waves of pain were rising in me.

Several men were standing in the entrance of the storeroom and I called to them to leave, but they understood not a word and remained, looking on stupidly. They all were Englishmen, and I wondered how I could have surrounded myself at such a time with foreigners.

The bearded man called to his friends to hold me down and, though I protested, they took me by the shoulders. Then he knelt and pressed in with his thumbs on either side of the shaft, took the stump between his teeth, and drew back his head. I screamed. He drew again, and I bit at the sleeve of my hauberk. The shaft was coming out, but more slowly than I could bear.

I yelled at him to pull it out and tried to free my arms to do it myself. I could feel the point, which was barbed, tearing its way through my leg. Then it reached the skin and, with a sudden jerk, the Englishman pulled it out. 'Voici, voici!' he said to me as he held the thing up. The others slapped me on the shoulders. The

Englishman then bound my thigh with a piece of sacking, and he and his companions helped me outside.

The English knights were slaughtering the Turks. I yelled at them at once to stop, but none could understand me. They continued with their work as coldly and with as much indifference as if they were cleaning fish. I would have stopped them somehow, but at that moment I collapsed.

When I awoke again the stars were out. I was feverish but a cool night breeze soothed me. I lay upon a rampart of the fort, wrapped in a rough blanket, my leg heavy and throbbing. The courtyard below was crowded with corpses, and among them a few women who had accompanied the Turks to Harenc were being raped, the Englishmen standing in orderly lines to take their turns.

I was sick at heart, but there was nothing I could do. I lay back feeling helpless and exhausted, listening to the wails of the women. It sounded to me like the slaughtering of sheep, or the wind in the desert beyond Nicaea, mournful and full of emptiness. Just then the English knight approached me. He stood over me grimly, holding in his hand a length of iron which, I could see, was white hot. He motioned with his head and his companions pressed down my shoulders. The Englishman lowered the rod and poked it into my wound. I screamed, but he pushed it in, working it slowly back and forth until it emerged on the inner side. Then, as I howled and wept, he drew it out again. One of his companions handed him another. I stared at it in horror, and then I fainted.

FEBRUARY THE TWENTIETH

I can walk now with the aid of a crutch that Mansour has made for me. As soon as I was able, I went to the camp of the Englishmen to speak to their chief. I did not know his name, and had to ask several men before I learned that he is called Osbert of Ipswich. I demanded to be taken to him, but no one seemed to know where he was.

At last I found a knight who had been with me at Harenc, one of those who had held me down while the arrow was removed, and he agreed to lead me to this man. The English encampment, while neatly laid out, is intricate, consisting of many twisting allées and cunning pits where provisions are concealed, so that a stranger might easily lose himself without a guide. I supposed, as I hobbled along, that such was the intention.

My companion led me to a very crude but sprawling shelter, built more below the level of the ground than above, and made me understand I was to wait. He bent nearly double and entered and, in a few minutes, re-emerged followed by an exceedingly tall, thin man with a long face and a few wisps of hair stretched over his skull. This was Osbert, the chieftain of the English.

He invited me in broken Langue d'oïl to enter, but with my leg it was impossible. I thanked him and declined, and explained as simply as I could that I wished to protest about the behaviour of his men at Harenc.

'You mean the slaughter of the Turks?' he said.

'And the raping,' I replied.

'The raping?' he repeated in some surprise. 'Did they not behave properly? Did they not stand in line?' I assured him that they had, but that it made no difference to me, or to the women. 'Why,' he said haughtily, 'it makes all the difference in the world. We are not animals in Britain. We observe the forms.'

I was far too weak to argue. I requested that if, in future, I should have the pleasure to command his men, he instruct them to obey my orders. He assured me in some dudgeon that they most certainly would if they could understand them. I thanked him and left.

The English are a strange race indeed. They have as much in common with us as do the creatures of the sea. And God be thanked for the sea that separates our peoples.

MARCH THE FOURTH

Our condition improves, as does the weather. The destruction of the relief column has cheered our men, and the Cypriot ships dock regularly, bringing supplies. An English fleet has arrived from Constantinople, its ships heavy with the siege engines promised by Tatikios. It appears that we misjudged this Greek. Food is not plentiful but we are no longer starving. My leg aches a good deal and continues swollen. Mansour, with his usual care, bathes and massages it. Each evening he brings out a great deal of pus.

I have written no verse. It is odd. As I look back over it, I see that I have written about love and loss and the loftiness I felt above Nicaea. Here there is nothing of that. A siege is like a lingering death, a regimen so boring and mechanical that one goes through the motions of preserving one's life and inflicting death on the enemy with scarcely a thought.

Every morning the engines start up, flinging rocks and Greek fire into the city with a dull monotony that continues all the day. Our men have transferred the routine of their villages to this place where, instead of being about the business of living, they go about that of death. There are alarms, as when the Turks raid our supply carts on their way from the port, or when they launch excursions against our outposts through the Iron Gate. Then we have some bother as the men rouse themselves to drive them off. A few bodies are left behind and handfuls of wounded, whose pitiful cries are never absent from the camp.

We are like soldier ants here before the brown walls of Antioch. How I have come to hate those walls. Some of us tend to the machines, some to guard, some to transporting supplies, others to mending weapons. The sluggish back-and-forth movement of dirty, dispirited men never stops, not even at night. And through it all we observe the customs of our race: mass, confession, morning prayers, noontide prayers, evening prayers, feasts of the saints, holy days. We are ground down by this siege to the bare minimum of existence, yet every so often there is some ray of light — a soldier who keeps a garden, a knight who sets a challenge of strength or swordsmanship, and even music.

There are certain soldiers, clever men of the Auvergne, who have fashioned instruments from cast-off equipment. They have made rebecs and viols, pipes and mandolins, and they have banded together to make entertainment. Now that the rain has stopped and the evenings are tolerably warm they play for us, and I must confess they have become rather good.

They perform the *estampie real*[80] as well as any I have heard in France, and the man who sings the counter tenor, a big bearded fellow, is especially good. Last night he sang the *Parti de Mal* so movingly that many among us cried, especially at the words: 'I have left evil behind me, I have turned to a good life. God has called to us in His need, and no worthy man can fail Him. Those whom God allows to return will be greatly honoured. He who has loved faithfully must keep alive the memory of his love wherever he goes.'

Such moments remind us of the nature of our expedition even more so than the sermons of the priests. We have been so long at this work and have endured so much that we have become new men, perhaps not better than when we left, but surely different. And I think that, until we return to our homes, none of us will know the true nature and depth of that difference.

I think of home not at all these days. I would not have mentioned it here except that Mansour came in to tend to my leg and asked whether I were writing of it. I told him no.

'Do you never write to your wife, Effendi?' he asked as he unwrapped the wound. 'The English sailors could take your letters.'

The question hurt me. In two years I have not written to her,

---

80 A lively instrumental tune with a quick beat.

though other men have managed to send letters home. And the only word I have received from her plunged me into despair.

'Perhaps I should,' I said.

'You are angry with her?' The wound was tender, though coated with scab. 'Does this hurt you, Effendi?' Mansour asked as he kneaded the flesh around it.

'Not so much as before,' I replied. 'Yes, I was angry with my wife, but no more.'

'That is good,' Mansour said. 'You see, there is no pus. Just a little clear liquid, like tears. It is a good sign.' I thanked him for his solicitude. He bathed my thigh with a soft sponge while I thought calmly of Jehanne for the first time in weeks. 'With your permission?' Mansour said. I glanced down from my reverie.

'Oh, of course,' I replied. I pulled back my tunic and he washed my groin above the wound. I had had no erection save for night emissions since my drunken days in the port. Now I felt a vague stirring as he gently drew the sponge over my flesh. I realized that I had not been touched with tenderness in over two years, indeed, since before that time. I have not felt gentle fingers, have had no love caress, have not been handled like a man who is loved for longer than I can remember.

Involuntarily I sighed and laid back my head. Mansour went on, oblivious. What can such a creature know of lofty love? And what can he know of the guilt of love that drags it down to earth and chains it there with passion? What do I know of love who have never felt it except in my loins?

I have loved God, yes, but God is a dream, a wish, an exaltation. One can love God with the soul, but the mind remains a prisoner of the body, and the body remains a slave to lust. And so, while the soul is God and the love of God, man himself remains apart, a stranger, alone between heaven and earth.

Such thoughts did Mansour's ministrations provoke in me. Can man truly love in the flesh? Can the soul be made flesh? Can one truly join one's spirit with another? Or are we condemned to languish in the prison of our bodies, scratching at the walls to let in light, listening to the invisible songs outside?

'You are sorrowful, Effendi,' said Mansour.

I gazed at his withered face beneath the twisted turban. 'I am lonely,' I replied.

He glanced sidelong up at me a moment. It was rare that he allowed his eyes to meet mine. Then he said, 'With your permission,' and he carefully lowered my tunic to my knees. He got up to go.

'Mansour,' I said. He turned slightly. 'I will write to my wife. You will take the letter to the English captain.'

He bowed. 'Very well, Effendi,' he said, and went out.

MARCH THE SIXTH

Lord Raymond summoned us to say that the attacks of the Turks upon our supply columns have become intolerable. They take every opportunity to intercept the caravans from the port, sometimes in bold daylight raids, sometimes by treachery, as when they disguise themselves in captured clothing or even as monks and slit the throats of the sailors to make off with the loads. They must be starving in the city to devise such stratagems.

As a result, Lord Raymond has commanded a tower to be built on the riverbank to guard the road from Saint Symeon. Meanwhile he has ordered the transport guard doubled, and will himself command the squadron which will accompany the convoy of siege engines from the English ships. Should these be lost, our hopes for the spring assault will vanish with them.

MARCH THE NINTH

A fearsome time. On the morning following my last entry, Lord Raymond set out for the port with forty knights to fetch up the siege machines. Count Bohemund insisted upon accompanying him, from mistrust I suppose, taking with him another score of knights. By midday there was no sign of them, but at the thirteenth hour a messenger came at the gallop, shouting that the convoy had been attacked in strength, the siege machines had been captured, and Lords Raymond and Bohemund were slaughtered.

The words chilled me to my heart. My Lord dead, and Bohemund too? I ordered Mansour to bring Fatana and struck him on the face when he demurred. He slunk away and came back with the horse, but I felt no pity for him; all my thoughts were with Lord Raymond. Mansour helped me into the saddle. I took no time to put on mail but grabbed up my sword and shield, snatched a lance from a stand nearby and joined the other men who were rallying to the port.

The scene was horrible. Dozens of knights lay dead and wounded along the road. We did not stop, but rode straight on for the Turks who were labouring with the engines towards the Gate of Saint George. From the walls archers fired at us, but we were too far and the arrows fell among their fellows, further slowing them.

I was maddened, crazed. I galloped towards them, outstripping the other horsemen. The Turks saw us coming, let go the machines, and turned to fight. Some had lances but most short swords. I made for the man nearest me, lowered my lance and drove it through him. It broke as he fell, the bell jamming painfully against my ribs, nearly unseating me. I threw the stump of it down and waded in among the Turks.

'The engines!' someone yelled. 'Save the engines!' But I cared nothing for the engines. I swung at a Turk and my sword split his cheek. I caught another under the chin and opened his throat. A spear glanced off my leg. I turned and saw the man preparing to strike again. I kicked out and felt a terrible pain in my leg. He went down and I trampled him.

By now several hundred knights had joined the fight, but Turks were pouring from the city to aid the raiders, and the archers were reaching us now from the walls. By this time Count Godfrey had come up and he moved at once to seize the bridge and prevent more Turks from crossing. It was a hot, heavy fight but I was driven by fury. I fought not well but blindly; I wanted to kill as many of them as I could. I felt as though they had murdered my own father and I wanted them to die too.

I could see that the Turks were making for the gate and I shouted at the others to cut them off. We worked our way around behind them and threw ourselves across the road, blocking their path. By this time we had formed a circle entirely around the raiders and had cut them off from reinforcement. They were trapped against the machines they had sought to steal and we were driving them further and further within the circle. I felt the heady prospect of massacre.

Then I heard shouting from behind and when I turned I saw a miracle. My Lord Raymond was coming at the gallop, leading a handful of knights, his head naked, his white hair flowing, and beside him Count Bohemund, frothing at the mouth and shouting. They pitched in beside us and within the hour every Turk upon the field was dead.

I made my way to Raymond, exhilarated and exhausted. He frowned. 'Roger, you should not be horsed,' he greeted me. I told him I had thought him dead. 'All the more reason to spare yourself,' said he.

We rode back to the camp together and parties were immediately sent to fetch in the machines. We had lost upwards of a hundred knights, but the Turks upon the field, the dead and the wounded who were quickly killed, were numbered at thirteen hundred.

Lord Raymond helped me to my tent where Mansour took charge of me. My wound had opened again, and he fretted over it like a woman, declaring that I had undone all his good work. I did not care. 'You see,' I said to him, pointing, 'Lord Raymond lives. He has come back from the dead. We are not orphans.'

Mansour helped me to my tent and laid me down. I was dizzy but happy. The blood soaked my leggings and as he peeled them off the scabs came away with sucking sounds. But nothing mattered to me. My Lord was safe and I was content, though I had killed half a dozen men.

That night there was a stirring in the camp. I went outside to see. Men were standing on every side peering into the darkness towards where the battle had been. At first I thought they saw ghosts, for shapes were moving furtively along the road below the Saint George Gate. No one spoke. Shadows, at first one or two, then dozens, then scores, were moving among the corpses. 'Robbers?' I said to a man nearby.

He shook his head. 'Friends,' he replied.

It was true. The Turks had sent out parties to bury their dead, and not a man among us had the heart to stop them. By dawn every one of the thirteen hundred corpses had been buried. I thought it a noble thing on the part of our men, for the Turks worked unmolested all night long, reverently, without a sound. Perhaps some good will come of this fighting, I thought. Perhaps we strangers, with so little in common among us, have learned to respect one another.

But then, the next night, word having spread that the Turks bury their dead with silver and gold, scavengers went out from our own army to rob the graves. The next morning arms and legs and heads protruded from the soft earth, and the place that had seemed to me to be suddenly sacred was just as suddenly a rubbish heap of ideals.

MARCH THE FIFTEENTH

The siege engines, which cost so many lives, are being assembled, and Lord Raymond's tower is nearly finished. It is being built upon a hill next to a mosque. The Greek engineers wanted to demolish this structure and use the stones, but Raymond has given order that the mosque is not to be disturbed. Our supplies are growing and the weather continues fair. For the first time since I reached Antioch five months ago, I am hopeful.

We have had visitors. Two days past a fleet of slender ships with painted sails the shape of diamonds slid into the port. A parade of half-naked black men then appeared, carrying in a sedan a very noble-looking man in white robes, his shaved head topped by a gold skull cap. This was none other than al-Afdal the Magnificent, of whom none of us had heard, the Grand Vizier of Egypt, and emissary of the boy king al-Mustali. Our leaders greeted him in state, for the Greeks assure us that he is a very great man in his own country, and much revered among the heathens.

His mission was frank. He proposed to us an alliance whereby Egypt would provide for our army and make trouble along the Turks' southern borders, in return for which we would cede to Egypt the lower part of Syria. Since this would include Jerusalem our leaders declined, but for the first time the idea took hold among us that perhaps it is possible to treat with the Muslims.

To this point we had thought of them as one race. Now these Egyptians have made us realize that there are divisions among them, even as there are among Christians. We had assumed that every Muslim in the district would aid the Turks for the sake of religion; now we have reason to believe that there are rivalries among them which might be exploited.

It is a timely realization, for we have heard for some weeks a rumour that a powerful sultan called Ker-boga is raising armies in the east to relieve Antioch.[81] These rumours have been seconded by

81 Karbuqa or Kerbogha, was the atabeg of Mosul, and one of the most powerful and influential leaders of the Muslim world. A former slave, Karbuqa had risen to become the official 'father of the prince' of Mosul, the capital of Mesopotamia, in modern-day Iraq. Even in the eleventh century Mosul was famous for its oil, which was valued for its medicinal uses.

Tancred, who has rejoined our army, as well as by spies whom Bohemund has captured. We are told that the Muslim world is mounting a holy war to destroy us, and its leaders are calling troops from as far away as Persia and Mesopotamia.

The Bishop Adhémar has therefore sent a delegation to the emir at Damascus and to other cities to the south requesting their neutrality. In return, we are promising them no harm, and that we will respect their rights within their own territories. Surely if we can separate these heathens one from another, our work here will be easier. I only regret that we did not adopt this tactic earlier.

I am nearly crippled now and confined to my pavilion. Mansour has stripped away the winter coverings and cleaned the place out, and so it is not unpleasant for me to spend whole days upon my back following the progress of our preparations for the assault. I find in my convalescence that I have many friends in the army who come by from time to time to chat with me. Landry Gros and his countryman Fulk Rechin visit me from the Norman camp, as do the Germans with whom I caroused in the port. I confess that their visits cause me shame.

Bernard and Gérard also attend on me, bringing me 'treats' as they call them, all manner of nonsense from sweetmeats to children's toys. They are reformed completely, and have thanked me for my discipline. I think no more of it and tell them so. Bernard assures me that when we reach Jerusalem he will marry and go into trade. Gérard makes it always a point to speak of his wife. They are good men, and like all good men they are better for having fallen. And they have not deserted, as have so many of their kind, which I take as a tribute to myself. Perhaps I have done some good on this pilgrimage.

MARCH THE NINETEENTH
The Feast of Saint Joseph

We had a spectacle last night which I hope never to see repeated. Bohemund produced the spies whom he has captured, eight ragged, fearful-looking men much worn down with beatings and starvation. They are for the most part Armenians in the service of the Turks, though one was a Greek and another of mixed parentage. From them he had extracted all the information he was likely to get; it seems they have been reporting to Yagashan on our numbers, positions, morale, plans, and even our names and origins. This information, Bohemund declared, has been relayed to Ker-boga to aid him in his preparations to attack us.

The men of our army were naturally incensed and demanded their deaths. Bohemund had anticipated them. The spies were taken to a pit dug in the earth where fires had been prepared. Then, as the soldiers cheered, they were spitted and roasted alive. It was a horrible sight and I turned from it, but I could not escape the smell. It hung on the air like paste, and I snorted to get it out of my nostrils. It is said that some of our men ate flesh from the bodies. Bohemund assures us that there will be no more spies in our army. I am inclined to agree.

On this, the feast of the father of Our Saviour, my thoughts bend to my own father. I shall attend mass and pray for him to intercede with God at whose throne he stands that I may be a son worthy of his memory. I am making an effort to reform myself. I have engaged in no promiscuity, I keep a rein on my evil thoughts, I am attempting to restore the balance of my faith which has been shaken by events. Of the men I have slain I make my own repentance since the priest will not hear me confess their deaths as sins. 'They are pagans,' he says, 'and have no souls.' That may be, but I have a soul, and late at night it aches for what I have done.

APRIL THE FIRST

I have charged Mansour with the care of my horse during my convalescence. At first he declined to exercise her but I insisted that he run her daily. I am astonished to see how well he mounts; as if he had been bred to it. I suppose that among his people horsemanship is a skill, though it occurs to me now that I do not know who his people are. Indeed, although this man has served me for nearly a year I know almost nothing about him.

Our emissaries to the Turks have returned, and the news is disappointing. None of the emirs would give earnest of neutrality, though neither did they seem anxious to come to Antioch's relief. Better news has arrived from the north, however. The Emperor Alexius is moving with a large army to support us.

This is especially welcome as the rumours continue that Kerboga is assembling the Muslim host at Mosul. So insistent and elaborate are these rumours that they begin to have an effect upon the men. Some speak of a Turkish army of thirty thousand, while our own forces have now been reduced to some two thousand knights and eighteen thousand of foot. Of the knights, fewer than five hundred still have their mounts, and so we have sent to Baldwin at Edessa for horses, and are buying up every animal in the district.

I thank God that He has preserved Fatana so long and so well. With the increase of fodder and the regular exercise she regains her old form. Her flanks are full, her eyes are clear, the gloss is on her coat, and her old spirit and intelligence have returned to her. Just this morning she put her head in at my pavilion to wake me and enquire about my health. I assured her that I was well and would soon be testing her upon the hills and flat-out across the plain of Antioch. She brushed that challenge off with a snort and went on her way with Mansour.

Spring is truly here. Even wild flowers bloom about the camp, the view towards the harbour is fine, and a heaviness seems to have been lifted from the troops. Many are still boys, and the spring-time calls to them, but the Bishop of Le Puy has given strict orders that no women are to be allowed into the camp. A prostitute, seized the other night in the midst of venery, was stripped naked and hung upside down for an example. Everyone came to look, including the priests.

April the Twelfth

There have been rains, and the ditches about the camp fill up again. This is always unsettling, since body parts are invariably washed down into the camp, throwing the men into a gloomy mood. I woke this morning to find an arm and shoulder bobbing in the stream outside my door. It lay there, caught in the mud by its fingers, the shoulder blade, with its severed bone like a shank of meat, moving back and forth before the current. I wondered for a moment whose it was, and then kicked it clear with my foot and watched it slide away towards the river.

The Muslim cemetery on the heights above the city has been nearly washed away. Now there is a hill sprouting skeletons that whiten with every day. Some begin to glow under the moon as did the bones in the pass at Nicaea, a grim phosphorescence that catches the eye no matter how one tries to avoid it.

I am melancholy tonight and do not think I should write more since I fear my mood. I do not want to slip into depression on such a calm night. I want to enjoy it, especially the scent that is breeze-borne from the fields where the first grasses are growing, and that is so sweet it almost masks the odour of the dead.

Alexius is said to be at Dorylaeum – his is a slow progress – and Ker-boga is rumoured to be moving on Edessa. If Baldwin fails and the road to Antioch opens, it is then a question of who will arrive here first, the emperor or the Turk. Our fate approaches, one way or the other.

EASTER SUNDAY

Père Raimund of Aguillères preached a sermon today that has caused a stir in camp. Usually placid, even mystic, he was this morning in a foul mood. He declared that there have not been enough miracles among us lately, and that this is due to a lack of faith. Now it is true that men have reported miracles, including, as I recall, a goose that spoke, statues that bled or wept, wounds healed with the application of relics, and most recently, the lights in the sky following the earthquake.

Of these miracles I have myself witnessed only the last, and though I do believe that it was the souls of our dead ascending into heaven, the others I hold to be fictions or fancy. Nonetheless, the men set great store by them and they are harmless for the most part.

I say that they are harmless for the most part since I cannot forget the example of the little daughter of Baldwin who, in her dying days, was believed to have miraculous powers. The priests exploited her and the soldiers gave her not a minute's peace. I learned later that, after her death, her body was dug up and torn to bits for relics. There followed a brisk trade in the camp for babies' bones, with the result that no child for miles around was safe. Even the Bishop of Le Puy was scandalized, and threatened to excommunicate any soldier found with an infant body part upon his person.

After mass this morning, in the conclave with the nobles, Adhémar seconded Père Raimund, declaring that we must pray harder for miracles since they prove God's favour and raise the morale of the men. 'I want more!' he said. 'I don't care what they are or how you get them.' We left in some consternation, for nothing in our training as gentlemen and soldiers has prepared us to produce miracles.

What struck me more than this in Père Raimund's sermon was his reference to a journal. He stated that he has kept careful account of the miracles in this journal, the first indication I have had that anyone but myself and the renegade priest Fulcher has kept a journal. I call him renegade because he left with Baldwin and has not returned to us, and even when he was here he was imperious and haughty. Indeed, he used to threaten us with his book, saying that we would go down in eternity as scoundrels if he willed it so. For myself I know of no book that is eternal save the Scriptures, and so I assume Fulcher compares himself to their Author.

I am tempted to approach Père Raimund and ask to see his journal, but he has become so strange, so otherworldly, that one can scarcely speak to him. He has no shelter, but sits cross-legged on a mound with arms outstretched, day and night, rain or no. As often as not he speaks in tongues, and he smells so foul that it is difficult to be near him. No one goes to him for confession any more since you must kneel so far from him that you have to shout, and everyone hears your sins. His beard is very long and infested with vermin, and even his clothing wriggles with them when he is still. It is said he is longing for the stigmata, and some there are who swear they have seen the wounds upon him.[82] But he is so thin and frail that I doubt he has enough blood left in him to achieve it.

It has been instructive to live day after day with the clerics of this pilgrimage. At home they were familiar but distinct, a separate class, almost a separate species. As a child I thought there were four sexes in humanity — men, women, priests and nuns. And indeed we are brought up to revere them, which serves their purposes well since it confers on them a kind of nobility, whether they are born to it or not.

But living with them on the march and in camps, seeing their behaviour in every kind of situation from battle to daily chores, has

82 The stigmata: the so-called five wounds of Christ, a phenomenon ascribed to certain Christian mystics, in which the hands, feet and side spontaneously bleed.

altered my view of them. First and foremost they are men like me, in their weaknesses and strengths, and because of their lofty state even these are magnified. The worst of them are hypocrites, cowards and villains. The best are simply good men, who will stand with you in a fight and kneel with you in despair, and not put on any airs save the sanctity of Christian caring. I thought this of Adhémar until he unmasked himself, and I thought it of Aguillères until he mystified himself.[83] But I have been disabused.

Lately, however, I have found a priest who, I think, is a solid man and a worthy cleric, and to him have I been making my confession. He is, oddly enough, a Spaniard of Castille, Frey Alfonso of the monastery of Ripoll. He was once a landowner and soldier and took part in the campaigns against the Moors. In trophy of this he lacks an ear, and bears a purple scar upon his face. But his demeanour is one of great simplicity and frankness, and his words are always few and to the point. In short, he seems a true man of God.

Frey Alfonso speaks Provençal well, for he often had business in Montpellier, and we have had many and long talks in the evenings about the camp. He is chaplain to Diaz, lord of the Spanish knights, and is largely responsible for the piety and rectitude they have shown throughout the expedition. I would judge he is a man of forty, with a rich voice and a sonorous accent punctuated by the lisp of his native dialect. He wears a soldier's tunic and does not shave his hair, and is distinguishable from a common infantryman only by the simple wooden cross he wears around his neck.

Upon his first visit to my pavilion, after Mansour had served and left us, Frey Alfonso asked me about him. I told him what I had recently learned; that he was, as I had thought, a Circassian who has lived long in Syria, taking up Turkish ways and a Turkish name, that he spoke several languages and had worked at many trades, and that he had no family except, as he said, for me.

83 The expression here is deliberately chosen to convey a blend of mysticism and mystification, or confusion.

Frey Alfonso nodded, and then he said: 'His eyes are brown.' I remarked that I had never noticed. 'Usually those of Circassians are blue,' the priest said. 'But it is likely that he is of mixed parentage. He speaks quite excellent Provençal. Have you heard him speak his native language?' I replied that I had not. 'It is called Adigue, and I am told that it is quite beautiful. The Circassians are famous for their songs. You must have him sing for you sometime.'

We then continued our discussion of my wife, which we had begun some time before. Frey Alfonso agreed with Mansour that I ought to write to her, saying, 'She is not evil but profligate. It is not uncommon in the women of Europa, and it is a cross to many men. Do you intend to put her away?'

I answered that I could not make up my mind.

Frey Alfonso considered this. 'You have the benefit of this holy pilgrimage to rectify your soul,' he said at last, 'but she has no such advantage. She requires guidance and forgiveness of you, or she may remain in error. It would be un-Christian to deny it her. Then, if she continues in her sin, you may wish to put her away before God and the law. But remember,' he added, raising a finger, 'you may never again take wife so long as she lives.'

I have written a letter to Jehanne, which I have given to Mansour to take to the captain of the British fleet. It was a long and painful writing, which I started and destroyed many times.

I wrote that I have been tormented by doubts of her fidelity, and I demanded that she tell me the truth. I told her that, if my suspicions are justified, I am prepared to forgive her, provided that she cease her illicit relations, confess herself to the priest, and beg pardon of my mother and sister, whom she has disgraced. I further instructed her to speak daily to the priest, who will be her earnest of good conduct until I return, should God grant me that favour. If she does all this, nothing more will be said on the matter, and we will resume our lives together, although there will, of course, be no more intercourse between us. Otherwise, I concluded, she will be put away with no provision made for her.

It is a harsh judgement. I know well what divorce will mean for her. With no family of her own and no right to remarry, it would be a sentence of destitution, perhaps even of death. But in such matters there can be no middle ground, or marriage becomes a prison in which man and woman are forced to live, silent, suspicious, resentful.

The truth is, I do not wish to put her away, for I have no desire to live alone, and there is a tenderness in me for her which has become softer and stronger with distance and time. It is a longing that is not akin to lust so much as that which a brother might feel for his sister, or a father for his child. And indeed, my lust having been quenched in me, I do desire her now as a companion, one whom I have known, and who has known me, for many years.

As I write I wonder – can this be true? Would it be true were I to see her again, to touch her again? I think it may be so; I believe it. For I no longer desire sex as I did before, when it seemed impossible to live without it. I amuse myself these days with the memory of it. I will not have children with her and, so, why this sweating exercise? And yet, if sex was all the substance of our marriage, then to what should I look forward if not that? Having put that aside, what shall we be to one another?

She is not intelligent or cultivated. Indeed, she is hardly educated. What shall we talk of? Can I have with her the conversations I have had with my confessors and with my comrades – conversations about God and man and passion? No. I think that I have never had a conversation with Jehanne on anything of substance; I think I would not wish to do so. And so why should we remain together? And why do I not tell myself to put her away?

Is it because of Eustace? Is he a bond between us? Did not the passion flow from that guilt? But why does that guilt, having been confessed and done penance for, still haunt me? I have killed men with my arm, with my two hands, that I feel less remorse for than him whom I slaughtered with my lust. Is marriage a penance for me now? Is that why I cannot let her go? Is she the sponge to my sin; is she, as Alfonso said, my cross?

Involuntarily I glance at my shoulder. There is the scarlet Cross, much faded and worn, that she sewed upon my tunic. But in doing so, was she sewing herself into my pilgrimage? Is my true pilgrimage, with its faint hope of salvation, my marriage to her? And if I break it off, do I then condemn myself to hell?

Hell in life, with hope of salvation. Or release in life with certainty of hell. Is that the choice I face? And if so, what have I done that might merit it? It is right that the Church forbids divorce, for divorce condemns us to death, either here or in the next life. I thought to run after Mansour and fetch my letter back. But it is too late – it is sent. And it being sent, God will that I may not survive this pilgrimage.

MAY THE SIXTH

Ker-boga has invested Edessa with an army said to number fifty-thousand men. The news has caused tumult in our camp. Couriers have been dispatched to Alexius, of whom we have had no news since he entered the plain beyond Dorylaeum. We could not possibly withstand an onslaught by such a force, especially as it will be backed by an attack from the city. We will be caught in between and crushed. Not a man of us will be left alive.

Men desert now in such numbers that we cannot stop them. The situation we face is so grave that a council was called to determine, not whether we should attempt an escape, but who would lead it. None of the commanders – Lord Raymond, Bohemund, Godfrey, Robert of Normandy or Robert of Flanders – would agree to lead a retreat. Only Hugh of Vermandois came forward, but he was deemed too unreliable. It was therefore decided that, if Edessa falls, Stephen of Blois will take command of the withdrawal. It is ironic in the extreme: Baldwin was thought a traitor, eager only for his own profit; now the future of our entire expedition is in his hands. Withstand, Baldwin, for our sakes as well as your own.

MAY THE TENTH

Things move rapidly and darkly now. The bishop has proclaimed excommunication and eternal damnation irreversible to any man who deserts. This has eased the flow somewhat, though not entirely: some there are who will rather face the wrath of God than of Kerboga. It is said that the Christians he has captured around Edessa have been mutilated horribly. They have been flogged, flayed, boiled, emasculated, or sold into slavery. Every captive has a Cross branded on his face as a sign of his condition, and those so marked are entitled to be abused by everyone through whose hands they pass.

I have never seen our men so ill content. They grumble openly at their commanders with real venom, and not good-naturedly as they had used to do. I have even heard reports of commanders being attacked by their men. They say that we have led them into a trap, that we have sacrificed them for a dream of priests. The Marseillais under my command behave no better. At first I tried reasoning with them, and when that failed, resorted to threats. But nothing save the prospect of damnation sways their minds. To that end I have had Frey Alfonso speak to them, as both a soldier and a priest. That they are still susceptible to my authority is due in large part to his influence.

Edessa, meanwhile, continues to hold, but all news from Baldwin is cut off by the Turkish siege. There will be a council tonight, called by Count Bohemund. What he will propose short of abandoning the expedition I cannot imagine. I see now that I was wrong to scoff at Père Raimund's call for miracles.

MAY THE ELEVENTH

The council last night was a scene of great contention. Count Bohemund declared that the Emperor Alexius has ceased his advance and is waiting to learn whether we will take Antioch or be annihilated by Ker-boga. In the former case he will march quickly to claim the city; in the latter, he will withdraw and treat with the Turks to retain the possessions we have won.

None of us could deny the truth of it. Bohemund turned to the Bishop Adhémar. 'Where are the reinforcements your Greek priest promised us in his appeal? And what of the food he has sent? Hardly a feast, for which you, bishop, surrendered your authority. And now the emperor is waiting either to pick our purses or our bones.'

Even Lord Raymond, who is determined not to break his oath to Alexius, admitted that the Greeks had likely abandoned us.

'So, the light has finally dawned,' Bohemund gloated. Lord Raymond asked him what he proposed. 'Just this: that we take Antioch before the heathen arrives.'

Count Godfrey pushed back his stool in disgust. 'A brilliant idea,' he said. 'Why has none of us thought of that in seven months?'

Bohemund ignored his sarcasm. 'If you will not grant me the city outright,' he said, 'then pledge me this: Whoever enters Antioch first shall possess her.'

'And what of our oaths to the emperor?' Lord Raymond asked. 'He will surely not be the first, by your own words.'

Bohemund nodded at him. It was a question he had prepared for. 'Indeed,' he said. 'So let those who still hold to their oaths agree to this: If Alexius does not send to claim the city, then it shall belong to him who enters first.'

There was silence. Godfrey exchanged a glance with the others and then he said: 'It seems a fair proposition. If Alexius doesn't

want the damn place, then how else to decide except by priority?'
He turned to Adhémar. 'What does the papal legate say?'

The bishop glanced sidelong at Bohemund. 'It is to be prayed
on,' he replied. And with that the matter was left, though Bohemund
smiled in the manner of a man who knows he has won.

On the way back to our encampment, Lord Raymond was deep
in thought. I asked him finally what troubled him.

'Bohemund has some scheme. He would not make such a
proposal unless he was sure that he would profit by it. You recall
the roasting of the spies?' I answered that I should not soon forget
it. 'Why was it done?' he mused. 'Was it for the benefit of the
Turks, or for our benefit?'

I asked him what he meant but he would say no more.

MAY THE TWENTY-FIRST

Word has reached us, though we do not know whether to credit it,
that Ker-boga has broken off the siege of Edessa and is preparing
to move on Antioch. So far we have contained this report among
ourselves, fearing the effect it may have upon the army. The Bishop
Adhémar went so far as to swear each leader to secrecy. Meanwhile,
I am to ride to Edessa with two knights to reconnoitre. I write this
hastily, for I want to be away as soon as night falls. I shall leave
this book here in the care of Mansour, with instructions that he is
to send it to my mother should I fail to return.

MAY THE TWENTY-EIGHTH

I have just come from my Lord Raymond's pavilion, where I made
my report to him, the Bishop Adhémar, and Count Godfrey. What
I told them, briefly, was this.

For my reconnaissance to Edessa I took with me two knights,

Peter of Roaix and Marcel Couvreur, both of the retinue of Lord Raymond. We pushed our horses as hard as we dared, avoiding all towns including the Christian ones, and came within sight of Edessa on the evening of the third day. We remained upon the heights of the Euphrates' western fork from which the spectacle was spread out before us like a painting.

The Turkish army was immense, dotted with striped pavilions of silk and speckled with long pennants of scarlet and gold. The horses were numerous and fresh, and the knights well-equipped. There were legions of archers and many thousands of infantry who wore leather armour such as we had never seen among the Turks. I supposed that they were Persians, for their skin was fair and their beards cropped short as I have seen them depicted.

My companions groaned at the sight, and I must confess that my heart too sank within me. This was a potent host, led by the greatest emirs of Islam, freshly recruited, soundly provisioned, and assembled for the express purpose of destroying us.

We remained all the next day to watch their operations and calculate their numbers. By nightfall, it was clear that they were preparing to quit their siege and take the road. Scouts had been sent out to reconnoitre and the smaller pavilions were being struck. We kept well back for fear of being discovered by the scouts and waited for dark. Then, as we were preparing to leave, we heard horses approaching.

'Christians!' Marcel exclaimed, but just as they came towards us – two knights with their swords slung over their backs for fast riding – they were attacked by Turks. They had no time to arm themselves, and the Turks, eight or ten in number, cut them down in an instant. Two Turks dropped from their horses and slit the men's throats. Couvreur drew his sword but I grabbed him and held him back. 'We cannot risk discovery,' I whispered to him. 'Besides, it is too late.'

We waited until the Turks had left and then made our way

carefully to the men. They bore the colours of Baldwin, and both were dead.

'Couriers,' said Peter of Roaix.

We set off at once, swinging well to the north to avoid Saruj and the road to Antioch. We crossed the western branch of the river below Bira and turned south again. On the seventh day we were back at our camp.

'So Ker-boga has abandoned Edessa,' Lord Raymond said when I had finished.

'But it remains in Baldwin's hands,' the Bishop Adhémar pointed out.

I gave my opinion that the city is so beaten down there is no hope for assistance from Count Baldwin. Godfrey asked my estimate of the Turks' strength. 'Thirty to forty thousand,' I replied, 'and they are even now on the road to Antioch. They will arrive in seven or eight days' time.'

I cannot describe the gloom in that pavilion, which is exceeded only by the mood of the army. Despite the oath of secrecy, someone has put out the news of Ker-boga's approach, throwing the men into panic. In desperation, the bishop has posted the Tafurs around the camp to prevent desertions, with orders to kill those who try to flee. This stratagem has worked, for the men are even more terrified of the Tafurs than of the Turks.

I must now dress and attend a meeting of the council.

MAY THE THIRTY-FIRST

Stephen of Blois is preparing for the withdrawal, reckoning up the number of our troops, organizing our supplies, and planning the route of the escape. It is no easy task to quit a siege of seven months, and he is beside himself with care.

There was a council last night in the Bishop Adhémar's pavilion, attended only by the leading nobles: my Lord Raymond, Count

Godfrey, Bohemund, Robert of Flanders, Robert of Normandy, Stephen of Blois and Hugh of Vermandois. I was invited to repeat my report. It was met with a heavy silence.

It was Adhémar who spoke. 'It seems that we have no choice,' he said with a sigh. 'We shall withdraw into Armenia and await reinforcement.'

'And what if we take Antioch?' Bohemund put in.

'An assault would only weaken us further, and there is absolutely no guarantee of success,' the bishop replied.

'I am not talking about an assault,' Bohemund said, 'but I am guaranteeing success.' Count Godfrey asked what he meant. 'Your answer first,' Bohemund responded. 'You said that you would pray on my proposal. What have you decided?'

The Bishop Adhémar stood and with difficulty answered: 'In the name of His Holiness the Pope, I consent that whoever enters Antioch first shall possess it. Provided the emperor makes no claim.'

Bohemund nodded in satisfaction. 'Godfrey?'

The count gave a dismissive wave of his hand. 'I've already said yes.'

'Raymond?'

There was no help for it. It was withdraw and abandon the expedition, or accede to Bohemund's request. 'You will send to Alexius?' Lord Raymond said.

'You may send to him yourself. As soon as the city has fallen.'

My Lord gazed at him a long moment, grimly. 'Very well,' he replied.

'Good,' Bohemund grunted. 'Then it's settled.'

Count Godfrey asked for his plan. Bohemund lowered his voice. 'I have been in contact with a captain of the Turkish guard who commands the Two Sisters, the towers that flank the Gates of Saint George and of the Bridge. He has agreed to sell me the city for a price.' Bohemund turned to Lord Raymond. 'I think you have gold, Raymond?'

'That is for the welfare of my troops,' Lord Raymond replied.

'Then in God's name,' Bohemund said, 'give it to me now.'

Thus was a desperate plan agreed on. I accompanied my Lord to his pavilion, where he fetched out his treasure box. Heartbroken, he delivered it to Bohemund. For two years his careful husbandry of this treasure has kept the Provençals alive when others starved, has paid their wages when others went without, has bribed our knights to remain while others deserted. Now it will be used to purchase Antioch.

June the Second

It will be today or not at all. Bohemund, fearful of spies, has forbidden us to tell anyone of the plan. His traitor waits within the walls, no doubt more anxious than ourselves. The army has been told that we will take the road to Edessa to intercept Kerboga on the march and give him battle. All the men think it folly, and Stephen of Blois, who has so assiduously prepared the escape, considers it mad. He insists on going through with the first stages of his plan, by which he will withdraw the French troops of Hugh of Vermandois towards Alexandretta. None of us was surprised that Prince Hugh should have volunteered for the hazardous undertaking of being the first to leave the city.

My Lord Raymond argued hotly that Count Stephen should abandon the withdrawal, but Bohemund just as hotly refused, saying that we would do better without the French at our backs. Thus, while a part of the army prepares to retreat, the rest are preparing to advance. Surely never has an army undertaken such a campaign.

Everyone is angry, and most are baffled. I had practically to bully my men into line, threatening them with damnation and cajoling them with vague promises of a quick victory. They must have thought me insane. Mansour said nothing, but set about preparing my equipment and Fatana with questioning glances at me. I kept aloof. No one must suspect what we are about.

We will set out before sunset so that the Turks in Antioch can see us going. Deception lies at the heart of this scheme, and everything – our army, our lives, our sacred pilgrimage – depends upon an anonymous Turk within the walls of Antioch. If he deceives us, we will all of us be destroyed. By this time tomorrow night I may be flayed alive or sold into slavery in the East. And yet I go about my preparations as coolly as ever I did upon the practice field, or in the meadows of Provence. I hate this war by treachery. I would rather face my enemy and measure him and kill him or be killed by him. But to balance victory upon a lie – that is helplessness.

The same, later

I write hastily. We have reached the shore of the Lake of Antioch, where in February we had our great battle. The army now being out of sight of the city walls, and the night having fallen, we shall double back to the north and west, and approach the Gates of Saint George and the Bridge.

My Lord Raymond has just now come to me with an urgent commission of great importance. At the middle of the night a squadron of our men is to climb into the city, abetted by Count Bohemund's traitor. At first Bohemund wanted to send only his Normans of Sicily, but neither Godfrey nor the Bishop Adhémar nor my Lord will trust him to that extent. They insist that the squadron must include men of all the armies. Lord Raymond told me that Bohemund fumed and cursed, but at last agreed. Thus, I am to accompany the troops who will invade the city and open the gates to our men.

It is an honour, if a sudden one, and I am not entirely sure what is expected of me. I go now to meet with Bohemund and receive my instructions.

JUNE THE FOURTH

I suppose I should explain what has happened in some detail, though, to be frank, I have not much heart for it.

The night of our assault I accompanied Lord Raymond to a conference with Count Bohemund and the other leaders. The Count was in a state of agitation. He spat when he saw me and called me a nuisance, and I think he would have slapped me with his gloves had not Count Godfrey caught him short and told him to convey the instructions.

There were sixty knights and nobles gathered upon a knoll overlooking the River Orontes. The moon was nearly full, and we watched as Bohemund spread out a parchment on which was crudely sketched a map of the city's walls. As I listened, I noted my companions: they were a cross-section of the army – Normans, Germans, Britons, Spaniards and Italians. Our leader was to be a knight of Rome who spoke Greek, the choice, evidently, of the Bishop Adhémar.

'Now listen, you bastards,' Count Bohemund began, 'our man's name is Firouz. He'll lower a ladder to you. Once you're in, you send to me. You're to do nothing until I arrive. Any man of you that makes a move without me will answer with his balls. You understand? Now get yourselves off. And leave your shields, for Christ's sake. Take nothing that will make noise.'

We mounted and set out for the western wall. The rear guard of the army was still on the road and as we passed along the ranks of troops we heard them mutter at the stupidity of counter-marching. 'Say,' a man called out to me, 'is this the road to hell?'

There was a gap a hundred rods wide between our front ranks and the Sisters. The men were packed so tightly in that none could sit or kneel. We left our horses and made our way to the front, following the river bank as far as the outermost shelters of our old encampment. The Italian gestured us to follow him.

We slipped in among the abandoned shelters, moving like shadows from one tent to another, keeping low and making no sound. The walls of Antioch loomed before us, growing taller and more forbidding as we approached. In seven months I had never ventured so near the battlements. They seemed to pierce the sky, and from their towers we could hear the steps and voices of the Turks. The night was frighteningly still, and every sound seemed amplified. By the time we cleared the camp, we were crawling on our bellies.

'To the right, the right,' the Italian said, and then repeated it in four languages. We followed him up a narrow ditch, and had not gone ten rods before I realized that we were crawling through the cemetery of the Turks. Those same bones whose glow I had watched at night were now all around us, and we had to move with care so as not to disturb them. Arms and chests and heads protruded, many still with flesh and clothes, and some with eyes that stared after us as we passed.

'*Aspettate,*' our leader said, and I repeated it behind me: 'Wait.'

We were at the ditch beneath the wall. The Italian slipped into the water silently. He could not touch bottom, and so he slung his sword across his back and swam towards the farther bank. We each in turn did likewise. As I was preparing to wade in, a young Lorrainer knight grabbed at my sleeve. 'Sir,' he whispered, 'I cannot swim.'

I could not leave him, and so I gestured him to take my shoulders. We slid down the bank together and I started across, the youth clinging to my back, more frightened by the water than by the Turks. He was heavy and dragged me down, so that I had to roll near onto my side and kick with all my strength to keep from drowning. As he clutched at me I started to choke. 'I'll go back, sir,' he panted into my ear. I told him to shut up. When we reached the farther bank he kissed it.

It was an hour before all sixty of us were assembled under the wall. The towers shot straight up into the night sky, dusted with the blue of moonlight, imperturbable, featureless, and surprisingly cool to the touch. The Italian pressed his forehead against the stone. '*Antioco!*' he breathed. We all crossed ourselves.

We crouched against the wall and watched the Hunter revolve.[84] At last the Italian got up and began to make his way along the base in search of the ladder. In a few minutes his whisper came from out of the darkness: '*Veniamo!*'

We crept along the wall to where he waited at the foot of a leather ladder that twisted up into the dark. We all glanced at it uncertainly. My old companion Landry Gros was first to climb, and then I followed on his heels. The ladder sagged and swayed so that I was sure it would break. I felt a man start up behind me and I took the risk of calling to him to stay back. When I was up, I waved for the next to follow. Meanwhile, Landry Gros was crouching beside a man in the shadows, gesturing and trying to communicate in strained whispers. 'Where's that damned Italian?' he said at last to me. The answer came from the ladder: 'Shut your filthy mouth!'

The Italian slipped up and over the wall and dropped to his knees. 'Firouz!' he whispered. An urgent voice replied. The traitor crept to the parapet and peered over. He gasped and turned to the Italian with a contorted face. I heard the name Bohemund thrown back and forth. Landry Gros demanded to know what he said.

'He says we are not enough, and he wants Lord Bohemund,' the Italian answered. More men were slipping over the wall now, and crouching on the parapet.

'Send to him,' Landry Gros said. Our leader leaned over the wall and called in Italian to a man who was halfway up the ladder. This man at once let himself drop, and I saw him disappear towards the ditch.

Firouz stood fretting as the other men climbed up to us. He was much as I expected – a small, thin man with yellow eyes and

84 The Hunter: The constellation Orion, by the position of which they could estimate the time.

a slick moustache, who glanced about and wrung his hands in terror. At last, when all of our men were up, he led us to the summit of the Sisters. There a watch of Turks stood at ease, their weapons stacked before them.

Firouz whispered to the Italian, who turned to us. 'These we must kill,' he said. Landry Gros and his Normans moved forward quickly. In less than a minute they had strangled the Turks without a sound. The Gate of the Bridge was in our hands.

We followed Firouz across the tower and along the wall towards the Gate of Saint George. This time the Germans took the lead, cutting the throats of the watch with their daggers. Now we occupied the western wall for its entire length between the Two Sisters.

'Bohemund!' Firouz suddenly exclaimed. I glanced over the wall. Count Bohemund, his sword slung across his back, was climbing the ladder. We waved to him that it was safe, and he gestured back for us to stay where we were. Then, as we watched, a rung came away in his hands, then another, and the ladder began to give way. For a frightening moment Count Bohemund clung to it, then he fell headlong among its pieces. Firouz let out a moan and turned his eyes to heaven.

'We must get down!' we told him. But Firouz was beside himself with fear. 'He doesn't understand,' said the Italian.

'Let me translate,' Landry Gros grunted, and he punched Firouz full in the face. The traitor stared at him in horror, then put his hand to his nose. Blood gushed out between his fingers. 'Down,' Landry Gros repeated, pointing to the courtyard.

Firouz wiped at the blood with his sleeve and led us to a winding staircase. We emerged in a passage off the courtyard lined with doors. On some of them crosses had been chalked. Landry Gros asked the Italian how we would open the gates. 'See the crosses,' the Italian translated as the traitor sobbed the reply. 'Rouse the inhabitants.'

We made our way silently along the passage, tapping at the marked doors. From each a man emerged, armed, his face wound in a scarf. Without a word they joined us as Firouz led us across the courtyard towards the gates. While we stood guard, the men of Antioch took charge of the mechanisms. A minute passed, then two. Then I saw figures moving towards us.

'Hurry,' Landry Gros whispered. Firouz let out a whimper. Turks of the guard approached from across the courtyard; there was not a second to lose. If they sent up the alarm the whole city would be upon us. Landry Gros stepped forward; there were four Turks, heavily armed. The young Lorrainer knight hurried after him.

I heard a gruff command from the Turks. Landry Gros walked towards them quickly but without concern. When they caught sight of his face in the moonlight they rushed him. Landry Gros swung at the first man's throat. The young French knight threw himself upon the second man. The others turned to flee, but half a dozen of our men were on them, wrestling them to the ground and slashing at their throats to silence them.

The Turk struggling with the youth let up a cry, and in a second more I saw the young knight roll over with a dagger in his breast. Landry Gros stabbed the Turk in the side, then cut off his head. Lights were appearing in the windows now and Firouz was shouting at the men labouring at the gates. I ordered our knights to form a defensive line. More Turks were swarming into the courtyard pulling on their clothes. There were voices on the walls above us, an arrow whizzed by my head.

Firouz dropped to his knees beside me and began praying. I kicked at him with my heel. The Turks were organizing themselves for a charge. Faces appeared all around us, women and children gaping at the spectacle. I yelled 'Prepare!' and several other voices took it up.

Just then, behind us, there was a massive creaking. Involuntarily we turned. The Gate of Saint George was swinging open, and silver moonlight reflected from the moat spilled in. In the next instant a shout came from the Gate of the Bridge as it too opened.

The Turks stood still, their weapons frozen in their hands, and then all at once they sent up a cry of despair. Behind us a thousand men came cheering over the bridges and into the city. The Turks scattered, alarms sounded from the walls, all the houses were lighted now. We stood aside, for our men were pouring in, screaming, waggling their weapons, converging on the centre of the courtyard like the fists of a great beast. Count Bohemund ran past, limping and cursing, and then the Normans and the Tafurs. The knights all around me were cheering. A few brave Turks approached us and were instantly cut down. After seven months of siege our men were overwhelming Antioch, not so much an army as a riot, not so much soldiers as prisoners freed and on a rampage.

JUNE THE FIFTH

I was interrupted last night by matters that I shall relate in due course. Here I continue the narrative from where I left it off, though I have not much time.

No sooner were our men inside the walls of Antioch than they began murdering the inhabitants. The slaughter was quickly out of control, led by Bohemund and his Tafurs crying, 'Kill the rats!' People were dragged from their houses and shops or slain where they hid; men, women, children, the old, the sick. No one was spared, neither Turk nor Greek nor Jew.

When it was clear that the gate was safe, I set out into the city to do what I could to stop the killing. A few of the nobles were shouting at their men to form ranks, but only a man or two obeyed. I saw the body of Firouz in the courtyard not far from where we had made our stand. It was horribly mutilated, with gashes on every limb. From within the houses I could hear the wails of women and the terrified screeches of the children. A few fires broke out, and it is a miracle that the city was not burned to the ground.

The Turkish garrison, meanwhile, had abandoned the citizens and fled to the citadel atop the mountain. Many were killed as they tried to escape, but several hundred reached the fortress. The Spanish knights, who were still under command, attempted an assault but were beaten back.

Below, all was chaos. I tried to stop a group of Normans who were pillaging a district in the shadow of the palace. They were maddened and would not even hear me. At last I grasped the arm of one of their knights and invoked the name of their chief, Fulk Rechin. He paused for a moment as though suddenly sobered, then turned on me with a look of shame and fear in his eyes, and struck me in the chest with the hilt of his sword.

I was stunned more than hurt, and I fell back while he disappeared into a house with a low door. I followed him in, nearly blind with fury. Inside I found him grappling at the arm of an occupant who was hiding under the bedclothes. I commanded him to stop, and when he turned to strike me again, I swung with my sword and caught him on the side of the face with the flat. He went down, unconscious.

I moved to the bed and pulled back the covers. There, crouching like a child, was a small woman swathed from head to foot in robes. She yelled to me in Turkish and raised her hands to protect herself, for I must have appeared a terrible sight. Footsteps came to the door. I told her to be still and threw the covers over her again. Three or four soldiers were barging in but I shouted at them to get out and waved my sword. They disappeared and I bolted the door.

When I turned again, the woman was crouching behind me with a curved dagger. She slashed at me but I avoided it, and when she came at me again I grabbed her wrist and twisted the knife from her grip. Her eyes above the veil stared in horror at me, then in resignation. She dropped to her knees. 'Please, Faranj,' she said in French, 'kill me if you will, but do not violate me.'

Her accent was heavy but her words were so precise that I had the impression it was a speech she had rehearsed. I told her I would do neither, that I was a nobleman of France.

'The city is full of your noblemen,' she said bitterly.

I asked whether there was anyone else in the house. She told me that everyone had fled but her. I said that I would remain with her to protect her, but by her eyes I could see that she did not believe me. She glanced again at the dagger, and so I moved carefully to it, keeping her in view, and picked it up. With that she seemed to go limp, and she turned her face away and began to weep.

I remained in the house all night, seated on the floor with my sword across my knees, while the rioting and murder continued. By dawn it had nearly burnt itself out. The woman was asleep in a corner. I went to her and shook her shoulder. She started awake, her eyes filled with fear. I told her that I must go out to find my Lord and to fetch my servant. She stared at me, unable, I suppose, to believe that she was alive and unharmed. I handed her the dagger and told her to bolt the door and admit no one but me.

'My name is Roger,' I told her.

'Faranj,' she said. 'You are Faranj?'

I realized that she meant French and I said yes. 'Roger . . . Faranj,' I repeated.

Outside, Antioch was a desperate sight. The side streets and the marketplace were piled with corpses; all had been stabbed or clubbed, though some had been burned. Many were stripped naked; not a piece of jewellery remained to them. The houses and shops had been looted. Doors gaped open, shutters had been torn from their hinges, goods lay everywhere. A white flag with a red cross flew above the Gate of Saint George and a few sentries, Provençals I was glad to see, stood guard upon the walls. Below was nothing but death and ruin.

I found Lord Raymond not far away, at the palace of the emir. His pennant stood outside the narrow gate leading to the courtyard, where his pavilion had been pitched. Praise God, he had managed to control our men, and now they stood guard over the building, which dominated the quarter where I had spent the night. I reported myself to him, and he kissed me on both cheeks.

'I had feared that you were dead,' he said. He looked old and ill and, as he embraced me, he leaned heavily upon my shoulders. I explained briefly what had happened. 'Worse is to come, I think,' he replied. 'Ker-boga has reached the Lake of Antioch. He will be here tomorrow. We must organize our army and prepare for a fight or, God help us, for a siege.'

Now it was we who were trapped in Antioch, and our men in such a condition that the city would fall easily to Ker-boga. I told Lord Raymond that I would take charge of the western gates. He replied that Godfrey and Robert of Flanders had rallied their men and were sealing off the northern and eastern walls. 'The Turks still hold the southern wall,' he said, pointing to the citadel where the emir's flag flew. 'We will send Bohemund up there as soon as we can find him. It is his people who have to answer for what has happened. He is a king of corpses now.'

I had to move quickly to secure the gates. I gathered my Marseillais and a few of the knights, organized them into squadrons, and posted them. We literally ran from one point to the next, and my orders were simple: the gates were to be opened for no one save Lord Raymond or myself. As I was returning to the palace, Mansour came running to meet me. 'Thank God you are safe, Effendi!' he called.

He was shaken by the condition of the city, and I could see that he had been crying. I grabbed his elbow and hurried him to the house with the low door. There was no answer to my knock and so I called that it was Roger, Faranj. The bolt slid back and we stepped into the darkness. The woman stood behind the door, peering at us.

I had no time for explanations. I quickly instructed Mansour to remain with her and to admit no one but myself. There was shouting now in the streets and the sound of our trumpets, rallying the men. The Norman infantry was making its way towards the southern wall, led by a few mounted men. I caught sight of the Bishop Adhémar, a sword in his hand, arguing furiously with a group of nobles. Lord Raymond was walking towards me assisted by two knights. I hurried to meet him. His face was red with fever, and his breath came panting. 'Ker-boga approaches,' he said.

We climbed to the top of the Sisters by the very stairs I had descended three nights before. From the higher of the two towers we could see the length of the plain of Antioch. There, to the north-east, the vanguard of the Turkish army was making its way down the river road. The line of white-robed cavalry, studded with black pennants upon their lances, wound back to the shore of the lake and disappeared beyond its glittering arm. We could hear their drums and pipes, and the voices of their priests calling praises to God. I felt the hearts of our men sink as they looked on.

'My God,' a boy near me said, 'all this way we've come. It seems a pity.'

JUNE THE EIGHTH

I have posted Gérard and Bernard to watch over the house with the low door. I am there now, and shall continue my account as quickly as I can, for there is a council tonight, and it is likely to be a long one.

For the moment the Normans besiege the citadel, but Bohemund is furious that he, the King of Antioch, has been given this task. The army of Ker-boga has nearly surrounded the city, and has established contact with the Turks in the citadel. The troops there are led by the son of the emir, whose father was captured by Armenians trying to flee the city. They cut off his head and brought it to us, and now it stands upon a spear atop the Gate of the Bridge.

When the Turks in the citadel saw what it was they set up a wail of mourning that has not stopped for two days. The emir's son, whose name is Samadolo,[85] has sent to us for his father's head so that he may be buried whole and enter into paradise. The Bishop Adhémar replied that, head or no, the emir would not be welcome there, and refused to deliver it. And so it remains upon the tower of the gate, where carrion crows tear at it.

As I write this, the woman sits in silence and stares at me. We have offered her food but she has refused, and has neither moved nor bared her face in the six days that I have been here. Mansour has tried to speak to her in Turkish, Armenian and Greek, but she ignores him. He tells me that she is of mixed parentage, for her eyes, though brown, have green flecks in them.

I think that she must feel she is a prisoner in her own house, but though I have told her it is not so, it still is not safe to go out. Very few women are left alive in Antioch, and these are in constant danger. But what is worse is the condition of the streets. We have begun to burn the thousands of corpses, but they decay rapidly in the heat and their stench and that of the fires make it difficult to move about. No one can go out of doors without a perfumed cloth over his face, and the smoke from the burning heaps stings the eyes. Flies and vermin are everywhere, all the wells are polluted, and the sight of the dead, especially of the children, is terrible.

What is more, the Turks have begun firing stones over the walls. These land among the piles of corpses and send them flying. I know of at least one man who was killed by a corpse flung through the air with such force that it broke his back. There is a pall over the city day and night, and the ashes that drift down like dirty snow are those of the dead.

I must go now to the council. The decisions that are made

---

85 Shams ad-Daula. He had been sent to Ridwan of Aleppo, Duqaq of Damascus and Karbuqa to plead for help for his father. Over Shams's objections, Karbuqa relieved him of command of the citadel. A note on the Turkish army: Though called for a jihad, or holy war, the army was deeply split along lines of fealty and politics. These divisions would play a role in their subsequent operations.

tonight may determine our fate. I wonder at this woman. She seems young and, judging from the few words she spoke to me, she may be educated. I should at least like to know her name.

JUNE THE NINTH

The council of last night was a rancorous affair. Count Bohemund was the last to arrive and his entrance was dramatic. He staggered in clutching a wound in his side, his hands covered with blood. He had attempted to storm the citadel earlier in the day, was repulsed, and was struck by an arrow. He cursed at us mightily for failing to support him, but the truth is that all of our armies were busy organizing the defences of the city.

At Bohemund's insistence it was decided that each army will take it in turn to blockade the citadel, with Lord Raymond taking the first watch. He has refused, however, to give up the palace of the emir to Bohemund, declaring that, since we have not yet heard from the Emperor Alexius, Bohemund does not have the right to rule.

This instantly touched off an argument over who should be detached to go to the emperor, since any attempt to escape the city now will be a dangerous undertaking. After much discussion it was decided that a squadron under the command of the Count of Clermont should attempt it.[86] He will slip out at night by the Iron Gate, as the Turks had so often done, and make his way to Stephen of Blois, who is said to be at Tarsus.

Normally, Count Stephen might attempt to raise the siege, attacking the Turks from the rear. But the irony is that he escaped with Hugh of Vermandois's men, and they are the least fit to attempt our rescue. Consequently, an appeal is to be made to the

---

86 In fact, three nobles attempted the escape: William and Aubrey of Grant-Mesnil, as well as Lambert of Clermont. They succeeded in reaching the port of Saint Symeon, where the pirate Guynemer took them to Tarsus. From there William and Stephen of Blois set out to contact Alexius.

Emperor Alexius to come up at once with the Byzantine army and take command of the city.

Meanwhile, we are to gather all of the city's supplies and place them under guard in the Cathedral of Saint Peter, which Adhémar has re-sanctified after its desecration by the Turks. To this end every house and shop in Antioch is being searched, and though there is no doubt in my mind that the surviving citizens will suffer greatly in the process, it cannot be helped. I have placed the seal of my Lord Raymond upon the house with the low door, for I have pledged safety to its occupant and mean to keep my pledge.

I have moved my quarters into the palace of the emir, which Lord Raymond has ordered me to keep from Bohemund. I write this now in an antechamber of a fabulous hall where dignitaries were once received by the emir. The floor and walls of my room are covered with carpets bearing designs of such delicacy and intricacy that I can scarcely take my eyes from them. I think that it is wrong to call these people heathens and barbarians. To produce such beauty, their minds must surely be lighted by God.

There is one particular carpet that delights me. It is woven in royal blue and gold, framed in flowers, and its centrepiece is a hanging votive light. The nap is shimmering and smooth like a cat's fur. I keep it by my bed and often run my fingers on it. Were it not that I am here for salvation and not plunder, I would most certainly take it back to Lunel. But I must admit I am sorely tempted, for it is one of the most beautiful things that I have ever seen.

JUNE THE TENTH

This morning, very early, the peasant boy Bartholomew came to me with a curious request. 'I must see Lord Raymond at once,' he said. I told him I had no time for such nonsense, for I was even then organizing the parties to search for food. Bartholomew grabbed my sleeve. 'Sir,' he said, 'I have seen the Christ.' I demanded to know what he meant. 'And Saint Andrew, too,' he said.

'When?' I asked him.

'This morning, sir. Saint Andrew told me to go to Lord Raymond with a message. And from him to the Bishop of Le Puy.'

There was an earnestness in his voice which, together with the ecstasy I had seen in his face after the battle, persuaded me to hear him out. 'No disrespect, sir,' he said, 'but I am commanded to speak to Lord Raymond and Bishop Adhémar and no one else.'

I fixed him carefully with my eyes. 'Bartholomew,' I said, 'his Lordship is very busy. He has the cares of all the army on his shoulders. You understand that he is not to be disturbed except for the gravest cause.'

'I'm not disturbing him, sir,' the boy replied. 'It is the Christ Our Lord who commands me.'

I looked at him a moment longer. His eyes were not his own, but filled with depths I could not fathom. 'Very well,' I said. 'I must make report to Lord Raymond and I will take you with me. But if this is lunacy, I myself will beat you for it. You understand?'

He smiled at me, the gaps in all his teeth showing. 'I have no understanding any more,' he said. 'Thank God.'

I fetched a mule for him and had Fatana brought. I took up the pennant of Lord Raymond and we set off through the winding streets of Antioch towards the citadel. Already soldiers were ransacking the houses, and the citizens called out to me their petitions and their curses as I passed. Bartholomew rode behind me in silence with an expression of great solemnity upon his simple face. The closer we came to our siege line, the more I wondered at myself for bringing him. It was stupidity surely, and yet, there was something about the boy, about the darkness in his eyes, that troubled me.

Below the citadel upon the peak of Mount Silpius our men were labouring to build a breastwork so that, should the Turks above attack in concert with an assault upon the walls, we should have a position to defend. I found Lord Raymond barely able to stand, directing the work with his usual calm command. He greeted me kindly as I rode up to him. I made a brief report upon the situation in the palace quarter and then, with apologies, I told him that my squire begged leave to speak with him.

'Speak to me?' Lord Raymond said. 'Your squire?'

I explained in a few words about Bartholomew, that he had been buried alive in Nicaea and since that time had been subject to visions and ecstasies. 'My Lord, he has seen . . .' I hesitated to finish.

'Yes?' Lord Raymond said.

'He has seen the Christ,' I said. 'There is a message for you.'

Lord Raymond peered at me. I think that had we endured less together than we have, he would have dismissed me with an oath. Instead he asked that the boy be brought. I gestured to Bartholomew and to my amazement and consternation, he prostrated himself before Lord Raymond.

'My sovereign Lord,' he breathed. Soldiers were pushing past bearing stones for the breastwork and had to step over him. I told him gruffly to get up. 'Oh no, sir,' he replied with a smile of wonder on his face, 'it's just as Saint Andrew told me.'

Lord Raymond scowled at me. 'You said nothing about Saint Andrew.'

'It appears he has seen him too.'

'Boy,' Lord Raymond said, 'what have you to tell me?'

'Wondrous things, my Lord,' Bartholomew began, and then in a single breath he panted out: 'Christ Jesus, our Blessed Saviour, and Saint Andrew His disciple, will reveal to me the resting place of the Holy Lance, with which our Saviour's side was pierced upon the Cross. And he commands that you go to Bishop Adhémar and tell him this, that we may search for it. For with its help alone can we be saved from the danger that threatens us, and our army shall proceed in triumph to Jerusalem.'

Lord Raymond raised a silver eyebrow. 'Come here, boy.'

Bartholomew stood timidly and approached him. Lord Raymond took his chin in a firm grip. 'Where are you from?' he asked.

'Lunel,' the boy replied. 'The town of my master, Duke Roger.'

Raymond glanced at me. I nodded. He asked the boy how many visions he had had. 'Four of Christ, my Lord, and of Saint Andrew, six.'

'And what did he look like? The Saviour, I mean.'

'Like the statues, my Lord. Except his hair was softer.'

'And Saint Andrew?'

To my surprise, Bartholomew turned and smiled at me. 'Like my master Roger,' said he. 'Though Saint Andrew's face is never severe. And, oh,' he added, 'he lacks the moustache.'

'It was Christ who spoke to you?' Lord Raymond asked.

'Saint Andrew, my Lord,' the boy replied. 'Our Saviour stands always in the back, and never says a word.'

'And what language does Saint Andrew speak?'

'Oh, it's not speaking,' Bartholomew corrected. 'It's more like knowing. Like pouring out directly to my mind. It's a marvellous thing, my Lord, like looking at a flower. You don't speak to it, you take it in, just all at once. He doesn't talk – it's just there, all in your mind at once.'

Lord Raymond released his grip on the boy's face. 'Very well,' he said, more to me than him. 'We shall refer this to the Bishop Adhémar. Far be it from me to stand in the way of divine intervention, especially under such circumstances as these.'

I escorted Bartholomew to the cathedral, where we found the Bishop Adhémar preoccupied with the organization of the supplies. The nave had not yet been cleansed of the stable wastes left by the Turks, and with the storing of the sacks of grain and bales of hay, the cathedral resembled a vaulted barn. It was with great difficulty that I managed to get the bishop's attention, and with even more that I explained my errand.

'The Holy Lance?' Adhémar repeated. 'That which drew the blood of Christ?'

'The same,' I said. He told me to bring the boy.

What followed was an interrogation as stern as that given to any thief. Adhémar demanded to know how he, an illiterate peasant, dared make such a claim. Bartholomew responded: 'Because you have allowed the army of Christ to descend into such debauchery and sinfulness. Because you have not been a pastor to His flock, but have allowed them to behave like wolves, killing the innocent and plundering their homes. Because you, in your pride, have forgotten the humility of Christ, who made of Himself a simple peasant for our sakes.'

I could see the veins in the bishop's forehead pulsing; I think he would have struck the boy if he had dared. Instead, he regarded him with a rage that was scarcely controlled. 'Show me the Lance,' he demanded.

'In five days it will be revealed to me,' Bartholomew replied. 'Then I shall lead you to it for the glory of God and the victory of our pilgrimage. In the meantime we all must fast.'

Thus was the matter left. I rode back with the boy in silence to the palace of the emir. 'Bartholomew,' I said to him as he dismounted from the mule, 'it is a heavy responsibility you take upon yourself. Are you quite sure, boy, of what you are doing?'

Again he smiled at me. 'I am sure of nothing, master,' he replied, 'except that Saint Andrew speaks kindly to me, and that the face of Our Lord is a beautiful thing to behold.'

JUNE THE THIRTEENTH

The Turks have pressed their siege to within a few hundred paces of the walls. They have occupied our old camp and the slopes before the Gates of Saint George and the Bridge as well. Except for the Iron Gate, through which our emissaries escaped, we are entirely surrounded. We have seen them reinforcing the citadel, slipping in over the mountaintop at night. Their assault cannot be far off now.

Meanwhile we have gathered all the provisions we can find, and they are scant enough. We cannot withstand a siege of more than a few weeks, and so everything now depends upon the emperor. This morning all the ships were gone from the harbour, a fact that has depressed the morale of our men a great deal. It seems now that everything and everyone is deserting us.

Meanwhile, Adhémar informed the leaders of the vision of Bartholomew. Though the question was hotly debated, all agreed that the matter should be kept secret until some proof be found. However, this morning Père Raimund of Aguillères stood up in the marketplace and declared at the top of his voice that he has seen the Christ, and that the Holy Lance is to be found within the city. Within an hour the news had spread of Bartholomew's visitation, and now the entire army is demanding that we search for the sacred relic.

A hasty council was called this afternoon, at which the Bishop Adhémar insisted that we not risk the humiliation of a false miracle. Count Bohemund spoke up at once. 'Damn-it, priest,' he said, 'this army is in need of something. If the boy says fast, let's fast, and if he says search, let's search. I for one accept the vision as authentic, and will swear an oath upon it.'

And with that he marched down to the marketplace where the soldiers were assembled around Père Raimund and took his oath that he will not leave the city until the Lance is found. This was met with wild cheering, and soon every man was swearing. Seeing it, the Bishop Adhémar had no choice but to declare the fast and to take the oath himself, as did all the nobles in turn. And so now we are committed to the vision, for good or ill.

I have been twice to the house with the low door. The woman now eats but still she has not spoken. Mansour tells me that she prays often in the Turkish way, but that she does so in silence. He has seen her face, and says it is beautiful. When I arrive, however, she is always veiled.

I find that my mind wanders to her in those moments when I

have time to think. I reflect upon the words she spoke to me. They were said in terror; pleas that I not harm her. 'The city is full of your nobles,' she said, meaning that she could trust none of us. But surely she trusts me now. I have saved and protected and provided for her, giving her food even from my own table. For the moment I can do no more, but Mansour remains with her, and I question him closely every evening when he comes to wait upon me. What is the source of my curiosity about her? It must be the mystery of her, and the way her fear-struck eyes bored into me.

June the Fourteenth

I was upon the wall inspecting the guard when a great wonder occurred. Just after sunset a comet appeared in the southern sky.[87] It grew brighter as it came towards us, then suddenly it turned and fell directly into the Turkish camp, scattering the horses and throwing the Turks into confusion. All at once our men fell to their knees to thank God for this sign that He is with us. I too was struck with amazement, for what could it be but a sign from God, and I knelt with them to pray. One of the priests began a hymn which the soldiers on the wall took up, and soon the whole city was ringing with the De Profundis.

Can it be that this comes in response to our fast? Can it be that Bartholomew, the tailor's son of Lunel town, *has* been blessed with a vision of Christ? Indeed, in our perilous condition, only divine intervention can save us. It may be, after all, that our army has pleased God, and that our sufferings may yet be rewarded with victory.

Tonight, thinking perhaps that the comet favoured them, the

---

87 This meteor is mentioned in all of the chronicles, including accounts of Muslim historians. It appears to have been part of the prelude to a period of intense solar activity called the medieval maximum which began about the year 1120. cf. J. Riley-Smith, *The Crusades, a Short History* (New Haven: Yale, 1987), p. 38.

Turks made an assault against the Sisters and were driven back. This has further strengthened our men's belief in the vision, and now everyone waits for tomorrow, when Bartholomew has been promised the revelation of the Lance. I must admit that I too am filled with hope that God may make some miracle for us, for there is no word of the emperor, and only God can save us now.

For some reason I decided to go to the house with the low door and tell the woman what had happened. I found her preparing a supper of barley cakes, broth, and dried figs. When she saw me she snatched the veil up to her face and turned away. I asked Mansour to leave us.

'You can understand me,' I said to her. 'I know that you speak our language. I shall respect your silence if you wish, but I must tell you that the next few days may decide our fate and that of the city. Today God has sent a sign that seems to favour us. But if we are wrong, if the city falls, I wish you to know that I will do whatever I can to see that no harm comes to you.'

She did not respond nor even turn to face me. I felt I ought to say something else, and so I added: 'If the Turks are victorious, I hope that you will not think ill of me or of my people. I pray you will not.'

She remained unmoving another moment, and then she reached down, picked up a tiny cup with no handle, turned, and offered it to me. I took it carefully, for it was a delicate thing lined in gold.

'Tea,' she said.

I thanked her and drank. She then placed bowls upon the table and set out her food. She motioned me to sit. I did so and she served me without a word. Then she sat opposite me, folded her hands in her lap and lowered her head.

'You will not eat?' I asked.

'When you have gone, Faranj,' came the reply. Her veil trembled slightly as she spoke.

As I ate I noticed that she glanced up at me from time to time, though as soon as she caught my eyes she lowered hers. I saw for the first time that they are oddly shaped, like those of the merchants of Asia whom I have seen in the market towns.

'You are Turk?' I asked her.

Still she did not raise her head. 'My mother was Turk.'

'And your father?'

'Tatar.'

'It is a name with which I am not familiar,' I told her. She did not reply. I asked whether I might know her name.

There was a moment's silence while she decided. At last she said, 'Yasmin.'

'Yasmin,' I repeated. 'Like the flower that blooms at night?'

'If you will, Faranj,' she said.

I asked for more tea and she got up to fetch it. Despite her loose robes, I could see that she is slender, below average in height, and graceful in her movements. She brought a bowl with a lid and poured for me while I held the cup. Her hands are small and finely shaped, with the nails cut short. She saw me looking at her hands and she drew away, nearly spilling the tea. Then she began to tremble.

'What is wrong?' I asked. To my surprise she was crying. I stood and she shrank back.

'Please, Faranj,' said she, 'you did not violate me and I am grateful. But you must leave me. I beg you in the name of God.' Her body was as taut as tuned strings and she shook from head to foot. I put down the cup and left.

It has been a long and puzzling day, from the sign this evening, to the attack tonight, to my supper with the woman Yasmin. I feel I should no longer go to the house, yet the nearness of her bore a scent to me that I had long forgotten, a fragrance of holiness and wonder every bit as foreign and unexpected as the comet.

June the Fifteenth

This morning thousands of soldiers waited in the square before the cathedral for the boy Bartholomew. No one made a sound. I stood beside Lord Raymond, who is so ill that he must be carried in a chair. The other leaders stood upon the steps in their crowns and battle colours, with the Bishop Adhémar at their head. I had expected him to be in his solemn vestments, but instead he wore a simple monk's robe and his head was bare.

Bartholomew appeared from a side street and walked silently towards the bishop, not at all distracted by the multitude of soldiers nor the presence of the nobility. He was followed by Père Raimund of Aguillères, who muttered prayers to himself and beat his breast like a madman. He was a spectacle: his eyes were wild, his hair was thick with filth, and his robes were in tatters. Had he appeared in any town of Provence in such a condition, he would have been taken in charge.

Bartholomew went straight up to the Bishop Adhémar, bent to kiss his ring, and then stood smiling. There was an awkward silence before the bishop said, 'Well, boy, what have you to tell us?'

'The resting place of the Lance,' he replied.

'It has been revealed to you?' the bishop asked.

'Oh, yes, Your Grace,' Bartholomew said with a radiant smile. 'It lies within.'

Bishop Adhémar glanced around. 'In the cathedral?'

'Beneath the floor. I shall show you the spot if you will.'

Adhémar stepped aside and allowed the boy to pass. We all followed him into the church and the doors were barred behind us. Bartholomew knelt below the high altar, one hand pressed to his heart, the other pointing to the floor. 'Just here,' he said.

Adhémar called for knights, and half a dozen came in. The bishop directed them to pull up the stones and dig.

We glanced among ourselves as the knights began their work.

Bartholomew stood to one side smiling and rolling his head in a strange half-conscious way. Père Raimund pushed his way inside and prostrated himself near where the knights were digging, babbling prayers and writhing on the filthy floor.

Adhémar called for tools to be brought and more men. Soon a dozen knights were digging a trench as large as a grave and nearly as deep. The soil was flinty and dry. Bohemund stood by in his Sicilian finery, fuming at them. 'Goddamn-it,' he growled, 'can't you do any better than that?' Adhémar scowled at him. Bohemund shot him a look. 'If it was liquor they'd find it quick enough,' he said.

An hour went by and then two. The trench was now deeper than the height of a man and the dirt was being thrown up in handfuls. I kept glancing at Bartholomew, but he appeared wholly unconcerned and merely stood by, lolling his head in the same rhythmical way. Père Raimund, however, was becoming agitated. He was grunting like an animal and shrieking so that Adhémar threatened to put him outside.

Count Godfrey stooped to speak to Lord Raymond. 'You know what'll happen if this is false fire,' he said. Raymond nodded gravely.

By midday the trench was as long as the altar and well above the knights' heads. At last the bishop called to them to stop. They laid down their tools and crawled out, panting and wiping the grime from their faces.

'Bartholomew,' Adhémar said. 'It is not here.'

The boy shook himself as if roused from a dream. He smiled at us with great tranquillity. 'Digging cannot bring it to light,' he said. 'Prayer can.'

We glanced at one another and then, following Adhémar's example, we dropped to our knees.

'Father,' Adhémar began, 'we have heard the command of Your Son. We have abandoned all that we have and followed Him. We have come into this holy land to save His tomb from desecration, to walk in His steps, to open the way for His servants who will come after us. Now we are surrounded by Your enemies. Those of us who have shed their blood and those who stand ready to do so cry out to You for mercy. If it be Your holy will, we beseech You to raise up to us from the bottom of this pit Our Saviour's Holy Lance.'

Bartholomew, who had not knelt, cocked his head at these last words as if they were familiar to him. 'Yes,' he said, stepping to the edge of the trench. 'The bottom of this pit. Look. There it is.'

We all got up and pressed to the edge, and indeed, there at the very bottom, a point of metal protruded from the earth. Père Raimund of Aguillères pushed to the front, let out a scream, and threw himself headfirst into the trench. There he began thrusting his chest against the earth, trying to impale himself upon the point, yelling 'Take me! Take me!'

'Get him out of there,' Adhémar ordered, and the knights pulled him roughly from the hole. At that Bartholomew stepped forward. 'I'll fetch it out,' he said. Bohemund took his arms and lowered him into the trench. The boy knelt, scratched carefully at the earth, and lifted from it the shaft of a Roman pilum.[88] He held it up to us. The Bishop Adhémar bent to take it.

'The lance that drew the blood of Christ,' he said with great solemnity. We all fell to our knees. Below, in the hole, Bartholomew stood smiling tranquilly.

The effect on the army has been dramatic; all are now convinced that Christ Himself is leading us, and that we cannot fail. Bartholomew has told the bishop that we are to continue the fast until our sins are purged, and then we must attack the Turks, whom we shall defeat with the aid of the saints and angels and the spirits of our fallen comrades. Normally it would be folly to engage the Turks outside the walls, but not a man of us doubts that it must be so.

Tomorrow there will be a procession of the Lance throughout the city. Meanwhile, though it is now far into the night, the bells

---

88 A pilum was the shorter and heavier of the two spears carried by Roman soldiers. Normally it was about three feet long with a six-inch blade. It was used for stabbing rather than throwing.

still ring and the city resounds with hymns of thanksgiving and praise. Not since the day of our departure has the army been so joyful. It is a miracle. It is as though we have been reborn.

JUNE THE TWENTY-THIRD

Some of the Turks have begun to retreat. We have seen detachments of cavalry and foot leaving the camp and disappearing to the east. Why this should be I cannot say, but it gives heart to our men.[89]

Our fasting has ended, but we can scarcely tell the difference. There is little food left in the city, and some of our men have nothing at all. They have taken to eating the bark from the trees, or boiling it to make broth. Our animals, much reduced by the siege, are now dying at an alarming rate. The Bishop Adhémar has ordered an inventory of horses which are fit to ride, and we have discovered that scarcely one hundred remain. Among them is Fatana, whom I labour to save. There have been days when I have gone without food for her sake. She has carried me this far; I will not see her die.

I am very tired, and my leg wound has begun to pain me again. I think I will continue this tomorrow.

JUNE THE TWENTY-FIFTH

I have been unable to walk without pain for two days. Peter of Roaix now performs my duties, attending to the defence of the walls and keeping Bohemund from the palace. I have seen him lurking about sometimes, eyeing the courtyard like a jealous suitor.

89 The Muslim army was being rent with dissention, led primarily by Duqaq of Damascus who may have feared Karbuqa more than he feared the Crusaders. Some Muslim historians suggest that Duqaq joined the army precisely to sabotage it and prevent Karbuqa from taking control of Syria.

I think were he ever to find it unguarded he would occupy it and turn us out. Count Raymond remains at the citadel, and is so ill with fever that he cannot come down.

We have had bad news from the north: the Emperor Alexius has retreated into the interior of Anatolia with the Greek army. There will be no help for us from that quarter, though, indeed, I think we never expected any. Still the news has been hard on us, though the men retain their faith in the Holy Lance.

JUNE THE TWENTY-SIXTH

Count Bohemund has taken command of the armies. This was decided by the Bishop Adhémar in view of Lord Raymond's worsening condition. Bohemund presented himself at the palace this morning, demanding that I cede it to him as his headquarters. I refused. He shook his fist at me and swore that I would be his enemy. I told him that I was very sorry to hear it, but I should rather be his enemy than a traitor to my Lord.

'You know that Alexius has retreated,' he said. 'That means he has declined to take the city. By your Lord's own admission, it is therefore mine.'

'When he tells me so, I shall be happy to yield it to you,' I responded.

'Your master is dying,' said he.

'That may be as God wills,' I answered. 'But if he dies without telling me to yield, then I will stay here until I meet him again at the Judgement.'

Bohemund bared his teeth at me. 'That may be sooner than you think,' said he.

The desertions of the Turks continue. It has been decided to send an emissary to them to propose a truce. We will offer to leave them unmolested if they quit the siege. Peter the Hermit has volunteered to convey the message. It is a brave act, since the Turks have not guaranteed safe passage. Perhaps he hopes by it to redeem himself before the army.

The same, later

I was interrupted in my writing by a knock upon my door. It was the woman Yasmin, dressed from head to foot in black. I was astonished to see her. She stood at the door a long moment in silence. Then she said, 'You are not well, Faranj?'

I had lain in my bed for three days and was ashamed of my condition. I asked her to leave. Instead she stepped into the room.

'I have brought you food,' she said. She took from beneath her robes a woven basket and carried it to my bed. I set aside the writing desk and tried as well as I could to arrange myself.

'You will not disturb yourself,' she told me, and laid the basket on the carpet by my side. She did not move, but remained standing by the bed with her head bowed. I gazed at her a long time. I did not know what to say. The silence seemed to surround us. Then she gathered up her skirts and turned to go.

'Thank you,' I said.

She paused. 'You are welcome,' came her reply.

I was anxious that she not leave and so I said, 'It was dangerous for you to come.'

She turned to me again. I could see nothing of her but the glimmering of her eyes in the candle light. 'Since the finding of the relic much has changed.'

'You have heard of that?'

'Indeed, Faranj, everyone has heard. You are a superstitious people.'

'For us it is a matter of faith,' I said.

'Then I shall praise God for your faith, since I may now cross the street of my own city without fear.' She did not seem inclined to go and so I begged her to sit down. She would not. 'Faranj,' she began hesitantly, 'you have protected me. For that I must be grateful.'

It seemed a grudging acknowledgement and so I said, 'I could have killed you.'

She bowed slightly. 'Indeed, Faranj, I understand that it is your duty to kill everything that does not agree with you.'

The answer amused me; she was nothing if not bold. I took up the basket. 'Will you eat with me?'

'I cannot. You are an infidel. It would soil me,' she said.

I felt insulted by the reply. 'Our Lord Jesus Christ said that it is not what goes into a man's mouth that soils him, but what comes out of his heart. Have you not received kindness from my heart?'

She considered this a moment. 'It is not a matter of the mouth or of the heart, Faranj,' she said. 'It is a matter of the soul.'

'Very well,' I replied. I began to eat and she watched me from the corners of her eyes. She had prepared the grain which is called semoule with raisins rolled in the leaves of grapes. 'It is very good,' I told her. She bowed again in acknowledgement.

She did not move the whole time I ate, but stood in perfect silence. It was surely the strangest supper I have ever had: in the tiny room of the emir's palace, surrounded by golden carpets, under the eyes of a veiled woman whose face I have never seen.

When I finished she approached the bed and knelt. From beneath her robes she produced a linen handkerchief that was moist with perfume. I looked at her, uncomprehending. She took my hands and began to wipe them.

Her touch softened me at once. I felt a warmth flow through me, and I breathed in the fragrance that clung to her like mystery. She was now close enough to the candles that I could just discern the outline of her face beneath the veil. It was youthful and smooth, and laced with deep shadows. I watched her in wonder as she anointed each of my fingers in turn. Again she stood. 'I will leave you,' said she.

'You will come again?' I asked without thinking.

'No,' she replied.

'Then do not leave.'

She stood over me in silence, and I thought that beneath the darkness of her robes her body trembled. 'What would you have of me, Faranj?' she whispered.

'To see your face,' I said.

She gazed down at me a long while and then reached up her hand and undid the clasp of the veil. It fell, and I beheld her face for the first time. It was not beautiful, but there was within it a frankness, almost a solemnity, that struck me. She could not be more than twenty, and yet her presence is that of an older woman, one who has thought and felt much longer.

Her eyes are wide-set, deep and very dark, the under-lids straight but the upper arched like those of an Asiatic. Her brows are fine, slightly curving, scarcely more than a shadow. Her face is a simple oval, without a shade of subtlety or sensuousness. Her forehead is very high, framed by the scarf of severe purple, almost black, that she always wears. Her lips are rather thin and down-curved at the ends. Her nose is small with a slight crook. Her skin is not swarthy as I had expected, but rather, tinged with darkness. Her neck is very slender.

And yet it was her eyes that caught me, and the gaze that they contained. It was not sad but serious. I was impressed deeply that there was much and of importance behind her eyes. It was as though I could see the soul alive in them, and it sobered me.

I stood and she stepped back. I raised my hand to remove the scarf from her hair but she said, 'You may not touch me, Faranj.' I was reminded suddenly of the words of Christ to the women after His resurrection: 'Touch me not.' I lowered my hand.

I thanked her for her concern and for having come.

'Your servant says there will be a battle,' she said. I told her it was true. 'Then I will pray for you.'

'I have never had Muslim prayers in a battle,' I told her.

'You would rather I not?' she asked, raising a brow slightly. I answered that I would be grateful. 'Then, with your permission, I shall pray for you.' She reached for her veil. 'Now I will leave you,' she said. She raised it again to her face, crossed her hands upon her bosom, and bowed. Then she was gone.

I shall not sleep tonight.

JULY THE FIRST

What can I say of the wonders of these days? On Sunday we opened the Gate of Saint George and advanced to meet the Turks. We could muster only a hundred horsemen and so, despite my leg, I armed myself to take the place of Lord Raymond. We set out before dawn led by the priests in their vestments, and the Bishop Adhémar who bore the Holy Lance.

We expected them to attack at any moment, to cut us down as we crossed the bridge into the camp. But as Bartholomew had been promised, they did not come. There is no explanation for it but an act of God, since there were forty thousand of them and scarcely ten thousand of us. They could have butchered us piecemeal. Instead, as the dawn light rose, we could see them watching from their tents while we formed our lines.

It was the plan of Bohemund that every squadron, upon crossing the bridge, should move by the flank to make room. This we accomplished in perfect order while the priests sang hymns and the men upon the walls watched in amazement. And then the greatest wonder of all occurred.

From the mountaintop a mist began to descend before us. 'Look,' the soldiers whispered, 'it is the angels and the saints and the spirits of our dead come to fight with us.'

And indeed it was a sight most remarkable, for the fog came down in clouds that billowed and pulsed. Behind it we fanned out into a front scarcely more than half a league in width, stretching from the slopes of Silpius to the Orontes River. By this time the Turks had formed to meet us, but they could see nothing through the fog. Count Bohemund threw a company of foot upon the slopes to prevent them flanking us, and gave the order to advance.

Our lines started forward in perfect formation. We entered the fog in wonder, and many there were who saw the shapes of men long dead, of friends and kin and townsmen who spoke to them as they passed. Names were called, voices on every side, some in amazement, some in joy. By the time we emerged, nearly every man's face was wet with tears. I saw such expressions of ecstasy in the eyes of our soldiers as never an army has borne while making its way towards death. For the first time in battle I felt my soul uplifted. This was war, yes, but it was glorious. The glory of God was upon us that day.

The Turks stood stark still as we came on. And then, praise God, they turned and fled. On seeing this our men sent up a cheer and pursued them. Many Turks were struck down among the shelters, and others trying to ford the river. The battle was over in an hour, and we stood upon the bank and watched them disappear in their thousands across the plain of Antioch towards the lake. The Bishop Adhémar brought up the Lance, and we all fell to our knees and prayed.

The vision of Bartholomew had forbidden us to kill the prisoners or to plunder their camp, and so we stripped them and set them free and made our way back inside the walls. We had lost not a single man. Antioch is free. The road to Jerusalem is open.

The citadel surrendered tonight and there is feasting in the city, but while the soldiers sang their songs and the bells rang out, I made my way to the house with the low door. When I entered, the woman Yasmin was seated by a lamp, fingering beads. She rose but did not veil herself. For an instant I thought I saw in her eyes a look of relief, but it was gone so quickly I could not be sure. 'I thank God that you are well, Faranj,' she said.

'Your prayers kept me safe.'

She took up a bowl of water and a strip of linen trimmed with lace. 'I have prepared supper for you, but if you have spilled blood, you must first purify yourself.'

I could not help but smile. 'I have not,' I told her. 'They fled.'

She lowered her eyes and nodded, then motioned me to sit on the floor by the low table. Again the meal was simple, and again she did not eat.

'Antioch is ours,' I told her. 'What will you do?'

'With your permission, Faranj . . .' she began. I could see the discomfort in her expression. 'I have spoken with your servant. He says that I may wait upon you. I may prepare your food and wash your clothing and attend to the beauty of your horse.'

'Is that what you did before we arrived?' I asked. 'Were you a servant?'

She looked at me fully in the eyes for the first time. 'I am a poet,' she replied with dignity. 'I created verse for my lord the emir – him whose head you were pleased to place upon the wall.' She lowered her gaze again. 'That is why I live here at the palace gate.'

'I see,' I said. 'Very well. You shall attend me. And you will also write for me.'

She frowned. 'That I cannot, for I can neither read nor write in French.'

'Then you shall write and read to me in your language. And I shall see that you do not want.'

She inclined her head in thought. 'As you wish, Faranj,' she said at last. She fetched tea for me and, saying that she must attend to her night prayers, withdrew to the inner room.

I remained a little longer to finish the meal and went out. Soldiers crowded the square, celebrating. From the shadows at the side of the house Mansour approached me. 'Your horse is well,' he said. I thanked him. He hesitated and then added: 'She was in anguish today.'

I said nothing in reply. But the words moved me deeply, and I felt a joy stir in my heart far deeper than that of our victory.

July the Ninth

A pestilence has stricken the town.[90] It is due no doubt to the many corpses and the polluted wells. It spreads through the army, and man after man falls ill. The Bishop Adhémar is stricken. I am immune, having been tempered by it on the march.

Food remains scarce; the market is nearly deserted. Forage parties have scavenged for leagues around, and have not scrupled to attack the market towns, with the result that even the Armenians have deserted us in fear. An English ship arrived at Saint Symeon with supplies, but the crew was nearly slaughtered by the garrison of the town as they unloaded, and none of the provisions reached us. Now no ship will put in.

Antioch is a desolate place. Men drop down in the streets and die. Every house is shuttered. Where lately there was so much faith and rejoicing, now there is feverish discontent. Some speak out against the Holy Lance, especially among the Normans. This anger is whipped up by Bohemund, who is so obsessed with taking Antioch for himself that he turns us against one another. There have been fights among the men of different armies. To my mind Count Bohemund has much to answer for.

My Lord Raymond has returned from the citadel which the Normans have occupied. Secretly, but with careful design, Bohemund has taken possession of the entire city except the palace quarter and the Gate of the Bridge, which we still hold. Now it is Norman against Provençal, with the others looking on to see the result. Meanwhile Adhémar, who alone could reconcile the nobles, lies ill in the cathedral.

Yesterday Fulk Rechin came to me in the street with Landry Gros and other Normans. Their minds have been poisoned by Bohemund and they threatened me, saying that we must give up

90 An epidemic of typhoid fever. Since Roger had already survived an attack, it is possible that, as he says, he had developed an immunity to it.

the palace or we will pay for it. I fixed my eyes on my old companion Landry Gros and asked whether he was of that mind.

'You're better out of it, Escrivel,' he said, hardly able to look at me.

'And what of our oath?' I asked. 'What of Jerusalem?'

'We'll make a kingdom here,' he replied, 'so that others may come and finish the work we've started.'

'Cowards leave their duty to other men,' I said. I turned to go but he took my arm.

'Escrivel,' he whispered, 'if the bishop dies our expedition will be finished. Then it will be each for himself. I have no wish for harm to come to you, but it will if you stand fast.'

I took his hand from my arm and thanked him for his concern. 'But if standing for one's duty means harm,' I added, 'then harm is welcome.' I should have said 'inevitable', for I do not welcome a battle with the Normans.

JULY THE TWENTY-FIFTH

Today the Bishop Adhémar called the chief nobles to a council. No words were exchanged as we assembled at the cathedral. The atmosphere was grim. Lord Raymond, who has recovered, would not even look at Bohemund. As for the others, they kept their distance. Even Godfrey, normally boisterous and frank, held his peace.

We were conducted by a monk into Adhémar's bedchamber, which is off the sanctuary. I was shocked by his condition; he is clearly in the final stages of the fever. His skin is nearly transparent so that the blood vessels can be seen throbbing beneath it. There are livid circles around his eyes and his voice is scarcely a whisper.

'Soldiers of Christ,' he addressed us. We stood as close to him as we dared, keeping our distance from one another. 'I charge you with the liberation of the Holy Sepulchre. We are ten days' ride from Jerusalem. You must go.'

Count Bohemund spoke up in a voice that startled us. 'Adhémar of Le Puy,' he said, 'which of us shall have Antioch?'

Adhémar raised his eyes to him. Then he lifted his hand and pointed with a finger, first at one noble, then at another. At last he brought his hand back to his chest and touched the image of the Christ upon the crucifix he wore around his neck. 'Only He,' he said.

'Damn-it, bishop,' Bohemund growled, 'you have to decide.'

'Leave him in peace,' said Lord Raymond.

'Oh, that would suit you,' Bohemund spat.

Adhémar raised his hand again. 'Forgive one another,' he said. Then he pointed to Lord Raymond. 'Take up the Lance and they will follow it to Jerusalem.'

'I shall,' Lord Raymond replied.

'Why him?' Bohemund demanded. 'Who was first into Antioch? Who drove the bloody Turks away? I have more claim to lead this pilgrimage than he does.'

Adhémar fixed him with his feverish eyes. 'You do not believe in the Lance,' he said.

Bohemund looked as though he had been slapped. 'Who? Me? Didn't I put the damn thing right up front when we attacked Kerboga? If ever there was an act of faith, that was it. What the hell's faith worth if you don't win?'

Adhémar was too weak to go on, and the monks in charge of him begged us to leave. Bohemund wanted to continue, but Count Godfrey and Duke Robert led him out.

The Holy Lance lay upon a cloth of purple on the cathedral's high altar. Lord Raymond genuflected, climbed the steps, and took it in his arms. When he turned, Bohemund was glowering at him. 'Don't think that trinket will save you,' he said.

Tonight when I appeared at the house of Yasmin for supper, she could tell at once I was disturbed. She said nothing as she laid the meal for me, setting down the copper bowls and gold-lined cups without a sound. As always she stood nearby while I ate.

'Please,' I said to her, 'sit down.' To my surprise she did, folding her hands into her robes. I was irritated and did not mask it well. 'It is my pleasure that you eat with me,' I said.

She pressed her lips together, then bowed her head. She took a bit of fig paste between her fingers and spread it on a wedge of flat, dry bread. I watched as she put it into her mouth.

'That didn't soil you, did it?' said I.

She did not look up. 'There is no discipline in your army,' she observed quietly. I asked what she meant. 'Your imam, Al-hemur, is dying. Soon your soldiers will be at one another's throats.'

I was astonished. 'How do you know this?' I asked.

'This morning in the market a soldier put his hand into my bosom. A noble standing near said nothing and the soldier laughed at him as he felt me.' I was outraged and demanded to know who these men were, what colours they wore. She shook her head. 'It is no matter,' she said. 'Your people have killed so many, it was a little thing.'

I told her that from now on she was to have a guard whenever she left the house. Then a horrible thought crossed my mind. 'He did not . . . harm you?' I asked.

'No, Faranj, he did not.' Then she stood. 'I went to the market to buy paper. I have written a verse for you.' She went into the inner room and returned with a sheet of grey parchment. 'With your permission,' she said, resuming her place at the table. I nodded.

She read in the language of the Turks, which I had only ever heard from prisoners or shouted by desperate men in fights. I had thought it coarse and primitive, but as she recited her lines I heard for the first time the melodiousness of it. There were catches in the throat, but they were lilting and not guttural as I had heard them before. The rising and falling of the tones and the many rolling 'l' and 'r' sounds were like music.

The verse was not long. When she finished she placed the parchment in her lap and lowered her eyes timidly. I thanked her. 'What does it mean?' I asked.

'In the poem, sound and meaning are one,' she replied. 'It should be like the wind or the sea.'

I persisted. 'What are the words?'

'It is of a master, a religious man, who has a servant, but the servant does not know how to please him. Then one night he hears the master praying: "I am such a sinful man, only death can atone for it." And the servant, hearing this, is filled with joy, and takes his own life.'

'It is a sad poem,' I remarked.

She frowned severely. 'Oh, no,' she said. 'It is a song of joy. It is a song of your Christ.'

'I see,' I said. But I did not, and still do not. She is a strange creature. She was right to tell me not to touch her, and I have no wish to. Yet I do want to listen to her, for her mind intrigues me. I have never known the like, and I cannot help but wonder who she is and what hands of life have shaped her.[91]

AUGUST THE FIRST

Adhémar of Le Puy is dead. He expired this morning of the pestilence. What happened then can scarcely be believed.

His retinue, which included not only monks but a hand-picked guard of knights from Picardy, were attacked by Bohemund's Normans. They fought viciously over the corpse, pulling it this way and that while they thrust at one another with their daggers. At last the Normans prevailed and made off with the body, which they took to the stronghold of Bohemund in the north of the city. It seems that, having lost the Holy Lance to Lord Raymond, he was determined to seize the body of Adhémar as a kind of counter relic.

91 The expression here, *de quals mans la vida l'a dolada e limada*, derives from pottery-making. In effect, Roger compares her to a vessel turned upon a wheel and formed by the potter's hands. It is an unexpected image; the first of many he will employ in describing her.

Now the Bishop of Le Puy, the legate of His Holy Father the Pope, lies in state in the great mosque of Antioch, which Bohemund has had consecrated as a church. We have not been allowed to view the body, but I am told that he rests in solemn vestments beneath arches decorated with the words of the pagan prophet and which, until lately, had resounded with the chants of Turks.

Lord Raymond was distressed to hear the news and called me to his rooms. 'Roger,' he said, 'the pilgrimage has not been in more danger than now. Bohemund has so fragmented the armies that we cannot move on Jerusalem, and worse is to come. He will not forbear fighting among ourselves if it will serve his purpose.'

I felt I should make bold to tell him what I truly thought. 'Then why not cede Antioch to him, re-unite the army, and move on?' I urged.

I feared that he would chastise me. Instead, he simply nodded wearily. 'Perhaps I should,' he said. 'Perhaps it is God's will. And yet . . .'

He stood slowly. He was in his nightshirt, and his thin white legs shone in the candle light. I have never seen a man so old, so weighted down with care. In that moment, as he made his way towards the little table on which he kept a stoup of wine, I felt as close to him as ever I had been. He, who is the Lord to whom I owe my fealty, has long since become a friend, indeed, has been a father. Now I saw him as an old, old man in need of help to cross the room.

I took the pitcher and poured for him. He glanced at me and smiled, a kindly smile in his eyes and on his lips, and then he lowered himself again onto the bed. 'All that we have done,' he said, 'all the killings, all the suffering, all the sin, can only be atoned for by one thing – our honour. Surrender that, and we are nothing more than brigands with crosses on our cloaks. It is honour that separates the act of duty from the act of necessity. It is honour that saves us in our lives, as grace saves us in our deaths. Honour makes us men; without honour we are worse than beasts. For beasts kill and suffer and do harm without thought.'

He raised a finger suddenly and his voice was firm. 'Man is the creature that thinks and acts with honour. Anything less is to be spat upon,' he declared. Then just as suddenly he lowered his voice again. 'I cannot violate my oath. Bohemund wishes to play a game of relics with me. Very well, we know where he stands. But where does God stand? I do not know. It is sufficient that I know where Raymond of Saint Gilles stands. With God's help, he stands upon his word.'

The funeral of the Bishop Adhémar will take place tomorrow in the cathedral. Already Bohemund has fortified the place as if it were a siege camp. Evidently he fears a battle, but Lord Raymond has decided that the Provençals shall hold our own service here in the palace quarter. This will enable us to avoid a confrontation, but our absence from the funeral will surely weaken our position.

AUGUST THE SIXTH

These past few days have seen manoeuvrings in the armies that no one would have credited at the Council of Clermont which called our pilgrimage. Bohemund has moved secretly to secure every quarter of the city except that which we hold. He has encouraged the other nobles to embark on expeditions, has relieved their garrisons, and has cut off food to those who resist.

The result is that Count Robert of Normandy has left to assist the English whose fleet has taken Lattakieh,[92] Tancred has withdrawn

---

92 Lattakieh (or Latakia), the southernmost port of the Byzantine empire, had been seized by the pirate Guynemer, then was taken from him by the same English fleet that had tried to provision Antioch. Robert of Normandy saw it only as a source of income and extorted heavy taxes from the citizens, who forced him to withdraw. It then reverted to the empire.

to his holdings in Cilicia, and Godfrey of Bouillon came yesterday to announce his decision to join his brother Baldwin at Edessa.

'The expedition is disintegrating before our eyes,' Lord Raymond remarked.

Godfrey seemed abashed. 'Damn-it, Raymond, half my men are down with the fever and the other half are starving. Baldwin's got food enough for all of us. Why don't you come?'

'Edessa is far from Jerusalem,' Lord Raymond replied.

'Well so's the grave, which is where we'll all end up if we stay here. Winter with us in Edessa, then we'll join up with Robert and take Jerusalem.'

'And what of Antioch?'

Godfrey lowered his voice. 'Leave it to Bohemund,' he said. 'It's a dunghill. Let him rot on it.'

Lord Raymond shook his head. 'There's a battle raging here for the soul of this pilgrimage. I can't walk away from it.'

Godfrey looked a long time at him. His face had filled out again and his blue eyes had the look of gentle frankness I had first seen when the two friends met in Macedonia. 'Listen, Raymond,' he said, 'we're neither of us getting younger. Why fight battles we can avoid? If you really want to save this pilgrimage, come away from Antioch. Bohemund's got the bit between his teeth. Let him have his filthy city.' He jabbed at Lord Raymond's arm. 'We'll be lords of Jerusalem and he'll be king of the corpses.'

Lord Raymond smiled at him. 'I'll consider it,' said he.

Godfrey beamed. 'They say that Ma-arat's ripe for the picking; go and take it. That'll put an apple up the Norman's arse; he won't like a fortress on his flank. Meanwhile, I'm going to take my brother Baldwin's trousers down and give him a good spanking. And I may just take his kingdom for good measure. You know, he's got himself twelve wives, which is surprising since he hasn't a prick to speak of. You come and visit us when you've taken Ma-arat. We'll make some bastards for King Baldwin.'

He got up to go. Lord Raymond called after him. 'Stay away

from the bears,' he said, and Godfrey burst into good-hearted laughter.

With the departure of Count Godfrey's troops, Antioch is divided between the Normans and us. Bohemund has now put it about that the Holy Lance is a fraud, and that he will carry the body of Adhémar to Jerusalem as the only true relic of the pilgrimage. On our side, we have doubled the guards upon the wall, about the palace, and on the Gate of the Bridge, which will be our only escape should we be attacked.

AUGUST THE FIFTEENTH
The Feast of the Assumption

Two years since I left my home. I remember my departure: the solemnity of my mother, the sweetness of my sister, and the spectacle of Jehanne grabbing at my legs. I wonder what they think of me today. By now Uc of Lunel town must have returned, and my letter must have reached them. They know that I still live. Does my wife care? I do not know.

I mentioned her to the woman Yasmin at supper tonight. She asked me to describe her. A man always feels a pleasure at describing his woman to a stranger, no matter the state of their relations. 'She is not so slender as you,' I told her. 'Her body is fuller, and though she is dark, she is not as dark as you. Her eyes are grey but her skin is pale like that of the women of Provence.'

'What of her hair?' she asked.

'Very long and soft, and in colour almost black.' She was gazing at me with her dark eyes. I asked: 'What colour is yours?'

She looked down. 'Brown,' she said simply.

'May I see it?'

'That would not be right,' she answered. 'Only to my husband may I expose my hair.'

The words struck me. 'You are married?' I asked.

'No,' she replied. 'I was betrothed, but he is gone away.'

The curiosity I had felt about her now took hold of me. Until that moment I had not realized how intense it was. 'What manner of man was he?' I asked.

'He was the son of the emir,' she said. The answer surprised me and I told her so. 'It was the pleasure of my lord the emir that we marry. In that way I might better serve his household.'

'Did you love him?' I asked.

'No,' she said. 'But love is not among us what it is for you. Men and women must marry, children must be born. It is the will of God. The will of man is secondary. And that of woman, even less.'

I searched her eyes. 'Do you believe that?' I asked.

She looked at me a moment. 'Among us, women marry when they come of age. I did not,' she said.

'Where are your parents?'

'They are in the cemetery beyond the wall. That which your men were pleased to loot.' I told her that I was sorry. 'It is no matter,' she replied. 'They are in paradise. At least, my mother is. My father did not wish to go.' I asked how that could be. 'He never cared for the company of hypocrites,' was her reply.

I could not help but laugh, but her face remained as serious as ever. 'My father was Tatar. He was of the northern mountains, beyond the great sea that is called Kakus. He was a prince of his tribe, and wild as the wind. He rode with a scimitar between his teeth and stirrups made from the hair of his enemies. He was taught as a boy to obey no law but that of his own heart, and to measure a man by his eyes and not his words. He often said to me that words are nothing but lies.'

'How came he to Antioch?' I asked.

'His younger brother, whom he loved, betrayed him. They fought a long war in the mountains and at last my father captured him. He put the dagger to his brother's throat and said: "Now could I kill you and now become king. But whom shall I trust if you, my brother, have turned on me?" And so he let his brother rule and he became a wanderer, preferring to live among strangers who cared nothing for him than among kin who claimed to love him and yet would kill him for power.'

'So you are a princess,' I said.

'It is a meaningless idea,' she replied simply. 'A musement to be hung by the fire. Have you children, Faranj?' she asked.

I said that I did not, but added, 'Though my wife has.'

She frowned. 'You are not a father to them?'

'Their father is dead,' I told her.

'Indeed, he is, if you choose not to be their father,' she replied. This time it was I who frowned. Yasmin blushed. 'I speak too frankly,' she said. 'It is a fault reserved for men. Forgive me, Faranj.'

'No,' I said. 'I admire your frankness. I appreciate it.'

She nodded faintly. 'You love your wife?' she asked.

The question irritated me and I said, 'I should have accepted your apology.' Again she lowered her eyes.

I sighed and leaned back against the wall. Upon it hung a carpet like those in the palace, and I fancied it was a gift from the emir or from his son. 'No,' I told her, 'it is a matter I have disputed with myself. I don't know why it should be, but I feel that I can speak in front of you as though to myself.' Her eyes were fixed on me; she studied me as I spoke. 'It is a difficult thing between us. I loved her . . . for her body. I worshipped her in that way. But I never knew her. Do you understand?'

'You will permit, Faranj?' she said. I urged her to speak. 'The soul is not in the body. You may search for it there, but you will find only yourself. Loneliness is there, but not the soul. In marriage it is the soul that one seeks.'

'You seem quite knowledgeable,' I said facetiously, 'though you have never been married.'

'Neither, I think, have you,' she replied.

Later, when I returned to the palace, all were asleep. I made a quick inspection of the guard and then retired to my room. I undressed, for the nights are sultry, and though the insects annoy it is impossible to sleep in even a nightshirt.

I had not been asleep long when I heard a footfall near my bed. I started awake and reached for the dagger beneath my pillow. 'Who is it?' I demanded. There was a little moonlight through the high, round windows, and I could just make out a figure, small and slight, standing at my feet.

'Adhémar of Le Puy,' came the response. I recognized the voice at once – it was the bishop. A shock went through me, my heart raced. The figure did not move. I pulled myself up.

'You are dead,' I whispered.

'I am in hellfire,' the figure said. I felt myself go cold. I was not dreaming. The figure advanced, coming right up to the bed where it just caught the sallow moonlight. It was Bartholomew. His face was still, as in a trance. His eyes were closed.

'Boy,' I said.

They opened. They were the eyes of Adhémar. 'Roger,' said he, 'forgiveness is not enough. I suffer still, though not forever.' His voice was sorrowful and weary. I asked what he wished of me. 'The city belongs to him who claims it,' came the voice, 'so long as his aim remains Jerusalem. Our soldiers must repent and leave at once or they will never reach the holy place. Leave my body in the cathedral. Go to Jerusalem.'

He turned to go. I was terrified, almost giddy with fear, yet I called to him: 'Adhémar, what of my father?'

He stopped, turning back to gaze at me. I would have known those eyes in life or death. 'I released him, as I said,' was the reply. 'Now you must pray for me.'

He disappeared into the darkness, and by the time I found myself enough to follow him, he was gone.

I went at once to Lord Raymond and woke him, relating to him what had happened. We talked long into the night. At last he

said that we must go to Bohemund, for such a portent could not
be kept from him.

'You will give him the city?' I asked.

'If he will go with me to Jerusalem,' Lord Raymond replied. 'If
not, then he must answer to God, not me.'

AUGUST THE NINETEENTH

So much has happened. The parlay that took place following the
visitation of Bartholomew was a stormy one. Bohemund welcomed
the sanctioning of his claim to the city and then fumed and cursed
at the idea that it be dependent on his cooperating in the advance
on Jerusalem. He accused my Lord Raymond and me of having
invented that part in terms so strong that I immediately swore an
oath that I had spoken the truth.

'More of your oaths,' Bohemund scoffed at me. 'You southerners
set great store by them.'

'God sets store by them,' I retorted.

At that the king of Sicily blasphemed. 'Jerusalem belongs to
God,' he said, 'but Antioch belongs to me.'

Thus there is no reasoning with him. Since he has cut off our
supplies, Lord Raymond has had no choice but to leave with about
half our force on a foraging expedition. Almost as soon as he had
gone, Bohemund too departed, to take up the occupation of the
towns held by his nephew. It appears that he wishes to extend his
kingdom of Antioch at Tancred's expense.

I have been left in charge in the city, with instructions to hold
the palace quarter at all costs. And so I spend my days organizing the
defence of the palace and the bridge, not against the infidel, but
against our own. Meanwhile the Genoese fleet has arrived and
supplies from Italy are at last reaching the city. None, however,
reach us. And so while the Normans feast, we starve.

I felt ashamed as I explained this to the woman Yasmin. I urged her to take up residence with her acquaintances in the northern quarter of the city, but she refuses to leave her home. She endures, and together with Mansour, does her best to provide for us. Now that all the leaders of our expedition have left, I am the senior noble in Antioch. How ironic that is, for I cannot even feed my men, and I am as much a prisoner of Christians as ever the Turks were.

I went into the market today in an attempt to cajole some provisions, and found that the slave trade has recommenced. Women and children from the towns taken by our troops are being sent to Antioch for sale. Armenians, Greeks, and even Muslims from the neutral cities come now to buy them. The profits go to Bohemund. Thus are we Christians, who have come to liberate these lands, engaged in the sale of humans. Adhémar was right to come back from the grave. We are far from grace here, and still farther from Jerusalem.

AUGUST THE TWENTY-SIXTH

Today is a fine day, with cool breezes and moist air from the sea. One would not think oneself in the desert of Syria, but in Provence. The olive trees that have not been cut down for firewood are in bloom, and there are flowers – the Rose of Sharon, which Ruth of Brindisi brought me – that blossom on the slopes of Mount Silpius. Today the air is clear and fresh and the city seems quiet.

I have not been happy in a long time, but have been weighted down with war and worry. My brow is permanently creased and I feel old. I shall be thirty-three this autumn. Normally I might expect ten or twelve more years of life, but I do not think it now. Yet today I was happy, for reasons I shall tell.

This morning after seeing to the guard I started for the market-place with a cart and a squad of soldiers. I always go about the town armed, and I took with me, as well as my sword, a dagger I have found within the palace. It is curved with a bone handle topped with bronze. It is a well-weighted weapon that moves quickly. I shall keep it so long as I am here.

I had not gone a dozen paces from the palace when a voice called to me. It was the woman Yasmin, swathed from head to toe in robes of purple near to black, her face veiled. She hurried after me with small steps and caught me up. 'I may accompany you, Faranj?' she said.

It is awkward for me to be seen about the city with a woman. I have no desire for scandal, especially among the Normans who would make sport of it. But for that very reason I told her yes, and she fell in step with me.

The market is reviving. In addition to the slavers there are now farmers from Armenia and goods merchants from the towns, as well as the sailors of the Genoese fleet. Slowly the city is resuming its life. I had in my purse a dozen gold bezants from the treasury of Lord Raymond, which he recovered after the murder of the traitor Firouz. These coins buy food sufficient for our men. So far the Normans have not interfered, but I think that cannot last.

The woman seemed to have friends among the merchants with whom she bartered. At one point I saw her take a golden torque[93] from her arm to exchange for grapes. She has not much of value in her home, and so I stepped between her and the merchant, an old woman, and handed over a few copper coins. Yasmin turned to me. 'You may not,' she said firmly.

'I have,' I told her.

Her eyes were angry. 'Then this is yours,' she said, and she pressed the torque into my hand.

When I had done and the cart was loaded I looked for her but she had disappeared into the market. I ordered my men to return to the palace and went to search for her. All the women of Antioch were out, and the market was bobbing with veiled heads and robed

93 A stiff woven bracelet usually worn over the upper arm.

backs. I had despaired of ever finding her when a hand touched my arm. I turned. It was she. 'Faranj?' she said.

'I thought I had lost you,' I told her.

'But you with your scarlet cross and sword and chestnut hair are not easily lost,' she observed. 'There is a sight for you, Faranj, that you should see.' I asked her to explain, but instead she motioned me to follow her. We walked out of the market towards the slopes, then up among the narrow streets of a quarter filled with villas. These are large whitewashed homes, each with a garden enclosed by walls. Many of these walls have been broken down and the gardens stripped for fruit and firewood.

Above them the streets twist and rise towards smaller dwellings, those of farmers and herders who have terraced the upper slopes with low walls of rock. Indeed, up to the citadel the ground is steep and rocky, with outcroppings of the rough, white, porous stone of which the mountain is made.

I panted as I followed her for, going everywhere on horse, I am unused to such exercise. But Yasmin made her silent way, preceding me by a few steps, never slackening her pace, but glancing back occasionally at me. I smiled at her to hide my weariness, but once or twice I thought I caught the amusement in her eyes. At last we came to a terrace upon which a few Christians of Antioch knelt in prayer. Yasmin stopped and waited for me.

We were well above the lower city, and in the clear day the countryside shone for leagues about. 'There,' she said, pointing, 'Saint Symeon, the harbour, and the Italian ships.'

I looked out over the walls to the tower that Lord Raymond had built and the port where I had spent such dismal days and nights. There were the remains of our camp, and the cemeteries of our men and of the Turks.

'And there,' Yasmin said, 'Harenc, where your men slaughtered the garrison and raped the women. And there, the road to Ravendan, from which we watched your army come, and that of the emiri.'

'You know the country well,' I remarked.

She peered at me. 'It is the land of my birth, Faranj. Could you not stand upon the battlements of your castle and name every town and road and tree?'

'I have no castle,' I told her. 'Merely a manor house.'

'I am sorry, Faranj,' she said with a slight bow. 'I had thought you more grand.'

It was a challenge, one of many she offered me in her understated way, and I took it up. 'I am grand enough to be a leader of the army that has taken your city,' I remarked. She looked at me a moment, then turned and led me towards the mouth of a cave in the rock wall of the terrace. The opening was morticed round and decorated with flowers.

'You must enter,' said Yasmin with a gesture towards the cave. The sleeve of her purple robe hung down so that I could see her forearm to her elbow. She quickly lowered it. I asked what the cave might be. 'The grotto of the saint,' she said. 'It is where your bishop Peter worshipped in the days of the Roman persecution. It is where the Christians hid themselves and where, indeed, they took the name of Christian.'

'Can it be?' I said.

'Even so.'

I started in. She did not follow. 'I cannot leave you alone here,' I told her. 'It is not safe.'

'This is not a holy place for me,' she replied.

I put out my hand to her. 'Then there is no reason not to enter,' I said. She hesitated and then took the fingers of my hand.

We descended a long and sloping passage into a cavern half in darkness. The ceiling was smooth and dry like the inside of a shell, and it inclined towards a simple stone altar.

'In this place the bishop Peter conducted your rite of mass,' Yasmin whispered to me.

'At that altar?' I asked.

She shook her head. 'It was erected in my childhood by the pilgrims.'

I walked to the centre of the cavern, bending my head beneath the slanting roof, and ran my eyes about the place. Here, in this crude room, the first chosen of Christ, the Rock upon which our Church was founded, himself said mass. Here he broke the bread and shared it with disciples who lived at the time of Christ, who may have known Him as Peter had, who had heard His voice and breathed the air with Him and looked into His eyes.

I bent my knee, took out my sword, raised the cruciform to my lips and kissed it. I closed my eyes to imagine the scene: the earliest Christians, led by Simon Peter, with the words of Our Saviour still in their ears, sharing out the bread of life in this cave. It was the first holy place of my pilgrimage and I wished to savour it, but the voice of Yasmin came from the shadows.

'There is more, Faranj,' she said. 'Come with me.'

I rose and followed her into a farther passage, where it was necessary to bend nearly double. Beyond it lay a second chamber, deep within the hillside. This was even darker than the first and narrower, with a musty scent.

'You can see?' she whispered. My eyes had not adjusted. 'There, along the walls.'

I peered hard into the darkness and in a few moments shapes began to appear on shelves hewn from the rock. At first I could not make them out, and thought them artefacts carefully arranged. Then, gradually, I realized they were skeletons, each upon its back, the arms crossed, some skulls turned towards me, gaping.

'During the persecutions, many died here,' Yasmin breathed into my ear. 'The bodies remained. It is not the only room. There are others, there, and there.' She pointed to more passages branching off to right and left.

I stepped to one of the skeletons and gazed at it. Here was my spiritual ancestor, small and slight, perhaps a woman, with narrow ribs and delicate neck and a calm roundness to the sockets of the eyes. She might have waited on the Lord or heard Him speak and seen the truth in Him and followed it to her death in this perfumed dark. It was a solemn and sobering thought – should I have the courage and the faith to accept such a death in His name? Will another, a thousand years from now, look on me and think: This was a faithful servant of the Lord?

And then I thought: Where has she gone – the person that once animated these bones, that moved in this flesh, that walked these stones and came out of the sunshine of Antioch never to emerge? Where is she now? Gone? Gone where? To what rest or life? To what silence or reward? She lived as I live. She died as I shall die. What is she now? An angel? A ghost? A memory? Did her faith die with her, or did it bear her up to eternity?

And then I thought of my father, and that the Bishop Adhémar, speaking through Bartholomew, had said he was in paradise. I knelt beside the bones of the woman and asked her, if she could see my father, to say to him that I am well, and acting as rightfully as I can, and trying to bear his line with dignity. And then I whispered, 'If you cannot . . . if you cannot . . .'

Yasmin laid a hand on my shoulder. 'Faranj, we may go now.'

I stood and looked at her. In the faint light she was almost invisible, save for her eyes and her small hands. 'You do not believe in the power of this place?' I said.

'It is not my truth,' came the reply.

'Then why do you whisper? Do you think they can hear us?'

Her eyes were fixed on me. 'You have said that you respect my beliefs,' she answered. 'I shall respect yours.'

As we returned to the palace quarter she spoke of her childhood in the city, of the places where she had played and of the people she had known. Often she pointed to a house, saying there lived so-and-so, and concluding, 'They were killed by your men.'

It irritated me and so I told her of the atrocities of the Turks that I had seen: the men mutilated, disembowelled, emasculated, the women and children at Nicaea. She replied: 'Would it have happened had you not come?'

'It is a matter of faith,' I retorted.

'Faith does not kill,' she replied. 'It gives courage.'

'To fight for what you believe in.'

'To suffer for what you believe. Not to kill for it.'

And so we talked all the way from the slopes of Mount Silpius down to the palace quarter. By the time we arrived at the house with the low door, I was angry with her and admired her all the more. It was, I realized, such a conversation as I had never had with a woman. She had beliefs, principles, ideas, and she fought for them. And I realized that I was proud to be with her, to be seen with her walking the streets of Antioch, she in her long robes and hidden face, in her confidence and poise, and in her defiance. For it is defiance in a woman to argue with a man, not about emotions but ideas; not about what she feels, but what she knows to be the truth. And here I, Roger of Lunel, was walking with a Turkish woman through the streets of Peter's city, arguing heatedly of faith. It was exhilarating, it was uplifting, it was a happiness I had never had with a woman.

'You are educated,' I said as we turned into the street before the palace gate.

'My mother taught me,' she replied. 'And my father, who could neither read nor write, insisted. I used to read poetry to him at night. It was his joy; he often wept. Not for the poetry, but for the daughter who could read it. He kissed my forehead. He valued my mind.'

'You loved your father?'

'Yes, Faranj, very much.'

'I never knew my own.'

'That is a pity. A father is the rock that you climb to be free.'

'And a mother?'

'The voice that tells you to go on.'

I looked at her a long moment, or rather, I looked at her eyes. 'You are very wise,' I said.

'I am a fool,' she answered, 'for I am alone.' And then she turned and went into her house.

I wish I had met her long ago. There have been miracles on this pilgrimage – some real, some frauds. I think she may be the miracle that has happened to me. I think she may be an angel sent from God to teach me. What? I long to know.

August the Thirtieth

There was a mass sung in the cathedral tonight that moved me deeply. It was antiphony, two choirs conversing with each other about God. From the plainsong it evolved into a discourse, and from the discourse into a celebration, spiralling unto the heavens. Above the altos the counter tenor soared, lilting and lifting in gilded tones that spun my soul like gold. I did not take the host, for in that spiral tone I felt myself commingled with my God. It was enough, it was unnecessary to devour Him. I had been devoured by Him.

I must bring Yasmin to hear this. She will understand, I think.

September the Fourth

My mother is dead. Mansour came to me this morning in great agitation. A ship has arrived from Pisa bearing letters from Provence. Mine was from my sister, the Duchess of Sète. It seems that Uc of Lunel town reached Provence and announced that I had died. This report was seconded by Hugh of Vermandois, who assured Stephen of Blois that we at Antioch were lost.

The news struck my mother so that she fell ill and did not recover. My wife, Jehanne, immediately applied to the bishop for my rights. As of my sister's writing, no decision had been made, but Gauburge did not believe the report and wrote to me. And so I read the news of my own death, and of the eagerness of my wife to have it a settled matter.

It is a strange thing, to think of oneself declared dead to the world. Now that my mother is gone, and my wife so eager to inter me, perhaps it is just as well. I cannot find it in me to be angry. I am not even surprised. But I mourn the loss of my mother, and shall have the priests say a mass for her in Antioch. Perhaps Saint Peter will welcome her to paradise. Perhaps, even as I write this, she is with my father. For she never did harm to a living soul. And she loved me to distraction, who did little but harm to her.

September the Fifth

Last night, after writing in my book, I was so restless that I found myself at the entrance to the house with the low door. Bernard and Gérard, standing at their post, peered at me from the corners of their eyes but I ignored them. The truth was, I did not wish to be alone.

It was late but she admitted me. I greeted her and sat in silence. She regarded me a long time, and then she brought me tea. She poured, not taking her eyes from me. At last she said: 'You are disturbed, Faranj.' I did not reply. 'Do you wish me to read to you?' I nodded.

She took up her paper, that which she had bought in the market the day the soldier abused her. I always think of it when she reads to me. She loosed her veil and held the paper to the candle light. I scarcely heard her. My mother has been dead these six months and I did not know. She died of grieving for her son, who is still alive. She died of my absence.

The woman Yasmin continued to read. Her voice was low and mournful, and it suited my mood. There was a woeful, wistful tone to her poem that joined with me. 'I will never see you again,' my mother said the day I left. I thought back as hard as I could – had I not felt the moment of her death? Is it possible for someone so close to pass without a rustle?

The woman Yasmin put aside her papers. She looked at me in the yellow light, a curious expression in her eyes. I turned aside.

'You are crying, Faranj?' she asked.

I tried to answer her but I could not. I felt her gaze on me, and wiped at my eyes. Then she stood and walked to where I sat upon the floor and knelt by me.

'Faranj?' she said quietly. She put out her hand to me and touched my shoulder. And in a moment she was holding me, stroking my head and whispering to me. And I was crying in her arms like a lost child, like a child that has lost its parents and does not know where to find them.

September the Eleventh

Lord Raymond has returned, as have the other nobles save for Bohemund. It is said that he lies ill in Cilicia. My Lord brought few provisions. He told me that the fighting and constant movement of the armies had laid waste to Syria, and that crops are scarce. It is his view that we should move as soon as possible on Jerusalem, for it is said that the yield in Palestine has been good and that the people there are well disposed towards us.

Count Godfrey arrived with fanfare. His mules bore bulging sacks which, when they were emptied, proved to contain the heads of hundreds of Turks he has killed on his expedition. The heads rolled out onto the market square, emptying the place in seconds. Women and children fled in disgust, and I must say that I too was disquieted, for the heads were much shrunken and decayed. They tumbled out like coconuts trailing long strands of wiry hair, and making the same hollow sound upon the cobbles. Count Godfrey laughed to see the citizens flee. And though he poked me in the ribs and pointed, I could not join in his laughter.

As soon as Bohemund returns there will be a council, the chief subject of which will be Jerusalem. This is only right, for it is

Jerusalem that brought us here, and to Jerusalem alone that we are bound.

Lord Raymond is much reduced with campaigning. He is now in his fifty-seventh year. There are heavy folds of skin below his eyes, and his face is flecked with the brown spots of worry and care. His hair never returned after the fever so that he goes about everywhere with a woven cap upon his head, which gives him the appearance of an aged abbot. He has lost much weight and is inclined to stoop, a thing he never did. God forgive me, but I hope that Bohemund succumbs to the fever, so that we may move on from here under the leadership of Lord Raymond. He cannot take much more of Antioch and his clashes with the Normans.

In his pavilion tonight Lord Raymond told me that he has taken Rugia, to the south on the Orontes. This isolates Ma-arat, which he intends to seize as his base for moving into Palestine. It was while returning from Rugia that our army was attacked by the Hash-hashin.[94] These are brigands specially trained in the art of silent warfare. They descend upon the column under darkness, strangle men at random or cut their throats, and then retire without a sound. This has a profound effect upon the others, who cannot sleep and are unwilling either to stand guard or scout the column. They are much to be feared as we move south, says my Lord.

SEPTEMBER THE FOURTEENTH

Count Bohemund has returned and there has been a council. Needless to say, it was a tumultuous affair. To be brief, a decision was

94 Hash-hashin or Assassins: a heretical Islamic sect that practised political assassination as a tool of terror. They were led by Sheikh Sinan, known as The Old Man of the Mountain, and were headquartered at the fortress of Masyaf. Their name derived from the fact that they were said to be under the influence of hashish when they committed their murders. I am indebted for this to Prof. J. R. Hougan of the University of Wisconsin, Madison. For more, see his excellent study, *The Butcher's Opera: The Assassin in History* (Malcom Bell and Sons, 1989).

taken, against the wishes of my Lord, to send to Pope Urban and invite him to take possession of Antioch. Failing this, it will fall to Count Bohemund's control. It is a ruse, as we all understand, for the Holy Father is not likely to transfer his see from Rome to Antioch, despite the fact that Saint Peter presided here. Thus we move a step closer to ceding the town to Bohemund.

Another step was taken as soon as Bohemund returned. The Greek patriarch, John, whom we had seen abused and tortured by the Turks, took advantage of Bohemund's absence to assert his authority. Unhappy man, he did not count on the Norman's stern resolve. He has suddenly disappeared, and though we make protest to Bohemund, no trace can be found of him. He is no doubt in a prison in the Norman quarter. He may even be dead, though I pray it is not so. But nothing would surprise me now.

As for Jerusalem, it was decided that we shall set out as soon as possible after the worst of the hot weather. This is welcome news, and its effect upon the army is palpable. Lacking direction these many weeks, the men have become surly and undisciplined. Their arms have fallen into disuse and their training has lapsed. Now it revives, together with their spirits.

For my own part, I spent much of the day practising falling off my horse and mounting again, armed and mailed, without assistance. At one point I caught the woman Yasmin watching me with laughter in her eyes. Though it annoyed me, I could not help but smile, for it was the first time I had seen her laugh.

I started towards her to explain what I was doing, but I was such a formidable figure, I suppose, in my mail and coif, my sword and shield, that she withdrew into her house and locked the door.

Lord Raymond has departed again, this time with Robert of Flanders to take Kafar-tab and Serap. That done, we shall control the approaches to Palestine. Bohemund has not yet heard of it, but I fear that when he does there will be trouble.

Tonight I went to the house with the low door. I am aware that the soldiers gossip about my visits to the woman, but I do not care. I would not forgo my talks with her for anything, for they divert my mind and lift my spirits, although they also irritate me sometimes beyond endurance.

She is much and widely read. She possesses books in several languages and can quote from them. Her knowledge of mathematics, astronomy and natural science far outstrips my own. She has French from her mother who attended to pilgrims in the days before the Turks sealed off Jerusalem. She has also Armenian, Greek, and some Hebrew. She has read the Scriptures in the original, and was amused to learn that I have read them only in Latin, and that not in their entirety.

She has spoken to me of her book, the Koran, and I find that it has much in common with our Scriptures. The Muslims recognize Jesus, it seems, though not as God incarnate, but as a prophet and a holy man. This is novelty to me, for never had I conversed with a woman who does not accept the Christ. Yet she is a deep and moral person, whose depths and morality flourish in the absence of His divinity. It is so curious to me: I had not thought it possible to exist outside the one true faith except in savagery. And yet I find more of faith and civility in this pagan woman than in the bishops I have known.

I must say to my book that now that I am orphaned, and know that my wife has buried me, my relations with this woman of the East mean ever more. I cling to them as to a human hand, one that keeps me steady and upright, and in the warmth of whose touch I find both comfort and stimulation.

SEPTEMBER THE TWENTIETH

We have had news from Palestine that may be of great import. Guynemer the pirate has returned from Tripoli where he learned that, following the defeat of Ker-boga, the Egyptian army invaded Palestine and has taken Jerusalem. Thus the Turks no longer control the Holy City. What this may mean for the future of our pilgrimage is uncertain, but there are those among the nobles who now regret that we did not treat with the Egyptian ambassador when he visited us during the siege.

Today I made confession to Frey Alfonso. He asked about my relations with the woman Yasmin and I found myself speaking of her at length and with great enthusiasm. When I had finished, Alfonso asked whether I were not in love with her. The question caught me short.

'What makes you say that?' I asked.

'You speak as a lover speaks of the beloved,' he replied. 'With ardour and dignity. With passion and pride. You praise her mind and her character. You value her companionship.'

Such a thing had never occurred to me. I had thought of lovers only in terms of carnality. That was the bond that defined them; that was the measure of their love. But this ... this was how I regarded my father, or Lord Raymond, or my stepfather Gilles. I had never felt this for a woman. And yet I feel it for her – the Turk, the infidel, the enemy of God.

This pilgrimage is full of puzzles, and each puzzle is unexpected, and all that is unexpected brims with wonder.

SEPTEMBER THE TWENTY-NINTH

I have had many conversations with Yasmin. In them I have opened my heart to her. I have told her of my relations with Jehanne, though I did not mention Eustace nor my wife's barrenness caused by our sin. I told of the letter that I wrote to her, and of the letter from my sister, and how my wife has sought to have me declared dead. I was deeply moved as I spoke of it, and she heard me out in silence, though with understanding in her eyes. I was grateful for that silence, as I was for her understanding.

At last I encouraged her to speak. 'What do you think of me?' I said.

She glanced away a moment, her dark eyes growing pensive. 'May I speak plainly, Faranj?' she asked. I told her I had never known her to speak otherwise. She said: 'I think of you as a man between two worlds, in neither of which is he at peace.'

'What two worlds?' I asked.

She regarded me a long moment, as if deciding whether to go on; as if calculating the effect of an explanation. 'That in which you live and that in which you wish to live,' she answered. 'You as you are and you as you see yourself. Your requirements and your desires. Your truth and *the* truth. Your body and your soul. Provence and Jerusalem.'

Having said this she lowered her eyes and awaited my response. I could make none. I felt as though I had been struck a blow – but a blow of great gentleness. A caring blow, such as a physician gives to a child to dislodge a bone from its throat. A firm and needful blow.

I gazed at her a long while. There were two candles burning, and between them she sat, her legs folded beneath her, her hands concealed within her robes, her head scarfed. Suddenly she did seem to me beautiful, but with a distant, hidden beauty that lay behind her face as her face had lain behind her veil. I longed to touch her, but instead I asked: 'And how may I reconcile these worlds?'

She did not look up. Her voice, when she spoke, was almost inaudible, as if she revealed a secret. 'By understanding that neither of them exists.'

I leaned back and brushed at my moustaches to hide my smile. 'But if neither exists,' I said, 'how can I be between them?'

She shook her head firmly and a little sadly. 'It will not do, Faranj. You cannot reason it out. If you try, you will indeed be lost.' Again I asked her to explain. 'It cannot be explained,' she answered, with impatience in her voice. 'It is not *of* explanation.'

'Then how should I understand?' I insisted, feeling myself grow impatient.

'Faranj,' she said, 'you are like a man beating his head against the cathedral wall, demanding to be let in.' She shook her head faintly. 'But you cannot force your way.' She raised herself and took a paper from the shelf. 'If you will, I have written a poem.'

'Read it,' I said. 'Please.'

She read as ever in her lilting way, running the syllables over her tongue, never taking her eyes from the page. I listened to the foreign music of her verse and then begged a translation.

She put the paper aside. 'It is the story of a prince who comes from a distant land in search of a dream. He fights many battles, kills many men, whores many women. Then, on the threshold of his dream, he meets a woman. She is a foreigner, ignorant of his ways, a little frightened of him, but she sees his heart. She knows that above all he is lonely, and she invites him to stay the night. They talk at length. It is as if they had known each other from before. His words are in her mouth, and hers in his.'

I could not take my eyes from her as she spoke. 'Go on,' I said.

'In the morning he leaves. He searches everywhere for his dream, but never can he take the woman from his thoughts. At last he returns and finds that she has borne his child, a daughter, and that she has called her "Helim". That is, in our language, "dream". And he embraces them both and remains with them.'

'This story is true?' I asked. I was desperate that she would say it was of me.

'It is of my father,' she replied.

I nodded, feeling chastened. I rose to go.

'Faranj,' she said, 'what will become of Antioch?' I told her that I did not know, but that I thought it would belong to Count Bohemund. 'He is the small man with the eyes of a thief?' I agreed that he was. 'Then it will go hard with us.' I told her she would be safe so long as Lord Raymond held the palace quarter. She considered this. 'He is a strong man, your master Sanjili?'

'He is.'

'And you will go where he goes?'

'Everywhere.'

She nodded. 'It is as it should be. But Faranj, you will tell me in advance should you decide to leave?'

'I have no intention of leaving,' I answered. I wanted with all my heart to add the word 'you' but I could not.

'But you will tell me?'

'Yes,' I said, and I went out.

The city was quiet. Above, upon the slopes of Mount Silpius, lights burned in the citadel where Bohemund kept counsel with himself. Below in the palace quarter a few lamps shone in houses shuttered against the deep uncertainty of Antioch. In the house with the low door one candle and then the other was extinguished as the woman Yasmin wrapped herself in darkness. I had never felt my heart so full nor so heavy.

I made my way back to the palace where Mansour squatted in the doorway of my room. 'I will undress you, Effendi?' he asked. I answered that I would attend to myself. He peered hard at me in the dark. 'It is very hot, Effendi,' he said. 'You should sit awhile and allow me stroke your forehead.'

I wondered at his words, for they seemed so kindly and so odd. And then I realized that he might be jealous of the woman Yasmin, for all the time I spent with her, allowing her to attend me. I patted his shoulder. 'You are a good servant,' I said. 'A good friend. You are irreplaceable.'

He bent nearly double and thanked me in his effusive way and wished me a good night. I lay a long time thinking on her, though frequently a thought of Mansour would intrude. He has nearly saved my life a dozen times since Nicaea, I reflected. I must be more careful of his feelings.

And then I thought of myself, that I should be concerned about the feelings of a servant who had been no more than a beggar when I took him in. What unaccustomed sensibility has this pilgrimage sewn in me? What tenderness of the heart has it exposed to the air? Why do I feel so full of expectation, and yet so vulnerable to loss, as though I were on the verge of a great joy which also is great danger?

October the Eleventh

Lord Raymond has once again set out with the greater part of the army. This time he joins with Count Godfrey to seize the fortified town of Azaz which controls the road to Edessa. In this way they will secure a line by which Count Baldwin may support our move into Palestine. It is sound strategy but poor politics, for Bohemund sees an alliance forming between Raymond and Godfrey on the one hand and the king of Edessa on the other. This time he has determined not to leave Antioch, and I fear that his presence may mean hardship for the Provençals.

Our situation has again become acute. There is little food in the city and less in our quarter. For the most part my garrison is made up of invalided men and unhorsed knights, neither of which makes for willing soldiers. The knights resent being reduced to the level of infantry, and the infantry resent being bullied by the knights. I spend most of my time settling quarrels and disciplining insubordinate or unruly men. The Normans no doubt realize this and delight in it. And Bohemund eyes the palace hungrily.

Of what does my garrison consist? Four hundred infantry, of whom fifty are ill and unable to stand guard. Eighty knights, of whom fully half find liquor though they can find no food. I have instituted a regimen of drills, combat trials, and weapons exercise under the supervision of Guillaume Ermingar, a most excellent knight of the Camargue.[95] The men turn out surly in the daytime heat, but he soon has them in form, and I must say they

---

95 A swampy region in the south of France.

present tolerably well at inspection. All the while the Normans watch us with mockery and taunts, like black crows upon the branches.

OCTOBER THE NINETEENTH

Today I achieve the age of thirty-three, that of Christ at the time of His death. To mark the day I invited the woman Yasmin to attend with me a sung mass in the cathedral. She was very loath to go until I told her that it would do me an honour as it was my birthday.

Bearing the colours of Lunel we rode with an escort of knights to the cathedral, I upon Fatana and she upon a mule. At the entrance to the market square we crossed the Norman lines, for so I must describe the guard posts with which they have ringed the palace quarter. The Normans watched us pass in silence, but then, as we turned into the square, I heard one of them remark, 'There goes the southerner with his whore.'

I stopped and turned. 'You there,' I called, pointing to the man, a squat, bearded knight in leather-covered mail. 'What did you say?'

He glanced sidelong at his companions and replied, 'I said the wind is southerly off the shore.' He laughed, as did the others.

I walked Fatana back towards him. 'It is not bad enough that you are a coward,' I said, 'but you are a liar as well.'

He straightened himself and reached for his weapon. I drew mine and struck him over the head and he dropped to his knees. With this my men also drew, and there would have been a fight but for the intervention of a Norman noble. He chastised his men and told me to move on. I said that I wanted an apology for the woman.

He squinted at her. 'For a Turk?'

'For the poet of my household,' I replied.

The Norman rolled his eyes in consternation, then kicked the knight and ordered him to apologize. He did so, and we went on.

Yasmin came up beside me. 'You should not, Faranj,' she said. 'I do not merit such trouble.'

'You ride under the colours of my house,' I told her. 'They must be defended or none of us is safe.'

She was extremely shy to be in the cathedral, which was filled with soldiers and the Christians of the town. She insisted on remaining at the back until the music started, when she began to move forward so that she might be closer to the choir. As I expected, she listened rapt as they made their way among the Kyrie, the Gloria, the Credo and the Sanctus. When I started up the aisle she clutched at my arm, but I told her I was only going to take the sacrament. When I returned, she looked closely into my face to see what change the communion had made.

Later we spoke of the mass, and though she was most enthusiastic about the music, she expressed her perplexity at the liturgy. She mimicked the standing and kneeling of the faithful and the gestures of the priest. Though I should not have done, I laughed with her as she grimaced and waved her arms. The more I laughed, the more animated she became. Then I declared that the prayers of the Turks were no better, and I knelt and banged my head upon the floor and wailed and groaned until she too was laughing. Then she grew suddenly serious. 'One should not mock the religion of another,' she said, shaking a finger at me. But in the next instant her face began to tremble and she broke into laughter again.

I have rarely enjoyed a supper so much as ours of that evening. When it was done, she placed before me a set of chess more intricately and cleverly carved than any I had ever seen. I play only indifferently, but she taught me many new strategies, and though she defeated me every time, I did not tire of the game. At last, when it was very late, she returned the set to its mahogany box. Reluctantly I rose to go.

'Thank you, Faranj, for this day. It is the happiest I have had in many months.' I did not wish to leave and told her so. She gazed at me a long while in her solemn way. I took a step towards her. She raised her hand. 'There is poetry between us,' she said. 'Let that suffice.'

'You said you were a fool for being alone,' I replied. 'Do you remember?'

'Yes.'

'There is no need,' I whispered.

I watched the moods sweep over her narrow eyes before she spoke. 'There is love and there is loneliness. All that lies between is delusion. I do not delude myself, Faranj. Neither should you. If you have not love, then learn to cherish loneliness.'

'Do you cherish it?' I asked.

'I am learning,' was her reply.

Again I said, 'There is no need.'

'Faranj,' she responded quietly in her language, 'God be with you this night.'

'And He with you,' I said, also in her language.

I allowed Mansour to prepare me for bed. He takes pleasure in it, and I was needful of a caring attention. But all the while as he undressed me, sponged me, and raised the nightdress to my head, I thought of her.

As I got into bed, Mansour remarked, 'You seem peaceful, Effendi.' I admitted that I was. 'I am pleased,' he said, 'but, forgive me — you do not pray tonight?'

I told him that I would, and after he had gone out, taking the candle, I whispered her name in the darkness. And I slept.

OCTOBER THE TWENTY-THIRD

I have written to my wife informing her that I am not dead. Similarly, I have sent letters to the Bishop of Montpellier and to

Rome, whereto any claims on her part must be forwarded. Of course, I may be dead by the time these letters arrive, but at least as of their date she will be deprived of any action against me. Too, they will serve to ensure that before she can secure my rights, an enquiry will be made whether I am dead or no.

My letter to Jehanne was brusque and to the point, scarcely more than a few lines. I sealed it with the signet of my ring, though I had the devil's own time to find wax, and had it at last from the woman Yasmin who keeps a small quantity of it. She used it to seal the letters of the late emir, which he had her write for him since her hand is very fine.

Even though I do not read the script of the Turks, I can see that her letters are well-formed and the lines perfectly even. It is indicative of her character, I think, for in everything she takes care and moves with grace. This is unlike my wife, whose manner is excess. Even her letter, which I look at sometimes in spite of myself, shows a want of moderation. The writing is large and broad and no care was taken to see that the lines were straight. I feel that I should be insulted that she took so little time over the one letter she saw fit to send to me in two years.

It is true I did not write to her, but I was in constant struggle, preoccupied with worry for my men, my Lord, and my commission. I have fought battles, commanded troops, and nearly died a dozen times, faced hunger, despair and loneliness, while she has remained at home with time enough to enlist the charitable aid of the Duke of Arles's son – a boy no less than ten years her junior! She should be thinking of the grave – her grave, not mine – instead of luxury with a youth who has scarcely his beard. I am disgusted; I will write no more about it.

NOVEMBER THE THIRD

The nobles have returned and a general council has been held in the cathedral. It is the first of our expedition, and the result was extraordinary as I shall tell.

Bohemund had decorated the cathedral with all the flags and pennants of the army, as well as those captured from the Turks. The high altar was magnificent with golden candlesticks and starched linen. All the nobles were present in the sanctuary, each in the colours and crown of his house. The nave was crowded with knights and common soldiers, more than a thousand in number, fully one man in ten of the army. Thousands more stood outside.

Bohemund began, as expected, by asserting his rights to the city. There was stirring among the soldiers as he spoke. Lord Raymond rose to dispute his claim and to remind us of our oaths to the emperor. The restlessness increased. Each of the nobles then spoke in turn, some supporting Bohemund, some Raymond, until, at last, the soldiers began to grumble openly.

At that the peasant Bartholomew stood and all fell silent. The boy walked up the centre aisle to the sanctuary gate, turned to the assembly, spread his arms and declared: 'There is only one prince here, and that is Christ. There is only one city in the world, and that is Jerusalem.'

With that the church erupted in cheers. The doors were thrown open and more men crowded in chanting 'Jerusalem, Jerusalem!' In a moment the whole cathedral was resounding with the word and nothing the nobles did could silence it.

Lord Raymond leaned to my ear. 'It seems they want us to lead them to Jerusalem,' he said. And he too took up the cheer, while Bohemund stood fuming.

Some of the men, who had appointed themselves as spokesmen, informed us that the army would tear down the walls of Antioch if we did not set a date to depart for the Holy City. The upshot was that it was decided to resume the pilgrimage during the course of this month. By that time the matter of Antioch will have to be resolved one way or another.

Much as I dislike to admit it, for it almost condones mutiny, the men are right. Antioch has become a curse to this expedition. We have languished here a year at great expense to the army. And yet Lord Raymond is also right: Antioch cannot simply be ceded to Bohemund; it would be too dangerous a precedent. And though Alexius has been scant help to us, we do not dare estrange him since he alone is capable of guarding our rear against the attacks that must come sooner or later.

Tonight I took supper with Lord Raymond together with Peter of Roaix and Guillaume Ermingar. He thanked us for our service, citing me in particular for my command of the quarter in his absence. He told us that he intends to depart again, both to forage for the garrison and to continue to secure the route to Jerusalem. He has taken the town of Al-bara, where he has installed a Latin bishop, the first in the East. He will use Al-bara as a base to besiege Ma-arat. Once that is in our hands, our flank will be secure all the way to the County of Tripoli.

Guillaume and Peter were enthusiastic, but I was perplexed. We have assured the army that we will move on Jerusalem this month, yet Lord Raymond intends a siege of Ma-arat. This will take a month at least, perhaps longer. I did not raise the question at supper, but spoke of it when I was alone with him afterwards.

'There can be no movement on Jerusalem so long as Antioch remains uncertain,' he confided in me. 'It must either be in the hands of the emperor or in the hands of the expedition.'

'We cannot take the city from Bohemund,' I replied. 'And if Alexius does not come—'

Lord Raymond interrupted. 'That is what Ma-arat is for. We must have a fortress in our rear that we control. You know that Bohemund will not allow the passage of supplies from Edessa to Palestine. Ma-arat will be our Antioch. With Ma-arat we will have a line of supply to the north, and Antioch becomes irrelevant. And so you see, Roger, far from impeding the march to Jerusalem, capturing Ma-arat will make it possible.'

I said that I doubted the army would support the delay. Lord Raymond stood, holding his cup of wine, and began pacing grimly. 'That is my only fear,' he said. 'Bohemund has turned our men against one another and sewn such discord in the army as the Turks could never do. It's the enemy inside the walls that does the most damage. Think of the traitor Firouz.'

He paused, deep in thought. 'I have an idea — one that may remove Bohemund's influence whether he holds Antioch or not . . .' he began. Then he smiled at me. 'But he shall not have Antioch so long as you are here.' He invited me to drink with him. 'I understand you have a new servant,' he remarked when he had filled our cups. I replied that it was so. 'A Turk?' he asked slyly.

'A woman,' I answered. 'She writes poetry for me.'

He raised an eyebrow. 'Indeed. That is a luxury.' Then he gestured with his cup to the torque I wore on my wrist. 'And she gives you gifts?'

'A payment, for food,' I explained.

Raymond squinted at me. 'A female servant who pays you. Now there is a mystery of the East.' I was discomfited by the talk of her and he could see it. He put a hand on my shoulder. 'Roger, I know something of your heart,' he said. 'I know something of your life. But I ask you as a friend to remember: there is only one cleft for us in this world, and that is the Sepulchre. For that we must sacrifice all other joys, all other pleasures.'

I assured him that I had been correct in my dealings with the woman. He nodded approvingly. 'That is well,' he said, 'for the soldiers are divided and malcontent, and we must not give scandal to them. They must look at us and say: The head is steady if the legs are not. Otherwise, Jerusalem will remain a dream.'

The words struck me, and I thought of Yasmin's story of the foreigner and his dream. 'He met a woman,' she had said. And though she told me that the story was of her father, I could not deny how it sounded a note in my own heart.

NOVEMBER THE TENTH

Lord Raymond left five days ago, and I have resumed my duties in command of the palace quarter. After inspecting the guard this evening I went to the house with the low door for supper. To my surprise, Yasmin was veiled, and remained so throughout. She spoke little, and I thought I saw her stumble as she brought the tea. She insisted that nothing was wrong and read to me after the meal. I watched her closely, for her eyes seemed unnaturally bright. Her poem was of the winter, and she wrote at length and cleverly of snow, which she has never seen. She imagines it as white fur, or bandages among the trees. When she had finished she said, 'Now tell me, Faranj, what it is truly like.'

I took up a sheet of her paper, tore it into small pieces, and scattered them over her. 'Like that,' I said.

She picked them up carefully and held them in her hands. 'French snow,' she said, smiling. 'Like paper.'

'It will not melt,' I told her.

'Then I will keep it,' she replied, and she put the pieces carefully away in her carved box.

The Normans have cut us off entirely. It is dangerous now to go into the market; several of my men have been beaten. I have protested to Bohemund and the reply startles me. It seems that the Normans have issued coins bearing Bohemund's image, which alone can be redeemed for food in Antioch. Needless to say, these coins are not available to us. Our few supplies are now nearly exhausted. It is clear that the Normans intend to starve us out of the city. If Lord Raymond does not return soon with forage, we will be in a difficult state indeed.

November the Twelfth

This evening when I arrived at the house with the low door, I found Yasmin unconscious. She lay upon the cushions of her room still dressed in her robes as I had left her two days ago. Her face was flushed and her forehead was hot to the touch. I called at once for Mansour who told me, as I feared, that she has the fever. I was frantic.

'You will bring the doctor, Effendi?' Mansour said, stripping off his coat. 'I will prepare her.' He removed the veil from her face and lowered her scarf. For the first time I saw her hair and was startled by how short it had been cut. Then he began removing her robes. 'You will go, Effendi?' Mansour repeated. I hurried out.

The doctor, a stupid man from Toulouse, was useless, of course. He bled her, which failed utterly to revive her and I think has only weakened her. He tells me she may remain unconscious for two or three days. I retorted that I knew as much from my own experience. His dignity was offended. 'You could call the priest,' he said, 'if she had a soul.' I threw him out.

I shall leave Mansour with her during the day and I shall remain in the house at night. From our walk to the grotto of Saint Peter I know she is strong. I count on her strength to sustain her. She lies in the inner room as I write, and I can just make out her face. It is composed, though I resist the idea that it is the composure of death.

I do not allow myself to think it, but I am terrified that she will die. She is my friend and companion. She teaches me and causes me to think, and I have shared secrets and laughed with her. She must live. I am an orphan and have no children – I would gladly trade my life for hers. That will be my prayer tonight – that if God wills, He take my life and spare hers. For though she is an unbeliever, I know of no evil she has done, and there are mountains of it on my head.

November the Fifteenth

It is turning cooler. I have known fevers to subside with the cold, and so I long for winter, though usually it depresses me. I am in the house with the low door, where Yasmin still lies unconscious. Her sleep is no longer quiet, however, but is tormented with dreams. Suddenly she will blurt out some phrase in her language, or she will lie muttering words or simply sounds, over and over. At such times I hold her hand or press my palm to her forehead to restrain her, for it is as though she tries to rise or to reach up with her arms towards some vision.

I was thus once, and the Bishop Adhémar watched with me or, rather, he spied on me in my delirium. I suppose I too could see into her soul if I could understand her language. But I am glad that I cannot, for it is fearsome to look into the soul of another, particularly of one for whom you have feeling. Thus her secrets, whatever they may be, remain with her. If I am to learn them, I would rather she told me them herself in quiet conversation over supper, or in the course of a poem.

How I miss her company, yet how happy I am to be able to attend on her. And how curious that is – I the lord, happy to attend upon my servant. But in truth she never was my servant. I called her so but I never considered her as such. How then did I think of her? As a friend. Yet I have never had a woman friend before.

In her fever she is beautiful, strange as that may sound. She struggles against it, and in her struggle all the character rushes to her face. There are strong lines between her brows, and when she twists her head upon the pillow I can see the defiance in her face. It is heroic, this struggle that she wages, and all my soul and my strength go out to her to help her. She must win – she will win. I believe in her.

Each night I pray by her bedside. I speak to God frankly, and not in the formulae of the Church. I tell Him what this woman means to me, that she has helped me to become a better person, that she has touched my soul. And then I try to merge my soul with hers to give her strength, and I feel, after an hour or more of this, that I can accomplish it little by little.

If I remain very still and concentrate, if I cross my hands upon my breast and focus my mind, I feel that I can effect a movement in myself – I do not know how else to say it – in which a deep stillness comes over me, like water seeping in, and gradually everything is silent save her breathing, and my breathing which comes into rhythm with hers. Then I almost feel as though my soul is merging with her own, so strong is the connection between us.

At such moments she seems to calm a little and to relax, and her breath comes more evenly. At first I could effect this feeling for only a moment or two, but I become more practised at it and can sustain it longer now. It is, I think, the first time in my life I truly pray, the first time I understand something of what prayer is. And it occurs, as so much on this pilgrimage, at the most unlikely time and in the most unexpected way – at the bedside of a Turkish woman, whose people we have come to kill and from them take the Holy Land. Indeed, if I had to say what God is now, I would say that He is strangeness.

NOVEMBER THE SEVENTEENTH

I have ordered all the supplies left in the palace quarter deposited in the great hall of Yagashan. The result was scant, though the men were under strict injunction that anyone who held back would be flogged in public. Indeed, we did find a poor boy who had hidden half a dozen boiled eggs, and he was flogged, though it strained my heart to do it. But every man's life now depends on how fairly we allot what is left. I have written ceaseless notes of protest to

Bohemund, invoking the name of Lord Raymond, but without effect. I shall go to him personally to plead for Christian conduct.

My men are reduced to half a cake of barley and two handfuls of meal a day, together with such dried fruit and fish as can be spared. The sick, whose number increases daily, are given double share, but this provokes resentment among the others. Why should the sick, who are like to die, have more, they ask. I am hard-pressed to answer, for the more I deprive the healthy men the quicker they grow ill, and the more I am obliged to ration for the sick. It is a strange, un-Christian logic: give to those who are needy and the more needy you will have.

As a noble I am entitled to double ration, which I carefully take despite myself. I eat what I need and give the rest to Mansour to hoard up against Yasmin's recovery. She has been unconscious for five days and has grown frighteningly thin. When she awakes, as I know she will, she will require food.

A little I keep aside for Fatana, who also loses flesh. Yet her too will I keep alive though my own health suffer for it. I do not exercise her, nor do I dare to take her out for fear that the men, in their extremity, will slaughter her. But every night I visit her to talk to her and feed her with my own hands. There are only sixteen horses left in the palace quarter, and of them only she is fit to ride. She has been faithful and strong, and I will bring her through; my duty demands no less.

NOVEMBER THE EIGHTEENTH

Tonight as I was returning to my room from the house with the low door I encountered a figure standing in the courtyard. I drew my sword and challenged, and was astonished to see Count Bohemund step into the light.

'Roger of Lunel,' he said, his little eyes glowing, 'it seems you want to see me.'

The words made me understand that there were spies in my entourage. 'Indeed, I intend a visit,' I replied.

'Well, speak,' he said, spreading out his short arms. 'We were always on good terms. Do you remember Constantinople when we saw Alexius? In the cathedral of, what was it, Saint Shitface? You laughed along with me at their ridiculous show.'

I told him I did remember it. 'But there is nothing funny here,' I added.

Bohemund frowned at me. 'You bring it on yourself, and on your men,' he said. 'And on your Turkish woman.'

I ignored the remark, though it outraged me. 'We are the army of Christ,' I retorted. 'You are starving the soldiers of Christ — men who have fought alongside you, who have risked their lives with you for the sake of our pilgrimage.'

Bohemund approached me, coming almost to my face. He peered closely at me. There was perfume on his moustaches, which disgusted me. 'Roger, you believe in this pilgrimage no more than I,' he said slowly. 'From the first you've doubted it. Don't deny it — Adhémar told me so. He also told me a thing or two about your past. It seems you're here to atone for a certain murder. Well, would you have the murder of your men on your conscience as well?'

I would have struck him had he not been my superior in rank. Instead I said: 'My conscience is no business of yours. You are a traitor to our cause.'

Bohemund laughed. 'Now that's Raymond talking. You have to get that old man out of your blood. I'll make this bargain with you, man to man: give me the palace quarter and I'll open the market to you, everything your men need, and your woman. I'll even send my doctors to her. They're not our French idiots either, but Arabs, and you'd be amazed what they can do.'

I said nothing. He took my arm. 'Roger, a few streets, a Turkish heathen building — I'll have it one day anyway. You can tell Raymond I bought it from you — he'll understand that with all his gold.'

Then he narrowed his eyes suddenly. 'Otherwise they'll starve, Roger. All of them. And you'll have to answer for it.'

Formerly I would have dismissed him haughtily. But now I heard myself say that I would consider the matter. Bohemund brought his fist down on my shoulder amicably. 'That's the spirit,' he said. 'Now, I've learned that Raymond is besieging Ma-arat, oh, yes, you needn't try to deny it. So I intend to join him there, just so he doesn't get the upper hand. I'm leaving day after tomorrow. You'll have my answer for me by then?'

I replied that I would.

'Good,' he said. Then he lowered his voice and went on. 'We're going to Jerusalem. That much is settled, for if we don't we'll have a mutiny on our hands. The only question is, who will lead us. You know as well as I that the leadership depends on Antioch. Impress me, Roger, and I won't forget you.' With that he flashed an evil smile and left me.

What shall I do? I have never in my life been unfaithful to my Lord. Yet he is distant and Bohemund is here, and my friend Yasmin lies dying, and I am alone. Alone save for a God whose stone face on the heavens never answers except to impose some new unhappiness upon us.

November the Twentieth

It has been a trying two days. I received a summons to the quarters of Bohemund, which are in the great mosque in the north of the city. Just as the Turks desecrated our cathedral with their animals, so Bohemund desecrates their church with his. I was to attend upon the Count after evensong.

I spent most of the day among my men, seeing to the distribution of food. The ration to the sick has been systemically pillaged and it was only with great difficulty that I and Peter of Roaix managed to identify the thieves. They were two of my Marseillais, former shopkeepers in whom I thought I could trust. Peter was for hanging them, but I chose instead to have them branded with irons and made to stand under guard in the courtyard with placards round their necks. Every man who passes spits on them, and they are called the most vile names. It is no less than they deserve.

The men must mount guard with full equipments all day, and it is more than some can bear. The weaker men I have put on the walls, for I fear no attack from outside. The stronger ones guard the streets and outer buildings of the quarter. My own bodyguard is made up of six knights, all men whom I have known since the pilgrimage began. They were with me on the forced march to Antioch, and I have absolute confidence in them. It moves me to tears sometimes to watch them eat the filthy little ration they receive, to see them pick the insects from it, to know that they savour cakes the rats refuse. Yet through it all they remain as loyal as the Pope's guards.

But there is worse to come. The Normans have cut off our water. There are only two wells in the quarter, and so water, too, is now rationed. Of the three hundred infantry and thirty knights left to me, three score are sick, ten with fever; a dozen more are invalided from wounds, most lack proper equipment, and there are fewer than a dozen horses. What is more, there are some two hundred citizens in the quarter – mostly women and children – of whom a third have fever. And with it all, one foolish doctor, no medicaments, and few supplies. I am not so much a commander of a garrison as the warden of a prison hospital.

Every morning I send out small parties of men to forage. Most never return. Indeed, the temptation to desert this place is great. Those who do return I embrace as though they were members of my own family. Loyalty, when it takes hold, is a powerful emotion. Only love surpasses it. And in return for the loyalty of these poor soldiers, I do feel love.

I thought long and hard about what I should say to Bohemund and decided to offer a compromise: he could take the emir's palace as his headquarters, but he must leave the rest of the quarter to us. In that way, I reckoned, the barrier between ourselves and the city would be broken, and we might resupply ourselves at the market. It was, I knew, a violation of my trust to Lord Raymond, but it was the best judgement I could render, and my good judgement I also owe to him. If Bohemund were to refuse my compromise, which I thought him like to do, I would have no choice but to capitulate.

When I had the garrison quieted for the night I equipped myself for battle, with mail and surcoat, sword and dagger, and left the palace. Soldiers huddled around fires in the yard, their lances stacked as neatly as in any camp of Provence, speaking in undertones. They saluted me as I passed.

I turned into the street and had a thought to stop in at the house with the low door. Gérard and Bernard stood guard and seemed surprised to see me armed.

'You're going to the Norman, sir?' Gérard asked. I told him yes. 'Kick him in the arse for me, will you, sir, and tell him this quarter's a piece of Provence.'

The bravery of it struck me deeply. I was going to surrender, and yet here were my starving soldiers telling me to resist. I thanked him for his words and went in.

Mansour was asleep upon the carpets of the parlour floor. I did not wake him but went into the inner room. She lay exactly as I had last seen her, in a linen shift, her short hair wet about her face.

I knelt beside the bed, inclined my head, and prayed as I had so often done. I felt the calm creep over me and the soul spread out of me towards her. No words, no concepts, no awareness, only the silent offering of my strength to her.

I do not know how long I remained so, but at a certain moment, full unexpected, I felt a hand touch the back of my head. I was frighted and the fear broke the spell of my concentration. I raised my head to see her gazing down at me. It was the first time in seven days that her eyes were open. 'Faranj?' she said.

I took her hand. I felt a joy sweep over me. 'Yes,' was all that I could manage.

'I am tired.'

I nearly laughed. 'You have slept so long,' I said. I pressed my hand to her forehead. It was hot, though not so hot as before.

'I am thirsty.'

I hurried into the outer room and shook Mansour. 'She is awake,' I whispered.

'God be praised,' he said.

'Fetch water.'

She drank with difficulty, I holding up her head. From above upon the citadel came the sound of bells denoting the close of evensong.

'I must go,' I told her. 'But I shall be back quickly.'

She reached out for my hand. 'I dreamt of you, Faranj,' she said. 'I felt you with me. I was falling and you held me up. Your hands were on my waist.'

'Yes,' I said.

A groom was waiting with Fatana. I took the colours of my house and started for the citadel. From side streets and across the darkened squares the Normans peered at me as I passed. I ignored them, keeping my eyes upon the lighted tower of the great mosque, where Bohemund awaited me.

Their horses were tethered in the nave, chomping idly at piles of straw among the gilded arches. In the apartments of the loft Bohemund's bodyguard stood starkly, decorated in their necklaces of teeth and bones, their surcoats trimmed in human hair. Each bore upon his shoulder the scarlet Cross, the same as mine. Yet we are no army so long as Antioch divides us.

I was shown into Bohemund's quarters. They had been the dwelling of the Muslim high priest, and though austere, they were expansive, with low ceilings and artfully carved windows. The walls were covered in long shelving which was lined with thousands of beautifully bound books. The floor was deep in carpet.

A fire was blazing in the hearth. Bohemund stood with his back to me, talking loudly and gesticulating to two men. One was elderly and bearded, the other, very young. Both were wound in the severe black robes of Greek priests. Bohemund turned and smiled.

'Here! Here's the very man I was telling you about,' he said to them. 'Count Raymond's man, the Duke of Lunel.'

I bowed to the priests. 'Roger,' Bohemund went on, 'let me introduce you. This is John, the Patriarch of the Greeks. You've seen him in a cage, I think, hanging from the wall. And this,' he said, indicating the young man, 'this is Christoph, he's, well, not to put too fine a point on it, he's John's concubine.'

Bohemund broke into laughter and the other two laughed politely with him. Evidently they could not understand what he was saying. 'I'm giving John back his throne,' Bohemund explained. 'He's tickled to death. He can't wait to start getting even with the Syrians and Armenians who collaborated with the Turks. I've assigned him fifty men to roust them out and hang them. Really, Roger, he's as giddy as a schoolgirl over it.'

'And in return?' I asked.

'Always the cynic,' Bohemund chided. 'Well, in truth, he's going to anoint me king. Make it all legitimate, you understand. Just a formality. But you see how that will clarify things. Just let me get rid of them and we'll talk.'

He dismissed the patriarch and his companion with elaborate bows and gestures. They too bowed, their black veils sweeping down across their faces. When they had gone, Bohemund remarked, 'Buggers, do you believe it? All these Greeks. I'm surprised any of them has children. Well, you settle yourself there on those cushions and we'll talk. I'll put more logs on the fire.'

He stepped to the shelves and took from them two or three books. 'No good for anything else,' he said. 'Look.' He opened one. It was filled with tightly woven manuscript in magnificent hand, the letters twined and decorated, the leaves an immaculate white linen. Bohemund tossed them onto the fire. 'Heathen lies,' he said. 'Best to burn them.'

He invited me again to sit, but I declined. 'As you like,' he said, settling himself among the cushions. 'Now, to business. Once the patriarch's anointed me, there's no place fit to govern from except the palace. So, knowing how proud you are, and what a fine house you come from, and how loyal you are to old Raymond and so forth, I'm prepared to make this offer: you give up the palace and keep everything else. You see, that way it's John that's ordered it, not me, and we all know how careful Raymond is of relations with the Greeks. So it's not like you've ceded the place to me – technically it'll belong to Alexius, which is what your master wants.'

He left off smiling with his hands spread wide. For him the matter was self-evident. And indeed, it was the very compromise I had conceived myself, with the added advantage of the approval of the patriarch. 'Well?' Bohemund said.

'No,' I replied.

'No? What do you mean, no?' he huffed.

'Respectfully, no.'

Bohemund stood. 'This is sinful, it's just pride, and pride is a terrible sin. No, it's not even pride, it's stubbornness.' He came closer to me, levelling the gaze of his narrow little eyes on me. 'Your father was stubborn,' he went on between his teeth, 'and the bishops tore him apart. You don't want to go that way, Roger. No one will thank you for it, and you'll have nothing to show for it neither.'

'I wish you good night,' I said, and I started out of the room.

'Roger!' he shouted after me. 'I leave tomorrow to take Ma-arat from your lord. He'll have nothing and neither will you! Not your Goddamned palace quarter, not your pride, not even your Turkish whore! Nothing will be left, Roger. Nothing!'

I rode back to the palace quarter feeling freer than I had in weeks. It is not, perhaps, a bit of Provence as Gérard had said, but it is where I stand upon my honour, and that, wherever it may be, is home to a man. It is the place where my countrymen suffer for the sake of duty, and the place we have pledged to defend. Honour does not choose its battlegrounds, men do, and they plant their honour there like flags. Honour does not choose its battles, men do, and so long as they bring their honour to them, there is nothing to fear, for it does not matter whether they win or lose.

Suddenly, as I rode back, Antioch was transformed from a curse upon the expedition to the very soul of it; from a place of misery I had longed to quit to a place of honour where I would gladly die. For the first time in the pilgrimage I felt I was fulfilling my sacred oath – and yet it was not against Turkish infidels, but against Christian ones. Not against unbelievers, but against disbelievers.

I dismounted before the house with the low door. Gérard saluted me. 'Well, sir?' he said.

'I did as you asked,' I told him.

'Good,' he grunted.

Mansour greeted me within. 'She has lain awake waiting for you,' he said. Then he paused, peering at me in the darkened room.

'Yes?' I asked, afraid there was bad news.

'Never have I seen such devotion,' Mansour said, and I thought he was near to tears. He stepped quickly aside and bowed so deeply that I could not see his face.

Yasmin put out her arms to me as I entered. 'You are well?' she asked, a frown of worry on her face.

I took her hand. 'I am not the one who has been ill.'

'Your servant told me that you went to see the count with the eyes of a thief.'

'He will not steal from us,' I told her.

She lay back, closing her eyes. 'I am happy,' she said. Then, as if remembering something urgent she added, 'You have seen my hair.'

I put my hand up to stroke it. 'It is beautiful, like a young boy's,' I said.

She smiled. 'I was ashamed to show it you.'

'You said only your husband has the right to see it.'

'Indeed,' she replied.

That was last night. Tonight I remain in my quarters, for there is much to do. The wells have been poisoned; several women and children lie dead. Even as I was speaking to Bohemund, his agents in the quarter were at work. They have broken into the storage, burst the sacks, and urinated on the grain, they have set fires in the houses and killed half a dozen horses. I have given order that anyone acting suspiciously is to be arrested and brought to me. Bohemund is very clever in his use of spies; but I profited from the lesson he gave in roasting the agents of the emir. If I catch his men, they will pay a heavy price.

I have commanded that every drop of liquid in the quarter be confiscated and brought to the palace where it will be stored in the emir's cellar. Anyone approaching it without a written warrant from me is to be killed. Children are to be provided for first, then the sick, afterwards soldiers fit for service, then the others. Our horses shall be measured out a share which is to be increased as men die.

Bohemund left Antioch this morning with all his banners flying and with music of bugles and drums. I watched with my men from the wall. As he passed the Gate of the Bridge he saluted me. Then he posted a hundred knights to seal off the gate.

This is a war such as I have never fought. My fine words of yesterday are well enough; they may sustain me, but I cannot give them to the others to eat and drink.

NOVEMBER THE TWENTY-FIFTH

I must write smaller, for there are not many pages left in this book. I never thought when I began it that it would grow so long and, indeed, I have no idea when and how it shall end. I have a second book, in which I keep careful accounts of the men, their condition, and their rations.[96] Every day I tally up the sick, the dead, and those who are like to die. I mark down the food given to each man by weight and kind, and the medicament, if any, given to him. It is trying for me, for even at home I struggled to keep my accounts, and was content to leave them to Jehanne, who tended to them dutifully. I think women are more practical souls than men, more inclined to the minutiae of life, leaving us to our grand visions, such as they are.

It seems to me that nature has cast us this way, with complementary gifts and interlocking concerns.[97] Indeed, sometimes I think that nature has divided humanity in half, with all its potencies and weaknesses, so that a man cannot be full without a mate. Perhaps what we perceive as oddness or contrariness in a woman is nothing more than our other selves estranged. Those who resist, resist from selfishness and fear. Those who embrace, embrace in hope and recollection. For do not the doctors tell us that in the womb we were both male and female? Must there not then be a memory of our other selves embedded in our flesh? Is that not why young men are so silly and childish in their pursuit of women – since that which we seek we never were ourselves except as infants?

This is idle thinking, but I indulge it as an antidote to the reality I face all day. Of the men in my care, half now are unfit for duty. I have made count: 334 of infantry and 39 knights; 72 infantry and 8 knights have died, 105 of infantry are ill (17 with the fever), as are 16 knights (3 with fever). This gives me a force of 157 of infantry and 15 knights still fit for duty.

Were the Normans to attack us we should collapse in an hour. That they have not done so is due to the fact that Bohemund does not dare to attack Christian soldiers so long as Lord Raymond has influence in the army. But should Ma-arat fall to Bohemund, he

---

96 Unfortunately, this book has been lost.
97 The expression here is *ab bezonhas entrebescadas*. This is a term of carpentry that might be translated as 'tongue and groove'. The Occitan dictionary suggests that the word *bezonha* may also mean 'copulation'.

would not hesitate. Thus I await news from Ma-arat as I would of our own fate.

I find some time each evening to spend with the woman Yasmin. It is well to be tender after such long hours of grimness. Every man needs to be tender in order to be strong. Those who value strength alone are fools – we must be tender to be men. He who fights and cannot feel never wins anything worth possessing. She has taught me that.

She remains weak and slips into and out of consciousness. The fever has so reduced her that she cannot rise, and she is as thin as any prisoner I have ever seen mistreated. Mansour cares for her with great kindness. He is very clever at concocting soups for her to eat. As she grows stronger she must have solid food, though what we shall find for her I cannot tell.

Now to the point I have been avoiding. This afternoon my Marseillaises came running to me in great excitement, declaring that a spy had been apprehended. They said he had been found in the storage counting the sacks of grain, and when they questioned him, roughly, he admitted that it was to make report to the Normans. I ordered the man brought before me in the courtyard. It was Bernard.

Of the men I brought with me from Lunel, only he and Gérard are left. I asked whether it were true. He lowered his eyes. I demanded to know why. 'I was hungry and scared,' he replied. I retorted that we all are hungry and scared. He raised his eyes to me in spite. 'You're a lord, you don't know what it is. You hold our lives in your hands and play with us. You tell us when to stand and when to sit, and who we can sleep with. But your belly's never empty, nor your bed.'

I felt the rage well up in me. I had threatened that any spy caught within the quarter would be flayed. I gave the order.

Half a dozen knights came forward. They took the terrified youth by his arms and legs and carried him to the portal of the yard. There they stripped him and tied him upside down so that his fingers just reached the ground. Daggers came out. He screamed for mercy. Then Gérard stepped forward, pushing his way past the knights. I watched as he knelt beside his companion.

'Gérard,' the youth pleaded, 'help me.'

'I'll see you in heaven, my boy,' Gérard replied, and he kissed him.

In the next moment the knights were at work. They sliced round his ankles and ripped the flesh down to his groin. Then they opened his belly and pulled it down. Bernard howled and screamed but I watched it with my jaw set. Women and children dead, my own men dying, my trust in him betrayed. I watched it all, and when it was done I gave order that he be left there as an example. For I do not want to have to do it again.

And so you see, dear book, what I have become. I am no different from a Turk, or from Bohemund for that matter. And since we are all the same, none dare be different. Once the wheel is set in motion you must go round with it or you will be crushed.

NOVEMBER THE THIRTIETH

Our supplies are nearly exhausted. I have petitioned the Normans to allow the citizens to join their friends and relatives elsewhere in the city, but they refuse. They know that the people are a drain on our resources, and that their presence hastens our capitulation. They suffer more terribly than our troops, for they are less used than we to deprivation. It is the children who sorrow me most. Nearly all of them are dead, and they are buried quickly in pathetic little muslin bags at the foot of the wall. Above each grave is a marker, either a cross, a crescent, or the simple cairn of the Coptic Christians made of white stones piled in a shrinking square. The weeping of the women never ceases now.

My care, increasingly, is for Yasmin who, though she has

overcome the fever, remains dangerously weak. She needs food, especially meat, which is simply unavailable. Every animal has long since been butchered except for a few of the destriers. But now, one by one, the knights consume their horses.

Every bit of them is used. Men who have suffered long with their mounts now divert their sorrow into thrift. The flesh is carefully dissected, the organs are preserved, the gut and sinew are used for soup, even the bones are boiled, and boiled again until they are smooth as steel. Then they are split open and the marrow drawn out, and from this a pudding is made. And finally the bones themselves are pounded into powder and mixed with water to make a gruel. I have seen men fighting over hooves as if they were jewels, and I have seen them, too weak to rally, have the hooves taken from them by other men who had stood by watching.

We speak in the evening, Yasmin and I, and I savour the moments. She told me last night that Mansour goes without food to feed her and I chastised him for it. He swore he will obey, but I do not believe him. He grows nearly as thin as she.

God, this is an awful time. How have we deserved this at the hands of Christians? I am tempted to fight our way out of the city but we have not the strength. My only hope is that Lord Raymond will return before the lot of us succumb. I do not question him; he acts for the good of the expedition. We are the light left burning in the window. But if he does not soon return, the house will be in darkness.

DECEMBER THE THIRD

I have killed my horse. Mansour prepares the meat. I shall not leave my rooms today.

DECEMBER THE SEVENTH

Yasmin grows stronger. She has meat and soup with giblets, and very clever puddings that Mansour prepares. I take none of it, but it is a joy to see how she improves.

DECEMBER THE TWELFTH

Let me set down what I was not able to previously.

On Thursday last, it being clear that the woman Yasmin would not recover if she had no solid food, I determined to sacrifice my destrier. I prayed much upon the matter and thought on it, and in the end my mind was clear. Fatana herself could not have lasted much longer. She was horribly reduced in flesh and I often found her unsteady on her legs.

After compline I went out to her. I took with me my sword, sharpened and polished as if for surrender to a king. I spoke to her, saying: 'Fatana, you have borne me in every battle, you have borne with me every hardship, you have never failed me nor have you ever betrayed my trust. You are as true a friend as any man that I have ever known; you are as sweet a companion as any woman. I believe that you will understand now why I must kill you. Your flesh will nourish one whom I hold dear, your blood will give her strength as it has strengthened me. And if there is a God who has a care for animals and men, you and I will be reunited in heaven, where you need never be shod again and I will wear no spur. And we will gallop on the clouds together for all eternity.'

I saluted her and then I cut her throat. She looked at me quizzically a moment, rolled up her eyes, folded her legs beneath her, and sank onto her breast. I held her while the life ran out of her and her body shuddered with its leaving, and her flanks grew cold.

Then Mansour came in with a curved knife and a saw, looking as grim as I have ever seen him. I left him to it. The last thing I heard before I locked myself in was the sawing of the bone.

Now I go afoot like a common soldier. My saddle I have burned as well as her caparison. The ashes of my colours that she has borne I keep with me. The rest is smoke.

December the Nineteenth

Ma-arat has fallen. We prepare for the Nativity.

December the Twenty-fourth

On this day, when I went to the house with the low door, Yasmin stood to greet me. She had robed herself but wore no scarf. She took a step and then another, and then she fell into my arms.

'Faranj,' she said, 'I live.' And then she looked at me deeply and added, 'My life is yours.'

'No,' I told her, 'it is yours.'

'Then I give it to you, for your Nativity.'

We held each other a long while, then I helped her back to her bed. I settled her among the covers, smoothed her hair, and started to rise. She took my sleeve and held me back.

'I bid you stay with me,' she said, 'that we may welcome your holy day together with the dawn.'

I looked at her a long while, searching her eyes. Her gaze never wavered. 'Be with me,' she said at last.

'I will,' I answered.

December the Twenty-fifth
The Nativity of Our Saviour

We celebrated mass in the palace court this morning. It was a sorry little affair. Few men were able to attend. Many watched from the windows where they lay. There was no bread for the communion, and so the priest distributed laurel leaves which we held in our mouths. There was neither water nor wine.

Our water supply is finished. Mansour has managed to husband the liquids of Fatana wonderfully, so that Yasmin does not go thirsty. I have seen him straining the blood through silk over and over until a pale pink liquid distils. With this he makes tea for her. I should not have thought it would last this long.

He now is my worry. He can scarcely get about, so weak has he become. He has the meat of Fatana to draw on, yet he continues to go down. I thought to cheer him for the Nativity, and so I gave him as a gift my old tunic, with the cross upon the shoulder.

'There,' I said, 'you are a proper pilgrim now.' He took it from me, lowered his face to it, and began sobbing. 'Here,' I told him, 'today is a celebration.'

To my surprise his eyes filled with hurt and anger. 'I had a life!' he said. 'Now I have nothing. I shall die and no one will remember.'

I took his arm. 'I won't let you die,' I said.

He pulled away, wiping at his tears. 'I should have died years ago. I should never have met you. I wish to God that I had never met you.' With that he collapsed onto the floor, pulling the tunic over his head.

I was astounded, but I left him to his strange and private grief. I have known this man only in relation to myself. But of his own life, of the past he carries within him, I am ignorant.

DECEMBER THE TWENTY-EIGHTH
The Feast of the Holy Innocents

I do not know what I ought to say here. I shall confine myself to setting down what has happened.

Yesterday morning word came from Ma-arat that open warfare has broken out between Lord Raymond and Count Bohemund. After taking the town on the eleventh, the army gave itself over to the wholesale slaughter of the population. The two leaders being at odds, no one could control them. Every man, woman and child was murdered, many being burned to death within their churches and mosques.

When that died down, the soldiers fell to fighting among themselves. At last, to prevent this, Raymond and Bohemund reached an accord. The city has been put into the hands of the bishop of Al-bara, he whom Lord Raymond appointed, while Raymond himself has left for Rugia. Bohemund, meanwhile, returns to Antioch, having failed yet again to force Raymond to give up our quarter. Instead, we are to be provisioned until such time as we can join Lord Raymond on the march to Palestine.

I was overjoyed at this news, and hastened to convey it to my men, who received it with happy tears and prayers. We have prevailed in spite of everything.

I hurried to the house with the low door to tell Yasmin. I found her in the outer room, attending to Mansour. He lay upon the carpets, his knees drawn up, little more than a skeleton.

'He is dying, Faranj,' she whispered to me.

'How can that be?' I said.

'Look.' She pulled back the sleeve of his blouse, and I was stunned by what I saw. Along each forearm were thin gashes, three or four in parallel, just over the veins.

'What does it mean?' I asked.

Yasmin looked at me evenly. 'It means he has been letting his own blood,' she said. 'To give to me.'

The realization raced through my mind. Where had he found the liquid? Why had he gone down so quickly? All at once I understood. I gathered him up in my arms and carried him to the palace, where I laid him on my own bed. He stirred a little and opened his eyes.

'We've won,' I told him. 'We shall have food and water soon.'

'Effendi,' Mansour said. His voice was scarcely more than a whisper. 'How long have I called you that?'

'From the beginning,' I answered. 'From Nicaea.'

He shook his head a little. 'Not from the beginning. Not in Provence.'

I thought he was delirious. I told him to rest, and that I would care for him as he had cared for Yasmin.

'You love her,' he said. 'That is why I did it, Roger. Because you love her.' I asked him why he called me Roger. 'That is how I knew you then,' he said, 'before this life.'

'What do you mean?' I asked.

He smiled at me, his empty gums shrunken and blue. 'In the days on your estate. And on mine, when I wiped your brow. In the village at the festival, when I burst in on you . . .'

I stood and stepped away from him. He struggled to lift himself a little, his eyes fixed on me, gleaming unnaturally. 'You never loved my wife,' he said. 'I suspected it then, but when I read your book, I was sure. But this woman you truly love. And so, from love of you, I have given my life to save hers.'

I stared at him. The face was shrunken and brown and scarred with wrinkles, but as I gazed at him, slowly, as if a glass were clearing of breath, I recognized him.

'Eustace,' I said.

He closed his eyes and fell back. 'I had buried myself in the East. But when I heard you were in Nicaea I came to you. I could not resist,' he said.

I took him by the shoulders and raised him. I was frantic. 'I came on this pilgrimage to atone for your death,' I told him. 'Why have you done this to me?'

'To be with you, to serve you, made me happy. To die for your happiness is my reward.' Tears again came into his eyes. 'I know what you have suffered on my account. Forgive me, Roger.'

I laid him down again. 'Eustace,' I said, 'it is I who have sinned against you. It is I who ask forgiveness.'

He put his hand on mine. It was as light as leaves. 'I forgive you,' he said. And then: 'Please . . .'

'Yes?' I asked.

He whispered, 'Kiss me.'

I leaned to him and pressed my lips to his. When I withdrew, he was smiling again. 'I said that I should never have met you,' he breathed. 'But I am glad I found you. I had thought of you so often . . .'

His voice trailed off and he slipped into unconsciousness. He lingered for two days, and this morning he died, without a further word.

I have buried him outside the walls of Antioch in the graveyard reserved for our nobles. I had his colours placed upon the stone. Today was the first day we have been allowed outside the city. Yasmin accompanied me to the grave. It was a fine, clear day, and we lingered a long while on the hillside breathing the fresh air of the sea.

JANUARY THE SECOND
The Year of the Incarnation of Our Saviour 1099

Thus begins the third year of our pilgrimage. With it comes a terrible report from Ma-arat. The citizenry there, knowing that our army would take the place, destroyed all the stocks of grain and poisoned the wells, hoping to drive our soldiers away. Instead, in their desperation, the soldiers have begun to devour the dead that lie everywhere in the streets. We are at a loss to believe it for, even in our extremity, we never considered such barbarity. Yet news of it spreads everywhere throughout the district.

For our own part, conditions improve. Bohemund has returned and has honoured, though grudgingly, his pledge to Lord Raymond to lift the siege. Supplies begin to reach us and many are saved; for those who did not survive we have said a mass. To my mind, however, it does not suffice. They ought not to have died at the hands of their own comrades.

I have thought long and hard on the matter of Eustace. When he drowned himself, or made us believe he had, my life changed. I knew I never would be at peace again until his death was settled. Then to learn that he still lived, that my marriage was invalid, that I had come all this way for nothing . . .

I remember the words he shouted that night of the festival: 'You have taken him from me!' Yes, he loved me then with an unholy love, as I loved Jehanne with an unholy love. Everything that came from that lust was sinful. I see it now – that is why she has declared me dead, for the wages of sin are death. And yet I never married her – she was never my wife – for her husband still lived.

I had a realization today, provoked by that which the Bishop Adhémar said to me when he thought he was dying. He said that every mass he had celebrated, every sacrament he had taken, was a mortal sin because the basis of his priesthood was a fraud. And yet the basis of my marriage was a fraud. And so I must go to Frey Alfonso and confess my marriage to him as a sin and be done with it. And thus may I be free to join with her to whom God and this pilgrimage have brought me.

January the Fifth

Now that I go about the city I see that the men are mutinous. They have had their fill of Antioch and the politics of the leaders, and they wish to move on. 'I didn't come to die in Antioch,' I heard one man, a Burgundian soldier, say. 'I came to kill for Jerusalem.'

I did not go to mass today. I shall explain why.

As I intended, I spoke to Frey Alfonso, confessing everything to him. We were in the garden of a mosque, where the winter flowers, which the Turks call the tears of Allah, were in bloom. He heard me out and then walked a little way from me in thought. He wore a new robe, starched and pressed, and looked more the priest than I had ever seen him. 'You have slept with this woman?' he asked.

'Yes,' I said.

'Why did you not confess it to me?'

'Because I do not consider it a sin.'

'You confess your marriage as a sin but your relations with this woman are no sin?' he said. He walked back to me. His beard was clipped short and razored carefully along his cheeks. Evidently he has not suffered at all as we have. 'Roger,' he said, 'when you believed you were married, she was your wife. Now you believe you never married, and she is not your wife.' He shook his head. 'Marriage is not a state of mind – it is a condition of the soul.'

'That is why I know it was not valid,' I said. 'We were married in the flesh, but never in the soul.'

'And this Turkish woman? She is of the soul?'

'Yes,' I told him. 'We have been through life and death together. We have faced starvation and sickness, we have shared the secrets of our souls.'

'Then you have told her about Eustace?'

'No,' I admitted. 'But I will.'

'So you have *not* shared the secret of your soul with her, yet you have slept with her,' he said in a biting tone. I told him that I had come to confess, not to argue with him. 'Then confess your adultery, that I may give you absolution,' he replied.

'What passed between us was not adultery,' I insisted.

Alfonso looked at me in frustration. 'Say what you want to your Provençal priests, but I am your friend. If you came to me to confess it was because you wanted the truth. And the truth is, you have a wife in Provence.'

'She has declared me dead.'

He beat the air with his hands in exasperation. 'But you are not dead, just as Eustace was not. The matter is complex, but until the Church decides, she is your wife.'

I shook my head. 'My wife is here in Antioch. If marriage has any meaning, then she and I are wed.'

'No, Roger, it will not do,' the priest replied. 'Wanting is not enough. Believing is not enough. There remains the law. The death of Eustace has freed you from nothing; it has undone nothing. You have a wife under the law of the Church.'

I felt myself grow angry with him; there was truth in what he said and I resented it. 'Have you not seen what we have done on this expedition?' I asked him. 'Have you not seen the corpses mutilated, burned, the towns in ruins, the women raped and the children murdered?'

'You know I have seen it all,' he responded quietly.

'And is that the law of the Church?' I demanded. 'The Church makes laws to suit itself and breaks them to suit itself – otherwise this holy expedition would be impossible. Should the law of the Church then guide our private lives? Our souls are our own, Alfonso, and I know in my own soul that the love I bear for this woman is genuine, and that if God has brought me to this place it was so that I might find her and join with her.'

He heard me out in silence. Then he answered: 'I agree with everything you have said, Roger. Except that our souls are our own. Our souls are God's. Our souls *are* God; the God in us. You must be very sure that your will accords with His before you separate yourself from His Church. No, Roger, imperfect as it may seem on earth, the law of God is perfect in heaven. And though I am your friend, I cannot tell you that this love of yours smells to me of perfection.'

'It is as perfect as I expect to find on earth,' I retorted.

He sighed. 'Then you must aim higher.' He took me by the arm. 'Now, my friend, confess adultery to me and I will absolve you.'

I told him no and left him. The next morning at mass he refused me the sacrament. I did not go to mass today.

January the Ninth

Not a day goes by that I am not with her. I wish I spoke her language, for when she reads to me it sounds very beautiful, but I would like to follow the words with her. So much is in one's language; it is the garment that our souls wear, the jewellery and decoration of our true selves. To know one in another language is to see through glass. And so I am striving to learn her language.

It is very strange. There is no verb 'to be' in it, nor any articles, and the letters move from right to left, the opposite of our own. It strikes me as a more fluid, organic tongue, unlike our rigid, mechanical one. I have begun to read her book, the Koran. I struggle with it verse by verse, but it is a struggle not with words, but to open the door to her soul.

Sometimes we sleep together, sometimes not. There is no urgency about it. The sex between us is not sex, but the searching out of mystery, the dark elusive life that lies behind our life. If it were only sex it would be sin. But sex it is not — it is a selflessness, a longing to be free of self, a striving to be more than self. It is like the love of God for man; the love of Christ for His Church. Surely this is the point of our pilgrimage: to give oneself for love, to lose one's self in love. To be another, to become that which we love, to sacrifice oneself as the Saviour sacrificed Himself for those in whose name He took His flesh.

January the Eleventh

I am for all intents and purposes excommunicate. I could go to another priest, confess my sins, receive absolution and take the sacrament. But I know that this would be hypocrisy. What is a priest's blessing compared to that which already exists between us? I could confess to old Père Alain, Guillaume Ermingar's chaplain, who is deaf. All the nobles go to him when they have sinned excessively. But that, too, would be hypocrisy, and so, let the priests do what they may.

Yet it weighs heavy on me. The men begin to notice and, I am certain, to talk among themselves. Will they follow a lord who is estranged from the Holy Church? I do not know. Will this affect my position within the pilgrimage? Am I prepared to abandon it for her?

I know the answer is yes. The purpose of the pilgrimage is to bring me close to God and this she has done. How will more murdered Turks add to my salvation? What difference will another battle make? I can apply to the bishop to annul my marriage; my wife's husband was never dead, and so our vows were never sanctified. But even had he been at the bottom of the river, there was never sanctity in our marriage. The matter is clear: the woman had a husband when I married her, we had no issue; we never married.

Women and children arrive in Antioch from Ma-arat, several hundred of them, and thus the tales of massacre are exaggerated. They are to be sold as slaves. The Arabs from the east gobble them up; they are taken away in chains. God knows what becomes of them.

JANUARY THE THIRTEENTH

I opened my heart to Yasmin last night. I told her all, from the beginning. She heard me out in silence for the most part, only asking a question here and there. She showed great respect. When I had finished, she asked, 'What do you wish of me, Faranj?'

The question surprised me. 'Nothing,' I replied.

'That is well,' she said, and she lowered her eyes.

I waited. She did not speak. At last I asked whether there was nothing she wished to say. She glanced up at me. 'Is the taking of the sacrament important to you?' she asked.

I hesitated. 'Yes,' I said.

'Then you must make confession.'

She sat upon the floor with her legs folded beneath her. I knelt beside her and took her hands. 'There is no sin between us,' I told her. 'I believe that with my whole heart.'

'And the sacrament?' she said.

I fixed her eyes. 'What we have is a sacrament far greater than those of the Church.'

'And so,' she said, 'you doubt your Church. Our relations cause you doubt.'

I was struck to silence by her words. The puzzle of the Jew of Brindisi came back to me with force: that the sin of doubt is rooted in the flesh.

'What do you mean?' I asked her.

She gazed calmly at me. 'You prize love above faith, Faranj. But faith is necessary for love. You cannot love until you know what you believe.'

'I believe in the love I have for you,' I said.

She smiled quietly. 'It is not the beloved in which you believe. It is that which stands behind the beloved. Do not pretend to me that you do not understand that, Faranj. It is not me you love; it is that which you seek in me.'

'No,' I stated. 'It is you I love. You alone. I have no care for anything else.'

She took her hand from mine and lifted it to my cheek. She touched me with great tenderness, and yet I felt a solicitude in her touch which disquieted me. 'I am nothing but a glass,' she said. 'Perhaps a clearer glass than others, but nonetheless a glass through which you look to that which calls you.'

'I was called by you,' I said.

Again she smiled. 'I am not so arrogant as to think that all this violence, all this suffering, all this upheaval, was for me. And you are not so naive as to think it. There is a greater purpose here, Faranj. You are caught in it. Were you to remain with me, I would become a hook in your back, and you would strain and tug, and you would end by hating me.'

'Never,' I told her. 'Never that. There is no purpose here but to be with you. If I must abandon the Church I shall. If I must abandon the expedition I shall. But I will not abandon you.'

'It is not the Church nor the expedition,' she replied. 'It is yourself. And that you cannot abandon. I say again: it is a question of truth, Faranj, without which there is no love.'

'What truth then?' I demanded.

'Only you can find that out,' she answered. 'And it is not here. It awaits you elsewhere.'

'Where?'

She lowered her eyes again. 'Perhaps . . .' she began, 'perhaps in Jerusalem. Perhaps in your holy tomb.'

I stood. I was angry despite myself. I did not want to hear what she said for I feared it might be true. I had what I wanted in my hand, and I felt it eluding me, freeing itself from my grasp. 'What of your poem?' I asked. 'The one about the man who sought his dream and found a woman?'

'I told you, that was of my father.'

'But is it not also of me? Am I not a foreigner, have I not come from a distant place, fought battles. And found you?'

'That is true,' she said.

'And so?'

She looked up at me in great seriousness. 'And so, according to the logic of the poem, you will leave.'

'I will not leave,' I told her.

'That is as God wills,' she replied.

I asked her why she said this. She rose, went to the shelf where she kept her paper, and took from atop the leaves a message sealed in wax. I recognized the seal of Lord Raymond at once.

'It was brought by your countryman Ermingar from your master Sanjili,' said Yasmin.

I opened it and read. It was a summons to join Lord Raymond at once at Kafar-tab, from which the army would begin the advance upon Jerusalem. I asked if Guillaume had told her what it said.

She nodded. 'I have prepared your things.'

'You knew this before I spoke?'

'Indeed,' she replied.

'Then why did you not tell me?'

'You asked me to listen. Are you not glad that you spoke to me?'

'Yes,' I said. 'Because now you understand why I will not go.'

'I understand why you do not want to go,' she said. 'But I also understand why you must go. Faranj, your lord summons you. You are a man bound by duty. This decision has already been made, as was the decision that we should meet.'

'I do not believe in fate,' I said.

'You believed in it when it suited your purpose. You cannot disbelieve now.' She paused, then she placed her fingers on my tunic where she had mended an old tear. 'There are your two worlds, Faranj: belief and disbelief. You move between them fitfully, because you do not know where the truth lies. It lies in you.'

I felt a bitterness in me. I wished to wound her, or at least to prove her wrong. 'You said that neither world exists. Belief and disbelief – they do not exist?'

'You speak of the faithful and the infidel, the Christian and the Turk,' she replied. 'Neither exists – except in your mind. And so you seek reasons in your mind to kill, but in your soul you know it is a lie. Find truth, Faranj, and there your soul will be.'

I stepped back and glared at her a long time. 'Very well,' I said. 'I'll go. And I'll kill more of your people. But that will not be in my mind – that will be on my hands. And at the end of it, what will I find?'

There were tears in her eyes. 'If I knew, I would spare you that,' she said.

I turned to go. At the door, I paused. 'You have never told me that you love me,' I said.

'No,' she replied.

'Do you?'

She lowered her eyes a moment, then looked at me. 'Words, Faranj, are lies,' she said.

January the Thirtieth
The Plain of Buqaia

Let me report what has happened, as I have had little time and less inclination to write. We quitted Antioch, thank God, on the fifteenth and made a forced march to Kafar-tab. Lord Raymond was surprised at the small number of our troops. I had left nearly half in the city, which is now entirely in the hands of Bohemund. Lord Raymond's force, likewise, has been much reduced, both by the siege of Ma-arat and the succeeding famine.

We have been joined by the armies of Tancred, Robert of Normandy, the Spanish, Germans, English, and other Northerners. Godfrey and Robert of Flanders remain in Antioch and Baldwin at Edessa. Our entire force is now no more than seven thousand, of whom nine hundred are knights and nobles. It is not a large army but at least it is unified. Thus the great quarrel of the pilgrimage has been settled: Antioch to Bohemund, and the leadership to Raymond.

How has this march come about? By force. The soldiers at Ma-arat, tired of the quarrelling between Raymond and Bohemund, threatened to march to Jerusalem without the nobles. In response, Lord Raymond summoned all the nobles to Rugia and put to them a proposition. To each he would give a portion of his treasure, in return for their pledge to recognize him as leader. It was refused, and the expedition again fell into confusion.

The soldiers then took matters into their own hands. Knowing that Raymond was about to return to Ma-arat, which had become his base, they destroyed the city. Everything was burned, the population was scattered, even the walls were destroyed stone by stone. It was an unmistakable signal. On the thirteenth, barefoot and penitent, Lord Raymond led the army from the ruins.

Since then we have marched uninterrupted either by Turks or by hunger. The emirs all about, having heard of the destruction of Ma-arat, have sent emissaries to treat with us, offering us safe passage, guides, access to their markets, and even horses. This last has been a great blessing to the army, since, for the first time since Nicaea, all of our knights and nobles are mounted.

I have found for myself an excellent animal, an Arabian mare of burnished brown with black mane and tail. She is spirited and quick, and has learned the regimen of a destrier easily. She is not so strong as was Fatana, but she makes up for it with intelligence and stamina. I am satisfied with her. I call her Helim.

Last week we reached the fortress of Masyaf, where the Hash-hashin abide. Lord Raymond had warned us of these killers and we were on our guard. But no sooner were we within sight of the mountain, topped by ragged battlements, than the overlord himself came out to parlay with us.

He is a very old man wound in white sheets, his head shaved, his brown skin wrinkled and spotted. He seemed to me drunk, for he swayed and closed his eyes as if dozing. I am told it is the effect of a drug which they take to give them courage. This was not courage, it was stupefaction. From what I know of him and his band, I favoured killing him on the spot and obliterating his sect. Instead, we accepted his offer of passage and a guide through the mountains. The guide smoked continuously at a short pipe and was so intoxicated that he led us in circles for two days before we beat him and sent him packing.

Three days ago we reached the citadel of al-Akrad.[98] Though we lack the men and equipment to force a siege, Lord Raymond felt that we had no choice but to take the place, for it represents a threat to our advance. The Normans, English, Scots and Galles led the assault, but no sooner had they reached the walls than the gates swung open and hundreds of sheep and goats poured out. It was a clever stratagem and it worked. The animals threw the front ranks into confusion, and the men quickly scattered, chasing after them down the slopes.

Lord Raymond was furious and declared that the Provençals would take the van next day. At dawn we formed up for the charge. The castle was strangely silent; not a man was to be seen upon the walls, not a sound came from within. We scrambled up the rocky slopes towards the main gate, expecting to receive a storm of arrows and stones at every moment.

None came. When we reached the gates we found them unbolted. The city was empty; the Turks had slipped out during the night. Thus the great assault on al-Akrad was ended: the Northerners have their milk and mutton and we have our stronghold.

I should say that I saw the woman Yasmin as I was riding out of Antioch or, rather, walking out of Antioch. She watched me

---

98 Hosn al-Akrad, or the Castle of the Kurds, was a fortress built upon a height that dominated the approaches to Palestine. After falling to the Christians it became known as Krak des Chevaliers, and it would remain a Crusader fortress for another two hundred years.

from the door of her house. Her face was veiled, but her eyes followed me and I believe she waved, though I did not look back. I move on; it is all one can do. The pain one carries always, though distance is a great deadener. But I do think of her constantly, and try to drive away the thoughts. The land hereabouts is very beautiful, with chalky hillsides dusted with olive and sage. I think she would enjoy it.

FEBRUARY THE NINETEENTH
Arqa

We arrived here five days ago after spending three weeks at al-Akrad. The men were reluctant to leave for there were ample stores in the castle and, once we were installed, merchants from the countryside came to sell us every kind of comfort, including women. But here at Arqa the men are again content. The fortress occupies a height above a fertile valley. There is plenty to eat, the air is warmer, and all the urgency felt in the hell-holes of Antioch and Ma-arat is forgotten. The men are fat and sluggish and our siege settles comfortably in.

Tancred has become a bother. He argued hotly against besieging this place and, indeed, it is not strictly necessary that we take it. We might have bypassed it altogether but Lord Raymond's intent is more political than tactical. We are in the County of Tripoli, and it is essential that we secure the cooperation of the emir, who is very powerful and controls the major port between Antioch and Jerusalem. Arqa is blackmail, forcing him to pay us tribute.

Meanwhile, a part of the army has been dispatched northwards to seize the port of Tortosa. With that, together with al-Akrad and Arqa, we will surround Tripoli on three sides. All this we accomplish with fewer than ten thousand men. Bohemund, Robert of Flanders and Godfrey of Bouillon remain at Antioch.

I have been reading back through this book. I am amazed. How young I was when we began – not young in age but in experience. I was obsessed with my marriage and my sins. Now all that seems so distant and damped down like an old fire. I convulsed like a man possessed, throwing myself this way and that; I agonized, fretted, did penance, prayed for signs. Now I am scoured out; I feel the scars on my insides but they do not ache. The flesh can take only so much pounding before it numbs, the mind a little more, the soul more still. Yet eventually all is dulled, the roughness on which we hung our passions wears down, the poses we struck in pride seem merely posturing. The heart becomes a pump and nothing more.

I have never felt fitter for a fight. It is not the soldier in his passion who is effective, but he in his emptiness. A cool hand kills more efficiently than a hot head. I see that I agonized over killing Turks; now it is a matter of regret and nothing else. I used to wonder at the siege machines in their dumb lethality – no hatred, no remorse. I have become one.

MARCH THE FIRST
Ash Wednesday

Tortosa has fallen to our men with an effect that no one had predicted: Bohemund, Robert of Flanders and Godfrey have started south to join us. Lord Raymond is both grateful and concerned; our battle cry now is, 'God grant us victory, before Bohemund arrives.'

Arqa remains stubborn; its defenders are exceedingly brave. We have set fires in the town, hanged our prisoners in full view, cut off their heads and put them up on pikes, desecrated the Muslim graveyard by making it our sinks, salted the fallow fields, and flung corpses dead of pestilence over the walls. Yet still they resist. Perhaps they fear what we will do should we actually take the place.

My pavilion is pitched in a grove of weeping acacias. A lovelier tree I have never seen. It braids itself to the ground in long branches of silver-grey hue that, in the moonlight and the breeze from off the sea, trill like water. Here among their graceful tendrils I feel secure, as though angels stand on guard, protecting me with their wings. I am melancholy tonight, and have written a verse. I shall record it here, for it moves me close to her whose absence I mourn despite my hard intentions.

> As fragrance on the night, as note
> Of lute heard dim in darkling wood;
> As candle glimpsed through gauze,
> As birdsong stilled by paw-pad;
> More than this, and more
> Than dozing after daydown,
> Flash of thought fuelled,
> Fraught with inspiration,
> Taught by heart to sing and soul
> To understand:
> I miss your holy hands.
>
> Thoughts turn to dross in absence
> Thicker than a mist,
> Lips cannot speak for dry
> of absent kiss. Arms do not
> Fold nor back incline;
> The mind is webbed, the flesh
> Is vacant of caress, the fingers
> Cold with memory of impress.
>
> If I could scent your hair
> Once more, and tune me
> To your walk; if I

Could taste the light and dark
Of you again and talk
The silence in your eyes,
And twine the silk small
Soothe of you about my brow,
Like rainspill on the bough,
I need no longer muse myself
To sleep and wake to day,
And say your name and
See your face,
And find you still
Away.

MARCH THE THIRD

Couriers tell us that Godfrey and Robert are at the port of Jabala, which they have taken after a brief siege. Learning of this, the governor of the port of Maraclea surrendered his town to them. We now control the coast from Lattakieh down to Tripoli.

I am not surprised to learn that Bohemund has turned back to Antioch. His obsession with that place does not abate. He heard a rumour that Alexius is marching south and hurried back to protect his prize. I do not expect to see him again on this expedition.

I have not mentioned that I have a new squire. His name is Mercure, though everyone calls him Maudire[99] because of his abominable language. He is a Corsican from the Panier district of Marseille, which I know to be a filthy, twisted warren of thieves and smugglers. I have taken him because he amuses me and can be controlled. I have beaten him twice severely, once with a length of chain, for stealing from me. The result is that he is perfectly tame

99 Maudire: to curse, pronounced *mo-deer*.

and reliable now, having received my message with all his scheming heart.

Though he is totally illiterate, he is not without brains, his upbringing among the whores and bandits of Marseille having taught him a self-reliance that is extraordinary. He has come on the pilgrimage, as he says, 'to get even with God', by which he means to settle his accounts so that he may live as evil a life as he wishes back in France.

He is not unattractive; indeed, women find him irresistible. He has a ready smile and an ingratiating manner. He is well-built, with a full face, trimmed moustache, and thick, oiled hair of which he is very solicitous. Often have I hunted him out only to find him preening, arranging his hair with a curry comb as carefully as a gentleman at court. Then I kick him and demand an apology, which he gives with comical bows. If he were to be killed by the Turks tomorrow I should not care, and the reverse is doubtless true. But in the meantime he diverts me.

Emissaries from the Egyptians in Jerusalem have arrived with a proposition for us. If we will agree to suspend our expedition, they will reopen the Holy City to pilgrimages. Lord Raymond will reject this offer of course, but it has given us some optimism since it appears to be an admission of weakness on their part.

There was an alarm in camp tonight. A band of horsemen approached from the north and were challenged by the outposts. They rode straight on, killing several of the pickets, and made for the pavilions of the nobles. At the drumbeat we all came out from our suppers to find half a dozen Turks on horseback, stripped to the waist, heads shaved, swinging at our men with short swords. The archers formed and brought them down. Each had a long scarf tied round his head with the word 'Ma-arat' upon it.

Their aim, it seems, was to take revenge for their city by murdering Lord Raymond. No doubt they expected to achieve salvation by their raid. I ordered their hands cut off and fed to the pigs, and had them hung up by hooks so they could watch until they died. It is the worst thing you can do to them, for, as the woman explained to me, no Muslim who has had contact with swine can enter paradise. And so they shall go to hell and our pigs will be fatter for it.

Lent begins. I must make my confession if I am to perform my Easter duty.[100] I shall confess my relations with the woman in order that I may receive the sacrament. According to the strict law of the Church my hope of paradise depends upon it, and whatever one might think, one ought not trifle with such things.

MARCH THE NINETEENTH

Counts Godfrey and Robert have joined us and there has been a terrible quarrel. The cause this time was Tancred, who was careful to speak to them before they saw Lord Raymond. Tancred has told them that Raymond has disregarded all advice – meaning his advice – laid sieges, assaulted fortresses, and in general behaved like a dictator to the detriment of our move on Jerusalem. After having spent two months in Antioch under the influence of Bohemund, they were not reluctant to believe this, and so the meeting with Lord Raymond was turbulent.

'Look here, Raymond,' Godfrey said, 'now that Adhémar's dead, no one man can claim leadership of the expedition.'

Lord Raymond was indignant. 'You wouldn't have left Antioch if I hadn't started south,' he huffed.

'And you wouldn't have started south if your men hadn't burned you out,' retorted Godfrey.

Even Robert of Flanders, normally a reserved man, was contentious, declaring that he had as much right to lead as Raymond. Ultimately the matter came down to the Holy Lance. Lord

100 Every Catholic is obliged by Church law to receive Holy Communion at least once a year, during the Easter season. Otherwise, he cannot be buried in consecrated ground, which is to say, he cannot expect to attain heaven.

Raymond declared that since he had possession of the Lance, the leadership was his. Godfrey and Robert then openly announced their doubt that it was genuine.

'You remember how the boy jumped down into the hole and picked it up,' Godfrey pointed out, 'after half a dozen knights found nothing.'

'But you swore your oath upon it,' Raymond replied.

Godfrey waved a hand. 'You know how it was – we needed something to bring the army together. All that oath business was Bohemund's idea, and a good one as it turned out. But things are different now. We're moving on Jerusalem. And as Bohemund says, we've got to be realistic.'

'Realistic?' Lord Raymond repeated. He seemed dumbfounded. 'What is realistic about our pilgrimage? It is an act of idealism, of faith.' He turned to Count Robert. 'Do you agree with this realism?'

I recalled our talk with Robert on Cyprus when he had warned us against Bohemund. He still bore the eye patch and the scars of that treachery. I could not believe that he would, in effect, take Bohemund's view.

'The Lance is not the issue,' he muttered. 'Only Jerusalem matters now.'

Lord Raymond stared at him in silence, and it seemed to me that he grew older as he stared. Robert avoided his gaze, and Godfrey merely shrugged like a peasant colluding in a swindle.

That was where the matter was left. Tancred has gone over to Godfrey's side, and has begun spreading rumours that the Lance is false and is propped up only by Lord Raymond's ambition. The result is that grumbling has begun again within the army, with the Northern troops denouncing the Provençals just as they had done in Antioch. The difference here is that we are conducting a siege, in which it is necessary for all the armies to cooperate. But cooperation is already breaking down so that, instead of being strengthened by the arrival of the Lorrainers and the Flemish, we are weakened by it. No doubt the Turkish spies have already reported this in Arqa.

I asked Maudire what he thought of the Lance and his response was enlightening. 'So long as everybody else believes in it, I'll believe in it,' he said. 'What's true is what works, and it got us this far.' I asked what he would do if the army ceased to believe in it. Maudire smoothed his hair with a grin. 'Then I'd be a fool to do any different, wouldn't I?' he answered.

There is not an ounce of faith in him, nor of doubt either. Neither world exists for him, though both may be useful at times. That is the practical man's attitude. Our problem is — has always been — that we are pilgrim-soldiers. Those are our two worlds, and we are caught in both of them. The challenge is to reconcile them, or to find the strength to live with the contradiction between them. But both worlds exist. The woman was wrong.

April the Third

The army is full of visions and fist fights. The priests of the Normans have signed a letter denouncing the Lance as a fraud. Their leader, Arnulf of Rohes, the chaplain of Count Robert of Normandy, was distributing this letter when he was attacked by Père Raimund of Aguillères. It was quite a spectacle, the two holy men rolling around in the mud in their vestments, scratching and biting at one another like women, while the Turks upon the walls cheered them on.

Scarcely a day goes by without some soldier or bishop announcing a new vision, either of Christ or of Adhémar or of Saint Mark. I have noticed that no one has visions of female saints nor of the Blessed Virgin. I think this is because the whores visit our camps, and so the men have no need of fancies. But indeed, it is Holy Week and the season for visions, so anything is to be expected.

At the centre of the controversy is the frail figure of Bartholomew. Since Antioch he has held an unusual position within the army, neither soldier nor cleric, neither peasant nor man of name.

Yet there are many who revere him, and equally as many who revile him. Two days ago he announced that Christ, Saint Peter and Saint Andrew had appeared to him to order an immediate assault on Arqa. Though Lord Raymond was willing the other leaders refused, and so we remain before the walls unable either to take them or abandon them.

Now today we received news from the Emperor Alexius. He writes that he intends to join us in the month of June and entreats us to go no farther until he arrives. At that time, he says, he will personally lead us to Jerusalem. This has intensified the quarrelling in the army, since no one but Lord Raymond believes that we should accept the emperor's proposal. The other nobles, without exception, dismiss it as worthless at best and, at worst, some form of treachery.

This fact has caused Lord Raymond to harden his attitude so that now he argues both for the Lance and for a delay to wait for Alexius. I do not think it is wise strategy, but rather, the result of my Lord's fear that the leadership is slipping away from him. Added to that is the stubbornness of old age. As the pilgrimage prolongs itself, he is less and less inclined to compromise. In matters of principle this is admirable, but in matters of strategy and politics it merely serves to isolate him. That, I think, is what the others hope for. It pains me to see Lord Raymond playing thus into their hands.

APRIL THE SEVENTH
Holy Thursday

I received the sacrament from Frey Alfonso this evening and hurried to a hasty conclave of the leaders. Imagine my surprise when I found not Raymond nor Godfrey nor Robert at the centre of it, but Bartholomew. Even greater was my surprise when I saw his face.

He was furious, his features tormented, his voice rising and falling as he fumed at the nobles: 'Christ Himself ordered you to attack the city and you did not obey! You allow your priests to speak against the Holy Lance, and you yourselves doubt my visions. Duke Roger!' he called, catching sight of me as I entered the pavilion. 'Did not the Bishop Adhémar speak to you through me?'

I glanced around the circle, uncertain what to say.

'Well?' Count Godfrey asked.

'It sounded like his voice,' I answered.

Bartholomew squinted at me. 'And so you too doubt me,' he said. 'Very well. You will put me to the test. Then you will know.'

'What test?' asked Godfrey.

'Of fire,' Bartholomew replied. 'You will create a passage of fire down which I will walk bearing the Holy Lance. If I live, you will know that what I say is true, and you will believe. If I die, then do as you wish, and God help you.'

He ran his eyes over us, unafraid, even arrogant. The idea that he was mad went through my mind. There was a long silence and then, with hardly any discussion, the matter was decided. The test will take place tomorrow, Good Friday, in the central allée of the camp.

Later I sent Maudire to fetch Bartholomew to my pavilion. He returned alone. 'The little bugger's refused,' he told me. 'Says he comes and goes for no man. Says he belongs to God. I'll fetch two or three soldiers, give him a good beating, and drag him here.' I told him that I would see to it.

I wrapped myself in my cloak and went to the boy's shelter. He was praying, though there was not about him the strange light I had seen at Antioch. When he had finished, I called to him. He glanced up at me and frowned.

'If you want to talk me out of it, don't bother,' he said.

I was affronted by his manner. 'I do not,' I told him.

'Then if you are here with some pleading of Lord Raymond, save your breath.'

'Bartholomew of Lunel,' I said, 'you forget who you are.'

He got up and advanced towards me, his fists clenched. 'You forget Who you serve,' he growled, 'you and the others. Christ has given you no messages, no saints have talked to you.' He struck his breast with his fists. 'They chose me, Bartholomew the tailor's son! Don't you forget that, my Lord Roger.' He was so wrought up that I scarcely recognized him. He stared at me with a horrible grimace on his face, his eyes wild, challenging.

'May I enter?' I asked him.

The question caught him by surprise. He stepped aside and I bent in under the flap of linen. His tent, though small, was crowded with artefacts, some of value, most trinkets. There were gold ornaments and jewelled chalices, as well as soldiers' belts and weapons. There were even toys such as the peasants make for their children, dolls of straw and cloth and ficellettes.[101] Bartholomew watched me, gloating.

'Offerings,' he declared. 'They give me goods of all kinds to pray for them, and for their kinfolk who are dead. I can't prevent it. The soldiers know my value if the nobles don't.'

'You have come a long way from Lunel town,' I remarked.

He smiled. 'God has raised me up and set me over all of you.'

'Have you heard from your father?' I asked him.

He squinted at me, mucus running from his nostrils. 'Why?'

'He should know what his son has become,' I said.

'And what have I become?' he asked slowly.

'That you must tell me, Bartholomew.'

He sat in a corner of the tent, wiping with a sleeve at his nose. 'Great, in the sight of God,' he said. 'At home I was nothing – now even the counts and bishops listen to me, a peasant who can neither read nor write. Only God could do that.'

'Indeed,' I said. 'And tomorrow, what will happen?'

Bartholomew spread his arms. 'I shall enter the flames, but not

101 Ficellettes: a game played with string and a wooden frame, rather like the modern cat's cradle.

alone. I shall walk through fire and God will preserve me. And then, bearing the Holy Lance, I shall lead the expedition to Jerusalem.'

'You?' I asked. 'And what of Lord Raymond?'

'He will follow me, and you, and all the others. Because God has picked me!' His eyes were glowing. 'Do you believe?'

'In what?' I asked.

'In all of it. All the stories of the Bible and of Christ. All the saints and bishops and priests. The indulgence, the Sepulchre – everything we came here for.'

'Why do you ask?' I said.

He smiled tightly at me. 'Because if you do not, because if it is nothing – you yourself, Duke Roger, are nothing. But if you do believe, then I am greater than you because God has put his finger on me.' Again he smiled, more darkly than before. 'And if that is true – if I, a peasant, am greater than you – then again you are nothing. For there is nothing less than a peasant in your world. Is that not true?'

I did not answer. Bartholomew cocked his head and grinned at me. 'Have you heard from your father?' he said, and laughed. I asked what he meant. 'That night in your room I brought you news of him. How did I know that, eh, Lord Roger? How did I know that he'd been released from purgatory? Tell me that.'

'I don't know,' I said.

He scrambled to his feet and came close to me. 'Because Adhémar told me. I was with him in purgatory, I smelled the sulphur and saw his sweat, and he shouted at me over the roaring of the flames to go to you. You who were my master and looked down your nose at me, and wouldn't even talk to me in the streets of Lunel town.'

'You had many talks with Adhémar in private,' I said. 'Perhaps he told you my secrets before he died.'

The boy turned away suddenly. 'No, no. I have been in the other world and come back. But when you go there, you will not return. You're jealous of me, Lord Roger. Why don't you admit it?'

He stood staring defiantly at me. I felt pity for him. 'It is not too late to change your mind,' I told him.

'There!' he said, 'I knew that was why you came. You want to deprive me of my chance! You are afraid of me!'

'No,' I said. 'I am afraid for you.'

'Well, you needn't be,' he scoffed. 'I know who I am, I know what is true. And I am prepared to put it to the test in the fire. Can you say as much, Duke Roger of Lunel?'

I admitted that I could not. He smiled triumphantly. 'I shall pray for you, boy,' I said as I turned to go.

Bartholomew grunted. 'And when you go into the fire,' he said, 'I shall pray for you, old man.'

I do not know what will happen tomorrow, but the consequences will be great for the pilgrimage. If God bears him up, then the Lance will be vindicated and Lord Raymond's position will be strengthened. If not, it will be a blow from which we may not recover. The leadership will be divided and the expedition will be a headless host deep in Turkish territory. Bartholomew was right: he will not enter the flames alone. We all will be with him.

APRIL THE EIGHTH
Good Friday

There was great excitement in the army today. Many of the soldiers shaved their heads in honour both of this solemn feast and of the test that was to come. Bartholomew did not appear all morning, nor was he at the noonday service. When it ended at three, the men rushed out to the allée to get the best places from which to view the spectacle. I returned to my pavilion to change into my old tunic and found Maudire huddling in his tent. His arms were full of money of every kind. 'What are you doing?' I demanded.

He jumped, spilling the coins. 'Shit, sir, that is, God save you, sir, it's wagers.'

'Wagers?'

'Of course, sir. Everybody's wagering on the test. The Normans have clubbed together and put up two hundred gold bezants. Course the bishops is holding that. I just took in the little wagers, sir. I've no desire to blaspheme, just to make a bit of profit on the prophet as it were . . .' I told him I had no wish to hear more.

By the time I reached the allée the fire was lighted. It burned in two rows, higher than a man's head and two rods long, making a footpath of roaring, sucking flame. I took my place next to Lord Raymond who stood at the front with the other nobles, his arms folded, his face grim.

The Bishop of Al-bara presided, flanked by half a dozen other bishops and a score of priests. Bartholomew, wearing only a rough woollen tunic, stood at the far end of the fire, bearing the Holy Lance in his two hands. On his face was an expression of ecstasy; indeed, he seemed transported, scarcely aware of the crowd of soldiers that pressed on every side around him. I glanced up at the walls of Arqa, where the Turks stood watching, as absorbed in the spectacle as we.

The bishop advanced, intoning the credo of the solemn mass. A boy beside him held a thurible from which incense wafted up into the trees, mingling with the smoke from the fire. Another held the holy water and aspergillum. When the bishop had finished he blessed the fire, which hissed as the water was sprinkled over it. Then he turned and blessed Bartholomew. I saw the boy's face twitch as the drops struck it, and for a moment he frowned as if annoyed.

The bishop gave the order for him to advance.

There was silence as Bartholomew reached the end of the row of flames. His face glowed orange and red, the hem of his tunic ruffled with the breathing of the fire. He glanced to left and right, taking in our faces, then he smiled, raised the Lance to his face, kissed it, and started in.

I could see him as he made his way among the flames. He was

battered from side to side as if in a high wind, the Lance swaying before him. Some men cried out, but others hushed them angrily. For a moment Bartholomew seemed to stagger and I feared that he would fall, but he continued on at a steady pace, the flames closing over his head.

'Where is he?' Lord Raymond said.

I could see his form through the wall of fire. He was still moving, though more quickly now. Every few moments he was visible among the flames and then he vanished again. Once the Lance appeared above them and the men cheered, 'He's doing it, he's doing it!'

Everyone pressed to the end of the fire row. We could just make out the boy's form approaching us, more slowly and unsteadily. 'My God, he's come through!' Duke Robert exclaimed, and he fell to his knees in prayer.

Bartholomew moved towards us, holding the Lance before him. 'Miracle, miracle!' men shouted. The Bishop of Al-bara stepped as close to the fire as he dared. Then as we watched, Bartholomew emerged from the flames, staggered a moment, and collapsed. The men pressed forward to touch him and the Lance. Counts Raymond and Godfrey pushed to the front. 'Is he alive?' demanded Godfrey.

Bartholomew lay upon his side, his hair smouldering, his face, arms and legs burned black. He was trembling and muttering, clutching the Lance to his chest. The bishop tried to take it from him but he pulled it back.

'What's he saying?' Godfrey asked.

The bishop bent his head to hear. 'He is asking for his master,' he said. Eyes turned towards me. I stepped to the boy's side and knelt. His flesh sizzled like steak and his whole body twitched. The smell was nauseating. 'He cannot see you,' the bishop told me. 'His eyes are burned out.'

I put my lips close to his ear and called his name. Bartholomew let loose a hand from the Lance. Black skin came away from his palm, adhering to the shaft. I took the hand in mine. He squeezed. 'I saw him in the flames,' he whispered to me.

'The Christ?' I asked.

'A child—'

'The Christ child?' I said.

'No ... you ...' he began, but suddenly the pain gripped him. His whole body convulsed, he let out a groan and pressed his face into the earth.

'Take him away,' Lord Raymond called.

Count Godfrey stepped to the front. 'I'll take him,' he declared. 'We need to see whether he lives.' Four knights lifted Bartholomew and carried him to the Lorrainer camp. I watched him go in silence, a limp black figure in their arms. Lord Raymond ordered that the Lance be brought to him. As we walked back to our encampment, he asked me what Bartholomew had said.

'Something about a child in the flames,' I told him.

'He saw the Christ child,' Lord Raymond said.

'Yes, it must have been that,' I agreed.

The test has done nothing to settle the army's doubts; indeed, it has magnified them. Some say that the fact the boy was burned disproves the Lance. Others point out that his tunic was not burned, and that the Lance survived intact. Still others claim that the Normans prevented him from emerging from the flames in order to win their wager. A few say that it is a miracle he survived at all. And everyone waits to see whether he will die.

April the Eighteenth

I have been reading the pages from my journal that deal with Eustace. What a duplicitous man he was. He took me in completely and used my trust in order to get near to me. I see that he handled my body, shared my secrets, witnessed my shame, and that I thanked him for it! He tricked us all into thinking he was dead, just as he tricked me into thinking he was my trusted servant.

Why I felt for him in his extremity I cannot now say. He was a man who had violated every bond of trust, from marriage to friendship to fealty. This pilgrimage was to assuage my guilt and wipe away my sin; for that have I suffered and caused others to suffer. And though Eustace saved my life more than once, he had no right to interfere with my penance.

How complex life is, and how strange it is that what we had thought was behind us suddenly appears before us in a new guise. Life is not a line but a tight spiral in which we move upwards, coil upon stacked coil, revisiting from a slightly different angle all that we have been and done. Progress we make surely, but it is slow and nostalgic. And to what end? And how may we break free?

Religion offers nothing but mystery, departures into that which we cannot know. We can only close our eyes like children and make the leap. 'Believe this and do not ask why,' religion says, and: 'Put your faith in this but do not try to understand.' And yet did not the woman say that the truth has no explanation, that it is not *of* explanation? But if the truth cannot be explained, how may we know it? And did she not say that you cannot love until you know the truth? How then may we love?

Eustace said with his dying breath that he gave his life for my happiness because he loved me. And yet all that he desired was unnatural. 'Kiss me,' he asked, and I did so and he died with a smile on his lips. But there is no truth in this – it is abomination. And yet he did nourish her whom I loved with his own blood in order that she might live. And is this not like to what Christ did in shedding His blood for us? Can it be that this unnatural creature was like Christ? He laid down his life for his friend's sake; he died and was alive again; he humbled himself to be the servant of him whom he loved. But did not Jehanne describe to me his sinful acts? Did she not tell me of his panting and slavering? This was not like Christ.

Yet Christ surely loves him as He loves all sinners. And Christ shed His blood for him as He did for all of us. And I saw no sin in him, only faithfulness and sacrifice. So perhaps he was more like Christ than I am. Perhaps this was a truer pilgrimage for him than it is for me, since he joined it out of secret love, and not from secret guilt as I did.

Now that he is dead, what has become of him? Has he earned the indulgence? Is he in heaven? He had no priest at his death; made no confession except to me. But he was a pilgrim, served with us, suffered with us. Do I truly believe that this pilgrimage alone earns paradise? Some, like me, have come in order to undo sin, and others, like Maudire, in order to do sin. Some die in grace, and others die scoundrels. Yet all are pilgrims, and so do they all gain heaven? And the Turks that we have killed – the innocents, the women and children – are they perforce in hell?

A Christian knight, with all his sins upon his head, kills a little pagan girl, a child who has never known sin. He goes to heaven, and she to hell. No, I do not believe it. If there is justice, if there is truth, then hell is his and heaven hers. For God took the child in her innocence and suffered the knight to endure to sinful age. He created both, knows both, loves both, and will gather her to Him and estrange the other.

That is truth if truth there is, and no pope, no bishop, no indulgence can undo it. We are damned by what we do, not by what we are. And we are saved by what we know to be the truth, not by what others tell us to believe.

April the Twenty-third

Bartholomew died this morning. Tancred immediately declared that the Lance is a fraud and that the leadership ought to be shared equally among all the senior nobles. At the council tonight Lord Raymond managed to postpone a formal decision on the matter.

He has, however, decided that we Provençals will assault Arqa on our own. By taking Arqa he hopes to restore his position or, failing that, to force the others to support our attack. When he announced this to us following the council, no one spoke. But I am sure that all felt as I did: this is an unwise move dictated not by strategy but by politics.

May the Third

I still live. I will first relate the attack on the city, and then recount the other event that has occurred which, I think, may be of far greater importance.

During the night prior to our assault we rolled our siege towers into position and the sappers made ready with ladders and ropes. The attack began at first light. The towers were heaved forward until they nearly touched the walls. The Turks, alerted to our plans, were ready with stones and arrows. Every man who ascended the towers was shot down, and the poor sappers could not approach within a rod of the walls without coming under a torrent of fire. It was a pitiful, forlorn gesture, and after two or three hours of it I could no longer hold back.

I gathered up a dozen knights and we made a dash for the nearest tower. Rocks and spears were falling everywhere around us. The man at my elbow went down with two arrows through his breast and before he hit the ground, three more had struck him. The Turks above were wild, howling and cursing at us. I managed to reach the shelter of the tower with most of my men and we started up.

The whole interior of the structure was hung with bodies, men dying of wounds, men dead. Two soldiers were struggling with the mechanism of the bridge as we reached the top. One gave a cry and fell to the ground, then the other stepped back, a shaft through his mouth. I could clearly see the Turks upon the wall; archers stood to the battlements firing arrow after arrow as men behind passed them forward. I shouted to Guillaume Ermingar to help me with the bridge, but as soon as he touched the mechanism he received an arrow in his arm and then another in his side. I grabbed him just as he was falling.

Below me soldiers tried to scale the ladders, but some were pushed over with long forks, others set on fire. The rain of missiles was incessant. Then, as I watched, half a dozen balls of Greek fire exploded within the tower beneath my feet, and in a moment the whole structure was in flames. The Turks cheered and increased their fire. The tower next to mine was now aflame and men were leaping even from the top.

I had to get down, but I could not leave Ermingar. I dragged him to the ladder. The flames were leaping almost to the top and the heat was intense. I had no choice. I carried my companion to the edge of the platform and rolled him off into the moat below. Then I jumped. It was not deep and my feet struck the bottom, sending a shock through my spine into the back of my skull. The concussion knocked the breath from me and I fought to reach the surface.

Stones were pouring down from the walls, splashing into the moat on which pools of Greek fire blazed. I searched for Guillaume and saw him a few rods off, struggling to keep his head up. I swam towards him and just as I reached him a rock came hurtling down and struck him full on the chest. I heard his ribs snap, he grunted and disappeared under the oily water.

I drew a breath and dived. I could see nothing, but groping with my hands I found him. I lunged for him and my hand entered his chest. When I came up and pulled him after me, his torso was ripped open. My fingers grappled inside the cavity of his chest as I struggled to save him, but his breastbone cut into my wrist so that I was forced to let him go. He lolled to one side and sank beneath the water. In my hand I still held his heart.

I was horrified by this more than by the rain of stones and arrows. I struck out for the bank as missiles splashed around me, pulled myself up, and ran as fast as I could for our lines. It was not until I stopped out of range of the walls that I realized that my whole body from my waist to the back of my neck ached with a dull pain.

After the burning of the towers the attack was called off. Not one other army had made a move to support us. They were, I suppose, waiting to see what would happen, and I cannot say that I blame them. Lord Raymond turned away from the spectacle with a look of dismay. He knows that the days of his leadership are numbered.

It was on the evening after our assault that the other event occurred. Lord Raymond was visiting me in my pavilion where I had lain since the battle, unable to rise. At first I thought I had broken my back, but the injury is not so serious. I have done some damage to my spine, and the pain forbids me to find a position in which I might rest. I am in a constant, nagging agony which the doctors can do nothing to relieve.

As my Lord was leaving we heard a commotion. Heralds from Count Godfrey appeared at the door of my pavilion, and then the Count himself. 'Look at this!' Godfrey bellowed. He handed a paper to Lord Raymond. I saw that it bore the seal of Alexius the emperor. Raymond read it through quickly. 'You see!' Godfrey exclaimed. 'He *has* betrayed us. There's the proof in his own bloody hand!'

Raymond sat beside my cot and handed the letter to me. It was in Greek and the language of the Turks, but beneath it someone, probably a priest, had written a translation. It was addressed to al-Afdal Shahinshah, vizier of the Fatimid empire. In it Alexius said that he no longer controlled the Franks, who had taken Antioch from him, and who sought to establish their own kingdoms in Syria. Alexius regretted that he could do nothing to aid his ally, Egypt, but he would try to delay the Franks long enough to allow the general Iftikhar to strengthen the garrison of Jerusalem.

'You wanted to wait for him,' Godfrey scoffed. 'He's digging our grave. What do you think of your oath now?'

Lord Raymond put his head in his hands. I have never seen him more downcast, but indeed, the death of Bartholomew, the failed assault, and this letter were a weight that even he could not bear. 'We will recall our forces from Tortosa and Maraclea,' he said quietly, 'and we will continue south.'

Godfrey nodded. 'And who shall take the lead?'

Raymond raised his eyes to him. 'We all shall, by the grace of God.'

Godfrey put a hand on his shoulder. 'It's the only way,' he said. 'No one man can bear the burden of this expedition.'

Raymond smiled at him sadly. 'It was supposed to be a blessing.'

'Blessing, curse . . .' Godfrey huffed. 'Who can tell the difference any more? Come on, we'll go to the other men.' Raymond rose to join him. Godfrey took his arm. 'Understand, Raymond,' he said, 'if I had to serve under any man, it would be you.'

'I think I will serve under you now,' Lord Raymond replied.

Godfrey shook his head. 'If they try to force it on me I won't take it. We'll march into Jerusalem as equals and we'll occupy it as equals, or we won't go at all.'

We await the return of our outposts from the coast. It will be a welcome respite for me, for I cannot ride in this condition. And though I cannot sleep either, that too is a respite, for I am sure that I would dream of water and bones.

MAY THE SIXTEENTH

We are camped outside of Tripoli in the most beautiful country I have seen in the East. The fields are covered in flowers and the land is rich and well tended. For a city so wealthy, and for so busy a port, its defences are quite poor; we could have taken the place with a full assault. But there is no need. The emir has made his peace with us, giving our leaders fifteen thousand gold bezants, twenty fine horses, and animals and provisions for our march. In short, he means to have us gone as soon as possible.

The nobles were invited to his palace the night of our arrival. We got good and truly drunk and the emir, a stout man with a spindly beard, swore that he will become a Christian if we drive the Fatimids from his kingdom. The next afternoon I awoke upon a bed of cushions in the company of three women, none of whom I recognized.

There has been little drilling in our camp. The men go about with flowers in their caps, gnawing on mutton bones and complaining of flux. Women are not in short supply. We are to leave tomorrow, though whether we can stir this army or not remains to be seen.

MAY THE TWENTY-SECOND

We are at the city of Tyre in the Kingdom of Jerusalem. Our passage has been undisturbed except at Sidon, where the garrison attacked us. We drove them off and destroyed their crops and vines so thoroughly that I am sure we shall have no more such trouble. The countryside grows more luxurious as we move south. Jerusalem must be a paradise, for the vines here are lush and green, the grain grows abundantly, the olive and fruit trees hang heavy with blossoms, and the soil yields easily to the hand.

There are poppies here with long, furry stalks upon which butterflies of every hue and pattern play. A warm breeze rises from the sea, that same blue sea which washes the shores of my home. The men are entranced. Surely this land is a blessed place, and an even greater blessing is that we are not obliged to fight for it. Blood upon these holy, happy slopes would be a sacrilege. Indeed it is a land for pilgrims, where thoughts of sanctity come readily to mind, and the scent of the ancient fragrant world is on the air.

The only dissonant note, and that a distant one, is the presence of the Egyptian fleet which lies offshore, glowering behind its striped sails and painted oars. They can do nothing but deny us occupation of the ports, and yet we have no need of them. The land provides for us and it is the interior that calls. We are content to wave at them from the heights above the town. Even now one of their sluggish galleons draws near to count our numbers. It looks like a great centipede upon the sea with bristling snout and spiked tail, its hundred legs skimming the wave tops to the beat of a lazy drum.

MAY THE THIRTIETH
Caesarea

Baldwin joined us from Edessa before we set out from Tyre. His force brings our numbers to about ten thousand. He strikes me as much changed. He has taken an Armenian mistress, a heavyset woman with a dark moustache, who has fattened him and softened the predatory expression of his face. I cannot help but feel that the loss of his wife and children has also contributed to this transition. Though his features are still dark and pinched and his voice a rasping pipe, he no longer bears himself with the haughtiness of his earlier days upon the pilgrimage. He has seen more of the world and its suffering, and it has blunted the nastiness in him.

Our stages remain easy. We made Acre on the twenty-third, Jaifa on the twenty-sixth, and celebrated Pentecost at Caesarea. These names begin to invoke the Scriptures. Saint Paul preached in Acre and was tried and imprisoned at Caesarea. Herod ruled here in the name of Augustus, in whose reign Christ was born. And here Saint Peter baptized the disciple Cornelius. Can it be that we have finally reached the Holy Land? And why did we tarry so long, seeing how lovely and accommodating it is?

I begin to see a change within the army as we prepare to turn inland towards Jerusalem. Men become more serious and pensive, as if the land itself provokes a mood in them. The vulgar edges of their conduct are rubbed off, the blandness of the life of camp takes on a deeper hue. They sense that their destiny is near. They feel, as for the first time, that their Lord awaits, a prisoner in His tomb, the liberation that they bring. For so long through so many trials have they approached this moment that it is as if the true intention of their pilgrimage had been forgot. Now it comes home to them in an undeniable scent upon the air, and the silhouette of naked mountains in the distance — mountains that framed the world of Christ, and where His footsteps and His words once echoed.

I remember the words of poor Bartholomew, whispered from his blackened lips, the breath of burnt lungs. He had seen a child in the flames, he said, and then he said the word 'you'. It has puzzled me since I heard it. Had he seen me as a child in the flames? Or had he meant to say more — 'You know it was the Christ' or 'You ought not have doubted me' or, 'You must believe me now'. Probably the last, for he did chastise my doubting him. Yet whatever I, or anyone, may believe about his visions or the Lance, it took courage to go through that fire, and great heart to have survived it as he did. To my mind he had his vindication, as bravery always vindicates the doubted soul.

And now I think what a time of redemption this pilgrimage has been. The Bishop Adhémar emerged from the long shadow of his sins, Peter the Hermit proved himself in going out alone to parlay with Ker-boga, Eustace returned to life in faithfulness and sacrifice. And what of me? Shall I likewise be born to a new life? I thought that with the woman I had. I was mistaken, as she herself told me. What redemption waits for me beyond the naked mountains of Judea that even now glow purple in the slipping sun?

June the Fourth
Ramleh

This was a Muslim town but the people all have fled. In their desperation they burned the ancient church of Saint George, which lies nearby at Lydda. Our leaders have vowed to rebuild it, since he is the patron saint of soldiers, and to create in this place a bishopric. No sooner was this decision announced than quarrels broke out over which army should supply the bishop. Lots were suggested, but it was decided that this was too profane a method to choose a bishop. At last, Robert of Normandy recommended a bout of sersten slaeg, and so soldiers from all the armies formed the circle. Not surprisingly the Normans won, and Robert of Rouen was chosen for the see.

We are now well inland, and the landscape begins to change. Sparser grows the vegetation that we enjoyed on the coast, the air is drier and the road begins to rise. Ahead of us lies the desert, stretching in great brown fingers towards the mountains. It soon will be the hottest time of year. Our progress to Jerusalem will not be easy. But more often the men sing hymns, and few complaints are heard now in the ranks.

On the road yesterday we passed a large, flat stone upon which, some priests said, Christ stopped to rest. From that point every man stooped to kiss it. When an Italian knight tried to prevent his escort from lingering to take their turns, he was pulled from his horse and beaten. It was nonsense, of course, but it causes me to wonder what the ardour in Jerusalem will be, where every stone is sacred and every pilgrim will be armed.

We are now two days' march from the Holy City. And near three years from home.

JUNE THE SIXTH

We take the rising road into the hills of Judea. This is truly the land of Christ. Our road is that to Emmaus, where the resurrected Saviour met His two disciples and explained the Scriptures to them. What would we not give now to hear that explanation. It might banish many mysteries, lighten many hearts. Yet we pilgrims who march in all our arms are like the disciples who said to Him: 'Are you the only stranger who has not heard what has happened here?' They thought they understood and that He was the stranger. I cannot help but feel that, like them, we are fools on the road to Emmaus, questioning our God about Himself.

It was while we were approaching the village of Latrun, where the encounter is said to have occurred, that messengers came galloping towards us. When they saw our column they dropped from their horses to their knees and began kissing the feet of the soldiers as they passed. Fulk Rechin was nearby and he ordered them to get up, saying, 'Damn-it, don't you have women where you come from?'

They were three ragged men, Christians, and they announced that they were from Bethlehem. The name brought our men up short. 'Bethlehem!' The word spread through the column like fire upon oil — the city of the Nativity. Fulk Rechin conducted them to Count Robert who immediately sent couriers up and down the column to call a council. 'They want troops to liberate their town,' Robert told the others. There was no hesitation. 'Who can we spare?' Count Godfrey asked. His brother Baldwin stepped forward and said, 'I'll go.'

'You'd give up Jerusalem?' Godfrey asked.

Baldwin smiled ironically. 'You'll still be there when I get back.' He turned to Tancred. 'What do you say, Sicilian? Shall we liberate the manger?' Tancred seemed to hesitate. 'Come on,' Baldwin said, 'your uncle's not here to piss on you now.'

Each is to take one hundred knights, secure Bethlehem, and

rejoin us at Jerusalem. And so the two rebel counts, who had quit the expedition to found their own kingdoms, have left once more to free Christ's birthplace.

As we started the column again dark clouds moved overhead, billowing at our backs. It began to drizzle, a warm, gentle rain that refreshed us as we marched. But soon it poured down, turning the road to slick, slimy mud. Scarcely anyone can keep his feet, and even the horses are having difficulty on the inclining path. I write this at a halt while we wait for the rain to slacken. Maudire holds a canvas over my head, cursing and stamping his feet. 'There's nothing in the Gospels about rain,' he just called to me over the downpour.

'There's nothing about you either,' I said back to him.

JUNE THE NINETEENTH

There are few pages left in this book. I had not thought to write in it again. I shall say what has happened and nothing more. What is to happen only God can tell, and for the moment He remains silent except to speak through fools whom no one can believe.

After the rain stopped our column moved on. We reached the slopes of the mountain that the pilgrims call Mountjoy at nightfall. It is topped by a mosque surrounded by battlements. Our scouts came galloping back to say that the place was deserted, and that from the summit they had seen Jerusalem.

There was no question of encampment for the night. We marched straight on, the men at first keeping to their columns, but soon dispersing to scramble up the rocky slopes, some running, some crawling on hands and knees. As we made our way the moon came out, riding on purple clouds. Then, while we watched, it began to disappear. Little by little it was swallowed up until nothing but a crescent remained. Then that too was eclipsed. 'It is the end of the Turks!' the men began to shout, and one by one, they fell onto their knees to pray.

Père Raimund of Aguillères went to the front. 'Come on,' he called, 'don't you want to see her? The most beautiful woman in the world — Jerusalem!'

We all followed him to the top of Mountjoy, crowding around the walls of the mosque. The moon was reappearing, and in the distance, upon a crest of rising valleys stood the Holy City. Its angled walls glistened with torches; its citadel, the Tower of David, sparkled with light from a thousand windows, and at its summit the Dome of the Rock shone broad and burnished in the moonlight.

The silence of our army was complete. No one spoke and every eye was fixed upon the city. Three years, a thousand leagues, twenty thousand deaths had brought us to this sacred place. It was too much for some, who began to weep. Many prayed in silence. No one moved.

At last I felt a grip upon my elbow. I turned. Lord Raymond stood beside me, gazing at Jerusalem. There were tears in his old eyes. 'We've done it, Roger,' he whispered. From behind us came a voice. 'Not yet.' It was Godfrey of Bouillon. He shook his head. 'But by God it's close enough for me,' he said, smiling.

We camped upon the broad summit of Mountjoy that night. Many of us did not sleep, content to watch the sun rise over Jerusalem, exchanging idle thoughts, congratulating one another. But all our thoughts were much the same: God has spared us to see this day; there must be meaning in it.

Sunrise revealed the enormity of the task that lay ahead. Jerusalem is well defended both by nature and by man. To the east it is protected by the valley of Kedron. To the south the long, sloping valley of Gehenna falls away with its unquenchable fires of burning refuse. A third valley skirts the western wall. Only on the southwest where the walls cross Mount Sion, and along the northern side, are the battlements approachable.

The walls themselves are doubled, the outer being low and

thick, separated by a broad, dry ditch from the inner, which are as
tall as those of Antioch. They are of the archaic style, with shallow,
squared towers and narrow embrasures. This offers some relief, but
even approaching them will cost us dear. They are manned, we can
see, by black-skinned troops in white robes.

As we were preparing to resume our march horsemen arrived
bearing messages. These were from the English and Genoese fleets
which had entered the harbour at Jaffa, the Egyptian navy having
withdrawn. They brought the good news that we are to have the
iron necessary to construct our siege engines and towers. They also
brought letters. To my surprise, one of these was for me. I unsealed
it with trembling fingers. 'Faranj,' it began, 'I have had one of your
priests write this letter for me. I do not think he will deceive, for
I have paid him well.' It went on to state that she was with child.

I read it over and over, growing more frantic and confused. The
last time we had lain together was near the new year, which meant
she must be close to her term. Yet the letter had been written only
a month ago. 'I am well,' she wrote, 'and filled with joy, though I
am afraid to be alone at such a time.' I could imagine her fear –
an unmarried woman with child by a Christian in the Antioch of
Bohemund. She has friends though no family, and she lives alone.
She must be terrified. What will become of her and the child?

The child . . . *My* child. The thought struck me with such force
that I was blinded to Jerusalem. I must go to her; I cannot leave
her in this state. I must be with them both.

The army was preparing to move. Maudire brought my shield
and my lance with its pennant. We were instructed to make a show
as we descended the hillside towards Jerusalem. The priests began
their hymns, the drums beat and the trumpets blew. The Provençals
marched in perfect alignment as if on the field of exercise. I mounted,
took the reins between the fingers of my mitt, and waited. They
slipped by, singing and waving their staffs. I began to fall back,
nudging Helim farther and farther behind the column until we were
alone. And then, when I was out of sight of the army, I threw

down my lance and spurred her, and in a moment we were careening headlong down the rocky slope back towards the road to Emmaus.

I had only the vaguest of plans. I would make for the port, find a ship, and sail to Saint Symeon. With luck I could arrive in five days. 'It seems the story *was* of you,' she had written. 'Perhaps I was too wise. Perhaps you were destined to return.' As I rode, whipping my panting horse, the clouds closed in again and it began to rain. I did not stop but pushed her until the downpour was so thick and the road so deep it was impossible to go on. By this time night was falling and I sought a shelter. Ahead of me was a blackened skeleton – the cathedral at Lydda. I turned off across the sodden field and made for it, determined to spend the night and make for Jaffa at first dawn.

The ruins were deserted. I walked Helim right into the gaping nave. A side chapel remained under cover and I tethered her there, brushed and blanketed her, and settled myself for the night behind the altar. My mind was reeling. I had deserted the expedition, but that did not faze me. I thought of her, her belly swollen with my child, alone in Antioch at the mercy of the Normans. How could I have left her? Why had I let her convince me to go? And what would I do when I returned to her?

I wrapped my cloak around me and cradled my sword against my chest. Rain slanted in on the square stones of the floor, dripped from the statues and glistened on the tall shards of the windows. Helim stood patiently by regarding me as if I were a madman. I would take Yasmin away as soon as the child was born. We would go to Constantinople and find passage back to Provence. I would divorce my wife, remove her from the house, and live with them.

I thought of her in my manor where I had lived so many years with Jehanne. I imagined her moving among the rooms and walking in the gardens. I wondered at the amazement of the peasants and the priests at the sight of this small Turkish woman in Lunel, crossing the town square, making her way to the market. The idea made me laugh and, as I fell asleep, I was smiling. After so long a pilgrimage, I felt at last that my path was clear.

A voice awakened me: 'Roger!'

I got to my feet. It was raining still, though more gently now. A figure approached along the dripping nave swathed in a purple cloak, the face obscured by a cowl. 'Who is it?' I demanded.

'Raymond of Toulouse,' came the response.

Lord Raymond stepped into the chapel, lowering his cowl. He had ridden all night; his face was splattered with mud and his cloak hung soaking. He scowled at me a moment, his silver brows a line across his forehead, his grey beard dripping. The day was breaking but it was steely cold and dull with rain.

'What do you want?' I said. My voice was trembling for I was freezing and alarmed. In all the hectic hours since the letter I had not given a thought to anything but Yasmin. Now to be confronted by my Lord threw me into frenzy.

He fixed his gaze on me. It was neither harsh nor accusatory. 'Your explanation,' he said.

I replied: 'I am a coward.'

Lord Raymond peered at me. 'I know you, Roger, and you are no coward.'

I felt my control slipping from me. 'I have left the woman I love. I have abandoned her and she is with child.'

He nodded slowly. 'And you will return to her now?' I told him that I must. He took a step closer to me but I recoiled. The gesture surprised him and he halted. The altar was between us; he rested a hand upon it. 'Roger,' he said, 'the army has need of you—'

I cut him off. 'She has need of me.'

'—and I have need of you.'

I gripped at my sword to steady myself. The rain had almost stopped and the empty church echoed with the water dripping from the beams. 'Remember Bartholomew?' I said. 'The child he saw within the flames was mine.'

'And what of Jerusalem?' he asked.

I shouted: 'Jerusalem be damned! This is life, not a dream! I have a child!'

Lord Raymond pulled his cloak about him. 'I too have children,' he said. 'Children I have left to make this journey. I hope to see them again one day, after my solemn oath to God has been fulfilled.'

I looked into his eyes a long moment, then I shook my head. 'You will not convince me,' I told him. 'I have seen oaths made and broken. I have listened to bishops lie. I have known nightmares with my eyes open. This thing that has happened to me is a miracle. It is the meaning of my pilgrimage.'

'Roger,' he said, 'I cannot let you break your pledge to God . . .'

Again I shouted at him: 'God calls me to Antioch! You cannot stop me.'

He came around the altar. Without thinking I levelled my sword at him. He stopped, stared at the blade, then at me. My hand was shaking as I held the point within an arm's length of his chest. 'I will kill you if I must,' I said.

He nodded. 'I believe you would.'

We stood confronting each other a long moment. From the corner of the chapel Helim snorted her impatience. At last Lord Raymond stepped away, holding out his arms. 'Very well,' he said. 'I will not prevent you. You have your destiny, I have mine. I had thought they were the same.'

'There never was a destiny,' I said.

'I meant the Sepulchre,' he responded. There was a sadness in his voice that touched me even in my tormented state. 'You recall when I was in my fever, I entrusted you with my legacy. It was this pilgrimage, for which so many have suffered, for which so many have died. Not our men only, Roger, but Jews and Turks, Armenians and Syrians. Oh, yes, I count them up as well. There are no enemies here, only fingers on the hand of God. And you now, in His palm, trying to escape.'

The sword was shaking more violently as I heard him out. I took it in both hands, but still I could not steady it.

'I have watched you all this time,' he went on, never taking his eyes from me. 'The rest of us have fought a holy war, but you have fought two — against the Turk and against yourself. Why did you come? To assuage a secret sin? So did we all. Yes, Roger, every one of us has come to atone for some silent sin. Me, for example. You know I came not for the pope or Adhémar or riches or a kingdom. Why then do you think I came?' I told him I did not know. 'I came from fear,' he said.

'You?' I asked, astounded.

'Yes,' he replied. 'I fear death more than I love God. I hoped by this pilgrimage to overcome that fear. I have not. I do not want to die, Roger. I have thought on it, and I do not think that death is fair. We live, we learn, we build. For what? So that death may claim it all, may take it all from us. Leaving us with what? A pair of wings and a beatific smile?' He shook his head. 'No. You are a corpse rotted in the ground and visited only by those who think of you at holy days. The truth is, Roger, I hate God. Because God created death, and death is all that I have to look forward to.'

I could not believe it. This man whom I had followed, whom I had worshipped, felt himself a slave to death and lived in fear of it, and hated God for it. 'Why then do you stay?' I asked him.

'What else is there to do?' he answered. 'To stay at home and die, or to liberate the Sepulchre and die: which is more likely to reward me? We are the whores of God, remember? I do His will, not mine, in hopes that He will not abandon me when my time comes. In hopes that He exists.'

'You don't believe?' I asked.

'I hope,' he said with a smile. 'I hope and I serve. Anything else is impossible.'

I put my sword away. 'I must go,' I said. I started towards my horse.

'Roger of Lunel!' he called. 'You are a father.'

The word stopped me short. No one had ever called me that.

I who had no father save in heaven now was a father upon the earth. 'Yes,' I said. I reached for Helim's reins.

'You are also a son,' he went on.

I turned to him. He stood beside the altar, the broken spine of a window crossed by a fallen lintel admitting the first rays of dawn above his silver head. 'And as you have the duty of a father, so you have the duty of a son.'

'What do you mean?' I asked.

He came to me and took my arm. 'If you leave this pilgrimage,' he said evenly, 'I will disinherit you.'

I stared at him. 'Disinherit?' I repeated.

He nodded. 'Jerusalem. The Sepulchre. That for which you were born. That which is your birthright. You have been a son to me, Roger. Turn your back on the Church, turn your back on Christ if you wish, but do not turn your back on me. For the truth is, unless you have been a son, you cannot be a father.'

The sun was etching its way in among the wet black beams and through the watered windows. High above our heads the morning mist rose up to heaven. I could not breathe, I could not think. I felt my heart swell with longing and remorse. I let go the reins and sat upon the soaking floor; Lord Raymond knelt beside me. I laid my head upon his shoulder and began crying, tears of bitterness and tears of resignation.

Since that time we have invested the walls of Jerusalem, we Provençals on the south-west before Mount Sion; Godfrey, Tancred, the Flemish and the Normans on the north. Four days ago we attempted an assault at the urging of a hermit of the Mount of Olives who, in a vision, had seen the Christ. It was a disaster in which we lost six hundred men, among them the peasant Gérard, the last of my retinue. We shall be wary of local visionaries in future. For the moment we are building our engines and towers.

I have given Maudire a letter and five gold bezants and sent him to Antioch with sailors from the Genoese fleet. He is to find the woman, deliver the letter, and return to me with word of her.

I have told him that if ever he feared a beating from me he will do this well and quickly.

We are camped in the place known as the City of David, along the Gihon Spring and Hezekiah's Tunnel. My pavilion overlooks the Pool of Siloam, where Jesus told the blind man He had healed to wash his eyes. It is a narrow cleft in rock hewn by the Israelites while under siege by the Assyrians. The water runs clear and undisturbed, but it has been poisoned by the Egyptians and several of our men lie dead in it. It seems a shame that such an ancient spring should be thus inaccessible to us.

JUNE THE TWENTY-NINTH

It does not go well for us. A hot desert windstorm blows, choking everything with dust. Animals left in the open drop dead in a few hours, their eyes abraded, their mouths caked with sand. We suffer terribly from thirst. Water now is fetched from the Jordan River and carried on the backs of camels in leather bags. Men pay everything they have for one of these bags.

Meanwhile the work of building the towers and engines goes on. The camp is like a vast, open chandler's shop thick with blowing dust. Men labour at the hammers and hand drills until they can no longer breathe, when others take their place. I too have taken my turn, sweating like a common labourer from sunrise to night. I do not grudge it, for it occupies my mind and drains my energy so that I can sleep.

On our side we build a huge tower upon wheels to be covered with skins against the Greek fire arrows of the Egyptians and Turks. Every animal that is not needed is killed, and those that die are immediately stripped. The blood is gathered in cisterns, then sealed in clay pots which are fired from our mangonels into the city. We are splattering Jerusalem with blood and bombarding it with the severed heads of animals to discourage the defenders. In return they taunt us from the walls. They hang crucifixes over the battlements on which they urinate. Statues of saints and holy images from the churches likewise are desecrated in our sight. It is a strange mental warfare between us.

The wind has blown for ten days. We are not used to it and we improvise means of protecting ourselves. Just now you could not tell the difference between the Turks and us, for we wear turbans and wind our faces with scarves. But the dust goes everywhere, in our clothing, in our food, our eyes, ears, noses and mouths, even in our privates. There are nights when I cannot urinate without pain because my member is infested with particles of dust almost invisible, and sharp as glass. Nothing stirs about the camp save from necessity, and those of us who move about resemble ghosts leaning against the wind.

On the northern wall Godfrey's men have constructed a battering ram. It is a tree trunk fitted with an iron snout that is suspended by chains. They have positioned it at the outer wall and their troops work it constantly, sixty men at a time swinging it to and fro. As it hammers against the wall it creates a thud-thud-thud which can be heard in our encampment, and which never ceases day or night.

It has driven more than one young soldier mad, that thud-thud-thud from dawn to dusk, muted by the blowing sand, measuring the daylight hours, hammering in our dreams. It is a kind of torture that never for a moment stops. Thud-thud-thud; I listen to it now as I write, the wind whipping the flanks of my pavilion, the yellow dust insinuating through the seams, gathering in the folds of the pages, choking out the candle. And all the while, thud-thud-thud as the walls reverberate like a surgeon tamping the exposed bone of a severed leg.

JULY THE FIFTH

News today that an Egyptian army approaches from the south. It is a rumour, but it is likely to be true. Before we arrived the garrison scattered their flocks rather than taking them inside the city, which means they did not anticipate a lengthy siege.

Our tower is nearly finished and our engines are already at work. We have succeeded in clearing the walls of Turks so that our sappers can start demolishing the outer wall. A rhythm has developed between the armies: their archers spring up to fire at our men and we reply with rocks. There is a space while our sappers labour at the wall, and then the Turks spring up again. In each exchange a dozen men are killed or hurt, and so it goes all day.

I was nearly killed this afternoon while working in the tower. It has surpassed the height of the inner wall and must weigh several tons. It is a massive vertical box crisscrossed with beams and shrouded in the skins of animals. The air inside is almost unbreathable, and no one can stand to work in it for more than an hour or two. I was near the top helping the Greek engineers to fix the ropes that control the bridge when one snapped at my feet. The blow knocked me over, and in the next instant I was being dragged towards the edge of the platform. A Greek grabbed at me and was pulled from his feet and then another grabbed at him, and in a moment there was a human chain stretching from the bridge right across the platform to where I lay half senseless, hanging over the edge.

The whole mechanism of pulleys and counterweights had come away and only my body prevented it from being lost over the side. The Greeks seemed more solicitous of the mechanism than of me, and by the time they finally got round to freeing me, the rope had dug so deeply into my leg that it had to be cut out of my flesh. I suffered the indignity of having to be lowered from the tower in a basket, and now I cannot walk without a crutch.

Peter of Roaix has been good enough to lend me one of his squires, a lad named Guibert. I had not wanted a squire, preferring to be alone and do for myself. But again I am an invalid, and the boy is quiet enough. I do not want to be idle, and I force myself to go out, for now that the wind has stopped there is much to keep one busy.

JULY THE NINTH

We have had much bother. A priest, Desiderius, a Norman with a reputation for visions, declared that he had seen the Bishop Adhémar, who still lingers in hellfire, and who commanded us to fast and make a pilgrimage around the city. The leaders met in council, considered the priest's claim soberly, and decided that there was no harm in it. As a result we have put on a fine spectacle for the Turks.

Yesterday, led by the clerics, the entire army assembled before Saint Stephen's Gate for the procession. Every man was barefoot – which suited me well for my ankle is still swollen – all wore simple tunics, their heads bare, few carried weapons. As the drums beat and the trumpets blew we processed singing hymns and praying under the great towers of the northern wall, past the mangonels of the Normans, around by the Jaffa Gate to our own lines, and on up to the Mount of Olives.

There, with tears in his eyes, Peter the Hermit announced that Pope Urban is ill and like to die. The news came as a shock to many. The Hermit insisted that the Holy Father lingers only to hear of our victory, which must not be delayed. Then Desiderius, who is fat and slobbers from thick lips, told us that Adhémar has promised we shall have Jerusalem in nine days.

The Mount of Olives, being a sacred place, has not been stripped of its trees, and I lay in the shade of one of them while the sermons groaned on, and watched a hawk make its winding way towards the north. By the time the service was ended and we were dismissed, I reckoned that it had come in sight of Antioch, and my heart went out to it.

JULY THE THIRTEENTH

The assault is to begin tonight. I am even now preparing myself. Guibert and the doctor have arranged a harness for my leg which enables me to walk. I doubt that I shall have to ride.

Maudire has returned from Antioch. He came in with the sailors bearing the severed arm of Saint George, a relic that we are to carry with us in our fight.

The woman has been sold into slavery. Bohemund is determined to rid the city of Turks and repopulate it with Christians. I did not take the news well, and beat Maudire with my fists demanding that he tell me where she had gone. It is impossible to know. She could be anywhere from Syria to Egypt to Europa.

There is nothing more to be said. I have lost both wife and child. Somewhere in this world will be a part of me that I will never know. And what is left here, with me? Nothing but Maudire who cowers in a corner, bleeding from a split lip. I have given him orders that if I do not survive, my possessions are to be burned and my horse, Helim, is to be butchered, the meat to be given to the prisoners of our army.

JULY THE FOURTEENTH

Everyone around me is dead, crushed by rocks or shot through with arrows. I lie in the ditch between the two walls surrounded by corpses. Last night the trumpets blew on both sides of the city and the sappers rushed forward to fill the ditch with the rubble from the outer wall. Every one was struck by missiles. Lord

Raymond stood upon the ruins of the wall waving handfuls of gold and offering it to any man who would replace them. He threw the gold upon the piles of rocks, and scores of soldiers crowded forward.

At the back we stood to the tower while the Turks poured down fire upon us. Their archers tried to set the tower ablaze but our men clambered up the sides to pull the burning arrows out with their bare hands. Our bowmen and our catapults returned the fire and the air grew thick with missiles. Down in the ditch a hundred, then two hundred men fell killed or wounded. Their bodies were immediately covered by rocks to make a passage for the tower.

At last Lord Raymond gave the signal and we moved the tower forward. Teams of mules strained at the ropes in front and fifty men pushed from behind. I shouted and encouraged them, swung my sword in the air, cursed and screamed like a madman. The great thing gave a lurch and then crept forward down the slope towards the ditch and onto the path of rocks.

We could hear the fighting on the opposite side of the city. The combined armies of Godfrey, the two Roberts and the Northerners, having breached the outer curtain with their battering ram, were moving their towers to the wall. From within Jerusalem smoke began to curl towards the sky, and then black billows were rising everywhere.

Down in the ditch the work grew harder. The tower tipped and swayed as it made its progress over the rocks. Bodies of our slain were crushed beneath its wheels, mules were falling, stunned by stones or shot two, three, ten times with arrows. As each fell it was cut away and rolled into the ditch.

Upon the walls the Egyptians and Turks fought frantically. They abandoned their catapults and began hurling stones by hand. Night had fallen and the whole scene was lighted by torches, the flaming arrow arcs, and the fires within the city. By the time the tower reached the inner wall not a mule was left alive, and a hundred men were labouring at the ropes. The Turks poured down Greek fire which clung to the skins, smouldering and filling the air with the stench of sulphur and burning hide. The ladders were brought and with a cheer our men raised them to the walls and began to scale. At once they were met with a hail of stones so intense that not a man could reach the battlements.

Meanwhile the Egyptians had thrown ropes over the summit of the tower and were trying to pull it over. On my order Peter of Roaix took a squad of knights up the ramps, scything at the ropes with their swords. More were thrown and more, and every one was severed. Peter hurled a shout of defiance at the Turks and on the instant a stone struck him on the head. He staggered to the edge of the platform and gripped the ropes. I yelled to him to get down but in that instant a quarrel[102] struck him full in the face. He threw up his hands and pitched forward off the tower, his body falling upon the rocks near where I stood.

I hurried to him. He lay upon his back, one arm twisted beneath him. The bolt had entered below his eye and come out behind his ear. His eyes were rolled back, but when I raised his head he looked at me. 'The Sepulchre. . . .' he said. I called to soldiers to carry him away, but by the time they lifted him he was dead.

The fighting went on deep into the night until both sides dropped down exhausted. Now we are trapped near the base of the wall, huddled around the tower which gives us some protection. Every so often the Turks will push a stone from atop the wall and there will be a dull concussion as it strikes a dead body, or a scream as it strikes a living one.

Maudire has just come up to bring me food. I shall give him this book to take back with him, for I think this will be the last assault. Either we will be over the wall tomorrow, or none of us will withdraw from here alive. I shall ask his forgiveness for the beating that I gave him yesterday. It was not his fault. All the fault – all of it – has been mine.

---

102 Quarrel: the bolt of a crossbow.

AUGUST THE FIRST
Jerusalem

An expedition under Lord Raymond will set out tomorrow to meet the Egyptian army. I am not going with it. Lord Raymond took my hand and wished me well. I am leaving Jerusalem.

What has happened? This.

We spent the night within the ditch below the wall and in the morning we resumed the assault. I was unable to climb the tower and so I took half a century of knights along the ditch to the Gate of Sion. There, crouching beneath our shields, we waited until the wall should be taken and the gate opened to us. During the night the Turks had replenished their ammunition, stripping the city of every kind of projectile. As we watched, the storm of stones and metal rained down upon our men, while from our lines the mangonels hurled boulder after boulder back at them.

A storming party mounted the tower, the Greeks let down the bridge, but the Turks were ready for it. They blocked it with beams and poured a heavy fire of arrows into the opening. Catapults were brought up to dislodge the beams, but at once they were flaming with Greek fire. Turks and Christians screamed at one another across a gap no wider than an ox cart. The fighting continued for an hour, then two, then three.

A flying squad was sent along the wall to dislodge us, but I called for catapults to scatter them. For the time being we were safe beneath the overhang of the bridge. Then from the far side of the city we heard a tremendous roar. The shouting increased, coming closer and growing more tumultuous. Godfrey had broken through and his men were pouring into Jerusalem. Within the hour the Egyptian general Iftikhar had sent messengers to Lord Raymond begging mercy for himself and his troops. Raymond quickly accepted, the tower bridge was let down, and our men streamed across onto the walls. In ten minutes more, the Gate of Sion opened.

I made my way up onto the bridge as the knights swirled past me into the city. I walked with difficulty. Inside, the garrison was fleeing for the Tower of David upon the citadel where Lord Raymond had pledged them sanctuary. The fighting had stopped, but not the killing.

Loosed upon Jerusalem our men were in a frenzy. They were killing everything that moved, man and woman, child and animal. I felt nothing as I made my way along the wide boulevard towards the centre of the city. I was exhausted, emptied, drained. I pulled off my helm and coif and let my swordpoint drag upon the ground at my feet. I walked as if in a dream, going deeper into the slaughtered city, not knowing where.

At last I came to a low wall, the wooden gate of which had been torn aside. Within was a broad court of raked earth inclining to a rock. At the base of it several knights knelt in prayer. It was, one told me, the rock of Golgotha, the place of crucifixion. I peered up at it a moment, squinting against the smoky sunlight, and then moved beyond it towards a rough stone vault half buried in the ground. After the mayhem of the city, this place was unnaturally quiet. A few soldiers knelt in tears outside the entrance. I regarded them, puzzled. None dared go in, and one of them clutched at my surcoat as I approached. 'The Sepulchre,' he whispered in awe.

I paused to gaze at it. There was no door, just a narrow cleft in the rock, and within, no light at all. I freed my surcoat from the soldier's grip and walked towards it. There were three rough-hewn steps. I bent my head and entered. The air smelled of chalk and, indeed, the walls were white. There was scarcely room to stand. The floor was earth, moist with darkness. I was alone within.

My leg ached where the rope had cut it, as did my back from the injury I received at Arqa. I lowered myself to the ground, stretched out my leg, adjusted my back with difficulty, and leaned against the wall. For a moment there was perfect silence. I closed my eyes and took a deep breath. I had not realized how very tired I was.

After a few minutes I opened my eyes again and looked about. There was nothing – just the darkness, the moist earth, and the musty smell of chalk. Was this the Sepulchre? Had I come all this way for this? I nearly laughed. There was nothing here, and I was at the centre of it. Here then was my truth – a narrow grave. I smiled. And then I lay upon my side, curled myself about my sword, and fell asleep.

I was awakened in the morning by priests demanding to know who I was. I told them I no longer knew. They pulled me roughly to my feet and took me out.

Beyond the low wall the killing had not stopped. The dead were everywhere, people butchered in their homes, in the public squares, in the shops and streets. Arms and legs and heads lay on all sides. Soldiers were going from house to house murdering and looting. It made no difference if the occupants were Christian, Muslim or Jew. No one was being spared.

I saw the pennant of Lord Raymond upon the citadel of the Tower of David and I made my way there. It was a formidable fortress with many twisting battlements and cube upon cube of towers, and every inch of it was filled with men both living and dead. The Egyptians to whom we had promised sanctuary were being slaughtered by the troops of Godfrey, who hoped to take the fortress for himself. Our men had rushed up to restrain them, and fighting had broken out between our troops and his.

At last Lord Raymond himself came up to take command. He began shouting orders for the killing to be stopped. Then he caught sight of me and climbed down off his horse. 'Roger, are you hurt?' he asked, coming to me. I shook my head. He smiled grimly. 'We've won,' he said.

'Won?' I answered.

'Yes, God be praised. Have you seen the Sepulchre?' I told him that I had. 'What . . .' he stammered out, 'what is it like?'

'Empty,' I replied.

It is said that fifty thousand people have perished at our hands. The bonfires burn day and night and still the streets are choked with corpses. Among them move the priests securing the holy places, while knights kneel everywhere in prayer, kissing stones or weeping over places where our Saviour stood or sat or did a miracle. The city is being stripped for relics. All the mosques and synagogues have been burned.

In the marketplace this morning the bishops presided over the torture of the Greek monks who tend the Sepulchre. It seems that they alone knew the whereabouts of the beam of the True Cross and had refused to give it up. They were stripped naked and white-hot irons were inserted into their rectums. Their eyelids were sliced off and their nipples excised, and still they would not talk. At last Arnulf of Rohes, he who had denounced the Lance, approached a young novice. He took the lad's penis in his jewelled glove and pressed a dagger to it. The other monks, all older men, begged him to keep silent. But the boy confessed. The beam was hidden in a secret niche within the chapel of the Holy Sepulchre. Now it travels with our army to meet the Egyptians.

The port of Jaffa is in our hands. I leave tomorrow for Antioch. From there God knows what will become of me. I close this book now, and do not know if I will write in it again.[103]

AUGUST, 1099
Antioch

I am having difficulty walking. The injuries to my leg and back as well as the old arrow wound have made me nearly a cripple. I returned to the house with the low door and found it occupied by

103 Editor's note: Here there is a space of several pages. The entries that follow appear to have been recorded at random. None is dated. In the cases where it is possible from the contents to guess at the dating and the location I have done so.

a family of Sicilian Christians. They knew nothing of the woman. I visited the slavers of the marketplace. One there was, a Muslim named Salah, who remembered a pregnant Turkish woman and thinks she was sold in a lot with other invalids to an emir of Baghdad. I shall attempt to reach that place, even though he tells me that once she has given birth she will again be sold, since her value will be increased by that of the child.

DECEMBER, 1099
Baghdad

The Nativity approaches, though in this city there is no place to celebrate it. I have suffered much at the hands of the Muslims. Twice have I been imprisoned, once in Damascus and a second time here in Baghdad. I know enough of the language now to make my way about, and I have learned from a physician that the child was born in September or October in the household of an emir named al-Mustazhir. When I approached him he had me thrown into prison. From there I wrote him petition upon petition begging for information.

At last he ordered me released and brought to him. His palace was splendid. He told me that the child was a boy and that, as soon as the woman was well enough to travel, they were delivered to a merchant of Basra.

MARCH THE NINETEENTH, 1100
Basra

It is the feast of the patron of fathers, the father of Christ, Saint Joseph. I have reached this place by very hard stages. My health gives out, as does my spirit. I have travelled deep into the land of the Muslims and can, from where I sit beneath an orange tree, see the Sea of Persia with its diamond sails and long boats of reeds.

They are gone. I found the merchant who brought them here, a man named Hassan. He is a careful keeper of records and he showed me the ledger where they were marked. On the twenty-first of January they were taken by a slaver to be resold in one of the markets of India. It is impossible to follow them. In any case, it is impossible for me.

I have lived these past months as a beggar, earning my way by telling the stories of our expedition. Some hearers give me coins; others spit on me. Now I shall make my way back to Provence, for I know not where else I should go.

AUTUMN, 1100

This will be the last of my book. I returned to Lunel by Brindisi and Marseille, arriving on the feast of the Assumption, exactly four years after having set out. As I expected, my death had long since been declared so that when I reached my house there was a great commotion. The peasants shrank from me, calling me a ghost. Jehanne fainted.

For a long time she refused to recognize me. She too has changed. She is thinner and has much more care of her appearance, for her husband, the Duke of Arles, sits on the council of King Henry of France. He was in Paris when I arrived, and she was preparing to join him there, for Prince Hugh of Vermandois is to lead a new pilgrimage. It has been called for by Godfrey of Bouillon, who was chosen to rule in the Holy City, but he since has died and Baldwin is now King of Jerusalem. Lord Raymond is to serve as adviser to the expedition, the purpose of which is to rescue Bohemund who has been taken captive by the Turks. The Duke of Arles will be second in command. Jehanne had planned to accompany him as far as Antioch, but my arrival threw her plans into confusion.

I have not contested the marriage. My health is poor and, my rights having been transferred to her husband, I have no resources. Nor do I wish to fight. I wish only to live upon my own land, and to die here in peace.

With the Duke's permission, I occupy a cottage on the property where once lived the peasant Gérard, he who attended my cisterns and fell before Jerusalem. It was much run-down but I have restored it with my own hands. I do such work about the estate as I am capable of, being careful to keep out of the way of the family. Nonetheless the children of Jehanne torment me, calling me 'cripple' and mimicking my gait. I pay them no mind. I have deserved more than this at the hands of children, and I think my soul is better for it.

Of the future I do not think. On the past I do not cease to reflect. The tomb was empty. So was I. There was nothing there, nor is there here. I have ridden a great storm; now I have sunk to the bottom of the sea where all is calm. Sometimes the sunlight reaches me in memories – a place, a poem, a pair of eyes. All that was violent is forgotten; all that remains is still.

I write this by a candle that has almost gone out below the window of my bedroom. On the hills beyond, the leaves turn even as I watch, the life flowing from them back into the earth, from where it will rise again in spring.

I shall sleep now and write no more. Tonight, as every night before I sleep, though I say no prayer, I will stretch out my hand for them, and I will take her fingers, and kiss his face that I have never seen, but that is always present to my mind.

POSTSCRIPT

Last summer, after finishing this work, I returned to Provence. With the help of Father Charles I located the site of Roger's house in the foothills just north of Lunel. It is possible, with some guidance and a little imagination, to picture the layout of the place. It must have been a large, comfortable home, built in a generous U on rising ground above a stream.

My intention, however, was to find his grave and do honour to the memory of the man whom I had come to know so well. It was not possible. Had he returned to his former state as Duke of Lunel, he would have been buried in the church where both Jehanne and her third husband, the Duke of Arles, now lie. But we must assume that Roger died in obscurity and had a commoner's burial.

With that in mind I visited the little ancient cemetery of Lunel which lies in a hollow of the hills above the town. There, within the high flint walls, I found stone markers dating from the seventeenth to the fourteenth centuries. None, however, was from the time of Roger.

I had brought with me a small bouquet of flowers – Iceland poppies, Rose of Sharon, and hyacinth, which Roger called the tears of Allah – tied in a bow of white and blue ribbon decorated with three gold stars. As I was leaving the cemetery I came across an unmarked grave beneath the branches of a weeping acacia that overhung the back wall. I stopped and gazed at it a long time. He had written about just such a place where he had camped at Arqa, saying that it was as if the wings of angels were protecting him.

I knelt and laid my flowers on the grave, said a silent prayer, and left. It was a gesture, nothing more. Perhaps he is there, perhaps not. Only God can tell.